BLOOD SCENARIO

BLOOD SCENARIO

Peter Spain

Coward, McCann & Geoghegan
New York

Library of Congress Cataloging in Publication Data

Spain, Peter.
  Blood scenario.

  I. Title.
PZ4.S73345Bl   1980   [PR6069.P28]   823'.9'14   79-24536
ISBN 0-698-11029-3

Printed in the United States of America

To Richard and Vivien

One

Saint Patrick's Day

The morning of March the seventeenth broke fine and clear, the air crisp with the champagne challenge only New York can offer, the sun hitting golden splinters off the buildings along Fifth Avenue. The finest Saint Patrick's Day for years. A great day, not just for the Irish but for all of New York.

The eighteenth unit of the parade had passed Fifty-fourth Street and drawn level with the St. Regis Hotel when the first bombs exploded. Seconds later there were more explosions, this time outside St. Thomas Episcopal Church at Fifth Avenue and West Fifty-third Street.

No one knew where the bombs had come from. Clouds of dense black smoke billowed down Fifth Avenue. Deafened by the noise and blinded by the smoke, spectators fought for refuge in stores and offices. Along the green line the city had painted from Forty-fourth Street to Eighty-sixth Street to honor the Irish on this, their special day, the dead and the still-living embraced each other in a welter of shattered bodies, swimming in a film of blood. Onlookers saw a young boy tossed high above the crowd by the force of the blast, his burning body melting and twisting like candle grease. A drum majorette lay ripped open from breastbone to crotch, her shapely legs still resplendent in shiny high-boots. Some marchers were literally blown to pieces. A woman's scalp was found lodged in a grating at the corner of Fifty-third Street like a sucked-out orange with bits of brain and gristle still adhering to it.

A writer for *New York* magazine happened to be standing on the sidewalk near St. Thomas Church. He said one of the explosions was like

9

a single searing coruscating eye of light. There was the illusion of the glare and heat coming first and then the noise afterwards—although they must have been simultaneous. I was lifted off my feet—and then I had a break in consciousness that might have lasted a minute. I wasn't seeing or hearing or breathing—and then I was in this hell of people, all of them shouting and shrieking in terror . . .

Within minutes the police were struggling to clear a path for the dozens of ambulances, lights flashing and sirens screaming, that were fighting to cross Manhattan. Teams of surgeons were hastily assembled at all of the major hospitals to await the arrival of the injured.

Two hours after the bombing the authorities took count. Fifty-seven people killed: thirty-two men, nineteen women, six children. Of ninety people taken to hospitals, nine would die, twelve lose limbs or be blinded. Certainly this was the worst act of terror ever perpetrated against the people of New York. Newscasters might mention recent outrages by Puerto Rican extremists, recall the bombing of La Guardia Airport at Christmas 1975, even dredge into history for the anarchist bomb that killed thirty-three at the House of Morgan after the first world war, but every past atrocity palled beside this one.

Dubbing it "The Saint Patrick's Day Massacre," a commentator labeled forever this day when joy was blasted into terror, when the blood of the innocent made the green turn red.

Later, everyone was to look for signs and omens to distinguish this from other Saint Patrick's Days. Hindsight made even the weather seem an ironic portent, its very perfection a mockery of what was to come.

But there were no omens. Everyone had been delighted that the weatherman was cooperating. As the mayor of New York said, "It's a beautiful Irish day." And, as they had done ever since their first parade in March 1762, the harps were marching. This Saint Patrick's morning there would be seventy-five parades stepping out in cities across the United States. In New York, everyone was getting ready to cheer two hundred and forty bands and one hundred and twenty thousand marchers in a show that was going to be bigger and better than ever.

The two hundred and forty bands' polished trumpets and tubas, tuned fifes and glockenspiels, tested the bellows of bagpipes. Drum majorettes twirled and pranced, especially the pompon club of Bishop Hogan High School. They were to mount a larger contingent this year. The New York City Police Department's Emerald Society Band was marching, as it always did. Wearing paper waistcoats with shamrocks on them, a thousand bartenders polished glasses against the thirsty aftermath. (Who was it said that on every Saint Pat's Day the Irish march up Fifth Avenue and fall down Third Avenue?) The beer had to run green or no one would drink it. And making Irish coffee was a test for any barman not raised in the Ould Country. (Warm the glass first and don't forget to put sugar in the cream.)

If the beer ran green, so did everything else. The riot of green that was Fifth Avenue surfeited the eye. Green flags and streamers, green balloons and green cigarettes. Men in Japanese-made green ties and green socks. Women in green chiffon dresses who wore green mascara and shouted "Erin go bragh!" White horses tinted green and ladies in green bowlers riding them. Children who waved little shillelaghs and toted miniature leprechauns with top hats and clay pipes. Old men who sported buttons that said "Kiss me, I'm Irish," and some younger men who wore buttons that said "I'm Irish and gay and Saint Patrick is my lover."

But behind this whole Irish fantasy—so close to the great heart of America—there lay meticulous planning. Discipline was implemented through the Line of March Committee, the Formation Committee, and the Grandstand Committee. Organization brought the hundred and twenty thousand marchers through a million laughing, clowning spectators, banned advertising and monitored the flags and banners. No yellow in the Irish flag: only orange, as in the flag given to the Young Irelanders in Paris in 1848. The American flag to be carried on the right shoulder, the Irish on the left. And, still the slogan on a hundred banners since it first appeared in 1948, ENGLAND GET OUT OF IRELAND as the motif of the whole parade.

This morning everything was happening as it always happened. The ceremonies had begun with mass at Saint Patrick's Cathedral. To the strains of "Garryowne na Glory" New York's fighting Sixty-ninth Regiment had filed up the aisle, Aer Lingus hostesses distributing shamrocks to the men as they took their seats. The regimental mascots, two huge Irish wolfhounds, waited outside.

The mayor arrived at eleven-thirty. A chic Aer Lingus hostess stepped forward and pinned a shamrock onto his lapel. He smiled and asked where she came from. An Irish member of his staff had him programmed for every county in Ireland, so when she said "Cork" the mayor came on with the old one about the General Post Office in Dublin being "stone outside and Cork inside"—a reference to the Corkmen's well-known habit of going to Dublin and grabbing all the best jobs.

Proudly waiting was a Corkman who had gone to New York instead. Patrolman Maurice O'Leary, born in Cork's Blackpool district, had joined the New York Police Department ten years before. Today he was to blow the whistle that would set one hundred and twenty thousand people marching.

And exactly at noon he did blow it, and the grand marshal, Police Commissioner Brefni O'Rourke, stepped out onto the green line to lead the parade.

At its head, as escorts to the grand marshal, marched the Mounted Police of the City of New York; followed by the Sixty-ninth Regiment; the Forty-second Division Band; the One Hundred and Ninety-ninth Army Band; and the Father Duffy Chapter, Rainbow Division, Overseas Veterans. Then the Holy Name Society of the New York City Police Department and then, escorted by the Emerald Society Band and the New York City Transit Police, the mayor himself.

As the parade moved along, the applause grew deafening—particularly for such familiar and well-loved groups as the Equestrian Ladies Aides to the grand marshal, the Equestrian Gentlemen Aides, the Cardinal Spellman High School Band, the New York Fire Department's Pipe and Drum Band, the All Girl Drum and Bugle Band from Yonkers, and the Bishop Lansing Band from Baltimore with their elegant white-powdered periwigs and Louis XIV costumes.

Every historical and political interest was represented among the thirty-three units of the parade, including the Ancient Order of Hibernians, the Wolfe Tone Club, the Catholic Daughters of America, the Irish Northern Aid Committee (Nor Aid), and Justice for Ulster.

Everyone was blinded by all the color and gaiety, the sheer bang and brio of the marching bands, but a political motif throbbed like a greater drumbeat behind the many drums. Aside from all the banners that demanded ENGLAND GET OUT OF IRELAND, there was the group of young men who wore only rough brown blankets against the sharp March air. They personalized the republican prisoners in H-block of the Maze Prison near Belfast; living in squalor and defiance in an attempt to gain political status. In classic republican parlance these men were "on the blanket": they went naked except for a blanket rather than wear prison garb. And, still with the theme of British repression in Northern Ireland, a group in the Justice for Ulster contingent marched in suits marked with the broad arrows of nineteenth-century convicts: they represented the many Irish republican prisoners held in British jails.

Grim as these symbols were, they didn't come alive for a lot of the spectators. What could this massive celebration have to do with the Irish Troubles you heard the newscasters talking about? The last year had been the bloodiest and most threatening since those Troubles began, yet here the music of fifes and glockenspiels still set feet a-tapping. The sun was out, and the Irish were marching. No one could see beyond the laughter and the pageantry to the horror that lay ahead.

And yet afterward some commentators chose to ask why the members of the Saint Patrick's Day parade committee had not anticipated the bombing. Did the organizers think the lighthearted shenanigans of a million New Yorkers on a day out could be separated from the dark facts of the present situation in Ireland? Certainly this last year it had become evident that a new campaign of terror was in progress, its effects not confined to Ireland itself.

The name "Loyalist Action" had first surfaced after the killing of twelve Armagh republicans on the way to a Sinn Fein Ardfheis in Dublin. Stopped by a Garda [police] car, the eight men and four women had climbed out of their minibus, thinking this a routine check. The bogus patrolmen had lined them up and then opened fire with automatic weapons, killing them all within two minutes. Later the wire services got a statement signed "Loyalist Action," saying that these people had been executed for giving support to IRA murderers.

Over the next few months there were other incidents. In Hamburg an arms dealer called Karl Asman was found hanged in his apartment. The next day Loyalist Action claimed responsibility for his death, although the Hamburg police had previously thought him a suicide. He had been executed, the statement said, because he had been supplying rifles to the IRA.

The next strike was particularly brutal. Fifty veterans of the Anglo-Irish War of Independence had gone on a pilgrimage to Lourdes (the youngest was seventy, the oldest ninety-one). Outside Tarbes their bus crashed and then exploded, killing all but seven of the veterans. Examining the wreck, experts found that the mileage gauge had been linked to an incendiary bomb attached to the exhaust. Once the bus achieved a certain mileage, the bomb ignited. Loyalist Action claimed in their statement that some of the veterans had links with the current republican movement in the south of Ireland.

Just before Christmas, firebombs were ignited during an evening program at an Irish Center in Kilburn in northwest London: in the ensuing panic twenty people died. In the first week of February of this year Terence Gye, a West of Ireland TD [member of the Irish parliament], in Washington to meet Congressman Mario Biaggi and members of his ad hoc committee on the North of Ireland, died in a car-bomb explosion described by the FBI as a carbon copy of the one that killed former Chilean foreign minister Orlando Letelier. Loyalist Action described Gye as an emissary from the Provisional IRA.

These incidents naturally provoked a backlash from republican factions. An Orange Hall in County Antrim was bombed—remarkably without loss of life. An explosive device was placed aboard a troop carrier leaving Aldergrove Airport in Belfast and eighty men of the Royal East Anglian Regiment were killed.

It was after this last incident that Dr. Christopher Dalziell of the London-based Institute for the Study of Conflict wrote that this ever-deepening spiral of atrocity-reprisal, atrocity-reprisal must inevitably propel a great part of Europe—not only Ireland—into anarchy. He went on to question the true motives of Loyalist Action. He had earlier endorsed the theory that whoever was behind "Loyalist Action" was employing a sophisticated and highly trained urban guerrilla group to act for them. Was it possible, Dalziell asked, that with this destructive spiral they hoped to provoke still more savage reprisals—rather like the Baader-Meinhof gang, who had been thought to be seeking an authoritarian backlash with general anarchy the ultimate aim?

Whether Dalziell's theories were correct or not, a pattern of murder was spreading like a stain of blood across the world. This Saint Patrick's morning it had reached New York.

☘ ☘ ☘

The ancient proverb that begins "A bear coughs at the North Pole . . ." mirrors a mystical belief in universal involvement. The bear coughs and a man dies of a heart attack in Brazil. Or a baby girl is born in Wellington, New Zealand. These events share a mysterious identity.

The Saint Patrick's Day Massacre killed some people and deeply marked or marred the lives of others. If some modern incarnation of the demon Asmodeus could have observed them in the days immediately before the Massacre, he would have found some of them much concerned with forthcoming events, but others profoundly indifferent.

Tom Dillon didn't expect this Saint Patrick's Day to have any particular significance for him—any more than any of the other Saint Pat's Days that had preceded it. Sure, he was Irish, but "nonpracticing" as he sometimes told his uncle, old Seamus Dillon.

He was in bed with a girl who called herself Linda Casaboud and they had just made love. She had talked right through it and now she went on talking.

"Good!" she said. "That was good, Dillon."

"Not just good. Terrific! The best."

It hadn't been, of course. What they had enjoyed was okay, but only okay. The violins hadn't played, to recall a phrase from the first happy days of his now-defunct marriage. (For how long had the violins played for him and Nancy? Three months? Two?) But Linda was acting a part and Tom hadn't the heart not to respond to her cues.

He reached over now and touched her nipples. "Nice!"

"It's nice you think they're nice, Dillon."

"Call me Tom, will you?"

"Dillon, I know money enters into this, our relationship, but I want to ask you something, and I want you to believe I'm sincere when I ask it, right?"

"Right."

She was frowning. "Dillon, they say a woman's gotta define her sexuality *as* a woman. Only way to do that is to make it with a man, right? But then, well, they say you get fucked over by sex without love, you're just an object for male lust, right?"

Tom smiled. "Linda, you're okay."

He shouldn't have dismissed it like that. But, however repugnant the phrase was, he was her john, hiring her to talk with, screw with, fill for him the emptiness of the next few days. So did he have to "relate to Linda as a person"—as she'd have put it herself?

Kindness—basic, stranger-in-the-street kindness—dictated that he should. Linda was pathetic: sixteen or seventeen and already a hooker, however soft and unprofessional her approach, shoring her ruins with outdated jargon from women's lib.

This pathos had attracted him at first. That, and a sense of anonymity, almost of mystery. Linda was small and dark and came from Southern California, that harsh yet seductive land of the Mojave and the Santa Ana that Tom, born in the East, always found fascinating.

Pathetic or not, strange he should patronize Linda. Thomas Augustine Dillon, thirty-two years old, former United States Marine, once described by *People* magazine as "restless and footloose ex-husband of chic, trend-chasing steel heiress Nancy Biddle Jones, now rumored to be involved with Gloria Steinem in the launching of a new magazine reflecting a less-explored aspect of women's liberation."

That had been some time ago and as with most of Nancy's enthusiasms, the magazine still hadn't gotten itself launched. But "restless" and "footloose" were still fair comment on Dillon. Why else would he shack up with a teenage hooker in this shabby anonymous motel on the coast near Carmel?

Tom suddenly felt chilled and pulled the covers over his nakedness. He tried to see himself as Linda must see him: a Black Irishman, six feet tall and one hundred and seventy-eight pounds—exactly his weight when he'd been inducted at boot camp. What did she think of him? Okay, he was just another trick to her, but had she appraised his still-taut stomach and still *in situ* hairline as well as his billfold? Or did hookers even notice? Was he just displaying the eternal, ludicrous vanity of the john?

The thought half amused, half irked him, and he turned to look at her. She got off the bed and walked across the room. He took in her long, clearly defined backbone and small buttocks, striped tallow-white against the bronze by the tiny bikini pants she'd worn.

She fumbled with the knobs of the TV, needing its compulsive chatter to fill even a moment's silence. And why not? Wasn't he using her for just the same purpose?

Tom closed his eyes and bunched himself up, fetuslike, willing himself into a tight ball of negation that rejected this place, this girl, this world. Maybe it was like that bitch Nancy had enjoyed telling him—that he was a man gripped in the vise of violent experiences he was not mature enough to relate to. A man still in thrall to the self-indulgent machismo shit that had sent him to Nam in the first place.

Maybe. But maybe not. The mood of self-lacerating soul-searching that had gripped America in the tail of Nam and Watergate had been all too opportune for Nancy. Rejecting Nam and those who had fought there enabled Nancy to reject Tom too, and that figured.

Fuck her anyway. He wasn't going to hang his head in shame for the motives—self-indulgence, machismo, or whatever—that had caused him to volunteer. He wasn't about to apologize for doing—okay, it was a cliché but it was true—what he had to do. Three tours of duty as a grunt in Nam had changed him, of course. They would have changed any man. But hundreds, thousands, of women had welcomed back husbands thus similarly changed—bloodstained, disoriented, haunted by pale dead faces in the night. Not women like Nancy, though: arrogant, destructively self-driven, high on women's liberation as if it were a newly discovered drug that created new and fascinating enmities.

Linda, watching a newscast, was calling.

"Dillon! Hey, Dillon . . ."

He didn't answer.

"Dillon—you know something? Tomorrow is Saint Patrick's Day."

"Really?"

"Bigger and better than ever before, they just said. Two hundred forty bands and a hundred twenty thousand marchers."

"That's formidable, Linda."

"I bet you seen the parade a lot of times, Dillon."

"Not a chance. Macy's parade, maybe. I'd go to that."

She laughed, and he closed his eyes again. Going to watch the parade had been a part of his childhood. They'd usually had places in a building on the corner of Fifty-sixth Street, across from Bonwit Teller; his mother had insisted on having places, although Tom had always sensed a certain hostility in her. Irish she might be and proud of it, but not the kind of Irish who enjoyed this kind of vulgar drumbeating and flag-waving. His father always appeared to enjoy the day as much as Tom or his brother Wendell did, and they enjoyed it a great deal.

All the same, Tom wasn't about to see any more Saint Patrick's Day parades. At this hour of his life he was inoculated against the maddening and irrational virus that can infect any American of Irish descent: the myth of Ireland. Either the myth of A Little Bit of Heaven peopled exclusively by leprechauns and dewy-eyed colleens, or the darker myth of Kathleen ni Houlihan still in pawn to her Saxon conqueror, waiting to be freed from her chains. Leave all of that ancient shit to his uncle, Seamus Dillon, a man almost as old as the century, an Irish-American who had actually fought on Irish soil in the Civil War of 1922, an untiring propagandist who raised millions of dollars for Irish republican causes (as well as making a few millions for himself from his own pharmaceutical firm), the founder of Justice for Ulster.

Yes, Uncle Seamus could have Ireland. Anyway, the old guy had the support of Tom's brother Wendell, and that was worth having. Despite his comparative youth, Senator Wendell Dillon had been a civil-rights pioneer, rivaling Paul O'Dwyer in his dedication to liberal causes. He had given his Uncle Seamus and Justice for Ulster substantial, though not unquestioning support. No doubt his detractors would say he was ass-licking for the Irish-American vote. But, saying that, they must know they were being naive. The Irish-American vote hardly existed in that sense anymore—certainly not for a politician like Wendell Dillon.

"Hey, Dillon," Linda was calling again.

"Yes?"

"You got no business to laugh at the Saint Patrick's Parade. You ought to be proud you're a harp."

She was smiling. "Dillon—I'm a harp too." She paused. "Casaboud—it's my father's name. My mother was Mary Kelly from Upper Darby in Philly."

Tom shook his head. "Tough shit. C'mon! Back to bed."

Frankie McNagan had certainly been concerned about forthcoming events. Fifteen minutes before they were due to land at Kennedy, she was gripped by panic at what lay ahead of her. Then she heard one of the two men sitting behind her mention "Ireland" and was immediately alert.

"I never know why people like Tip O'Neill and Governor Carey go on talking about that place." The voice was elderly, grumbling.

"I think we have to give them credit for some concern." This second voice was lighter, younger, and could have belonged to an Irishman who had lived a long time in the States. "You have to agree the situation is getting worse all the time."

"I don't know. Who gives a good goddamn, really? Anyway, beats me why the British don't just get out of there."

"It's not that simple—" the younger man began, but the older man cut him short with "It's an old-hat story to me—that Northern Ireland stuff!"

As the older man went on to grumble about the chairman of the Federal Reserve's attitude to the president's latest anti-inflation proposals, Frankie thought how strange that ten centuries of her country's suffering should be dismissed as old hat by someone who had just been in Ireland (this Aer Lingus 707 had left Shannon a few hours before). For a second she felt rage at the smugness that could yawn off a cause that was life and death to her. Then she forgot the grumbling voices behind her and thought again of the grueling tests ahead.

She wasn't so worried about her passport, although she wouldn't feel secure till she was through Immigration. The passport *must* be okay. O Dunnacha Duane had assured her of that when she last saw him in Dublin.

She had simply borrowed someone else's identity. The name on her passport was "Mary Ogham," and she had the real Mary Ogham's enthusiastic cooperation. Mary was twenty-five, the same age as Frankie, and a native of Newcastle West, County Limerick. A graduate of University College, Galway, she was a horticultural adviser with Mayo County Council. Her family had strong links with the Irish republican movement—known in Ireland simply as The Movement. When the Wednesday Committee chose Frankie for this vital mission to New York, they knew she would need a cover. Duane suggested she take the identity of someone like Mary Ogham, a republican sympathizer but not politically active. That meant her name did not appear on any police file in Ireland or America or anywhere else. As an added advantage, she had never held a passport. Two weeks ago she had applied for one, giving all her correct particulars (she and Frankie were physically very similar) but substituting Frankie's picture for her own. All passport photographs had to be verified by a professional person like a lawyer or clergyman, so Duane had invoked Father Maurice Wenham (known in the movement as "An tAthair Muiris"—Irish for "Father Maurice"), who had duly certified that the girl in the photograph was Mary Ogham.

No, the passport had to be okay. Frankie was more worried about the fact that she had not only taken over Mary's name, but her American relatives as well. In a few minutes she would meet Mary's cousins—the daughters of a family called O'Keeffe, who ran an "Irish pub" near the 207th Street Bridge at the northernmost tip of Manhattan. The three teenaged daughters had never met Mary Ogham, although their parents had, on their last visit to Ireland, when Mary was only six.

Mary told Frankie the O'Keeffes would accept her without question, but Frankie wasn't so sure. She knew she resembled Mary physically, but she had a dread of the O'Keeffes instinctively rejecting her as an imposter, thus wrecking this all-important mission. Mary had mentioned casually to Frankie that the O'Keeffe girls were crazy about anything Irish. They had won prizes for Irish dancing when they were kids, they followed Gaelic games with great interest. "More than I do," Frankie murmured. Mary wasn't so casual when she drilled Frankie in every ramification of the O'Keeffe and Ogham family trees. Names. Who had married whom and where they were living. The Irish passion for genealogy certainly crossed the Atlantic with the emigrants to burgeon among their descendants.

Of course Frankie was used to working—living—under a cover identity, but never before under the gaze of a whole family. She'd protested to Duane, but he thought Mary Ogham, a young Irish woman on vacation with her cousins in New York, excellent from a security point of view. But Frankie knew Duane's passion for "security" often only masked his plotter's love for the tortuous and mysterious. Staying with these stranger "cousins" could only increase the risks she was running. "What about my accent?" she demanded. (Her years in London with her mother had left her voice with some English nuances.) "Sure, just thicken the broth with the brogue a little," he retorted. Then, more seriously, he pointed out that since she was making contact with Seamus Dillon, a famous Irish republican in the States who had been under surveillance by the FBI for years, the O'Keeffes could provide an invaluable background for her if she were herself picked up and questioned by the FBI. The O'Keeffes were intensely respectable; lifelong Democrats with a token loyalty to the idea of Irish unity. Old Seamus Dillon had many friends in Ireland: what more likely than that Mary Ogham, visiting with her cousins in America, should be asked to bring him greetings from the Ould Country?

It sounded fine as Duane told it back in Dublin. Now she wasn't so sure. Suddenly she felt exhausted: consumed by her obsessive, aching sense of always being a conspirator, a fugitive. She had, after all, been on the lam from the Irish Special Branch for the past two years. That was a fact that had to take its toll.

But whom was she fooling? Didn't she, too, enjoy these paranoid games? Didn't she find some strange kind of fulfillment in her flight through this world of shifting masks?

She had to admit she did, ever since she had first met her husband, Francis McNagan. (He had the same name as her—he was "Francis," she "Frances"— which was why they were known in the movement as the Two Frankies, and why each of them referred to the other as the Other Frankie.) Falling in love with him, she had become a captive of the Irish republican dream—the vision of one Ireland, United, Gaelic, and Free, which was crystallized in the name of the small group to which she and the Other Frankie and Duane all belonged: Eireann Amhain.

No, in her heart she knew what was tormenting her: a mixture of uneasy passion and consuming guilt. The Other Frankie was in jail in England— convicted of a crime he hadn't committed—and while she appeared to be the classic Irish republican wife, regularly visiting her husband in the high-security wing of Parkhurst Prison, in every way loyal, she was in fact betraying him with his longtime comrade and political guru, O Dunnacha Duane. She still loved Frankie, she still wanted him—and yet she wanted Duane too.

She thought of their last time together in the apartment in Dublin Duane had borrowed from some anonymous friend: a drab academic's hideout near Trinity College, dusty with piled-up copies of *Proceedings of the Archaeological Society of Ireland* and cluttered with glass cases full of flint implements. She had exulted in Duane's body pressing down on her, as he took her on the shabby sofa; huge, black-bearded, buccaneerlike, and yet endlessly cerebral— talking, experimenting, even joking, all the times he caressed her, pierced her, enjoyed her. Somehow this lustful coldness was more exciting than the Other Frankie's silent, more conventional tenderness. Ice can burn sharper than fire.

And yet, a few hours afterward, as she sat waiting for the plane to take off at Shannon, the guilt sat like a leaden weight on her brain. Frankie was a prisoner deprived of everything, and most of all of love. Wasn't she inflicting the cruelest of insults upon him? She remembered how the Other Frankie had looked the last time she visited him in Parkhurst. Saying goodbye to him, she'd thought how pale he looked, almost fevered, his look of suffering overlaid by a grin that didn't fool anybody. What was he thinking? Did he guess?

Frankie settled herself back in her seat, a small, self-contained girl whose dark good looks had an inner, brooding quality that—according to the Other

Frankie—only just stopped her from being a full-blown Irish beauty in the Spanish style.

They were coming down into Jamaica Bay. The stewardesses were making the usual announcements.

Never mind Duane. Think about the O'Keeffes and the performance she was about to give for their benefit. Relax. Smile. More important, think about what she was going to say to Seamus Dillon.

"Yes," Wendell Dillon said, "the situation there is getting worse all the time. The country is steadily being pushed towards the brink."

"Then why doesn't the president intervene?" his wife, Cheryl, asked.

"An American initiative on Ireland?" Wendell smiled. "Any Dublin journalist has a column to fill, he comes up with that. Of course," he added, "the Irish in Ireland always exaggerate our interest in their affairs."

She nodded. "That's natural, I guess."

"And don't forget," he continued, "no American president has ever intervened directly in anything that concerns the British. Woodrow Wilson came the nearest. When we went into World War One he told them that self-government for Ireland would please the American people." Wendell paused. "Unfortunately Wilson was too much of an Anglophile to follow that through, and no president had bothered his ass about Ireland since."

"Of course," Cheryl said, "we have to admit there are places around the world where our intervention hasn't been the happiest thing that ever happened."

"Right," Wendell said and grinned wryly. He thought again how lucky he was to have her—Cheryl, his wife, his love, who ministered to his happiness in a thousand ways. Her alertness, her sensibility, never grew stale, never hardened into the routine mask of a Washington professional's wife.

"More coffee?" she asked and lifted the silver pot embossed with the device of her family. Genuine Southern gentry, the Sugdens, although Cheryl always mocked that by saying, "Yeah: real old Southern whiskey gentry." But you only had to see their old home, Battle Hill, on the direct line of Sherman's march to the sea: built of red, uneven slave bricks and fronted with classic white columns, at the end of a drive bordered with great magnolias. Perfect for yet another filming of *Gone With the Wind*, but the real thing. Style. Cheryl had it. Even this new house in Georgetown reflected her sense of the past enriching the present. How Wendell's mother loved the ambience Cheryl created here! She had been delighted by his marriage; indeed, she had approved the choices of both her sons. Both marriages had propitiated her oddly snobbish attitude toward Irish-Americans. She'd simply loved Tom allying himself with Nancy Biddle Jones, impeccably WASP, with roots reaching back to the Salem of Cotton Mather and his witch-burners; been ravished by Wendell's marriage to the only daughter of a fine ole Southern gentleman like Senator Sam Sugden. Not a drop of Irish blood in either gal—and that gratified Kathleen Dillon. She would have been less pleased if Tom or Wendell had married into one of the so-called First Irish Families—a Murry, a Cuddihy, a McDonnell, or even a Kennedy.

"Of course," Wendell went on, "having said that, I'll contradict myself like a good politician." He paused. "Sooner or later there *has* to be an initiative on Northern Ireland—and we have to make it. Who else?" He shook his head. "Something tells me the British wouldn't relish it coming from their beloved fellow Europeans. From the Germans? The French?"

"Hugh Carey," Cheryl said. "Tip O'Neill. And of course Teddy Kennedy. They've been saying it for years."

Wendell nodded. "Sure, it needed saying." He frowned. "But those guys are politicians—and politics is the art of the possible. They weren't thinking of this year or next. But someday—yes."

"When does that day come then?" she asked.

"When things get bad enough—when enough people die."

She nodded; didn't speak. Indeed, she looked a little abstracted. She must be tired, he thought, for one of the things he loved most about her was her inability to harbor boredom, even when he felt impelled to unburden himself of some dreary contretemps on Capitol Hill.

He glanced up at the wide mirror above the fireplace. There they were: Cheryl, Titian-haired, exquisite; himself, tall, fair, fresh-complexioned (his brother Tom was the Black Irishman of the family); the elegant couple who appreciate the Good things in an advertisement for a quality product.

He reflected that despite the fact that Irish terror was now spilling out across the world, there would probably be less interest in an American initiative on Ireland at this present time than there would have been when the Four Horsemen (as the New York *Times* had dubbed Edward Kennedy, Tip O'Neill, Hugh Carey, and Daniel Moynihan) had first appealed to Britain to move on Northern Ireland some years ago.

A colder wind was blowing—from every quarter—and nowhere was it more apparent than here in Washington. These days Wendell had moments, dark-night-of-the-soul moments, when he felt like a ghost here, in this town that had once intoxicated him with a thousand glittering choices.

That had been toward the end of the JFK era. A kind of magic had hung over everything then. No doubt some would tell you Camelot held within it the seeds of its own destruction, but for Wendell the magic had been real enough. Particularly for him, coming from a family that had money but no political edge. Inevitably it had been said that he'd gotten into the Senate through his father-in-law, Sam Sugden—and then had promptly kicked away the ladder the old man had provided. Well, Cheryl was the best judge of that and she'd never once reproached him. She had gone along with all of his causes—not only Ireland but Jews in Soviet Russia, Basque separatists, Israel, illegal immigrants in the States.

But now at the beginning of the eighties, the landscape had changed beyond recognition. In the present Senate, liberals were so scarce they walked like dodos. There was little doubt that today folks were obsessed with domestic ills—the energy crisis, high interest rates, above all inflation—and who could blame them? No wonder Wendell only half-joshingly quoted to Cheryl: "Othello's occupation's gone."

Now he said: "Not that any initiative could ever bring a United Ireland. Not in our lifetime. The best we could hope for would be a British withdrawal and then some kind of independent Northern Ireland state guaranteed by both the British and ourselves."

"Hasn't that been suggested already?"

"That's right." Wendell nodded. "Angus McStay, the Belfast MP, suggested it a year or two ago. Interesting thing—he got support from both Catholics *and* Protestants. Someone said it revived the spirit of Ninety-Eight."

"I know someone who wouldn't give it support," Cheryl said. "Your Uncle Seamus. For him it would be Ireland betrayed all over again."

Wendell grinned, delighted as always by the quick thrust of her mind. "Right."

"More coffee?" He shook his head this time and she poured herself a cup. Suddenly she said sharply, "Do you really have to go to New York tonight?"

"I really do. You know I'm marching in the parade."

"Marching up Fifth Avenue with a crowd of people banging drums and carrying banners. Honestly, Wendell, haven't you gotten a little beyond that?"

He shook his head. "I'm surprised you could ask me that. The day I get too rarefied, too goddamn pompous to march in that parade—"

She cut in. "I think it's just sentiment. Or rather, sentimentality. That's the basis of your whole relationship with your uncle."

"Cheryl!" he protested. "That's not true! Anyway, I have to speak at the

Loyal Sons of Saint Patrick Ball at the Americana tomorrow night. *That's* politics, if the parade isn't!"

She seemed to accept that; she didn't speak for a moment. Then she said, "Wendell—is there anything worrying you?"

"No. Of course not."

"I think there's something you're not telling me."

He didn't answer.

"I don't know," she said after a tiny pause, and suddenly opened her eyes wide, a trick she used when particularly concerned. They were turquoise and very beautiful. "I don't know what to think."

He still didn't answer. She was right—there *was* something—but he wasn't about to tell her what it was.

The strange thing was, this had been one of the few wholly spontaneous acts of his life, for he had always realized that a politician must invariably move with Hobbesian calculation—even when he appears to be acting on impulse. But on this occasion he had broken that rule and maybe it was about to cost him.

He could excuse himself when he thought of that time. Bloody Sunday in Derry was still vivid in everyone's mind. Violence in the North of Ireland was growing by the hour. There was talk of a massacre of Catholics by Protestant extremists. And his Uncle Seamus had been building up the foundation.

Wendell had never asked his uncle what he was doing. As a United States Senator he conceived it as his duty not to have knowledge of acts that were certainly illegal, but he was well aware that the old man was preparing for a Doomsday situation in Ireland (which was why the foundation came to be known as the doomsday foundation).

He remembered the night his uncle had called him—nearly five years ago. Wendell had spent the afternoon parrying a variety of Washington lobbyists and was having a quiet drink with Cheryl when Old Seamus called. Long distance. From New York, Wendell assumed, but it turned out Seamus was in Kansas City. Odd enough, but Seamus sounded quite relaxed. A good friend of his suddenly found himself in a slight dilemma. Nothing serious. Only delay could be awkward at this particular time. The friend was a decent fellow called O'Reilly from Cahirciveen in the County Kerry. Seamus had paused then, a little longer than was necessary, and Wendell only now appreciated that the pause was to make the nature of this affair clear. It was an "administrative problem," Seamus said. There was a man at Defense Systems Sales. Name was Austin Hogg. Clearance with the appropriate department for the goods O'Reilly was exporting was what was being sought. No, it would not do for Seamus to call Hogg. Wendell it would have to be . . .

Tired? Euphoric? Wendell couldn't remember what his mood had been that night five years ago. Certainly he hadn't considered refusing his uncle's request. Next morning he had called Hogg at the Defense Systems Sales Unit, identified himself, mentioned O'Reilly's "administrative problem"—and then more or less forgotten the whole thing.

Until three days ago. Then he had seen a news item—a tiny one but it seemed to leap toward him, burning at his eyes as if the words were set in molten metal—saying that Hogg had been subpoenaed before a grand jury. The granting of certain licenses was being investigated by the Treasury Department. Machine guns and rocket launchers officially destined for Iraq had been diverted elsewhere. The suggestion was that Hogg had used his position at Defense sales to facilitate abuse of the regulations regarding the export of arms. The grand jury also wished to subpoena an Iraqi diplomat, said to be involved with Hogg, but the diplomat had now conveniently been transferred to South Yemen.

That was it. A cloud no bigger than a man's hand that could still, in this post-Watergate America, mushroom and blot out the sun.

Or maybe not. Maybe the cloud would never get any bigger. There were scandals that never got off the ground. He certainly wouldn't worry Cheryl with this. Not yet.

☘ ☘ ☘

"Harps!" Malachi O'Farrell said. "I hate them, even though I'm one of them. All these New York dudes who become bog-trotting Irish peasants every seventeenth of March! Well, tomorrow they're gonna get it, and boy do they deserve it!"

Brenda Wilson didn't answer. She continued to lie on the bed, her thighs slightly parted, her mouth half open. She wore a tattered T-shirt and nothing else. Now she yawned and drew her knees up to her chin, swiveling around on her buttocks till she was facing him.

She wanted him to avert his eyes. Then she could jeer. Say something about some men becoming eunuchs for the kingdom of heaven's sake. That was why Malachi kept looking. Even though he felt like throwing up.

"You wouldn't understand," he said after a moment. "You're not Irish. And you're not a Catholic. You don't know what the Catholic Church is like, but I'll tell you. It's a power-grabbing oligarchy that puts little bugs into kids' heads around the time they're baptized—and then keeps them activated till it's time for the requiem mass and the conqueror worm!" He paused. "They never let you go."

He was silent, savoring his hatred like acid in his throat.

"And the more Irish, the more Catholic," he went on. "Yeah—that goes! That figures. Communion breakfasts at the Commodore and Emerald Society Balls at the Roosevelt—and then let's go and liberate Kathleen Mavoureen from the wicked pagan English." He shook his head. "Irish liberty? My own family—green fascists! What does the average Irish-American care about liberty even *here*—here in the States? Niggers and spicks get the fuck off the sidewalk—I'm on my way to mass!"

She spoke at last. "Okay, okay. But methinks you do protest too much."

"Well," he said in a quieter voice. "The president has announced his initiative. Could you hear it in here?"

"I was asleep."

"Now that he's spoken, everything can go ahead as planned."

"Wouldn't it have anyway?"

He shrugged and went into the next room without answering. Being chained to this bitch, this self-styled urban guerrilla, threatened to spoil an exciting and enjoyable assignment. But this was probably policy with Lang: he liked to team opposites together—even enemies, calculating that the tension between them gave their performance an extra edge. Besides, distrusting each other, they were less likely to depart in any particular from Lang's instructions.

It occurred to Malachi how much he would like to kill Brenda, grab her by the hair and bang her head against the wall. Or strangle her with that big candystriped bath towel—twisting and turning the towel, knowing that her face would get first red and then purple and that her eyes would pop like marbles and her tongue would stick out, enormous, black and putrescent like a rotted banana.

His body was strung taut: picturing, exulting. Then he clasped his hands and murmured, "Domine, non sum dignus"—the old pre-Communion prayer that went back to Origen and Chrysostom. Hating the Church as he did, Malachi still found some prayers useful as a kind of ju-ju to relax him.

Sure enough, after a moment he did feel more relaxed, but he continued to stand in the center of the room: a tall man in his middle thirties with the long upperlip and almost Egyptian cheekbones that distinguish some Irish faces. His thick black hair was beginning to gray.

He thought how everything in the room reflected Ben Mocatta, the owner. The star decals appliquéd into the sky-blue ceiling, the woolen rug, the old bamboo bookcase stuffed with yesterday's intellectual elite in battered paperback. It was all pitiable and futile and dead. Malachi despised Ben, but if he'd ever told that to Ben, the man would simply have looked puzzled—and interested. He'd have wanted to discuss it. Malachi loathed Ben's goddamn masochistic Jewish sensibility, though it had its uses. Who else would have lent him this crummy apartment at four hours' notice, no questions asked? Ben made a big deal of not asking questions: he was a "Nonjudging" person, to use his own phrase. A romantic like Ben loved the thought of helping a man on the lam, so Malachi had let him think the police still wanted him, Malachi, for questioning about the shooting of a Digger couple from San Francisco on Mulberry Street in 1968.

Ten after ten. Malachi ran down the stairs and into the street. He walked away fast for maybe fifty yards, then paused at the corner of Second Street and Avenue A. The night air struck cold. He stood for a moment, looking both ways, then started north up Avenue A. He shivered and hunched his shoulders as he walked. For Malachi these streets were plangent with memories of the sixties. The carving of the East Village out of the Lower East Side; the times he had met with folk-heroes like Jerry Rubin and Abbie Hoffman and achieved a mention in *The East Village Other*.

The pay telephone Malachi had chosen was dank and dirty and smelled of urine but at least it was working. If it hadn't been, the arrangement was for John Grunwald to call Malachi a half hour later at a bar on Sixth Street. But this booth was more anonymous and therefore preferable to a bar, even though the answers Malachi would give Grunwald would be entirely monosyllabic.

He studied the graffiti on the walls of the booth, variously celebrating incest, pedophilia, and shit-eating. It was 10:21 P.M. Grunwald might call any time up to 10:30. Then Malachi hoped to hear that the first stage of the Saint Patrick's Day operation was complete, leaving everything ready, primed, for the moment soon after noon tomorrow when he, Malachi, would press the button, burning and blasting those fools with their banners and slogans, their laughing and prancing and tinsel harps.

It hadn't been too hard to set up, really. As Lang had pointed out before Malachi had left Algiers, Malachi's own family background would give him entrée to the Irish-American circles mounting the parade. But it was also important that there be nothing to link him personally with the bombing. Two weeks ago Malachi had reestablished contact with his family. Turning up at their home out beyond the Pelham Parkway, he'd gotten the fatted calf treatment just as he'd expected. Seeing him resurface after eight or nine years in Mexico and Europe and God knows where else, not even his father was inclined to bug him with too many questions. And when Malachi just happened to mention that on his travels he had started going to mass again—feeling a kind of irresistible pull back to the sacraments—well, then he really was the Prodigal Son! Just to make his father's cup brim right over, he let drop that he had actually met some of the leaders of the Provisional IRA when in

Dublin; had even had a few drinks with one of them in one of their favored bars on Parnell Street. That really set the old man's adrenaline spurting. Born in Edgeworthstown, County Longford, he had retired after thirty years with the New York Central Railroad, and now all his vital energies were absorbed by a fanatical Catholicism and an obsessive interest in Gaelic games.

The O'Farrells belonged to all the Irish-American organizations—the Ancient Order of Hibernians, the Society for Irish Freedom, Justice for Ulster—and it would have been easy for Malachi to get the information he needed himself. But this of course he dared not do. The strategy, he had agreed with Lang, was to introduce an agent under a cover identity. This was an Irish Protestant named McVeagh, who had served with a Loyalist execution squad during the worst of the sectarian killing in Belfast. McVeagh adopted the identity of a Catholic called Liam Hannigan (who had been killed and left in a lime pit twenty miles outside Belfast). Hannigan-McVeagh had all the right answers—he was even able to sing the ballads his tribal enemies, the Catholics, sang across in the Falls—and of course these Irish republicans from Queens and Flatbush were thrilled to meet a real live IRA man from Ireland.

McVeagh had been able to find out where the musical instruments for the bands of the One Ireland League and Justice for Ulster were left the evening before the parade. (The One Ireland League had been picked at random: Justice for Ulster was the real target.) It had seemed unlikely to Malachi that the bandsmen would bring the heavier instruments like the big drums through the Manhattan traffic on the morning of the parade, but he was still relieved to hear from McVeagh that they would in fact be deposited at the AOH committee rooms on West Forty-fifth Street the previous evening.

This information obtained—McVeagh had pretended to be a musician, thinking of marching in the parade himself—his function was over. It was time for him to bow out and for John Grunwald to take over. Grunwald was—in no particular sequence—ex-army explosives expert, ex-Weatherman, and ex-FBI informer. Once Malachi knew where the drums were to be left, he contacted Grunwald (pretending to pick him up at a gay sauna notable for casual encounters). Grunwald was confident. No sweat, he indicated, for a professional like him to first burgle the AOH rooms and then get at the drums.

The actual charges to be placed inside each drum could not be large—obviously they couldn't add significantly to its weight or the bandsmen would notice.

Each of the big drums would contain 200 grams of a TNT-based mixture known as Composition B, with prefragmented spirally wound steel coil wrapped around it (in the side drums, 100 grams were used in exactly the same way).

Lang's explosives man, Bud Rosen, had designed these bombs after the U.S. Army M26 grenade, and had come up with a safety circuit that would allow them to be detonated only by a coded pulse peculiar to the remote-control equipment Malachi would carry. Malachi and Brenda Wilson had already conducted a rehearsal, tracing the parade's intended route up Fifth Avenue. Malachi walked up one side of the avenue while Brenda went up the other. Then, at the key points of St. Regis Hotel and St. Thomas Church, Malachi twice tested the radio-control device, transmitting a signal that switched on a tiny bulb that Brenda carried in her shopping bag. It worked perfectly.

Now Malachi was simply waiting for Grunwald to confirm that he had successfully entered the AOH rooms and set up everything in readiness for tomorrow. Of course the whole operation could have been botched, Watergate-style. Grunwald could have been caught in the act of burgling the committee rooms . . .

But Malachi reflected that when Lang planned something the luck seemed to hold. As Lang said, "You have to believe you're lucky. Otherwise you're dead."

In a sudden gust of exaltation Malachi flung open the door of the booth, letting the icy wind twirl the garbage around his legs. He felt such a sense of power bursting inside him that it must be apparent to others. He didn't care. Those long-haired derelicts and shivering Puerto Ricans mooning past—if only they knew who he was, what he was about to do! He wanted to shout at them, alert them, proclaim the existential beauty of tomorrow's deed.

And so the causal chain extends and tautens, gains new links. At the moment Patrolman O'Leary blows his whistle and sets the parade stepping up Fifth Avenue, Tom Dillon embraces Linda Casaboud in the Red Arrow Motel and wonders why pity so effectively kills desire; Frankie McNagan steps out smartly in the company of her supposed O'Keeffe cousins, marching with the Catholic Daughters of America; Senator Wendell Dillon leads the Justice for Ulster contingent, walking immediately behind the band; Malachi O'Farrell moves swiftly through the laughing, shamrock-toting crowds that throng the sidewalks, among them but not of them.

And so the parade moves on, speeded by laughter, marching proudly to the *oompah, oompah* of two hundred and forty bands as they play "Yankee Doodle Dandy" and "It's a Great Day for the Irish" and "The Battle Hymn of the Republic," basking in the great roar of applause that ebbs and flows like ocean tides.

Lang nodded. "Like I said: terror is theater."

The three of them—Rex Lang, Mark Durnan, and Leni Reffenstab—were sitting on the patio of the Villa Ben Kalah, a large house in El Biar, a suburb of Algiers. It was the moment of the North African dusk when light objects grow brighter and the dark, darker. Any second, night would come.

Lang said, "How many more times are they gonna mention the Kennedys?"

They had been listening to the newscasts on Radio Marseilles. The Frog commentators mostly ignored the political aspects of "Les bombes dans New York" and stuck to the human tragedies, notably "L'assassination du Senator Dillon," which they inevitably compared to the killings of John and Robert Kennedy. Lang had been listening with a half-smile on his face, rapidly summarizing the reports in English for Mark Durnan's benefit—Leni of course spoke French—but now he muttered "Shit!" and switched off.

Durnan said, "Looks like the operation was a success."

"We can judge that better when we get all the reviews." Lang grinned. "The fact that the French even mention it! They're the most insular bastards on earth."

"How many killed, Rex?" Leni Reffenstab asked.

"Fifty-seven," Lang said. "At the last count." He paused. "Not bad. They can't complain of that."

No one answered. Lang was eating a mandarin orange, and he leaned forward to spit a pip into an empty glass in front of him. Then he lolled back, a man just short of six feet tall, with a smooth, unlined face and thick, dust-colored hair cut on the short side. He might have been thirty-five years old, but hardly forty. American or apparently American, he spoke the ironed-out, mid-Atlantic English that can be heard in Dublin and Berlin as well as in Manhattan.

No doubt about Mark Durnan being American. With his muscular frame, his red hair and freckles, he had a directness of speech and movement, a forthright on-the-nose quality that made it hard to believe he was anything else. He was thirty, a veteran of the radical underground of the 1960s, of the occupation of Columbia University and the Days of Rage in Chicago. Most of his comrades of that time had resurfaced long ago. Awkward, obsolete survivors, they had thrown themselves on the mercy of a coldly different world. Durnan had done better: he had met Rex Lang.

Sprawled on the chair next to Lang, her full breasts thrusting against her silk shirt, her taut buttocks molded by tight jeans, with her long black tresses and olive skin Leni Reffenstab looked more Italian than German. She was twenty-nine and a newcomer to Lang's group, having arrived at the Villa Ben Kalah less than two months ago. The daughter of a wealthy industrial consultant in Hanover, she had been a member of the Movement Second June (so called after the death of student Benno Ohnesorg on June 2, 1967, and responsible for the kidnapping of Peter Lorenz, chairman of the West Berlin Christian Democrats). Lang had recruited Leni in Rotterdam. She had been hiding out there, alone and desperately short of money, sought by Interpol as a suspect in the killing of Dr. Hans-Martin Schleyer.

Lang leaned forward. "Hey! Any room service around here?"

Durnan clapped his hands sharply and called, "Keach!"

Immediately a tall man appeared at a doorway. He hurried across the patio, dragging himself forward with lurching, topheavy movements.

"Come on! Move it!" Durnan shouted.

Keach increased his pace till he stood in front of Lang—a dazed-looking giant, gasping for breath.

"Take these away." Lang indicated the empty wine bottle and dirty glasses.

Keach started to put the glasses onto a tray.

"Keach!" Lang hit him across the mouth with the flat of his hand. The noise of the blow struck across the patio like the crack of a whip. "Don't waste time washing those glasses, hear? Clean ones and another bottle!"

Keach was making snuffling, gobbling sounds that were clearly an attempt to speak. Picking up the tray, he turned and shuffled away across the patio.

"Rex," Leni protested, "I don't know how you can stand to have him around. That noise he makes!"

Lang smiled. "What would he find to say if he could talk? This way is better."

Lang was said to have met Keach when he was with the Montoneros in Argentina. The shambling giant had developed a doglike devotion toward Lang and had become a kind of personal servant to him during Lang's time with the *guerrilleros*. Apparently Keach had earlier been punished Tupamaro-style for some breach of security. A rubber band had been tied around his throat and the ends brought together and slowly twisted—not to strangle him but to break his thyroid.

Frowning, Leni watched Keach cross the patio. Lang grinned and said, "Anyone talks too much—that's what they get."

"Pour encourager les autres," Durnan added.

"That is a quotation, Mark?" Leni asked.

"Admiral Byng commanded the English fleet against the French in 1757. He lost the battle and so they shot him—to encourage the others!"

Lang laughed. "The British had balls in those days."

Night was coming down fast. Leni liked it out here, although everything suggested decay. The bougainvillea that gripped the broken flagstones. The fountain in the center of the patio that had ceased to flow. Soon they would be leaving here and going to Ireland. Leni wondered if Lang would feel any regret. Algiers had been his base for a long time.

She decided he wouldn't care. Life came to Lang in a series of expendable frames, momentarily vivid but self-destructing the next moment.

Keach was back with fresh glasses and another bottle of white wine. Lang nodded and Keach went off.

"Well," Lang said as he poured wine into Leni's and Durnan's glasses. "Loyalist Action got the action they paid for."

Durnan nodded. "Sure, Rex."

"Like to have seen it," Lang said. "From a chopper above the Avenue." He shook his head. "But Malachi had the greater claim, right? His finest hour."

They drank in silence for a few minutes. Then Lang said, "Who wants to guess what Leni is thinking?" He paused. "I know." He spoke now in a slight German accent that mocked hers: "For me, this action lacks an acceptable political rationale." He put his head to one side, regarding her sardonically. "Right, Leni?"

She shrugged, angry that he could read her so clearly. This was the way he maintained his ascendancy over everyone in the group: by his insight and by his apparent lack of all emotion. Distancing himself from others, he could command them. Only occasionally did he have to mention Sokatsu, the discipline he had adapted from that of the Japanese Red Army (Rengo Sekigun), one of whose members had said, "Once the process of Sokatsu starts, only death awaits you." Lang liked to quote that and remind everyone that Sokatsu had given Tsuneio Mori, the Japanese Red Army leader, powers of life and death over members of his group. Lang himself had never ordered anyone killed—yet. He had, however, inflicted a lot of pain and humiliation—always deserved.

After a moment Leni said, "Okay, Rex. Yes. I suppose that for me Saint Patrick's Day does lack an acceptable rationale."

"Because we're getting paid?"

She pouted and didn't answer.

Lang said, "Rengo Sekigun has undertaken operations for other organizations in the past and they have been paid." He paused. "I don't have to tell *you*, Leni. Lod Airport. The Hague Raid."

Leni gestured. "But think who was paying them! The PFLP [Popular Front for the Liberation of Palestine]. And then think of who is paying you. Loyalist Action!"

Lang smiled. "I might remind you that the same broker handled all that business. Theirs and ours."

Lang was referring to Georges Camoumim, the mysterious Syrian-born millionaire who had been described by *Newsweek* as an "international broker in terror," although they didn't name him. The same piece also alleged he was the man the DST [Direction de la surveillance du territoire: the French equivalent of the FBI] most wanted to arrest, although they had always failed to get any evidence against him that would stand up in court. French spooks considered Camoumim's International Fellowship organization (ostensibly designed to recruit and train activists to work in a nonviolent manner against tyrannical Third World regimes) was really funded by the KGB and served as a support network involving the PFLP, the Japanese Red Army, and possibly the Basque ETA [Eusakadi ta Askatasuna].

Leni didn't know or care how true any of this was. What she found hard to accept was the fact that Camoumim had first put Lang in touch with Loyalist Action, which had led to a series of contracts starting with the killing of the delegates to the Sinn Fein Ardfheis and culminating in the Saint Patrick's Day bombing in New York. Up to now she had never really voiced her dislike of Loyalist Action and its policy to Lang, guessing that he would already be aware of it.

Lang sounded amused. "After all these months you still don't approve of our contracts from Loyalist Action?"

Leni hesitated. "Rex—it's not for me—"

"You take sides. That's naive, Leni."

"So—I'm naive."

She smiled, noting how Durnan was sitting there, not saying anything, fearful of offending Lang.

"Of course," Lang continued, "Loyalist Action are a lot of goddamn fascist assholes—who doubts it? But, speaking pragmatically, their money smells the same as a liberal's. Their checks are met. 'First my belly, then your morality.' Brecht, right?" He paused. "But where you're being naive is in thinking that in executing these contracts we are fulfilling Loyalist Action's long-term aims." He shook his head. "*They* think we are, obviously, but they're wrong. No: in the long term we are contributing to a breakdown of the status quo in Ireland, creating a genuine condition of revolutionary flux."

Leni said, "You are a little subtle for me, Rex."

"Yeah. I thought maybe I might be." He didn't disguise the sneer in his voice. "Leni, you're a German. Perhaps it's a national characteristic to see things in black-and-white terms. You come from West Germany, the ultimate bourgeois society—and you want to stick a knife in its belly and watch the slime ooze out."

"You put it so elegantly, Rex."

"That's how it is, isn't it? But Ireland . . . Ireland isn't so simple. Ireland isn't just a country: it's a symbol, a state of mind. A lovely dreaming island of saints and scholars—or that's what it looks like if you happen to live in Pittsburgh or Detroit and had an Irish grandmother. An escape symbol. And of course a rebellion symbol—Brave Little Ireland throwing off the mighty English yoke." He nodded. "Yeah—Kathleen ni Houlihan—all things to all men."

"Right," Durnan added, clearly delighted he could chip in at last. "Like all those big-deal Irishmen who never leave New York."

"Now," Lang said, "Leni seems to think we have committed ourselves to a fascist stance in accepting these contracts for Loyalist Action. She forgets that we have been negotiating with the Wednesday Committee for nearly two months—and now sure as hell they're gonna plunge!" He paused. "As you know, the Wednesday Committee represents the exact antithesis of Loyalist Action. Loyalist Action wants the British connection maintained in Northern Ireland—mainly for economic reasons. The Wednesday Committee cherishes the republican dream: One Ireland—United, Gaelic, and Free."

"You are sure that the Wednesday Committee will buy your package, Rex?" Leni asked.

"How can they avoid it?" Lang demanded. "How can they *not* buy, the way things have been going?" He leaned back, appeared to relax. "Up to the time we accepted that first contract from Loyalist Action, the republican side always held the initiative in Ireland. They had all the nerve and expertise. They knew how to make the bombs and they knew where to deliver them. The best the Loyalist paramilitaries could do was shoot up Catholics in the backlots of Belfast." He paused. "We changed all that. Since the Orange hired us, we've got the Green dazzled and baffled—in retreat. Of course the Wednesday Committee have to hire us! Every strike we make for Loyalist Action makes that more certain." He grinned. "Beautiful! And when we're working for these two opposed forces—what do you think that's going to do for the status quo in Ireland?"

Now Lang spoke in a slow, almost dreamy tone, staring up at the silky darkness of the North African night. "That's what I mean about creating a situation of revolutionary flux. At the moment there exists in Ireland the ideal climate for violent change."

"But I thought things were good there now," Durnan said. "Since they went into the EEC?"

Lang shrugged. "The farmers in Ireland have done well out of it, sure, just as they have in France and Germany. But if the Irish farmers are happy, no one else is. The industrial workers resent the farmers making millions and paying hardly any taxes and they keep striking in protest." He paused. "And there's a deep frustration over national sovereignty and identity—aside from the North of Ireland. A lot of people fear that Ireland's future role is to provide beef ranches and tourist lebensraum for Germans and Dutchmen. They've exchanged their old British masters for new ones in Brussels." Lang's voice became taut, incisive. "In this situation, government hangs on a knife edge. You can insult the buried pride of a country for just so long—but sooner or later the boiler's gonna burst. Right now there's a great reservoir of anger and frustration just waiting to be unleashed."

"And we're about to unleash it?" Durnan asked.

Lang nodded.

"What you are telling us, Rex, is that we shall be selling guns to both sides?"

Lang nodded. "Just as soon as we finalize things with the Wednesday Committee. O Dunnacha Duane is sold on our package, I know that. And he can carry the others with him. He's sent a girl called Frankie McNagan to New York to see old Seamus Dillon about releasing the resources of the foundation."

"But wasn't old Dillon marching in the parade?" Durnan asked.

"Should have been," Lang answered. "At the head of Justice for Ulster, along with Wendell Dillon. He wasn't mentioned in the French newscasts—but that doesn't mean he's not dead. If he is—better yet! Then Duane gets to control the foundation."

Lang was smiling. Leni found herself staring into his eyes. They were pale green. In the dim light they seemed to glitter and yet to be transparent like glass. Leni had a peculiar sense of looking through them and seeing only emptiness inside.

☘ ☘ ☘

By August 1922 everything was going wrong for the republican, anti-Treaty forces. Landing from the sea, the Free State Army had taken Cork and Tralee; now the anti-Treaty troops had withdrawn from Clonmel, their last urban headquarters. Lacking artillery and an adequate supply system, all they could do now was fight the government of the newly created Irish Free State as guerrillas—constantly on the move, surviving through a strategy of ambush and surprise. Just like they had fought the British up to the signing of the Treaty in 1921.

Seamus Dillon, twenty-one years old and known as "the Yank," had been captured that morning with eight of his comrades. They had gotten separated from the rest of their detachment and were looking for a safe house that they believed lay somewhere in a certain square mile or so of the County Kilkenny. Seamus had a map reference all right, but it was clearly incorrect. However, he had been told by Jim Brennan, his commandant, that the house they were seeking lay at the end of a lane, amid tall beech trees, flanked by a haybarn built like a tower.

At last they had stumbled onto the lane—and there was the haybarn. They'd hurried forward eagerly, in their hunger and exhaustion forgetting to guard against a possible ambush—and had walked straight into a Free State patrol. Too late, they saw a Crossley truck, parked beside the barn. They were surrounded.

They had been locked up in a cowhouse at the rear of the barn. The day had passed somehow and it was now night. It was pitch dark and the floor was covered in sour-smelling dung. Two Free State sentries guarded the door. The nine republican prisoners had nothing to do but think. Think, inevitably, of the next morning and whether it would be their last.

At first their morale was good. They sang ballads like "Easter Week" and "Kevin Barry." Tim O'Leary from Cork gave them "The Boys of Fair Hill." But as the night wore on, their defiant chanting began to sound strained in the heavy, dung-smelling darkness. They kept wondering about the morning. Some Free State officers accepted that this civil war was being fought on a question of principle—as a protest against the Treaty with Britain accepted by Michael Collins and Arthur Griffith and the other signatories. These officers would treat captured IRA men as prisoners of war. But there were other Staters who held different views. There were ugly stories going around. Prisoners were often shot "trying to escape." The English visionary Erskine Childers had been executed on a trumped-up charge. A squad of republican prisoners had been blown up near the Ladies View in Killarney . . .

No wonder, then, that when the boldest rebel ballad began to sound hollow in their own ears, they eagerly agreed with Sean D'Arcy's suggestion that they recite the rosary. As each man said a decade in Irish, with the others making the familiar responses, each could feel the fear growing inside of him, freezing his heart.

Just before dawn the door of the cowhouse was opened. The muzzle of a submachine gun poked in like a snout in the hands of a Free State sergeant. The beam of a flashlight scanned their faces. The door closed again.

Soon after dawn—they could see the light growing through cracks in the door—Sean D'Arcy began shouting for the Staters to let them out for Jesus Christ's sake. He kept flinging himself against the door, shouting louder and louder.

Nothing happened. No one answered. Then, about ten minutes later, the door was flung open so suddenly that D'Arcy fell forward and outward, crashing against the leather-gaitered legs of the Free State sergeant.

The sergeant had six men with him. He ordered the prisoners out, then marched them around to the front of the farmhouse. There, drawn up in a single rank in the large empty yard, they confronted the cold gaze of a Free State major. He had a black curly mustache and carried a knobkerrie—so much a stereotype of the British regular officer that it was hard to believe he had been an IRA man fighting the British less than two years earlier.

The major nodded to the sergeant. The prisoners were made to stand in a circle. There was an armored car parked in a corner of the farmyard. The major walked over to it, got in, and was driven away. The sergeant wheeled around on his heel and disappeared into the house. A moment later he emerged again, a haversack slung across his shoulder. Out of this he took a small dark object. He stood regarding the prisoners, weighing this object in his hand. Seamus knew what it was. It was a hand grenade, a Mills bomb.

The sergeant had a harsh County Monaghan accent. "If youse fellas were English, we'd call this cricket practice," he said. He had a red, weather-roughened face; heavy brows and swollen dewlaps made his eyes almost invisible. "Listen to me now. This is what youse might call weapon training. Youse all know this Mills bomb is harmless till the pin is pulled—and what happens when the pin *is* pulled!"

Seamus saw that Sean D'Arcy was shaking uncontrollably; he looked as if he might throw up any moment.

"Now," the sergeant said, "one of these times I'm going to pull the pin out before I throw—and the man who catches it is going to be unlucky."

He lobbed the grenade straight at Seamus. Seamus caught it and with an instant reflex action lobbed it straight back at the sergeant, who caught it expertly.

"I can see you're a cricketer," the sergeant said. "Eton or Clongowes Wood?"

He threw the grenade at Con Murphy, who managed to catch it, but less expertly than Seamus.

This went on for some time. The sergeant began by working his way around the circle in leisurely fashion, throwing the grenade and getting it back from each man in turn. Then he began to speed things up. He would lob the bomb suddenly at random: once or twice a prisoner nearly dropped it. And all the time he kept up a jeering commentary: " 'Tis aisy to see youse ain't cricketers! A fucking hurley stick would be more in your line, I'm thinking . . . "

By now all the prisoners were beginning to show signs of strain: D'Alton and Con Murphy particularly. Twice D'Alton had almost dropped the grenade.

The sergeant's jeering voice went on: "I suppose we're all good Catholics here? How about a decade of the rosary now? In Irish of course!"

Seamus was sweating with fear. But he kept telling himself: He won't pull the pin out. He daren't. The bastard was just playing cat-and-mouse with them. He dare not pull it out because with a grenade exploding at such close quarters he would be killed himself.

The game went on. The prisoners were in a trance now, lobbing the bomb to and fro, hypnotized by the sergeant's jeering voice. "Won't be long now, you fucking rebel bastards. One of youse is sure to drop it! Any moment now . . . "

Seamus' action, when it came, was totally spontaneous, unthought of, pure reflex.

Relaxedly, almost offhandedly, the sergeant tossed the grenade. As if in a dream, miraculously free from fear, Seamus caught it. Then he pulled out the pin and hurled the grenade at the sergeant.

As he did so, he threw himself down on his face. He was aware of the roar of sound, the scorch of heat. He felt the kick of the blast on his face and neck. Men were screaming, shouting, writhing on the ground. Seamus dragged himself to his feet. He began to run. He went on running. Across fields and ditches. Then he found himself struggling up the side of a hill. Only then did he realize that there was no one following him. He dropped down exhausted into the long grass.

Now, fighting for breath, his heart beating so hard and so fast that it seemed it would burst his chest, he became aware of a salt, sticky liquid soaking his head, running down his neck. Only then, picking at something sticking to his cheek, did Seamus realize that he was covered in the sergeant's blood and brains, spattered all over him by the force of the explosion.

☘ ☘ ☘

Seamus came out of the dream like he always did—dazed and profoundly disoriented. Surfacing through layers of pain and fear that seemed like birth pangs, he spun in a muddle of agonizing symbols—faceless and terrifying.

One image predominated: a tree, black and gaunt and yet at the same time diseased. Like a cross, but a cross symbolizing evil: a crucifixion signaling not resurrection but torture and death.

He was awake now. He knew what he was looking at. The apparatus that had been set up to drip fresh blood into his veins. A bottle was fixed at the top of a pole at the end of his bed: struggling back to consciousness, he had seen it as a cancer strangling the life from some blackened, leafless tree.

It was the dream. It always stained his awakening with horrible images; left him shattered, clinging only to the fact that he was alive. He didn't have the dream so often anymore. Perhaps two or three times a year, and yet he never knew when sleep was going to confront him with that sadistic sergeant he had killed that morning nearly sixty years ago.

Anyway, he was alive. Just about. Seamus Dillon, aged seventy-nine, a resident of Manhattan, in bed in Doctors Hospital.

He was alive. He lifted his free arm (the other one had the needle in it, carrying the endless, revivifying flow of the drip) and then let it fall again. The flesh of his arm looked solid, healthy, his hand well-formed and not discolored by age. And yet he knew that there was that within him that would kill him: he was under sentence of death.

It was something he should have realized before. Suffering from aplastic anemia as he did. It was just that no one had ever spelled it out so bluntly as Dr. Hernandez that morning. The irony was, though, that if he hadn't collapsed at his apartment and been brought in here, he would have marched in the parade (as he'd done every Saint Patrick's Day for fifty years past) and would certainly have been killed along with his nephew Wendell. And with some of his most trusted workers for Justice for Ulster. Men like Frank McGuinness, Liam Horgan, Mick McGagan, and Timothy Cullinane. A woman like Elizabeth Hayes O'Neill. Burned and blasted into eternity in a second.

He wished he had been with them, kissed by the March sunshine, swinging along in step with his comrades, marching for Ireland and then, suddenly, being called on to die for it.

Yes: that would have been a good way to go. Better than the way Dr. Hernandez had prophesied this morning.

Having aplastic anemia meant that the red leucocytes in Seamus' blood were being continually overwhelmed by the white leucocytes. Hitherto, of course, the status quo had always been restored by a massive transfusion of new, healthy blood (this was happening now), but eventually the white leucocytes were going to win. Seamus now had to have his blood changed twice as often as he'd had to a year ago—every six weeks instead of every three months.

Dr. Hernandez hadn't been eager to tell him. She had hesitated, maybe wondering about this old, rich man who'd spent most of his life and a lot of his money for a country she'd probably never seen. But Seamus had growled: "Doctor! I have to know. Please."

"All right," she said, quite sharply—and strangely, at this moment he had been keenly aware of her beauty as a woman: cool, serene, in the manner of the Madonnas he had seen in Italian churches. "All right. I'll tell you."

She had then explained that his condition had probably reached a stage where the white leucocytes multiplied too fast for blood transfusions to be effective.

There it was. A term of weeks. Maybe months. Not years. She couldn't give him a year, in fact. At least now he wouldn't have to feel guilty at living on when Wendell and all those others had died. He didn't have so long to go himself.

Seamus sighed and leaned back against the pillows, a solid block of a man with thick white hair and steel-blue eyes that hadn't been dimmed by age. He was horribly aware of the needle thrust into his arm. It was saving his life, of course. But for how long? And for what?

He was really alone now. Childless himself, he had loved his nephews Wendell and Tom. Always, right from the time when they were tiny kids. He remembered the times when his brother John had brought his sons out to Seamus' summer house at Southampton, Long Island. Tom had always been the bigger and stronger; Wendell the calmer and more self-confident, with tidier clothes and cleaner face. Tom was the guy who talked back, who fired the stone through the transom, the natural heller.

Seamus had loved them both. He had enjoyed every golden moment of those long summer days at Southampton, and so had his wife, Magda. Maybe they suggested to her the kids she'd never had herself. Maybe.

She had been dead nearly seven years now. Sometimes it seemed much longer; sometimes hardly a day. Magda (named for the heroine of Sudermann's once-famous play) had come from a German Catholic family, a Hoosier beauty with blue eyes and golden hair. Her father had been a farmer in Indiana; when Magda was five years old he had sold out and become a brewer in Milwaukee. Seamus' mother would naturally have liked him to marry an Irish girl, but if this wasn't to be she would prefer a German-American. They were considered better Catholics than, say, Italian-Americans.

He and Magda had nearly forty years together, and yet now, although he said a Rosary for her every day, she had ceased to be vivid in his mind. He felt intense guilt at this, and yet there had always been something dead at the core of their relationship. He had known the reason, although neither of them had ever spoken of it.

Ireland. She'd been there with him, and pretended to care about it, but Seamus knew differently. Her indifference stood between them like a wall of ice. She rejected the dream he lived by, and sometimes he caught in her voice the note of a mother patiently enduring the prattle of a well-loved child. He couldn't blame her. All his life he had fought and schemed and begged for Ireland—and what was there to show? So many plots and plans and none of them had come to anything. Ireland was a lost cause. Sensible men grew up and recognized the fact. Fools and dreamers did not. Would things have been different if she had been Irish instead of German? Maybe not. A lot of Americans of Irish origins neglect their real heritage, choosing instead to wallow in a tourist operator's dream of leprechauns and donkey carts and black-shawled Mother Machrees.

So. His wife was dead; he had no child; what was left?

Money? He had several million dollars and he still owned several homes. The summer house in Southampton—hardly used now. A mansion on the Kenmare River in Kerry—he didn't use that very often either, and a Dutchman kept writing from Dublin, seeking to buy it. An apartment near the East River on Forty-fourth Street, where he mostly lived now, looked after by Hans and Karen Gruhl, an elderly German couple who lived in Yorkville but spent perhaps sixteen hours of the twenty-four attending on Seamus and his needs. Perhaps the Gruhls represented a kind of token responsibility for him. Magda had hired them almost thirty years ago. Karen Gruhl was pudgy and twinkling, the perfect hausfrau; Hans was tall and Prussian with a shaven head (after seeing a revival of *Sunset Boulevard* Tom insisted on calling him "Erich von Stroheim"). Seamus didn't really need the Gruhls full time anymore, but he didn't feel he could tell them that: they would be offended. In a way, old servants were like children who never grew up and went away; you had to go on looking after them, and of course Seamus would provide for the Gruhls after his death.

Would he have been happier if he hadn't sold his majority stockholding in Penrith Pharmaceuticals to the Rossman Corporation ten years ago?

A silly question. Rossman, that vast multinational Moloch, had swallowed Penrith like a whale gulping a minnow. Seamus doubted whether he'd have popped down their gullet quite as smoothly. Oh, they'd offered to make him an executive vice president, but he'd never even considered it. Apart from the fact that he would have been dazed by the sheer vastness of the Rossman operation, this had been the time when the Troubles had broken out again in the North of Ireland. Seamus had always given more hours every week to Ireland than to Penrith, but having sold out to Rossman, he now gave all his waking consciousness to propagandizing and fund-raising for the Irish cause:

crossing and recrossing the American continent, stomping through every State of the Union from Maine to California.

No, that was one road he couldn't walk again. Even though he'd had fun creating Penrith, building it up from nothing through the years. It had been such a small, highly personalized outfit—at least at the beginning. Seamus still felt excited when he remembered what his little team of researchers had achieved. Boradin 18, a cattle vaccine that had saved the lives of many animals. Luxinan, still the safest of the MAO inhibitor antidepressant drugs. But he knew a setup like Penrith could not possibly survive in today's economic climate.

So, a rich old man with nothing to buy, his very blood betraying him by running thin and rotten in his veins, Seamus Dillon took stock. Only a dream remained to him now: a dream of Ireland.

For as long as God allowed he would continue the fight, even though things looked as hopeless now as at any time during the last sixty years. The whole republican movement seemed demoralized by the successes of Loyalist Action, although Seamus had heard from Dublin that a messenger from O Dunnacha Duane was on the way to him, bringing certain proposals. Seamus couldn't imagine what these could be.

What was certain was that Justice for Ulster stood decimated by the loss of those who had died on Saint Patrick's Day. And Wendell—as long as Seamus lived, nothing could ever assuage that piercing sense of loss. Wendell had been so close to him; he had been a friend and adviser as well as a favorite nephew. Particularly adviser: Seamus had relied on Wendell to illuminate every devious Washington maneuver from Foggy Bottom through Sheridan Circle to the Capitol. Not that Wendell was ever indiscreet; ever compromised his own integrity as a United States Senator.

Integrity! Seamus closed his eyes, gripped by unease. How could he have forgotten?

Seamus had gotten the first hint of the threat to Wendell a few weeks ago when he attended a meeting of the Saint Patrick's Day Parade Committee at the Biltmore. The chairman of the committee, the redoubtable Judge Comerford, had been in his usual cracking form. Seamus regarded the meeting as a formality: everything would go like clockwork, as usual, thanks to the judge's genius for organization. He'd been about to leave when he had run into Liam Costelloe, of the AFL-CIO, with whom Seamus had enjoyed a half-joshing, half-antagonistic acquaintanceship for fifty years. The media liked to describe Costelloe as the last of the wardheelers, an Irish political boss cast in a magnificent, now obsolete mold. Conversation between him and Seamus these days tended to consist of a rollcall of mutual friends who had died since the two of them last met. Today, after the exchange of the usual ritual insults, Costelloe said, "Well, now the shit sails towards the fan!" He asked Seamus if he had seen the brief report of Hogg of Defense Systems Sales having to appear before the Grand Jury.

It took Seamus a moment to register that. Then he saw it all, in all its implications. Was it possible that in a moment of anxiety and weariness, the night he had called Wendell from Kansas City five years ago, he had betrayed Wendell? Smeared his reputation? Even destroyed him?

It had been Liam Costelloe who had told Seamus of Hogg in the first place, but that didn't matter now. Costelloe had always been good at getting out from under. Nor was Seamus so concerned for himself. It was Wendell who was at risk. Twice Seamus tried to call him at his home in Georgetown; he wasn't home either time. Seamus knew he should have taken a plane and gone to see Wendell, but he didn't. Perhaps he was still fooling himself that the worst would not happen.

And now Wendell was dead. Could Wendell himself have known about this? Maybe that had been what he wanted to talk about when he called Seamus on his arrival in New York on Saint Patrick's Eve. Karen Gruhl had taken the call. She had explained that Seamus had collapsed and been rushed to Doctors Hospital.

He would never know now. Wendell was dead.

Seamus would go on fighting. Native-born American though he was, Ireland had always been the true core of his life. Ireland. Kathleen ni Houlihan. Roisin Dubh. The Old Bitch. All his life he'd collected ballads as well as sung them—any ballad, from a seventeenth-century drinking-chant like "The Cruiskeen Lawn" to an emigrant's song like "Paddy Works on the Erie." But now he tried to soothe his spirit with an older verse, translated from the Irish by Padraic Pearse:

The Erne shall rise in rude torrents, hills shall be rent,
The sea shall roll in red waves, and blood be poured out
Every mountain glen in Ireland, and the bogs shall quake
Some day ere shall perish my Little Dark Rose.

The telephone booth still smelled of urine. Malachi stood poised for a moment before he lifted the receiver and dropped in the coin. This he was going to enjoy. Even the thought of Brenda sitting there back in Ben's apart-

ment couldn't spoil it for him. Twenty-four hours after the bombing, and wire
services around the world were still choked with supposition and comment;
TV screens still blocked by pundits pretending to know who was responsible.
They were all assholes, but they sure as hell came up with some good candi-
dates. The British SAS [Special Air Service], the Provisional IRA (hoping
people would think it was the SAS), the Puerto Rican nationalist FALN (hoping to attract the publicity they had recently lacked). Speculation went on
endlessly, although it must decline soon. Never mind. He, Malachi O'Farrell,
was going to set the wires buzzing again.

He got through at once. A girl responded, "Associated Press."

He wasn't sure whom to ask for. "News editor," he said.

After a moment another woman spoke: impatient, authoritative, this one.
"Yes?"

He'd intended an Irish brogue, but he couldn't really maintain it as he
read:

"This is a statement from Loyalist Action. We repeat that name: Loyalist
Action. We hereby claim responsibility for the bombing of the Fenian parade
in New York City on March seventeenth last, and we wish to point out that
this was a legitimate act of war directed against an ethnic group whom we, the
Loyal People of Ulster, the queen's subjects, must regard as enemies. The
so-called Irish American community in the United States have given millions
of dollars to the IRA, dollars which have been used to buy arms which have
killed and maimed thousands of Her Majesty's subjects in London, Belfast,
and other parts of the United Kingdom. But we must emphasize that revenge
is not our motive. This bombing was a warning: a warning that distance is no
protection. Hands off Ulster! This is a war that will be waged to the death.
Take heed that we, the Loyal People of Ulster, will never yield up our allegiance. God save the queen!"

"Your mother is a wonderful woman," Max Segal said.

Tom Dillon nodded. "Of course she is, Max. Do you think I need you to
tell me that?"

Max shrugged; didn't answer. His big dark eyes seemed to grow a little
brighter. He distrusts irony, Tom thought. He even fears it. All part of the price
for making it as big as he has.

They had met at Charlie Mac's on Third Avenue—a venue that jarred on
Tom when Max reminded him that his brother Wendell had breakfasted here

on Saint Patrick's morning, drinking Irish coffee and eating eggs and bacon and soda bread along with the mayor, Governor Carey, Governor Byrne of New Jersey, and other dignitaries. Thinking of this, Tom winced at the outsize shillelaghs and overdressed leprechauns hanging from the ceiling, the Tricolor and the Stars and Stripes hanging united over the bar, the portraits of Robert Emmet, Padraic Pearse, and Brendan Behan. But Max would like Charlie Mac's, Tom supposed. Probably because he was so deep into this question of ethnic roots beneath the surface of modern urban society—like, say, Max's Jewishness vis-à-vis Tom's Irishness.

Now Max assumed his persona of conservative, long-trusted family lawyer—belied a little by his youthful appearance and clear, ingenuous eye—and Tom felt absolutely certain of what he had suspected when they first met. He was here to convey some kind of message from Kathleen Dillon she preferred not to convey herself.

Max began by telling Tom a number of things he already knew. The holding corporation set up to handle the large capital sums accruing from the sale of the Dillon interests in Cleveland Steel back in 1962 had originally allowed for six stockholdings. One to John Dillon, father of Tom and Wendell (he had died soon after this trust was set up). One to his wife, Kathleen Dillon, in her own right. One each to Wendell and Tom. One—to Kathleen Dillon's annoyance—to Seamus Dillon. "But he's got his own Penrith Pharmaceuticals," she protested. "He's richer than any of us." She could never forgive Seamus, the eccentric, the fanatic Irish rebel, for being a more successful businessman than her own golf-playing, All-American husband.

The two remaining holdings had been designated in reserve for the education and general benefit of Tom and Wendell's children, assuming they had any.

"Okay," Tom said. "I know all this."

"Forgive me." Max smiled. "Most people have to be told these things more than once."

Max went on to explain that ever since her husband's death Mrs. Dillon had lived on the dividends from her own single stockholding. During her lifetime she could enjoy the income from her dead husband's holding: in fact she had made this over to Wendell, to further his political career. Now, through his death, that career was over. Cheryl and the children had the income from Wendell's own holding; plus, of course, that from the one designated for the children's welfare. "So," Max concluded, "your mother is considering allocating the income from your late father's holding to you."

"And the deal is?" Tom asked.

"There's no deal."

"My mother," Tom said, "always makes deals. I don't think she ever gave anything away. In her whole life." He paused. "I'm not talking about money."

Max nodded sympathetically. "I would expect you to say that."

Tom nodded; waited for Max to go on.

"I think"—Max hesitated—"she's only thinking of a change of direction for you. Tom—I think you could perhaps use that."

Tom stared down into the black heart of the Guinness he'd ordered to please Max. A change of direction? He had endured this discussion before. From Wendell; from his mother—many times; even, in the most oblique way possible, from Uncle Seamus. Allowing for individual styles and prejudices, each saw him as the cliché Vietnam veteran, unable to adjust to the world to which he had returned.

Tom never defended himself, never explained his reasons. Maybe because they were hard to formulate: more like feelings than reasons. That didn't make them less valid. It was a failure of motivation rather than of will. He couldn't see the point. With the income from his stockholding he certainly wasn't about to starve.

Apathy, maybe. Or a nicer word: acedia. He looked that up once and read that it meant spiritual apathy and indifference: sloth. Well, maybe. Maybe he just lacked anything or anybody to get excited about anymore.

It was the result of Nam of course. Each time you survived the death of a comrade, a drop of some vital sap was drained away from you. You were glad they'd left *you* alive, of course, even though your tenure could be terminated in a second by stepping onto a Claymore. These were difficult questions. Nuances. How explain them to anyone who hadn't been there? How little his mother knew him if she thought she could bribe him by offering him the income from another holding.

At the beginning she had hoped to squeeze him into a business suit and make him take a job suitable to his education and social status as a member of the Dillon family. She had suggested he join Amerigo—assuming a ghostly link still existing between the Dillons and the huge conglomerate that had bought Cleveland Steel from them. It wouldn't have worked, and Tom hadn't gone along with it.

But this time it seemed his mother wasn't thinking about business.

Max said, "You know Wendell was going to the Carrolton Inauguration in Dublin?"

"I knew that, yes."

"She wants you to go there. In his place."

Max paused.

"What?" Tom demanded.

"Is that so surprising?" Max asked. "The Carrolton project means a good deal to her. It meant a lot to your father too. And to Wendell."

Tom smiled. "Oh, yes. Mother sold us the Carrolls of Carrolton from the cradle on. You know why she's so keen on them? One of the oldest Irish-Catholic families—and she's related to them, or so she says." He paused. "She was a Quinlan of Philadelphia and they've got links with the FitzSimons family—Thomas FitzSimons was a delegate to the Constitutional Convention."

Tom paused. Max would really love all this, and here he was smiling and nodding encouragement.

"And so through the FitzSimons she's linked with the Carrolls," Tom went on. "And that makes her of pre-1830 Irish stock—not bog-Irish, Famine-Irish, like everyone else! And as you know"—Tom continued in his half-mocking, fake-professorial tone—"the Irish before 1830 were a small elite group. Social trend-setters like Mrs. Caton and Dominick Lynch!"

"Really?" Max nodded enthusiastically.

Mrs. Dillon took comfort in the fact that she was one of The Quinlans (and not "Them Quinlans," as old Seamus mockingly observed); it made her feel superior to her husband's family, the Dillons, who were certainly bog-Irish. Their forebear Michael Dillon had left Cobh (then called Queenstown) with his family in 1856, which made them Famine-Irish too.

"The Carrols came to Maryland in 1688," Tom continued. "There weren't many Irish Catholics in America then. There was a special tax on servants to prevent the importation of too many Irish papists! Charles Carroll of Carrolton was the only Catholic signatory of the Declaration of Independence; he was also the wealthiest. You can imagine how *that* appeals to my mother!"

It was true, Tom thought. This concept of the Carrolton Institute had been important to all of the Dillons—except himself. And most of all to his mother. Hers had been the emotional charge behind this project to memorialize Charles Carroll of Carrolton in an institution that would represent a focal point for Americans in search of the Irish traditions that helped shape the culture of the United States. Four major American universities had participated in planning the institute, which was to be located on the campus of University College, Dublin.

It would be in many respects a unique establishment, a pantheon of Gaelic studies. There would be a library, containing many rare works in print, in manuscript, and on microfilm; a theater, in which every kind of Irish drama would be re-created. A special department of Irish-American studies would initiate projects relating to the historical and sociological influence of the Irish on the development of the United States. The institute would also serve as a kind of clearinghouse: Irish academics would go to American universities on exchange schemes with American academics who would come to Ireland.

All this had been striven for through many years. John F. Kennedy's name had been on the letterhead of the Carrolton Committee's first appeal. At times it had seemed as if every brick of the building must be begged and parlayed for, but during recent years fund-raising had taken off. Some big corporate donors had come forward, and the buildings on the Dublin campus had been completed. The institute would be formally opened this coming summer.

Up to the Saint Patrick's Day bombing the Carrolton Inauguration had been regarded as a shedding of light on an otherwise darkening scene: a gesture of faith in the future. But now Loyalist Action had struck at the one occasion that—however theatrically and even frivolously—proclaims the link between Irish-Americans and their ancestors. There was still joy that the Carrolton Institute was at last to be opened, but it was clouded by the events of Saint Patrick's Day.

It had long been rumored that the president himself would attend the inauguration. Establishment figures from all over the world would certainly be there, many of them from the States. Indeed, the list of Americans to be invited included not only politicians but ecclesiastics, diplomats, and academics. Prominent among these last would be Professor Owen McKiernan of the Irish-American Cultural Institute, a longtime supporter of the Carrolton project. The cardinal archbishops of New York and Boston would be there, and so too would be writers and commentators as diverse as J. K. Galbraith, Gore Vidal, and William F. Buckley.

But indeed the guest list was international, encompassing distinguished names from all over the world. And of course the Irish establishment would be present in toto, ranging from the taoiseach [prime minister] and his cabinet down through bishops, professors, and judges to the larger industrial tycoons.

Tom found it easy to understand why Carrolton meant so much to his mother. And Wendell would have attended the ceremonies in a dual role: that of United States Senator and a member of the Dillon family.

"My mother's a romantic," Tom said. "Wendell would have gone as a Senator, what do I go as? It's ridiculous."

"You'd go as Tom Dillon," Max said, and smiled.

Tom didn't smile. He said, "Since she appears to have some crazy notion of using you as a plenipotentiary, pray inform her: No." He paused. "As to the extra money—something stronger than no!"

"Aside from the money," Max said, "why don't you go to Ireland anyway? You might enjoy it."

"Funny thing," Tom said. "A few weeks ago my uncle Seamus asked me to

go over there with him. He implied that this would be his last glimpse of the
Ould Sod."

"How is he? The bombing and all must have been a big shock to him."

"Okay. Pretty good, really." Tom frowned. "He hasn't talked much about it.
I think he's getting over it."

"Old men love life."

Tom nodded.

Max said, "Why don't you go with him? The tears of Kathleen ni Houlihan
watered your cradle. You can never escape her."

Tom grinned. "Wanna bet?"

They became aware of voices raised behind them, and then of other voices
saying "Shut up!" and "Let's hear it for Christ's sake!" Tom and Max turned
and saw that a TV set above the bar had been switched on. Normally you were
not exposed to television in Charlie Mac's.

"Hey, what goes on?" Max demanded, and a voice beside them hissed, "It's
the *president*."

As always the president spoke rather slowly, carefully enunciating every
word.

" . . . because we care for peace, because we believe, in Thomas Jeffer-
son's words, in exact and equal justice for all men, we are taking this step. We
are proposing this Initiative on Ireland because it is our belief that the time has
now arrived when it can be fruitfully made. The governments of both Great
Britain and the Irish Republic agree that the present situation demands that
narrow national interests must be set aside in favor of a wider aim: peace in
Northern Ireland." He paused. "Somehow, someone must end the brutal murders, the scenes of bloodshed that have occurred in a number of countries,
including—most recently and terribly—our own." He paused again. "You all
know to what I am referring. The terrible outrage that has already come to be
known as the Saint Patrick's Day Massacre. And at this point let me answer
one criticism that may be made. It may be said—just because this Initiative so
closely follows that terrible crime—that we are yielding to blackmail, giving
way in the face of violence. To this I firmly reply: no. It is not so. We are not
yielding to pressure: this administration will never back down before violent
deeds. It has taken weeks and even months of patient negotiation, in London,
in Dublin, and even in Washington, to lay the foundations on which, hopefully, this Initiative can be made. The fact that a long campaign of terror
happens to have culminated in an outrage in our own country is purely coin-
cidental . . . "

Max shook his head and whispered to Tom, "Tell that to the Republican
Party!"

The president went on to say that he wanted to answer another possible criticism: that once more, despite certain recent disastrous lessons, the United States was trying to act as policeman outside her own territorial boundaries. "To that I can only say," the president continued, "that on this occasion we simply want to act as peacemaker. We shall gain nothing in material terms. Ireland has no oil to sell us. Peace in Ireland will not diminish American inflation by one decimal point. Our countries are bound by the Irish blood that flows through the veins of twenty million Americans. But for me, there is one supreme consideration. This Initiative has to be made and the United States is the one country in the world that can make it." He paused. "I believe that if the day ever dawns when this great country abdicates its moral responsibility to the rest of the world, then that will be a bad day, a day of defeat for all of us."

Of course (the president said) neither he nor his advisers claimed that there was anything in the Initiative that had not been proposed before. This plan had surfaced in various forms more than once in recent years. Its essence was the separation of Northern Ireland from the United Kingdom. Northern Ireland would become an independent state and would be recognized as such. British forces would leave the North on an agreed time-scale, and both Britain and the Irish Republic would act as guarantors of the new six-county state. While not taking an active part in the negotiations, the United States would function as a benevolent midwife. A Bill of Rights would safeguard the interests of the Catholic minority, and the president personally pledged massive American support for this new Ulster state: loans, guarantees, and job-investment on a wide scale. On a scale, indeed, that could rival Marshall Aid in Europe after World War Two.

"We don't pretend that any of this will be easy," the president said. "Clearly we are not about to solve in a day a problem that has existed for so many years. There are many interests and loyalties involved, and I must stress that none of the groups involved—the Protestant loyalists, the Catholic nationalists, or the British or Irish governments—have yet agreed to this plan. What they *have* agreed—and this in itself represents tremendous progress—is to meet around a table and talk about it."

Inevitably, there had been suggestions of a Camp David-style summit. The president himself didn't see it that way. It had eventually been decided that the most appropriately neutral venue was the Isle of Man, almost equidistant between Britain and Ireland. A conference would be convened there in early summer. The president of the United States, the British prime minister, and the Irish Republic's taoiseach would all attend, as well as representatives of all the concerned groups in Northern Ireland.

The president added that the Irish taoiseach and the British prime minister would also be going on television to explain the Initiative just about now.

For a moment the president held the same expression: a half-smile, earnest, appealing, but not without humor. Then he said, "Thank you for listening to me. Good night."

As a babel of talk rose around them, Tom turned and said to Max, "My Uncle Seamus is gonna dismiss all of that with just one word. He'll say Ireland is being sold up the river again. He won't care about the British finally leaving, or the president promising Marshall Aid. Like Pearse, like the Fenians, he wants One Ireland." He grinned. "All or nothing at all."

☘ ☘ ☘

Naked except for towels, the three men were reclining on mattresses in the octagonal lounge of the hammam, the Turkish baths beside the mosque near the Jardin des Plantes. Two of the men were in their thirties—one blond with short dust-colored hair and a bronzed athletic body; the other bigger-boned, black-bearded. The third man was about sixty: slightly built and with a birdlike alertness. He was the host: he had just ordered mint tea, honey cakes, and Turkish delight.

Pretending to relax, O Dunnacha Duane, the black-bearded man, wondered when the real talking would begin. Any other time he would have enjoyed the secret, sweet-smelling atmosphere of the hammam. Like the garden of Haroun-Al-Raschid or a sultan's harem. But he was only in Paris for a few hours: there was a lot to discuss. Typical of Camoumim, though, to have them meet at the hammam. He would relish its exoticism and its anonymity—although Duane wondered if some of the naked forms they had encountered in their progress through the steam rooms had been French agents keeping watch on Camoumim, who had often been described, melodramatically, as the mastermind at the center of a spider's web of terrorist plotting. The French had never gotten anything on to him, though.

Camoumim had introduced the blond man to Duane simply as "Rex Lang, the man responsible for that tape." Duane would certainly have recognized Lang's voice from the cassette Camoumim had given him two weeks ago.

When a huge black servant had brought them the mint tea and the honey cakes, Camoumim got down to business. He was reclining on one elbow, sipping tea, quiet and calm, asserting, somehow, an implacable dignity.

"So," he said, "You listened to our tape?"

Duane nodded.

"I trust it is now destroyed?" Camoumim said.

"As you requested," Duane said.

Camoumim said, "We also listened to your tape. And then destroyed it," he added. "In theory, at least, we are in accord. But"—he shrugged—"between theory and practice a gulf looms."

He had changed his line a little since his last meeting with Duane two weeks ago in the bar at Orly Airport. Duane had boarded his plane back to Dublin convinced he had a deal, that Georges Camoumim believed the present situation offered a tactical opportunity to overthrow the government of Ireland. Duane had also gotten the impression that Camoumim saw the need for foreign help—"help" meaning skilled and highly motivated personnel backed up by large sums of money and the most modern and sophisticated equipment.

Now Camoumim had infused a note of doubt.

Duane said, "Mr. Lang, I'm impressed by your analysis of the situation in Ireland. Especially as you're not Irish yourself."

Lang grinned. "Could be *because* I'm not Irish myself?" Now be looked serious. "It's easy to discern the symptoms of strain in a small society like Ireland, with most of its potential concentrated in Dublin." He paused. "In my tape I describe the situation; stress the opportunity. In yours you explain how opportunities have existed in the past—and been lost. How this one will be lost if the same mistakes are made."

Duane nodded. "You agree with my assessment?"

"Sure," Lang said.

Camoumim said in his gentle, careful voice—as if he were picking up each word and polishing it—"I was much impressed by both tapes. So, as I stand a little detached in this matter, may I sum up?"

Lang nodded; didn't speak.

"You, Rex"—Camoumim looked toward Lang—"point out that in Ireland today there exist all the classic conditions for a coup d'etat. Among the masses of workers a discontent that vents itself in endless industrial disputes—banks, mailmen, public utilities—in Ireland nearly everyone is always on strike. And in addition, there is a crisis of national identity. Born not only of the British occupation, but also of the ridiculous stereotypes imposed on the Irish by other countries. They see Ireland as a phony Arcady, full of peasants smoking clay pipes and riding donkeys. However much the Americans and the Germans enjoy this fantasy of Ireland, you Irish know it is a lie, and this is bad for your morale as a nation." He frowned. "Would you agree, Rex, that whoever was responsible for the Saint Patrick's Day bombing in New York aimed to strike at these myths?"

Unexpectedly, Lang shook his head. "Whoever bombed that parade was just an animal. Nothing so theoretical as striking at myths . . . "

"Allowing for the difference in time," Duane said, "there is a requiem beginning in Saint Patrick's Cathedral just about now."

Camoumim nodded sympathetically. "Did I appear to speak lightly of this terrible deed? Forgive me. You have friends to mourn among the dead?"

In fact Duane had known none of the victims, and the only member of Justice for Ulster he knew was Seamus Dillon himself. When news of the bombing had first come through, it was assumed in Dublin that Seamus was dead. Later, when it was known that the old man had never marched at all but was in the hospital, it dawned on Duane that he was in some curious way disturbed to learn that Seamus was alive. He had adjusted to the thought of the old man dead—he realized with shock and horror—because it would have made everything so easy. Frankie McNagan could have returned from New York, her mission unfulfilled, and that wouldn't have mattered because, on Seamus' death, control of the foundation would almost certainly pass to Duane himself. Well, the old boy was alive and although Frankie might have a fight on her hands now convincing him to release the resources of the foundation, Duane was glad. He still felt guilty, though.

Camoumim was regarding him with his bright, birdlike eye. Duane said, "I mourn them all."

Lang smiled enigmatically. "That's a good answer," he said.

Camoumim said gently, "Their obsequies today will be magnificent. Mother Church does these things well. She has had plenty of practice."

☘ ☘ ☘

An hour later Duane turned out of the Rue Cuvier and onto the Quai Saint Bernard. He could still hear Lang's parting words: "Okay, Duane—you got yourself a deal. And don't worry—Ireland is a rotten apple ready to fall and we're gonna shake the tree!"

Duane walked quickly, weaving his way among the students and tourists who thronged the sidewalks. He had a deal, contingent on getting the foundation released. But even if old Seamus wouldn't play, they'd work something out, Lang said. Duane exulted that his plan was gradually gaining body and dimension, like an old-fashioned photograph coming into focus as it is developed in a darkroom.

He did a quick recap in his mind. Certain basic questions had already been dealt with by Lang and himself in the discussion tapes they had exchanged. Obviously the most basic question of all was whether Southern Ireland was ready for a military takeover. And, as a corollary, were they both agreed that only through such a takeover in the South could the Northern Six Counties ever be freed from British occupation? Both Lang and Duane, each on his own tape, independently, had answered, yes.

Another question, every bit as vital, was the proposition that this coup d'etat could not be effected by Irishmen alone. Foreign help was needed.

This necessity, indeed, had induced Duane to seek and make contact with Camoumim in the first place, through a man he had met at a conference of the Fourth International in Turin—though Duane wasn't a Trotskyite or even, strictly, a Marxist. Soon afterward Camoumim had indicated his willingness to meet. He was interested in Ireland, he said.

Duane had already told the Wednesday Committee that any action must depend on their getting the right kind of foreign help. There were precedents. What about the United Irishmen seeking French aid in 1798? Or Casement begging German arms in 1916? That was why he intended to go to Camoumim, whom he already knew by reputation—although he had no intention of telling the committee this till he had something finalized.

Now, this last hour, talking to Lang, Duane had been amazed and delighted to hear Lang express judgments that mirrored his own secret thinking. Quite independently, Lang endorsed Duane's reasons for seeking foreign aid in an Irish coup d'etat.

While the Irish were obsessed by the past—often confused and bedeviled by it—history certainly offered them one lesson. As Duane had told the Wednesday Committee the night he had revealed to them he was talking with Camoumim: "Put twelve Irishmen around a table and one of them has got to be Judas! Name any Irish rising in the last three centuries that hasn't been sabotaged by treachery." Duane looked around the room and read agreement in every face. "Partly, I suspect, this is something in our temperament, born of a thousand years of alternate slavery and rebellion; partly because Ireland is such a small country. If everyone doesn't exactly know everyone else, someone can always be found to tell you who anyone is. Outside of the cities a stranger sticks out like a Chinaman at the Court of Brian Boru. And in Dublin the Special Branch has tabs on most known republicans—yes, on *you* and *you* and *you!*" he'd added, counting around the crescent of faces before him. All were on file at Dublin Castle—documented, crossindexed, with reports of their current doings fed daily into the computer. They lived in fact on a kind of parole, provided they didn't engage in any overt subversive activity within the Irish Republic itself.

Duane himself had a file at the Castle—he knew that—but he had reason to hope that the hard men at C3 (Special Detective Unit) might not consider him too important. He had been one of the founders of the Trinity College Republican Club in the early 1960s, but since then he had been known only as a political journalist: a man of words rather than deeds. Soon after graduating he had published his biography of Wolfe Tone. It had been hailed as a definitive work, and on the strength of it he could have taught at any of a half-dozen universities in the States. But he had stayed in Dublin, conducting a popular Irish-language chat show, "Daoine Ag Caint" [People Talking], and occasionally writing pieces for London periodicals like the *New Statesman* and *Private Eye*.

Of course all of the Wednesday Committee were aware that their doings were recorded. Duane had only emphasized it because he had to convince them that they had to have foreign help. A small, highly trained task force that would execute a meticulously planned, split-second-timed coup d'etat in Dublin. For that to work they would have to be immune to the tittle-tattling treachery that dogs every plot by Irishmen to free Ireland; unknown, too, to Dublin Castle, who would know in advance of any unusual activity among known republicans and would pounce at once. Lang—Duane now knew—could and would provide such a task force.

Only two big questions remained. Two questions on which everything depended.

First: would the Wednesday Committee give their approval to this collaboration with Lang?

Second: would Frankie be able to persuade Seamus Dillon to release the resources of the doomsday foundation—the arms and explosives which would be used by Lang's spearhead group to effect the coup?

Duane felt confident enough to answer for the committee. In fact he had made a tentative arrangement for Lang to meet with the whole committee—probably at the Pan-Celtic Congress at Quimper in Brittany in about three weeks' time. (A venue that would have the advantage of being off Irish soil—no interference from the Special Branch—and also of being a cultural occasion which Irish republicans might plausibly attend without being suspected of political intent.)

Duane had gotten the committee's agreement in principle some time ago. The Saint Patrick's Day bombing and now the President's Initiative had enormously strengthened that agreement. The committee members all agreed with him that the Initiative was a monstrous attempt to underwrite with American dollars an injustice the British had perpetrated sixty years ago. The argument that at last the British would be leaving Ireland didn't impress any one of them. Half a loaf is never better than no bread.

Now they had to move fast: every day counted. The first blow had to be struck before anything was agreed at the Isle of Man Conference.

Duane had had some difficulty convincing the committee that it was necessary to hire a group like Lang's. And they had been even more reluctant to admit that the lightning strike should be against Dublin. Why not Belfast?

Finally Duane had convinced them. He had reminded them of the Civil War. "You know the IRA could have won against the Free Staters if it had struck hard and straight at Dublin instead of turning south. Seize Dublin and you must win!"

The committee had finally gone along with him, rather to his surprise. He had expected more opposition. But then it had been a kind of miracle getting all of these people here in the same room in the first place. He had to be amazed at his own powers of persuasion, inducing them to meet with each other at all. They were in every sense a mixed crowd, representing every shade of Irish republicanism. But they all loved Ireland. Duane had caught them at a moment of crisis, almost of despair. The movement (as they all called it) was reeling before the blows of Loyalist Action. The coup Duane proposed offered them a chance to achieve all they had ever dreamed of.

They called themselves the Wednesday Committee because they had first met on a Wednesday. Before he called that first meeting in Dublin, Duane had put out feelers among all of the diverse groups that made up the movement. Provisional Sinn Fein (the "Provos"); the "Stickies" (members of the old Official IRA); the IRSP (Irish Republican Socialist Party); Duane's own group, Eireann Amhain; Saor Eire; and other smaller factions. The Achilles' heel of the movement had always been what Seamus Dillon called the splinter syndrome: an urge to hive off into small independent groups. Forgetting the common enemy, Ireland will start fighting Irishman—which has helped keep the British in Ireland for a thousand years.

The committee's approval, then, was little more than a formality. But how would Frankie make out in New York?

He had sent her there not only because she was courageous and persuasive. She was also unknown to the authorities in the States and she could slip in under the cover identity of a respectable cipher like Mary Ogham. And of course from the point of view of persuading Old Seamus she had the supreme advantage of being Peadar Mahoney's daughter. Seamus Dillon hadn't seen Frankie since she was a babe in arms, but Duane knew he had a passionate admiration for old Peadar, truly a father-figure in the movement. If anyone could sway Seamus she could.

It was vital that she sway him. If he didn't release those arms and explosives, Duane would have to rethink his plans. He had let Lang think that Seamus' agreement was just a formality—but Dillon was a tough old bastard: it could be a lot more than that. He had his enemies in the movement; they would tell you there was a perverse streak in Dillon that sometimes surfaced with disastrous results. Duane had never confronted it, but he did sense in Seamus a possible distrust of intellectuals that might work against himself. Another reason for sending Frankie.

The foundation would represent a big factor when he finalized his deal with Lang. An enormous factor. The foundation would make the Wednesday Committee much less dependent on Lang: in money terms several million dollars less dependent. And of course it greatly increased their chances of success: it wouldn't be necessary for Lang to bring so much as a handgun into Ireland; the arms were already there, carefully concealed in a series of caches throughout the twenty-six counties (only Dillon knew where they were all located). Somehow Duane felt sure Frankie would convince Old Seamus. Peadar's daughter. Of course!

Everything was going right so far. And yet, as he submerged himself in the roar and thrust of the Boulevard Saint-Germain, Duane felt a chill. A ghostly awareness of a countdown going on somewhere. "Four . . . three . . . two . . ." He had the sense of being carried toward an abyss. Friends, lovers, children, smiled and waved at him as he moved faster and ever faster past them—but none of them realized that he was going over the edge.

He knew what it was. Like all Irishmen of his generation he had been reared on the familiar myths. Nineteen Sixteen. A Terrible Beauty Is Born. The Rattle of a Thompson Gun. But now he was to be put to the test.

For he was likely, had he been put on,
To have prov'd most royally.

How would *he* prove? How well he understood the gentle poet Padraic Pearse crying out for violence, proclaiming the necessity of spilling blood— even innocent blood. Duane had never killed a man; never even seen one killed. Nor had Pearse, up to Easter Week.

Locked in these thoughts, he negotiated the Pont Sully, only some hidden gyroscope within him saving him from being mangled amid the honking, thrusting cars. As he made the Quai de la Tournelle, he collided with a girl hurrying from the opposite direction. The impact had enough force to send them both spinning around, with a ridiculous, balletlike precision, only to thump against each other again, breast-to-breast, thigh-to-thigh, buttock-to-buttock.

Duane was mumbling apologies in French and the girl was mumbling something back, but he was hardly aware of what either of them was saying. Rather he was obsessively taking in the girl's long yellow hair, the complexion like poured cream, the jaunty nipples under the tight shirt, the crotch bursting through taut jeans. A second later the girl had gone, but it was as though a switch had been thrown inside Duane. He was filled with an obsessive, anonymous lust for this woman, any woman, all women. And he let himself yield to this, thankfully, ecstatically, letting it blot out his fears and doubts. He had always joked about being an old-fashioned lecher—"a dirty old man since the age of puberty"—but lately, through all his plotting, the countdown toward the moment when he must face the test, he had sought sex like a drug. That was why he never felt any guilt about being unfaithful to his wife—he thought of her with a kind of numb pity: "A shy creature emerging fearfully from the undergrowth; a character from *The Wind in the Willows* that Kenneth Grahame forgot to include," as he'd once described her. That was why he fucked Frankie McNagan so insatiably, forcing her to glory in her adultery, perversely denying their lovemaking any romantic gloss, making her agree they fucked merely for convenience, for physical release. At the same time—unknown to Frankie of course—he lacerated himself with feelings of guilt toward her husband, the Other Frankie, poor quixotic man, in jail in England for a crime he didn't commit.

He thought of Frankie now. He wished he were going to meet her in that grubby apartment near Trinity that Mick Lambert lent him (Lucky that Lambert seemed to be forever absent on archeological digs throughout Europe). He would make her sit naked in the broken, creaking armchair, and he would kneel before her, thrusting his head between her half-reluctant thighs . . .

Dry-mouthed, tense, but perfectly at ease, Duane stood at the corner of the Quai de la Tournelle. He'd better get a cab. Otherwise he'd be late at the Rue Monsieur.

This was the third time around that the huge black servant brought mint tea and honey cakes. Lang shook his head when they were offered to him.

"You were right," he said. "Duane is hooked on our scenario."

Camoumim nodded. "Of course." He smiled. "A clever man. But flawed. For instance, just now he told us he was going to the airport. But the flight he is catching does not leave Charles de Gaulle for another four hours. Duane has instead gone to an apartment on the Rue Monsieur where lives a first secretary of the Irish Embassy who is at present in Dublin, consulting with the Department of Foreign Affairs. His wife remains here."

Lang smiled too. "That Duane is one cunt-struck guy!" He paused. "I know he enjoys boffing other men's wives. But that's so straight these days it nearly wins a medal."

Camoumim said, "I think he is perhaps a Byronic figure in his own eyes. The romantic rebel who seeks a barricade to die on."

"You think?"

"For instance," Camoumim said, "he is obsessed always with betrayal. Cloak-and-dagger stuff. Loyalist Action, though you call them fascist assholes, are in some ways more realistic."

"They appreciated the publicity? Terror is theater?"

"Exactly!" Camoumim nodded. "What better than those bombs on Saint Patrick's Day, right in the heart of the greatest city in the world?"

Lang nodded. "Right."

"And soon you will kill that politician, that Irishman that Americans like?"

"Angus McStay?"

"Yes." Camoumim was smiling. "The Irishman behind the American Initiative. The murder that looked like a coronary."

Lang laughed. "Sure. But don't forget—Loyalist Action appears more consistent because its aims are simpler. The men behind Loyalist Action have power—they've always had it. This whole campaign we have mounted for them has been directed at those they consider might threaten that power. But"—he paused—"Duane and those others on the Wednesday Committee have never had power. They've dreamed of it, schemed for it—but never achieved it! They're plotters, visionaries." He grinned. "That's why you play them relaxed, nice and easy, give them the ole soft-sell."

He stood up, draping his towel around him.

Still lying on his mattress, Camoumim said, "I shall hear from you soon?"

"That's right," Lang replied. "I'm in Dublin from now on." He looked around at the stained-glass windows and Moroccan fretwork of the lounge and added, "Duane is gonna see me there a lot sooner than he expects."

🍀 🍀 🍀

On the morning of March 19, Senator Dillon and some other members of Justice for Ulster were to be buried after a requiem mass in Saint Patrick's Cathedral.

By 6 A.M. people were lining up on East Fifty-first Street outside, waiting in the cold. A few minutes later the doors were opened and they were allowed inside. The requiem would be at ten. Meanwhile anyone who wished could enter and say a prayer for the dead.

Senator Dillon had been by far the most prominent among those killed and now his body was encased in a mahogany coffin that lay on a black steel frame in the Lady Chapel of the cathedral. The casket remained sealed because (it was rumored) his body had been terribly mutilated in the explosion. His mother, Kathleen Dillon, had wanted him buried after a private requiem at St. Ignatius Loyola or St. Jean Baptiste, or perhaps at the Church of the Sacred Hearts of Jesus and Mary at Southampton, where he had married Cheryl Sugden fifteen years ago. But Cheryl had decided that this might seem to set Wendell apart from the other victims.

The early mourners who knelt before the coffins or moved vaguely around the great building looked as variegated and anonymous as any New York crowd. Young men and women who might have been students. Solid men with an Irish look, who might be bartenders from Brooklyn or busdrivers from The Bronx. A black man on crutches. Vague middle-aged women carrying plastic bags. Mostly they had a sober, collected air, but there were others who stared restlessly around, possessed by a kind of morbid eagerness—the tragedy buffs who lurk on the fringe of every doleful event.

"Keep your eyes down, Ben," Harry Lombard murmured. "You're praying, remember?"

Lombard and Greener had been here since the cathedral opened, ostensibly to look for any suspicious behavior among the mourners or (more likely) among the other aimless, anonymous people who kept drifting in and out.

"Tell me something," Greener demanded. "Why are we really here?"

Lombard didn't answer. Both of them knew that their immediate superior, Benstead—known to younger operatives as "I-remember-Hoover"—had a sense of drama worthy of his adored old chief. Their presence here this morning reflected that: the heroic G-men lurking in the shadows, mounting their vigil at the corse of the murdered Senator.

"Benstead is certainly a man of imagination," Greener said. "Does he think the bombers are gonna go down on their knees, say Kaddish for the guy?"

"Would you know them if they did?" Lombard asked.

"You know what?" Greener shot back in an exasperated tone. "This is a rare case of Benstead assholing to NYCPD. Just to show we care." He paused and then added, "This was a random act of terror by Puerto Rican fanatics."

"Benstead wouldn't agree," Lombard said. "He thinks Loyalist Action really exists, and was after old Dillon and his nephew." He paused. "That's why he reactivated this surveillance."

"Shit!" Greener said irritably.

Lombard glanced at the butterball form kneeling beside him. He knew Greener's incessant grumbling masked real concern. And old Ben was squat and jowly—the perfect coronary target. The lanky, asthenic Lombard really worked at not giving a shit. He didn't want to develop a heart condition or high blood pressure like so many agents did.

"Of course," he said soothingly, "we all know Benstead is a flaccid old prick. But once in a while he gets an intuition. The scintilla of an idea—"

"Scintilla, shit!" Greener mumbled.

Lombard was staring across to where Tom Dillon and his mother were kneeling: Tom Dillon's wide shoulders hunched forward; his mother ramrod-straight despite her years. Lombard said, "Switching surveillance to that other brother is Benstead's idea."

"Not on the file, is he?"

"Tom Dillon," Lombard said. "I remember he used to call the old guy, his uncle, when we had the bug on. Any time he was here in New York."

"What is the guy?"

"A nebbish. Vietnam veteran and he has the money, he makes a profession of it."

"Why the surveillance then?"

"He could have something going for the uncle too," Lombard said. "Sometimes I get this pricking in my thumbs."

Angus McStay sighed; shifted his position. Kneeling here in the echoing vastness of Saint Patrick's Cathedral, he kept thinking everyone was watching him. The people shuffling past—some of them looked sad and blank, others merely curious—all the time he expected one of them to point a finger, denounce him: "Hey, him there—that one kneeling there pretending to say the rosary! He's a Black Prod, so he is. Wouldn't you know it by the ugly black face of him?" And his own, back in Belfast. If they could see him now! A traitor he'd be for entering a Romish cathedral, a den of idolatry and papish iniquity.

Of course these pressures only bore down on you like this if you had been born in one of the sectarian ghettos of Derry or Belfast. It didn't matter which kind of ghetto—Catholic or Protestant—there would be the same siege mentality, the same readiness to shout "Traitor!" if anyone made any move toward reconciliation.

He knew it was all imagination. This was New York, and its tolerance was as vast as its indifference. Very different from the city he'd been born in. But he knew that however long he stayed in the States he could never escape Belfast, with its atmosphere of frozen tension, its British Army checkpoints, its gray skies and gray, dejected people.

What neither set of bigots would understand was that he had come here this morning on impulse—devastated as he was by feelings of pity and regret—giving his bodyguard, Tim Malone, the slip. McStay wasn't particularly a churchgoer anymore, although he had been brought up a good Presbyterian, but at least he had to come here and say a wee prayer for these poor people: cut down, blasted forever in their moment of innocent happiness.

Ever since those bombs had exploded on Fifth Avenue, McStay had felt a numbness as if a nerve had been severed in his brain. What had happened Saint Patrick's morning had been so hideous, so unexpected—and if you came from that misfortunate country called Ireland, so inevitable.

The irony for McStay lay in the fact that despite the president's disclaimer about not yielding to violence those bombs that morning had perhaps been the last straw, forcing change, movement, which all his years of patient lobbying had failed to achieve. How many times had he visited New York and Washington in the last four years, talking with Irish-American politicians, trying to convince them that only an American initiative along these lines could save Ireland from anarchy? Worse still had been his efforts to sway his fellow MPs in the British Parliament at Westminster. The Americans were, after all, heirs to the widest, most hopeful tradition in history. They cared in a way the Irish and the British didn't.

At least the Americans had given his ideas a positive response from the beginning. British politicians and diplomats were charming, but conditioned to a centuries-old technique of reducing the Irish Question to tea-table triviality. "The Irish? Delightful people, but—of course—absolutely mad!" The Irish politicians at Leinster House [the Irish parliament] and the diplomats at the Embassy on Sheridan Circle in Washington had an even trickier hand to play. Looking for consistency in Irish government policy was like tangling with the eight arms of an octopus. This ambivalence was personified in Conan O'Kelly, the minister for internal affairs. Suave, Trinity-trained, he wore his gallimaufry of different caps with the aplomb of a conjuror. His Appease-the-Brits cap, donned when he was seeking to persuade Irish-Americans not to give to organizations suspected of funding the IRA. His Ireland-helped-build-America cap, worn when appealing for American corporations to establish factories in the South of Ireland. And, in contrast to these, his we-are-now-good-Europeans cap, firmly in place when he made speeches pointing out that as members of the EEC, the Irish had now rejoined the Great European mainstream personified by Charlemagne and the late General de Gaulle: a tradition that made the Anglo-Saxon cultures of England and America appear merely trivial and barbarous. McStay was always dazzled by the sheer now-you-see-it-now-you-don't dexterity of O'Kelly's act.

Yes, the like of O'Kelly made the Irish-Americans look pretty straight-shooters. Not that they were any kind of pushover. They wanted to see the bottom line of any proposition, including that of McStay's plan for an independent Northern Ireland state. Now perhaps the bombs on Fifth Avenue had shown them what it was.

Not that American pressure alone could have effected much change in the British attitude. No: here again it seemed that this was a case of the last straw that breaks the camel's back—only with the British the straw had been, not the Saint Patrick's Day bombing, but the eighty soldiers who had died in the wreck of their troop carrier at Aldergrove Airport. Suddenly some hidden tank of rage overflowed: the mass of British people were demanding to know why all these boys had to be slaughtered, year after year. The Troops Out movement quadrupled its membership in a few weeks.

Suddenly McStay thought of Parnell. He had so nearly achieved what so many patriots had died for without spilling any blood at all. How different everything would have been if he had won. Home rule achieved at a time when the Northern Protestants could still have been absorbed into a single, harmonious Irish state. What a sea of troubles avoided! No Carson shouting "Ulster will fight and Ulster will be right!" No Easter Rising. No Partition. No Civil War. And—bringing the causal chain right up to its latest link—no Saint Patrick's Day Massacre.

McStay shifted uneasily. He still hadn't said his wee prayer for the dead. "Our Father which art in Heaven . . ."

"Which art . . ." The Catholics said "Who art . . ." Didn't they? Of such differences are hatreds compounded. He finished the Lord's Prayer but stayed kneeling, a big man with a heavy proconsular face framed in gray sideburns. His wife, Moira, said he looked like pictures of Oscar Wilde—"only more sensitive."

He closed his eyes and went on praying.

Frankie McNagan was kneeling a few rows back from Mrs. Dillon and her son Tom. She had identified the elderly woman and the big man from the photograph Duane (with his usual fanatic thoroughness) had given her before she left Dublin.

Frankie was tense, watching people pass in front of Wendell Dillon's coffin, pause, kneel, say a prayer. Mostly they must be strangers, stopping by out of compassion or curiosity.

She half closed her eyes, staring through enlaced fingers at the Dillons: they looked like china figurines, black and immovable, among the shadows of the Lady Chapel.

How exactly was she going to make contact with them? With Tom Dillon really: she had learned from Duane that he was friendly with his uncle Seamus Dillon, the man she was in New York to see. ("But no more than friendly," Duane had warned. "No political involvement that we've heard of.") A message conveyed through Tom Dillon seemed the best way of getting in touch with Old Seamus. Of course she had assumed he was dead, killed along with other members of Justice for Ulster. Then, when she saw his name wasn't listed, she had called his apartment. The phone had been answered by a man with a strong German accent. Mr. Dillon was in Doctors Hospital. No, he wasn't seeing visitors yet.

Frankie had thanked the man—a servant, presumably—and told him she would call again. There had been a wiretap on Seamus Dillon's apartment at one time, she knew: she didn't want to give the FBI any reason to take a voiceprint. So now Tom Dillon seemed the best—the only—channel of communication open to her.

How exactly do it, though? Intercept the Dillons at the end of the mass? Contrary to all her training, she was inclined to ad-lib this one, reacting according to the way the Dillons reacted.

Of course Duane would tell her she was crazy, coming here at all. And yet she felt so anonymous, kneeling here in this huge cathedral in this exciting but cold and menacing city.

Her feeling of anonymity had to be a delusion. Didn't the police always attend the funerals of murder victims in the hope that the killers wouldn't be able to stay away from the scene? Every foot of this building was probably staked out.

But how else was she to make contact with Old Dillon? Except through his nephew, and she would never grab him again if she missed him today.

Quite apart from that, she had wanted to come here. To thank God for her own deliverance from the bombs? (Not that the Catholic Daughters of America had been marching anywhere near Justice for Ulster.) Hardly. She hadn't been to mass for years. Her mother's fervent Catholicism hadn't taken, any more than the English rose persona her mother had tried to lay on her at the same time. Even as a child she'd sensed only blankness behind the solemn mumble of the mass.

Her mother had been Mary Clune, daughter of a small butcher in Tipperary town. At twenty-three she had met Peadar Mahoney, twenty years older, already a legend in his native city: the archetypal Irish rebel, the eternally mocking Dublin jackeen with a ballad on his lips and a gun in his pocket.

Maybe—Frankie was never clear about her parents' unlikely courtship— Mary Clune had caught this battered hero in a moment of weariness, exhausted by being on the run for years at a time, flitting from one safe house to another, arrested, interned, escaping, on the run again, arrested again, his life a strange seesaw between violent adventure and subtle politicking in the higher councils of the IRA. Maybe he had told the gentle, placid Mary Clune that he was tired of the fight, that he wanted the usual human fulfillments? A wife. Children. A home.

He got them all—his only child, Frankie, had been born a year after his marriage—but then he had tired of them. (Or so Frankie's mother maintained.) But Frankie realized—how well she understood it now!—that the fever for Irish freedom had gotten into Peadar's bloodstream years before: he was enchained by the eternal, death-nourished dreams of Tone and Pearse. When the tocsin sounded again with the IRA's 1953 attacks on British posts in border areas, Peadar had to respond. His wife had reproached him bitterly. Hadn't he given all this up? Had he no feelings of responsibility toward his wife and child?

Peadar retorted that no one ever resigned from the movement. There was only one way to leave the IRA—and she knew what he meant by that! An oath taken is an oath taken.

By early 1954 Mary Mahoney could stand it no longer. She left their home on Dublin's North Strand Road and took the infant Frankie to London. There over the next fifteen or sixteen years she sought to impose on Frankie a pattern of English living and thinking quite un-English in its intensity.

None of that, except her "English accent"—very useful since she had become a republican activist—had survived her falling in love with the Other Frankie.

She had been in her last year at the University of Sussex when she met him. She cherished vague ideas of doing journalism when she graduated; meanwhile she was enjoying the lectures of Quentin Bell, last scion of Bloomsbury, as he handed on the torch of mandarin aesthetics to a new generation.

Phyllis Batten had suggested they go over to Dublin for a weekend. She had theories about Irishmen being warmer and more instinctive than Englishmen. "For God's sake," she said, "aren't you bloody Irish yourself?" Amused, Frankie agreed to go.

In the Brazen Head they ran into a large party from Trinity. The Other Frankie was among them. Downing black pints of Guinness in a corner, they'd established a rapport at once. Francis McNagan was a postgraduate law student, he told her. He was hoping to establish a Peoples Law Center in Dublin similar to those operating in the States and more recently in England. Frankie had thought him vital and eloquent in a way that made the young men she met on the Sussex campus seem like scarcely animated dummies.

He had said abruptly, "I'm going to a funeral. Will you come?"

"A funeral?"

"What else?" he demanded. "Here we are, pouring black porter down our gullets, every God's one of us a pinchbeck Prometheus hurling defiance at the Fates! What more salutary than to be reminded of our ultimate futility? Besides, what more Irish than a funeral? All of us Irishmen are more than half in love with easeful death—that's the other side of the laughing, bubbling eloquence that has you captivated now!" He'd grinned suddenly, deflating himself and—she realized later—capturing her heart at the same moment.

All she could say was, "Who's being buried?"

"My brother," he said, suddenly tragic, unsmiling; instantly eliminating for her the babel of voices around them. "He was shot by British troops near Strabane in County Tyrone. Trying to get back across the border."

"Was he . . . in the IRA?"

"You mean the Provos, don't you, when you say that?" He paused, regarding her steadily. "No. Eireann Amhain. You've never heard of them, have you?"

She shook her head and he didn't explain further. They left straight after that, going to Mount Jerome Cemetery where thousands of Dubliners had assembled to do Michael McNagan honor. Every ritual tradition was observed. The rosary in Irish at the graveside. An honor guard in black berets and combat fatigues, their faces masked with dark glasses. And, at the end, a volley fired up at a rain-sodden sky.

Going away, she had said, amazed, "All those people. Are they all republicans? All IRA sympathizers?"

"At heart—yes!" Frankie said. "Even though ninety-nine percent of them vote for the old gombeen parties from the time of the Civil War—Fine Gael and Fianna Fail. They think that's the practical thing to do." He smiled reflectively. "Ireland—Ireland is a Sleeping Beauty and no fairy prince has even been able to kiss her awake. Not Emmet, not Tone, not Padraic Pearse!"

Neither spoke for a time and then he said accusingly, "I shouldn't have to tell *you* any of this. I know who you are. Frances Mahoney, daughter of Peadar Mahoney. I understand you haven't seen him for . . . what? Nineteen years? I must introduce him to you."

That was how it had all begun. Frankie had suddenly torn open a wound so deep and so long ignored that she had apparently forgotten its existence. In love with Frankie, it was an extra, overtopping happiness for her to rediscover her father too. He seemed like a stranger, but she loved him instantly, and she was awed to find how much Francis McNagan admired him. After fifty years of unremitting subversion against the state—the phrase was that of prosecuting counsel at the Special Criminal Court, and Peadar took it as an accolade—he was still living on North Strand Road, drawing his old-age pension, still subject to some surveillance from the Special Branch, still keeping his finger on every pulse of republican activity: a revered elder statesman of the movement.

Her marriage to the Other Frankie—and indeed, everything that had happened to her these last four years—now had for her the lopsided but compelling authority of a dream. Inevitably, she had joined Eireann Amhain which (she learned) was a small elite group with cells in London, Dublin, and Belfast. From caring little about Ireland, she had become an activist, ready to put her own and other lives on the line if the cause demanded it. Remembering her attitudes during her last year at Sussex, this made her smile. She was her own woman, intellectually disabused—and here she was letting herself be swayed, conditioned, by the beliefs of her husband and her father! What would her feminist friends say to that?

She didn't care much what they said, but she knew that in seeking to replace Irish weariness and corruption with vigor and hope, she was also working for the women of Ireland: the most deprived and put-down sisterhood in Europe.

She wondered with a sudden jerk of guilt what her feminist friends would think of the way she was treating the Other Frankie. He was a victim: monstrously betrayed and abused. Why did she have to betray him too?

He was a victim several times over. Of the British legal system. Of his comrades in Eireann Amhain. Of his own quixotic sense of loyalty. And not least (although he didn't know it) of her lustful adultery with Duane.

Francis McNagan had been sentenced to five years at the Old Bailey in London for being involved in the illegal shipment of arms. The arms in question—a hundred M16 carbines—had been bought from a legitimate dealer in Brussels. The British Special Branch—acting on a tipoff from the Belgian police—had found them in a trailer on Liverpool docks. They were intended for Belfast. The head of Eireann Amhain's cell there, Dick Grogan, wanted them for three-men assault teams throughout the North.

The Other Frankie had been in London at the time, studying the working of a People's Law Center in Whitechapel with a view to starting something similar in Dublin, along with some other young lawyers from Trinity.

The evidence to link him with the find was slender enough. The owner of the trailer was called Bob McIntyre: a sentimental fellow-traveler who lived in a London suburb. Worked over by the Special Branch, torn between losing all of his hard-won status quo in England and naming names—an offense visited with death in the movement—McIntyre tried to compromise. He named the Other Frankie, believing him to be in Dublin and therefore safe as he couldn't be extradited. But Frankie had been arrested leaving the law center on the Whitechapel Road.

The irony was that as a member of the Dublin cell he was not involved with this operation at all. But the police knew him as one of the leaders of Eireann Amhain in the South of Ireland. Held under the Prevention of Terrorism Act, Frankie had of course said nothing. As the evidence against him was purely circumstantial, if this had been another kind of case that might have gotten him off the hook. Not this time. The English police naturally react with fear and suspicion toward IRA suspects, labeling them guilty at once. A trained lawyer himself, the Other Frankie didn't deign to open his mouth in his ówn defense. He stayed silent, refusing in the classic republican tradition to recognize the court. Inevitably he was convicted, going down mute into the cells to start his five-year term.

The recriminations that followed had almost split Eireann Amhain apart. Duane, particularly, considered the Other Frankie's conviction a tragic waste. "He's a brilliant lawyer. Of course he could have defended himself." Duane had paused: black-bearded; bearlike yet gentle. He had gone on to blame Dick Grogan for not giving Frankie the okay to release at least *some* information to the police and thus confuse the issues before the court. "That mute of malice stuff—nonsense! And all Grogan's fault. That bloody man fancies himself as such a sea-green incorruptible!"

Frankie herself remained confused. She was crushed, dazed, with the injustice of it all—so dazed that even now she could not judge. Maybe the Other Frankie could have defended himself, as Duane believed; maybe Grogan was right and silence was all he could have offered without jeopardizing the cause.

Anyway, Grogan and Duane loathed each other with something more than rivalry. A polarization of opposites. Duane—tall, big-built, eloquent in word and gesture, relishing the drama of his life as he lived it. Grogan—small, neat, stylish in a self-consciously old-fashioned way: a dandy even. Opposites with only one thing in common: a burning conviction that Ireland had to be freed and that they would do it, even at the cost of their own lives.

Duane. Always her thoughts came back to him. The guilt that mounted inside her each time she visited her husband in Parkhurst jail, saw him smile goodbye, suffering, implacably resigned. And yet she knew that this in some perverse way enhanced what she had going with Duane. Fucking Duane, she felt an intoxicating sense of violation—no doubt what he intended her to feel. When he first asked her, he had set the mood by suggesting she seek the Other Frankie's permission. She had reacted with what she hoped looked like anger and then Duane had said, "You're a dedicated woman, Frankie. Dedicated to the cause for which your husband is currently incarcerated in an English jail. Do you think it's fair—to him, to your comrades, to yourself—to let yourself be crippled by sexual frustration?" When she hadn't replied he had added. "The Other Frankie is a realist, if you're not. He'd agree with me."

She had turned her back on Duane and walked out of the room. And then, three days later, she had given in. And the awful thing was, when Duane pulled her up to him, smiling, buccaneerlike, spreading her legs and driving into her savagely—why, then she had known a pleasure that was piercing, indescribable: a high unimaginable with the Other Frankie, the man she really loved.

Frankie rose from her knees, then checked herself. As soon as the Dillons made a move she would approach them. (She couldn't help wishing Tom Dillon were alone.) She would act emotional, overwrought. Play it like she had yielded to a sudden impulse to approach anyone of the Dillon family. After all, she was Mary Ogham from the County Limerick and her family were old friends of Seamus Dillon's. What more natural than to want to sympathize?

Of course Tom or his mother might react dumbly, or hostilely. Then she would have to think of some other way to get at the old man. She wasn't about to give up, whatever the difficulties. This was dodgy, knife-edged stuff, but she had her mission to perform.

"Hail Mary, full of grace, the Lord is with Thee. Blessed art Thou amongst women, and blessed is the fruit of Thy womb, Jesus."

Tom's lips kept moving in time with his mother's. The old tension was there between them, just as it had been when he was a boy. Always at mass she had monitored his outward show of devotion—and always found it wanting.

"Holy Mary, Mother of God, pray for us sinners, now and at the hour of our death . . ."

Tom's knees were aching. He tried to concentrate his thoughts on Wendell, conjuring up odd images from the days when they spent summer vacations at Uncle Seamus' house in Southampton. Wendell and himself running along the beach, plastered with a mixture of sand and seawater, happy summer clowns without past or future. Somehow, memories of the older Wendell were not valid in the same way. When Tom tried to evoke the adult Wendell—his first

TV appearance after being elected to the Senate; on various chat shows—all he got was cold, frozen images: lifeless stills. Only through childhood can one resurrect the dead.

Dead. His only brother. Lying there in that casket only feet away from him. In fact Tom had seen Wendell's body before they screwed the lid down on him, and he hadn't looked too bad, but the trouble was, Tom kept seeing everyone *except* Wendell. You get to have a lot of dead acquaintances after three tours in Nam. Whenever he tried to think of Wendell serenely and with love, his mind was blanketed by images of mutilation and decay. Blood and bone fragments; flesh flattened and frizzed black with fire. The dead—Cavs and grunts and VC alike—all of them stashed away in torn body-bags and given a grisly kind of resurrection by the heaving mass of flies that were feeding on them.

Maybe Nancy was right. He was burned-out, fucked-over, finished, by those three tours. Maybe—but then Nancy was hardly a detached observer. Once— only once, in the short period between his return from Indochina and their final parting—had Tom spoken to her of the war: attempted to convey something of what combat troops had suffered in, say, the Tet Offensive.

She hadn't spoken for a moment. Her pale face—once Tom had thought it had the delicate beauty of a mask by Dulac—was set in lines of rejection and disgust. "You know what?" she said. "Every day I find male self-pity more monstrous. For centuries you've wallowed in all you've suffered in your stupid manmade wars! Machismo shit! I said it before. You've dramatized it, blown it up—and then you've gone home to the poor women who're sitting waiting to console you. Breasts to lean on; wombs to defile with your seed!" Her eyes narrowed, grew mean. She was almost spitting her hatred now. "What about what those women were suffering while you were away being heroes? You didn't want to know, did you, any of you? I tell you, that young Marine you mentioned, the one that wouldn't stop screaming"—a twenty-year-old grunt on Tom's first tour, waking up in hospital to find his legs had gone— "I don't pity him. War may mutilate men's bodies; men have mutilated women's souls . . ."

He'd left her then. Gone out of the room without a word. He had the strange feeling that if he returned a half hour later she would still be talking— whether there was anyone to listen or not.

His mother was looking at him. Tom could sense that she was impatient, even irked. Probably with Cheryl. This was, in a sense, Wendell's last appearance on the political stage, and Mrs. Dillon would consider that his widow should be here by now. Cheryl would be in time for the requiem, of course, but that would hardly be the point for Mrs. Dillon.

He had to admit his mother still looked good. At seventy, plus a few months. Age had given her blond beauty a defiant, almost Viking quality. Even today, when Wendell's death must have laid what remained of her world in ruins, she was still in there, fighting. Tom had guessed that when he met her at the Drake Hotel this morning (she always stayed there on her less and less frequent visits to New York). She said, "Dreadful though it is, Wendell's death could mean a new beginning for all of us."

That was her oblique way of referring to what Max Segal had spoken of in Charlie Mac's bar last night—the suggestion that he go to Dublin to the Carrolton Inauguration in Wendell's place. The further suggestion that she make over to him the income that had previously subsidized Wendell's political career. Max hadn't said it, but she wouldn't offer that for just going to Dublin. Her expectations would come a whole lot higher. Could it be she'd gotten some grotesque notion of Tom going into politics himself? How far out in fantasy could this intelligent, cultivated, Catholic matriarch really get?

Of course solitude is conducive to fantasy, and his mother lived the life of a very wealthy anchorite. She had a house down at Coral Gables, and the climate suited her. She didn't seem to need people much. Her housekeeper, Mrs. McGuggin, anticipated all her needs with a sensitivity that was a kind of ESP. And in Miami lived the Very Reverend Monsignor William Taylor Warren— "Monsignor Bill" to the family as long as Tom could remember. Mrs. Dillon talked with Monsignor Bill most days; he came to visit with her—for confession or simply for chat—two or three times a week.

Neither Tom nor his mother would refer directly to her "new beginning" or Max's "change of direction"—which really meant the same thing. Purpose, control, injected into Tom's admittedly purposeless, rudderless life. But he wasn't about to accept any such control. From his mother or anyone else.

"Hey—what's she doing?" Greener demanded.

Mrs. Dillon had left her seat. Her son remained where he was. Slowly, she moved out of the Lady Chapel and into one of the main aisles. A yard or two on, she stopped and stood motionless: tall, statuesque, looking upward as her lips moved in prayer.

"What's she doing, for Chrissake?" Greener persisted.

Lombard said, "The stations of the cross. Like, she prays her way around the church."

"You a *Catholic*, Harry?"

"My wife was. My first wife."

"Irish?"

"Polish."

Tom could no longer see his mother. She had moved away, lost in the vastness of the cathedral as she made the stations.

On an impulse he moved forward and knelt on the cold flagstones before his brother's coffin.

"Mr. Dillon?"

It came as a whisper: tiny, intense, and clear.

"Excuse me."

He tried to look round; slewed awkwardly off his knees. He stood up.

"You are Tom Dillon?"

He nodded. This was a small dark girl: wide-eyed, almost gaunt with emotion. Before he could say anything she seized both his hands, murmuring, "I'm so sorry. About your brother. It was terrible . . . I was there marching . . . They had no chance at all."

She shuddered.

Tom still hadn't said anything. When she spoke again all the emotion had gone out of her voice: the words came quickly, cold and sharp as ice. "Your Uncle Seamus. I have to see him. I know he's in hospital but I came from Ireland to see him."

Tom said, "He's ill. I don't think you can."

"Tell him"—the force in her voice had her almost hissing the words, willing him, compelling him to listen—"tell him that Peadar Mahoney's daughter is here from Dublin. Tell him"—she hesitated—"that it concerns the foundation." She paused. "Say that. Say 'the foundation' and say 'Peadar Mahoney's daughter.' "

"I don't know," Tom said. "I can't promise he'd see you."

"Just say what I told you. Your uncle will see me."

"Who are you?" Tom demanded.

"You can tell him . . ." She paused. "Mary Ogham."

"All right," Tom said. "Where can I call you?"

"You can't," she said. "I mean—you'd better not." She grasped both his hands again with theatrical fervor and murmured, "You realize we're probably under observation?" Then she added, "Say a place. And a time."

"Noon tomorrow?"

She nodded. "Where?"

"Do you know . . ." Tom hesitated. "Luchow's on East Fourteenth Street?"

"I don't know anywhere in New York but I'll find it."

She was gone into the shadows. Still hypnotized by the intensity of this strange girl, Tom found himself wondering what had made him ask her to lunch.

☘ ☘ ☘

"And so, Rex," Sean O Morain said, "you can't tell us who the star of this movie is going to be?"

Lang shook his head slowly from side to side. "No way, Sean. Not at this moment. But let me just say—for 'star' read 'superstar.' "

Watching him in the monitor, Marta Troy thought: He knows what he's doing all right, but *what's* he doing? Everything he says stands up when he says it—and yet he's shitting the people. He's got to be. If this movie is as bankable as he says, if its really going into production any day now, why not level with O Morain? Say who he's got—if he's got anyone.

O Morain was nodding. "A superstar! How about that!" He paused. "But, Rex—I'm not about to let you go that easy! I'm going to name some names— and you're honor bound to tell me if I hit on the right one." He paused again, hamming it up with burlesque intensity. "It's Robert De Niro. Isn't it?"

Lang was shaking his head again, smiling, and Marta was reminded again how sunny and boyish his smile could be. "Sean!" he protested. "Much as I love you; much as I love all those Irish people who're watching us right now— name names I cannot!" He looked serious. "I dare not. I have an obligation to my associates and part of it is not to reveal the identity of the man who is gonna play the lead role in *Blood Scenario*." He paused. "As I say, he's not just a star, he's a superstar, and a lot of money hangs on a name like that. I used the phrase 'bankable' a moment ago. That means certain friends of mine have confidence in me and I can't betray them. There's big money involved here, even though *Blood Scenario* is a small-budget picture as pictures go today— maybe three million"—he shrugged—"could be three million, three, at the end of the day."

"Dollars?" O Morain asked.

"Dollars," Lang agreed.

"Well, Rex," O Morain said, "I suppose I'm dumb—I'm sure longtime viewers of this show will endorse that!—but you tell me you're about to start shooting in ten days, two weeks' time—"

"Right." Lang nodded.

"How can you? Without your star? Your *superstar*?"

Lang's smile grew broader. "Easy. We simply shoot around Mister X. Film those scenes in which he doesn't appear." He paused. "In this movie—in any movie—there's a lot of what I might call backup footage. Ancillary scenes."

"*Blood Scenario* will be made entirely in Ireland?"

"Right! In County Wicklow and various other locations throughout the twenty-six counties. And, indeed, right here in this city of Dublin."

I smell subterfuge, Marta thought, but poor old Sean is not the man to unveil it.

O Morain ran this "Weekend Show" every Sunday night, giving the viewers an Irish version of the kind of chat show popular in the States. As an emcee he was corny, obvious, and ridiculously indulgent of his guests. Marta was one of Sean's regulars, invited on the panel whenever he entertained anyone even remotely concerned with show business. Tonight Rex Lang was the guest of honor, parrying flattering questions, every inch that potent figure, the American director arrived in Ireland to make a movie.

Lang had called her before the show at her suite at Jury's Hotel. (How did he know she lived there?) He'd simply said "Marta," without saying who he was— she always knew his voice, anyway. She'd exclaimed, "You of all people!" and made her usual remark about their meetings being in a three-to-five-year cycle, determined by the stars. Marta was a Pisces and he was a Virgo and as far as she could make out, their mutual signs stood in disastrous confrontation.

Of course she was intrigued to see Rex here in Dublin. Over the phone he'd told her he was making a movie and that Bud Halsey was organizing the finance. (The last time she'd met Lang had been at Bud's house off Benedict Canyon.) Actually, Marta surmised, the finance could be the gray area that gave off the slight odor of subterfuge. The bottom line of this project was by no means clear to her. There were imponderables. For instance—had Rex Lang ever directed a movie before?

If Rex's presence intrigued her, Marta was positively electrified by the girl he had brought onto the show—without Sean's prior knowledge, she guessed. Rex had mentioned this girl when he called Marta at Jury's. Her real name was Leni Reffenstab, but "for various reasons" she would act in *Blood Scenario* as Gudrun Hebbel.

Leni Reffenstab or Gudrun Hebbel, she was a voluptuous-looking, olive-skinned creature that set Marta's thoughts drifting along certain delicious channels. (Why had Rex chosen to mention this girl before Marta had even seen her? What was going through *his* mind?) Leni wore an elegant cat-suit that modeled her splendid body better than nakedness; her long black tresses shone under the lights. Only Marta's iron professionalism kept her from staring at Leni in a way that would have embarrassed everyone.

"Do you agree, Marta?" O Morain asked.

Good Ole Sean, bringing her into the action at any cost. Trouble was, Marta had been so blinded by Leni's attractions that she wasn't sure what he had asked in the first place. No problem. Marta was too old a hand to be caught by a detail like that.

"Yeah . . . well . . ." She nodded her head several times to give herself pause, and of course Sean rephrased the question: "Is it inevitable that there should be tension between director and star—especially between a male director and a female star—and would you agree, as Rex has suggested, that a film may even gain from such tension?" Sean grinned and added, "For instance between Joseph Losey and a certain famous actress whose career has got some parallels with your own?"

Marta nodded. Losey vis-à-vis La Fonda was old hat, and she wasn't crazy about the comparisons between her and Jane that the commentators made. But that sort of shit was after all the staple of shows like this.

"No," she said. "I don't agree. Not really. For instance I believe there were even rumors of dissension between me and Gay Targ on the last film we worked on together."

"And they were false rumors?"

"My God," she said. "False as dicers' oaths! Gay is one sweet and sensitive man. Making *Harry Lorrequer* was a very rich experience for me."

In fact *Lorrequer* had been a foolish attempt to follow *Barry Lyndon* in the distinguished costume genre. A turkey: a real crock of shit. It had been Marta's last film. Because it had been made in Ireland it had seemed to offer a compromise between staying here and not working and returning to the States and confronting reality, professional and personal.

Lang said, "You know what Bergman said? He said he made his films with the help of eighteen friends. David Lean's comment was that he made his with ninety enemies."

"And you, Rex?" O Morain demanded.

"I think I'd better say"—Lang's grin was boyish, ingratiating—"with the help of twenty-nine very dear friends!"

There was a laugh at that. The other guest on the show, a black-bearded fellow called O Dunnacha Duane who hadn't said much up to now, went into a spiel about making a film really being a collective enterprise and how any concept of the director as *auteur* must be in conflict with that. Marta didn't know much about Duane, except that he had a show, "Daoine Ag Caint." On this one he was the usual obligatory gaelgoir, raising his voice against the vulgarity and materialism of the English and Americans that were polluting the clear stream of Irish culture.

Now Duane said, "Sean—don't you think we're being a little too theoretical? A bit too rarefied?" He smiled—leered would be more like it, thought Marta—at Leni, who sat sulky and silent across from him. "When we're confronted by such a beauty as Ms. Hebbel at close range."

"That's right," O Morain said. "Gudrun, tell us about yourself. Will this be the first time you've acted in English?"

"That is correct." She hadn't much of a German accent. She hadn't smiled once since she came on the show. Most young actresses on display smile continually: on-off-on like defective street signs. Marta thought: How beautiful she is. That chiseled profile. The hair blacker than a raven's wing. But also: how cold she looks. How cruel.

"I have not acted in a film before," Leni went on. "For the stage, yes. In a play by your own Irishman, Bernard Shaw. *You Never Can Tell.*"

"Fascinating!" O Morain exclaimed.

Lang said, "Her mother was a member of Brecht's Berliner Ensemble at the Schiffbauerdamm Theater. After Brecht's death, she escaped to the Federal Republic." He paused. "I mention this because in *Blood Scenario* Gudrun plays a student in revolt against the same West German stability and prosperity her mother risked her life to reach."

Sean O Morain was nodding sagely. "Fascinating—but look at that clock over there! Can you wind up by just telling us very briefly what *Blood Scenario* is about?"

Lang nodded. "Trouble is, I don't think any of my other work has been seen over here. I think I can best describe it in terms of the so-called underground cinema—"

"Rex!" O Morain cut in. "Time's a-wastin'!"

"*Blood Scenario* is a new departure for me," Lang said. "At one level it's an adventure story, a thriller. At another, a serious political comment." Lang paused. "A group of international guerrillas is hired to perform an operation against the British Army in the North of Ireland. They wear British uniforms and they take over from a real British Army unit at a strongpoint in the center of Belfast. That way they get to hold the whole city to ransom."

"Ingenious!" O Morain said. "What's the political comment?"

"That all revolutionary activity is now truly international. You in Ireland won't be able to keep your tribal wars to yourselves much longer."

"Tribal wars!" O Morain shook his head. "Okay, Rex—one last question: Are you going to use Irish performers?"

"Try to stop me!" Lang exclaimed. "I tell you: The Irish are natural actors. Go into any bar here in Dublin. Watch. Listen." He shook his head admiringly. "Why—it's *The Odyssey.* It's *The Canterbury Tales.* It's *Finnegan's Wake.*"

Marta realized that Leni was watching her. This gave her great pleasure coupled with a certain uneasiness. There was something *louche,* even sinister, about this girl. Was she an actress at all? The vibes she projected were powerful and disturbing. Marta realized that she felt toward Leni some of the fascination—and the fear—evoked by Lang himself.

All through the sex with Annabel Rayne, Marta kept thinking of Leni—and of Lang. As Annabel strove to pleasure her, her eager tongue thrusting, tasting, between her outspread thighs, Marta felt only impatience. There was something clumsy and unspontaneous about Annabel. Marta had sensed it at the very beginning. That slightly stammering English rose charm sure as hell had palled.

Later, Marta lay on the bed and watched Annabel walk naked into the bathroom. She had not realized before how ugly Annabel was in her movements: slow, almost lumbering. Marta thought of Leni, tormented by the contrast. Leni moved like a cat; her graceful nakedness was beyond imagining. She wondered what Leni was doing at this moment. Making it with Lang? Somehow she didn't think theirs was that kind of relationship.

Marta had wanted to go on for drinks and maybe dinner with Lang and Leni after their appearance on the "Weekend Show," but Lang had said they had to get back to Kilbrangan House, the big old mansion in County Wicklow he was making his headquarters. Disappointed, Marta had gone straight from the television studios at Donnybrook outside Dublin to this crummy apartment she kept in the Rialto district on the south side of the city. She lived in Jury's Hotel in Ballsbridge of course. She kept this place exclusively for sexual encounters, and no one knew of its existence—unless Marta took them there. The amusing thing was, she was sure this apartment had been used as a lovenest by the previous tenant too: the ceiling of the bedroom was covered by an enormous mirror. Lying here, listening to Annabel clonking about in the bathroom, Marta amused herself by posing for her own personal centerfold, up there in the mirror.

The face was okay. Yes, sir, the old Troy bone-structure was right there, like you saw it in portraits of her grandfather, Thomas Wilson Troy, generally acknowledged the finest Hamlet ever seen in America—better than Booth, better than Barrymore. The imperious, overlarge nose. The nearly Red Indian cheekbones. Not bad, considering the angst piled upon angst that had been her life these last ten years.

The body? Marta lay spreadeagled; opened her legs wide, snickering a little.

Like Germaine says: make friends with your vulva, right? Vulvas aside, she was too fat. No good anyone shitting her she was a Renoir woman. Her boobs were still magnificent, but they sagged a little. Her ass—well, that might be dubbed magnificent according to taste, but it was a long way from the perfect, pear-shaped "Miss America Ass" that Rudi Costelakis, the White-Russian-Greek-French director who'd been the first and by far the nicest of her husbands, had exulted in. (He'd always proclaimed himself an ass-man; native-born Americans were, he claimed, invariably tit-men.)

Looking at herself, Marta still liked herself. This was *her*, the real Marta Troy. In some secret magical way she even felt herself more desirable now—debauched and overripe as she was—than she'd been in the bloom of her young flesh. Men and women alike responded to her. Not that she'd screw with a man—it was axiomatic that male sexuality was aggression, an affront—but they still reacted to her. Women—ah, there weren't many women who could resist the kind of glamour she could project.

Yeah! She sat up suddenly, hunching her shoulders; stopped looking up at the mirror. All right, if she was still that good, why was she still here in Ireland rather than in New York or LA where the real action was?

It was obvious why too. That shitheel who'd done a profile on her for *New York* magazine had come close to the heart of her mystery when he compared her sojourn in Ireland with the Spanish exile of a famous star of an earlier generation—"only there are no bullfighters in Dublin."

It was obvious. She'd dropped out, through some failure of nerve, of will. Living in Ireland represented for her a kind of death.

An agreeable death, though. Never mind Celtic bitchery and Dublin's "daily spite." Marta loved the Irish way of accepting you at your own valuation (to your face, anyway). You didn't have to make it all over again each day like you had to in New York or LA or even London. Marta loved Dublin. From her suite in Jury's she had only to lift the telephone to plug herself into any one of a dozen tiny worlds. The media people at Radio Telefis Eirean at Donnybrook, shuttling between the studios and the bars where a lot of their real work was done. The politicians—the ministers and Dail deputies—and all their attendant parasites. The tax-exempt artists and writers, congregated in some ten square miles of County Wicklow and mostly so British that they wouldn't know a shamrock from a French letter at ten paces. The residue of the Anglo-Irish huntin' and shootin' and fuckin' set. Marta liked them all.

Here she was then, living out this pleasant death-in-life, and along comes Rex Lang. Was he going to act as a catalyst?

It was, of course, hyperbole to say that they met every three to five years, according to their mutual signs of the Zodiac. In fact they'd first met—it could be as long as six years ago. The war in Vietnam was still on. Not even La Fonda was active in more causes than Marta was at that time. Striking lettuce workers. Illegal immigrants. The Young Lords. Marta had hit the GI coffeehouse circuit even before Jane had. She'd been busted for handing out antiwar leaflets at Fort Jackson the same week as Fonda had been held at Fort Lewis.

That had been the time when she'd first met Lang at Natashia Chardin's beachhouse in Malibu. She'd gone along there in a mood normal to her at that time—blunted with fatigue, reacting to people with an edge of hysteria born of the fatigue. Natashia was the Eternal Madam, one of nature's bawds, procuring for everyone the person he or she most wanted procured, and it was easy to see why she had invited Marta along to meet Rex Lang. He had what was at that moment the extraordinary cachet of being on the lam from the army in Indochina. (Although, Marta thought, he didn't have the hungry look, the jangled agonized nervousness of a man on the lam.) Natashia had whispered that he had been commanding a company in Phu Yen province and had freaked out when ordered to cover up a massacre involving the population of a whole village ("worse than My Lai").

There was more yet. Escaping through Saigon and then through Laos, Lang had made his way to Latin America. There, he had become active with the *guerrilleros*. It was all rather vague, but certainly he had been in a number of interesting places at highly significant times. In Chile when Allende fell; in Uruguay with the Tupamaros. You could see how it would all grab Natashia, that impresario of fashionable revolt.

Marta tried to distance herself, told herself that this was all too romantic to be true, but confronting him, she had to admit the man was impressive. It wasn't just his looks. Maybe it was his style in general: clipped, elliptic, authoritative. Certainly Marta wasn't impressed because he was saying the things Natashia's guests wanted to hear at that time. How badly American multinationals behaved in Third World countries. How the State Department prostituted its consular agencies in such countries at the will of the CIA.

Living in her bright, shadowless Beverly Hills world, Marta considered herself a connoisseur of human falsity. But Lang had stature of some kind. He intrigued her.

He still intrigued her when she met him again, about a year later. The atmosphere in Hollywood had changed somewhat; the Zeitgeist was blowing from another quarter. Marta didn't go to Natashia's parties at the beachhouse so often anymore. But she went occasionally, and thus she met Lang again. Natashia still instinctively played the social bawd: presenting her guests in whatever persona seemed most fashionable that month or even that week.

Although radical chic was declining fast, she whispered to Marta that Lang had recently been involved in some Latin American activity; it was said with the Monteneros in Argentina.

But Lang never spoke of that. The Zeitgeist carried the conversation in a different direction. This was the aftermath of Helter Skelter in Southern California. A lot of talk was going around about the Family, about human sacrifices on lonesome beaches and bags of bones being found in the hills. And now a group centered on Lang was talking about snuff movies. Of course the very phrase "snuff movie" was new then, although Natashia's guests tried to imply that they'd seen so many that they were getting old hat. There was mention of a film of a human sacrifice that had taken place on a beach off Highway 1, near the county line, and Lang said, "The best snuff movies are like the best home movies—wholly spontaneous."

There was laughter at that, but Lang had spoken so coldly, in such a matter-of-fact way, that it got through to Marta at some uncomfortable level of her awareness. And then, later, after the party, Natashia told her that Lang had actually negotiated the sale of the human sacrifice movie, obtaining (it was said) one hundred thousand dollars from a New York "collector."

That was something Marta couldn't forget: it somehow intensified the sinister vibes she'd always gotten from Lang. Over the next three years she saw him occasionally, never at Natashia's, but at Mr. Chow's American or The Bistro. Sometimes he was at the Polo Lounge in the company of Franklin Brossard, the radical lawyer who first attracted attention with his theories about the Kennedy assassinations, and who had for so long been rumored to be preparing a Götterdämmerung greater than Watergate that no one believed in anymore. Marta noticed that Lang's dress had gotten more formal: custom-made jackets and once a blue business suit with a Countess Mara tie.

Her most recent meeting with him had been at Bud Halsey's. Technically an agent, Halsey functioned on an altogether more powerful plane than most agents. He liked to say that he married money and talent and no one ever wanted to divorce.

He lived off Benedict Canyon, and Marta's most recent meeting with Lang had occurred in Bud's Jacuzzi, a crescent-shaped pool with a control panel for brightening and dimming the lights and for turning on the various jets which could set it bubbling like a witches' caldron. Outsiders who would never be invited to share it said that Bud's Jacuzzi saw bigger money negotiated than Wall Street ever saw these days.

Marta hadn't been surprised when she found herself next to Lang in the bubbling water. Their meetings seemed inevitable. In fact, as she said, astrologically determined.

Something made her ask, "Making any good movies these days?"

He grinned boyishly.

"Natashia told you about that one, of course." He shook his head. "I didn't make it, though."

"Really?"

"Of course not!" But he spoke in a teasing way, so she didn't know what to believe. "You know—struck me afterwards—the aesthetics of the snuff movie must interest you, as a performer. That interaction of fantasy and reality. Carries the Method to the ultimate as far as the leading lady is concerned."

She didn't reply. As he spoke, she was conscious of his gaze upon her: piercing and yet curiously blind, empty.

That must be all of two years ago. And now Lang was in Dublin, going on O Morain's chat show. It made you wonder. Not only about Rex's credentials as a director, which no one in Dublin was about to investigate (if he'd been Irish, one of their own, they'd have been onto him at once), but also about the backing Halsey could be giving him.

Well, Marta wasn't going to rock the boat. Or anyway, not till she got to know Leni Reffenstab a good deal better.

The thought of Leni improved Marta's mood so much that she was quite mellow by the time Annabel condescended to come out of the bathroom. You had to admit the gal had a good body, though the face told you she was into her thirties. Tall and rangy, with boobs that still held up and long fair hair that Annabel would brush and brush for hours.

"Darling Marta," she said. "I'm sorry I was so long. You must have wondered what had happened to me."

"Darhling," Marta said in her Tallulah Bankhead voice, "ah was a-beginning to speculate on the various *possibilities* . . . But now you *is* here, honey— how about you just come back to bed, huh?"

✿ ✿ ✿

"So," Liam Costelloe said. "Now it hits the fan. Hogg comes before the grand jury two weeks from today."

"You think he'll talk?" Seamus Dillon asked.

Costelloe laughed. "Talk! A prima donna! The performance of the year and I shit you not!"

Seamus nodded. He wasn't going to let Costelloe see how deeply he'd gotten at him with this. "What a pity," he said, "that you ever mentioned Hogg's name to me the first day."

Costelloe shrugged. "'Twas done for dear old Ireland, Seamus boy! I couldn't read the tea leaves then, any more than you."

Seamus leaned back against the massed pillows. He was off the blood-drip now, but still confined to bed in this private room in Doctors Hospital.

"Of course," he said carefully, "what he's been subpoenaed for is the deal with the Iraqis."

Costelloe nodded. "Right," he said ironically. "And do you know where those machine guns and rocket launchers which had Iraqi end-user certificates issued for them finally landed?"

Seamus shook his head.

"Angola, that's where. And not for the use of the CIA's boy Holden Roberto either. No—it looks like that hardware went right to the MPLA, sponsored by the fucking Cubans, no less."

"Okay," Seamus said. "That's pretty heavy, isn't it? With a story like that—"

"You think everyone's gonna be so interested in the fucking Cuban connection that they'll forget to mention you or the late Senator?" Costelloe cut in with something like hostility in his voice. "Seamus, I gotta tell you: any sort of investigation like this is like someone complains of bellyache and they open him up and it's Big C!" He shook his head. "Once they start cutting, they're gonna find plenty!"

Seamus was silent. Don't let this ancient gorilla see how much this all hurt him. Let him talk away; let it ride. At this moment he didn't feel ambivalent about Liam Costelloe: he actually disliked him.

To signal a desire for silence, Seamus closed his eyes and made himself relax back against the pillows.

"I'm sorry, Seamus boy," Costelloe said. "Telling you all this, I'm not about to help you to recover . . ." He shook his head. "Like I always said, I think you're too sensitive for this kind of politics. You're a dreamer, Seamus." He spoke in a slow, ruminative tone. "You think of yourself as a soldier?" He shook his head. "I never knew Joe McGarrity wrong about a man. He once told me you should have been a poet, Seamus. A wandering bard. Turlough O'Carolan maybe. Blind Raftery with eyes on him!"

There was mockery in his voice, but Seamus knew where the shoe was pinching and didn't care. Mentioning Joe McGarrity, Costelloe showed his hand. He'd always been jealous of Seamus' friendship with McGarrity.

"The greatest recruiting officer the movement ever had in these United States," Costelloe went on. "A man of golden eloquence. That's how Joe described you to me."

Seamus remained silent. Costelloe was lying, as he was always prepared to do. Joe would never have discussed Seamus with Costelloe—or Costelloe with

Seamus either. Always Joe had remained the leader, holding all the threads of power in his hands. Costelloe might have cherished some fantasy about succeeding Joe in his unique ascendancy in the movement in the States.

McGarrity. Seamus figured he'd known Joe as well as he'd ever known anyone. McGarrity, that iron gallowglass of a man, longtime leader of Clan na Gael, a living link with dead giants like John Devoy, Luke Dillon (no relation to Seamus—a Fenian Guy Fawkes who had bombed the British Houses of Parliament), and of course the martyred Roger Casement. Yes, Seamus knew he wasn't the man Joe had been, but if McGarrity's mantle had descended on anyone, it had been on him, Seamus Dillon, and on no one else.

Costelloe's mind must have stayed on McGarrity too. Now he said, "One thing you have in common with Joe. You regard the Irish republican movement as your own personal bailiwick—and so did he!" Costelloe paused. "That might be okay in Joe's time. The harp vote meant something then—and no politico would dare move against the Clan." He shook his head. "Things is changed now, Seamus boy. Now you're vulnerable in a hundred ways." Costelloe had dropped his half-joshing, half-hostile manner. "You know who started this whole pizzaz on Hogg? The alcohol, tobacco, and firearms branch of the U.S. Treasury. And you must know they've been after *your* ass for a long time. Word is, they infiltrated Justice for Ulster in Boston last year, you knew it? With some help from your old friends in the Feds, I'd say." Costelloe shook his head. "Terrible thing to say, but could be, that bomb saved poor Wendell from having to answer some very nasty questions."

That was the truth, Seamus knew, and he couldn't blame Costelloe for telling it. He *was* vulnerable. Although surveillance on him had been at its worst toward the end of the Nixon era, he was always aware of hostile vibes from several directions at once. For example, every six months minor diplomats from the British and Irish embassies in Washington went to the U.S. Justice Department building in the federal triangle and consulted foreign agent's registration file Number 224172. In this the embassy officials would find the detailed return of Justice for Ulster, registered half-yearly to comply with federal laws. It wasn't that the Brits or the Irish hoped to prove that any of the dollars contributed to Justice for Ulster had gone to buy arms. No: they studied the file as a barometer of Irish-American support for the republican cause in Ireland.

That was a kind of invisible, painless harassment, of course. Other people had gotten it a lot worse than he had. Seamus had always been aware that being a millionaire was no disadvantage at all when it came to the more direct forms of interference. The fact that he was close to his nephew Wendell, a powerful and respected Senator, couldn't have been bad either. Of course, on a rather erratic, now-on-now-off basis, the FBI had spooked him for the last ten years. He even knew the agents who had been mostly assigned to his surveillance—Lombard and Greener—and if they sometimes appeared obsessed with the minutiae of his life, well, Seamus knew he didn't get the degree of harassment dished out to Irish republican fund-raisers who didn't happen to be president of a corporation like Penrith Pharmaceuticals.

Of course this present danger was another thing again. Hogg's testimony could start a chain reaction that might yet drag Seamus before the TV cameras at a grand jury hearing. He didn't care so much about himself. Old and dying as he was, what could they do to him in jail? In fact his arrest would be good counterpublicity to that goddamned President's Initiative. But what about the foundation? Suppose he were to die suddenly in police custody? He had to see O Dunnacha Duane in order to pass on the knowledge essential to Duane as his successor as trustee. And what of Wendell's reputation? That was what hurt most. Through a single act he could have stained Wendell's memory forever. No genuine liberal can ever appear to condone violence, in however just a cause, and for this reason Wendell had been careful never to ask Seamus anything about the foundation. And Seamus never mentioned it. And yet he had betrayed Wendell. Without intending to. In a moment of anxiety and weariness.

Looking back, it was obvious that Charlie O'Reilly couldn't have been in the desperate difficulty he said he was in. O'Reilly managed one of the smaller plants belonging to the Strategic Armaments Corporation near Manhattan, Kansas. He had been one of Seamus' first suppliers and Seamus was grateful for that. On this occasion all that was at stake was one hundred and fifty M16 Armalite rifles, intended to complete one of the early caches for the foundation. Normally such a quantity of arms would be included in a larger consignment covered by an end-user certificate from some Middle East country like Syria or Iraq and negotiated through a diplomat. (Although some of the deals that went to build up the foundation were black market transactions, with the goods simply smuggled out of the country.)

O'Reilly was in a panic because some kind of surprise audit was being conducted. The M16s would be unaccounted for—thus triggering off an investigation. Feeling old and tired and cornered—three days later he'd gone into Doctors Hospital for a blood change—Seamus had reacted to the fear in O'Reilly's voice.

He remembered Liam Costelloe had mentioned a man called Austin Hogg at the Defense Systems Sales Unit. Hogg had a reputation as a man who could fix things in the huge pullulating halfworld of Washington wheeling and dealing. But according to Costelloe it was better to approach him through someone who held office, however minor. As well as being on the take, Hogg was apparently some kind of a snob. That was why, in his fatigue and anxiety, Seamus had thought of Wendell. Talk about using a power hammer to crack a nut!

He realized that Costelloe was regarding him shrewdly. Suddenly Seamus' feeling of resentment evaporated. Costelloe had always been an ornery kind of a bastard, but he had to mean well, coming to visit with Seamus in the hospital. Anyway, Seamus knew this beetle-browed giant was as tired and defeated as he was himself. Once Liam Costelloe of the AFL-CIO had been a force to be reckoned with. Not quite a George Meany, but still one of the biggest of the powerbrokers, commanding thousands of votes. The last Democratic convention had ended that. Costelloe had been shown to be trading in a vacuum: a Samson shorn.

Seamus said, "You admire the President's Initiative so much, you'll be going over to Dublin to cheer him at the Carrolton Inauguration?"

"I don't particularly admire the Initiative," Costelloe sounded weary—"but it looks like it's the best trade-off we can get."

"Do you dare tell me that?" Seamus demanded.

"Politics is the art of the possible."

"Wendell used to say that."

There was a silence. Then Costelloe said, "Maybe you're the one who ought to go to Dublin? See Old Shannon's Face again? Why not?"

☘ ☘ ☘

"So!" Malachi O'Farrell said. "You're gonna interview McStay for a magazine. What's it called?" He paused. "*Screw* they used already. What about *Fuck?*" He grimaced and suddenly snapped his fingers. "I got it! *Cunt!*" He snickered. "What could be better for a feminist magazine? *Cunt:* organ of the militant feminist movement."

Brenda Wilson said coldly, "Shit, Malachi, it's too obvious, saying I want to interview him for a magazine."

"You got a better suggestion?" he demanded. "Break into his hotel room maybe, show him your pussy?"

"You know what, Malachi? You think everyone's a fool but yourself. McStay could be suspicious, check me out."

Malachi shook his head. "No. Trouble with you is, you've been freaked-out and fucked-up for so long you don't believe straight people even exist anymore. For straight people the obvious thing is the right thing—and a Northern

Ireland politician like Angus McStay is straighter than you could possibly imagine." He paused. "Back in Ireland they're always at least ten years behind us fortune-kissed citizens of the world's greatest democracy. McStay will have read about the liberation and penis-envy and bra-burning—like I say, they live in the past." He snickered. "He'll be as flattered as hell you wanna interview him for *Cunt*."

Brenda yawned, insultingly wide, without covering her mouth. "Okay," she conceded. "Could be the best way. That's how they got Trotsky, right?"

Malachi nodded. "Yeah, you could say so. Mercader played on his intellectual vanity. Got through all the fences, all the guards, like he was Superman."

"All we need is something that gets me into his room at the Gotham?"

"Right," Malachi agreed. "Lang even suggested this as being the best way." He relaxed a little as he went on, "A plus for us is we get him in a moment of euphoria. You know he was the guy who originally sold the idea of the President's Initiative? Mister Eminence Grise—and of course that's why Loyalist Action put out a contract. Okay, the Initiative has come about, the Saint Patrick's Day bombing was a nasty interlude, but he's still a success. He's relaxing, shooting the shit with guys like Hugh Carey and Tip O'Neill and them telling him what a diplomatist-behind-the-scenes he is." Malachi grinned. "Of course he'll love to tell you about himself."

"You think?" Brenda was lying stretched out on the old woolen rug. She was nude, as she always was when they were alone in the apartment. She would like him to refer to it—Malachi knew that—but he never would. She never tired, though: now she drew her knees up to her chin in her favorite thighs-apart position.

"You said he had a bodyguard?"

"An ex-cop from the Irish police force for God's sake! Not a real bodyguard."

She nodded. "He's got a suite?"

"Two rooms."

"But this bodyguard—"

"No problem. Just hint to McStay you'd rather talk with him in private." Malachi grinned. "He's sure to agree. He's real old-fashioned, McStay is. A gentleman. You wouldn't have met anyone like him before."

Brenda pouted, levered herself to her feet, and padded off into the bathroom, the surplus fat on her derriere jouncing to and fro. Malachi watched her with distaste. A faded blonde with drooping boobs and outsize ass, she looked like an aging hooker on the way down.

Except that she was coarser than any hooker he had ever known. Now she was going to use the john and she wouldn't close the door. That figured. Brenda was an animal—programmed to an animal cycle of copulating, eating, defecating. The fact that she was "educated"—the University of California at Berkeley for God's sake!—and could rap on about the theory of the Spectacle and quote Fanon and Marcuse and similar shit only put a gloss on the fact.

The seventies were over, but everything about Brenda was late-sixties radical. For instance, her parents: sober middle-class folks from Fairfield, California. Essence of the Middle America from whose loins sprang the generation of acid and revolt. Brenda had surely worked hard at fucking up their image of her as a golden-ringleted All-American pompon girl with luscious thighs and bouncing boobs. Before she was halfway toward graduation, she'd been screwing everything on campus and off it. Later, converted through reading George Jackson's *Blood in My Eye,* she was one of the white girls who fucked the spades in Vacaville's all-black jail as part of Colston Westbrook's unusual rehabilitation program. She also joined Unisight—which meant she might well have been recruited into the Symbionese Liberation Army and maybe died in the siege in Los Angeles. Before this could happen she got herself busted in connection with a dope burn. She beat that rap by splitting and going underground, and that had been her first step on the journey that had led her here, to Ben Mocatta's apartment south of Houston Street.

She called out now, "Hey, Malachi. *The Woman's Voice*—how about that for the title of the magazine?"

He ignored that. He didn't intend to let this bitch spoil his triumph in the successful planning and execution of the Saint Patrick's Day operation. His only regret was that Bud Rosen's bombs hadn't caused more casualties. Fucking harps! They deserved extinction on a scale that would make Hitler's job on the Jews look like amateur night.

Malachi knew his sudden reappearance—followed by his sudden disappearance—would make his parents suspicious. They couldn't connect him directly with the bombing, and of course they would never snitch on him, but they would wonder, agonize endlessly. Malachi rather wished he could tell them. Gloat, exult in the broken bodies, all the young flesh mangled by Rosen's Composition B. Ask his mother if she wanted him to pay for a month's mind for the dead at Saint Francis of Assisi on West Thirty-first Street, her favorite church.

But meanwhile he was stuck here with this one, this Brenda Wilson. Stupid to let her irk him. She was invincibly ignorant, in the Church's sense of the word. She enjoyed exposing her body, but she didn't realize how soon that body would put on corruption; how soon that flesh would be yielded up to the worms.

Two, three days more, though, and it would be over. Once Angus McStay was dead, he and Brenda would return to Ireland, joining Lang at his headquarters, Kilbrangan House in County Wicklow.

The thought cheered Malachi. He had done a good job. Lang had ordered; he had delivered. There was no one else Lang could have sent to New York. Mark Durnan was a Southern cracker who probably confused Saint Patrick's Day with Macy's Thanksgiving Parade. All the same, Malachi didn't want to be away too long. The German bitch, Leni Reffenstab—she was a new factor to be reckoned with. Malachi wanted to be back at Lang's side.

🍀 🍀 🍀

"New York can't be as terrible as people in Europe make out," Frankie McNagan said. "Else who'd live here?"

"Dirty, polluted, insolvent—that's New York," Tom Dillon said. "And yet millions of us do go on living here. And love it," he added.

"Including you?"

"Including me."

"Despite all that?"

"Call me Canute," Tom said. "Despite the rising tides of crime and decay, I'm too old to change my allegiance now."

"I could tell," she said. "The way you look around you. This is your town."

Tom smiled; nodded. "You could be right."

She was. This was his town. Squiring this dark, secret-seeming girl for the hour since they'd left Luchow's, he had displayed the *malgré lui* patriotism of the true New Yorker every block of the way. Even though everyone kept proclaiming New York a sick giant wounded unto death by his own folly and self-indulgence, Tom could never deny the irresistible vibes this town gave out. No matter who was on the take at City Hall or how high the trash overflowed the unemptied cans, this was still New York. Magnificent. Frightening. Unique. To quote his Uncle Seamus, himself quoting the legendary O. Henry: Baghdad-on-the-Subway.

"Anyway," Tom added, "my town or not, it's a pleasure showing it to you. You notice things."

"I was an only child. Only children notice things." Then she added, "What a pleasant place this is."

They were walking in Carl Schurz Park. Appropriately enough, since it was named for a German New Yorker, and Tom and Frankie had not long ago been eating Drei Mignons à la Berliner at Luchow's, absorbing that schmaltzy atmosphere of a *gemütliche* Munich beer hall. The German vibes had to be emanating from Old Seamus, still in bed in Doctors Hospital. Up to 1956 and the razing of the Third Avenue El, he had lived in a brownstone in Yorkville and it had been Seamus who first brought Tom and Wendell to Carl Schurz Park when they were small boys. Seamus always said he was soothed by the trees and flowers and the sight of children playing on the huge rocks, roaring alone on scooters and bicycles, digging in the sand.

Suddenly there was a silence between them, which neither Tom nor Frankie seemed impelled to break. Tom thought again how strange this girl was. Strange, not meaning odd or eccentric, but in the sense of falling into no category known to him, of eluding all the female stereotypes he already knew too well.

Still in silence, they walked across a wide expanse of grass. Children swirled around them, whooping and singing. Suddenly she stopped; looked around her. Tom wondered what she was looking at. Was she still dazed by the poetry of the Manhattan skyline? Those distant towers looming upward through the polluted air, kissed by a cold sun? He had the impression she was looking at something here in the park.

"Please don't be offended," he said, "but you don't strike me as very like the Irish girls I've met."

She laughed at that, opening her mouth wide to show very small and very regular teeth. "Tell me: what is an Irish girl like?" she asked. She frowned. "You mean the way I speak, don't you? I was brought up in London. My mother took me there when I was eighteen months old. If I'd been raised in Dublin I'd speak like my father does—like this, ya know?" She mimicked a cod-Dublin accent. "My mother tried very hard to make me English, and all through my childhood I suppose she was succeeding . . ." She grimaced. "Equally well, I suppose there had to be a reaction. It came when I met the man I married."

"I didn't know you were married." Ridiculously, Tom felt a slight sense of shock.

"Yes," she said. "I am married." She sounded numb, expressionless, and there was a silence between them again. Finally she said, "Reacting against my mother's indoctrination, I went to the other extreme. But in a way, I suppose, I'll always see Ireland from the outside."

"What do you think of the President's Initiative?"

She smiled and said in a dead, bright tone, "It's had a good press. It seems to have pleased everyone. Well—nearly everyone." A chill edged her voice. "Everybody your president thinks is worth pleasing."

"That's a little unfair, surely?"

"Is it? Would it be cynical to say that it's important for an American president to be seen to be doing *something*—never mind exactly what! The illusion
of presidential activity." She paused. "Anyway Ireland is hardly a big issue here
in the States, is it? Even to Irish-Americans, who think of it as Just a Little Bit
of Heaven Dropped Down to Earth One Day."

Tom laughed again. This girl really slapped it to you. "We're not all of us
that stupid, you know."

"I'm sorry. I wasn't suggesting you were." Now she struck sharp and cold as
a diamond. "It's just that the Initiative freezes all the ancient injustices, per-
petuates the status quo." She paused. "When all the talking is done at the Isle
of Man Conference, and the president has gone back to the White House,
everything will be pretty much as before. The British Army may be about to
leave—someday—but the same old gang will be in power. North and South.
They always are, in Ireland."

Tom smiled. "You sound exactly like my uncle."

She smiled too. "That figures."

It did. After all she was here on some cloak-and-dagger business arising out
of his uncle's endless plotting for the Irish cause. But this was the first time
Tom had met one of Seamus' fellow conspirators, and she wasn't what he
would have expected. But what *did* he expect? A grubby-looking Amazon in a
flak jacket, toting a machine gun? A Baader-Meinhof type?

Whatever he'd expected, he was intrigued with what he'd got. He hadn't
met a woman like this in a long time. And if it had hardly been necessary
yesterday to invite her to lunch at a second's acquaintance, it certainly hadn't
been necessary to go walking with her in Carl Schurz Park today. They could
have gone to visit with his uncle immediately after leaving Luchow's. The fact
was, Tom had put off going to the hospital for as long as possible. He wanted
to see more of this girl.

They had reached a point where the two small hills over which Carl Schurz
Park extends flatten out into the esplanade which forms the roof of East River
Drive. They moved forward till they stood together in the John Finlay Walk,
leaning against the black bars of the railing, staring at the river traffic—tugs,
freighters, garbage scows—sweeping past in a delicate mist which made them
appear closer than they really were. To the right loomed the Queensborough
Bridge; far to the left gleamed the arches of the Triborough Bridge.

"Like the view?" Tom asked.

She smiled and said, "The Seine and the Thames run yellow too."

"Kind of you to say so. It's amazing anything can move in the East River at
all, it's so polluted."

After a moment she turned, looked back, then faced Tom again. "They're still there," she said.

"What?"

She gestured. "There."

"What do you mean?"

"Those two men over there."

His gaze followed hers. Two men were standing some yards away from them. One was squat, dark; the other taller and perhaps a little older.

"You wondered what I was looking at just now," she said. "Sooner or later one always has to stop and stare at them."

" 'Them'?"

"That way you can always tell."

"What are you talking about?" Tom said.

"Spooks," she said. "FBI, police, Special Branch, whatever. Turn and look straight at them. Stare them out, as children would say. Any normal person would be embarrassed, but they always stare back. It's a kind of test." She grinned. "Don't look so surprised! You must know the FBI have had your uncle under surveillance for years. And you're the only member of the family he still sees. Well . . ." She shrugged. "They're probably onto you as a matter of routine."

"You're a . . . professional at this?" Tom asked.

"I suppose so. Never thought about that aspect."

Tom was silent. He remembered when he came home after his second tour in Nam his uncle had complained that his mail was being tampered with and that the FBI had a wiretap on his phone. Tom hadn't exactly disbelieved him, but he had wondered if his uncle wasn't dramatizing a little. Did anyone bother that much about IRA sympathizers in the States? The Feds would hardly accord them the bigshot treatment extended to Mafia dons.

"I noticed them soon after we left Luchow's," Frankie said. "I knew what they were—whenever I saw one, I saw the other, you know? The fat one kept a good way behind us; the tall one kept almost level, on the other side of the street." She paused. "That's called parallel pursuit. If one of them loses contact, the other keeps the tail. The crunch would have come if we had separated, but if they're any good they'd have been prepared for that."

Tom saw that the two men were talking together now: pretending to be two strangers chatting at random for a moment. Then they stopped talking. The fat one stared rather offensively at passersby; the tall one looked at a newspaper.

"They're not very good actors," Tom said.

Frankie smiled. "Cliché: They're just doing their job." Now she looked serious. "Isn't it about time we went to the hospital?"

"Don't you want to see the mayor's house?" Tom asked. "It's here in this park."

"The mayor can wait. But I can't wait to see your uncle."

🍀 🍀 🍀

"Jesus, Ben," Harry Lombard said. "I wish you had some control over your appetites."

Greener ignored him. "Holy shit! Look at that broad—yeah, the one with the little kid. They're walking away now . . ." He shook his head in wonder. "My God—*broad* is right! D'ya ever see such dimensions? Tell you what, Harry—jeans was a great invention. Tights were shit; tights were a retrograde step for the human race, right? But jeans! I never appreciated the marvelous diversity of the female ass till they started filling their jeans with it—I swear to God!"

"Ben!" Lombard protested. "You're gonna kill yourself. Think what this does to your blood pressure."

For the last few minutes their surveillance of Tom Dillon and the girl known as Mary Ogham had been halted while the couple lingered on the John Finlay Walk. Standing at Lombard's side—a slackening of procedure: agents were supposed to remain independent unless there was some reason for them to join forces—Greener had indulged in a commentary on the passing array of asses. With the discrimination of a connoisseur, he had greeted young apple-round asses snaking by in ski pants; celebrated more mature square-shaped asses bouncing along in tight jeans; even praised the still-voluptuous asses of older women proceeding circumspectly in matronly skirts. "The pantyline, Harry," Greener said. "Does it add or detract? That's a point you got to consider, Harry—"

"For Christ's sake, Ben!" Lombard cut in. He was frustrated enough with this surveillance without having to endure this shit. Old Ben sounded like he had problems which might be beyond the power of Mrs. Greener to resolve.

Lombard was frustrated because he wasn't getting anywhere, except physically, tagging around New York on the heels of this couple who seemed to be acting out the Happiness Sequence of a 1930s movie—meeting at a restaurant, wandering through Midtown, and now walking in the park. Where would they go next, for God's sake—Coney Island? So far they hadn't done one single suspicious thing except maybe—just maybe—the girl had shown some awareness of being followed. That would be an indication, but Lombard couldn't be sure.

He was frustrated that they could put nothing on the girl. He had felt suspicious when she accosted Tom Dillon in St. Patrick's Cathedral yesterday, and yet there was nothing to indicate that this was not a spontaneous gesture of grief. The girl had been tailed back to where she was staying, a bar on 207th Street in Inwood. Her name was Mary Ogham, an Irish national with an address in Westport, County Mayo; she was visiting with cousins, a family called O'Keeffe who ran the bar. He'd run a check on her with both Belfast and Dublin with no result. The Bureau in New York had nothing on the O'Keeffes either.

He felt less interested, now, in Tom Dillon, although he still agreed with Benstead that Loyalist Action was the kind of organization they claimed to be and that Seamus Dillon had been one of their designated targets. That was why he must be watched carefully—not least because another attempt might be made on his life, which could lead the Bureau to the perpetrators of the bombing.

It was easy to keep tags on Dillon while he remained in the hospital. Since Saint Patrick's Day he had been visited by a number of members of Justice for Ulster (a single visit in each case), a representative of the giant Rossman pharmaceutical firm which had taken over his Penrith outfit (a single courtesy call), Liam Costelloe of the AFL-CIO (one visit), Martin Macowen of Penrith Pharmaceuticals (Ireland), a subsidiary of the main Penrith corporation situated near Kenmare in County Kerry (one visit). (Seamus had retained control of this subsidiary, and Macowen, the general manager, came to the States several times a year.) Tom Dillon (three visits).

Analyzing these, Lombard decided that all of the members of Justice for Ulster were small-fry, visiting their leader out of *pietà* and a sense of relief at having survived themselves. Costelloe's visit was hardly significant either. True, he had once been a member of an IRA support group in the States, but he had been inactive a long time; in fact he was now a rather lukewarm supporter of the President's Initiative. Macowen might or might not be involved in Dillon's more doubtful activities; he lived and worked in Ireland and the Bureau hadn't had enough cooperation from the Irish Special Branch to tell.

That left Tom Dillon. He was practically Old Dillon's last surviving relative: what more natural than he should often visit with his uncle? And yet—as Lombard told Greener—he had this pricking in his thumbs. Tom Dillon had money; he hadn't worked at anything except screwing dames since he left the Marines; he was rootless, restless—just the type, Lombard reasoned, to get into Old Dillon's dangerous political scene.

Dillon and Ogham were still standing on the John Finlay Walk, silhouetted against the thin black line of the railing, bathed in a delicate mist from the river. Lombard noticed that Dillon had slipped his arm around Ogham's waist, although he soon took it away again. If they weren't just a boy and girl together discovering Manhattan, they were putting on a damn good performance.

What would they do next? Even if they went to see Old Dillon in Doctors Hospital, it still wouldn't prove anything. Ogham could claim to be a relative of Seamus Dillon's bringing him greetings from the old folks at home. Who was to say she wasn't?

Lombard wondered how Seamus Dillon was. He knew the man had to go into the hospital regularly for some kind of blood disease, but he didn't really know the score. Strange thing: he rather liked the old boy; hoped he wasn't about to give up the ghost. Old Dillon had made assholes of them all—everyone from Benstead downward. Of course, making an asshole out of Benstead was work of superfluity, but you couldn't help liking anyone who did.

That had been the night of the Big Boffola. A night to remember too: it had seen the Bureau's biggest-ever defeat in its struggle to halt the flow of arms from America to Ireland. With hindsight it was easy to see that they had fallen into a trap set by someone with a perfect appreciation of the Bill Benstead-J. Edgar Hoover mentality: a mentality vulnerable to melodrama, reveling in swift swoops and elaborate trackings-down. Once the scent of the chase was in his nostrils, Benstead's genuine expertise was worthless, his powers of analysis in abeyance.

Benstead and the bigger brass above him maintained that it was easier to penetrate the Irish-American IRA support-groups than the left-wing radical groups. That might be so. No doubt Cointelpro [Counterintelligence Program], Hoover's secret and often illegal war against political groups ranging from the Ku Klux Klan to the Fair Play for Cuba Committee had notched up some victories against the Irish-American fund-raising organizations. Why not? The people who gave their dollars to the Irish cause were mostly very respectable citizens. A lot easier to infiltrate than an outfit like the Black Panthers.

"This," Benstead had said, in his never-to-be-forgotten phrase, "is the Big Boffola. Probably the biggest consignment of illegal arms ever to leave the Port of New York. And we're gonna be there to intercept them, gentlemen. Yeah—this is the big one!"

Benstead had leaned back in his chair, rubbing his hands together in theatrical glee. He hadn't responded too well when Lombard pressed him as to the source of this tipoff. The intelligence in question (he implied) was so valuable that the name of he who snitched it must remain forever unspoken. The snitch had it that a large mixed consignment of arms was to be loaded onto scows moored between Hudson River piers 53 and 54. Later these arms were to be moved aboard an oceangoing freighter, which in turn would transfer them to an Irish trawler at an agreed meet on the high seas. Then the arms would be brought ashore at any one of a hundred lonely places on the rugged coastline of the Irish Republic. Not only would the consignment include a large number of M16 rifles (the type used by the U.S. Army in Vietnam, not the familiar sporting version mostly shipped to tbe Provisional IRA in Ireland), but also a huge quantity of small-arms ammunition, bandolier-packed. There would be Stirling machine guns, bazookas, and the latest Soviet-made RPG7 rocket launchers.

In Lombard's mind revolved a lot of questions he wouldn't ask. Most important: who was Benstead's snitch and who said he was to be believed anyway? Why load the arms directly onto scows on an open pier when many thousands of tons of arms had already been sent to Ireland in sealed freight containers with phony customs documents?

Old Dillon himself was said to be personally superintending the run. Again, Lombard didn't say it, but that contradicted Benstead's often-reiterated view that Seamus Dillon was one of the godfathers behind the scenes, manipulating the idealistic young and letting them take all the risks.

This accommodating snitch had not only given Benstead the date and location of the run, he had also told him its approximate time: around 10 P.M. A formidable reception committee would be waiting in the neighborhood of pier 53. Agents on foot, in cars: everyone linked by radio to Benstead in his command car. The whole schmear. Everything, as Ben Greener said, except bloodhounds.

Lombard and Greener were assigned to Seamus Dillon himself. As Benstead told them with an unexpected flash of humor, "He's gotten so used to seeing you two bums, he'd be lonesome without you."

The immediate question was whether Dillon would travel from his apartment to the West Side by limo or whether he would try to faze them by sneaking out and grabbing a cab (he'd hardly go by subway). But at 9:30 sharp, Hans Gruhl swung the big black Mercedes out of the carport and parked outside the apartment building. Then he stood rigidly at attention as he held the car door open for Seamus, infusing even this simple action with Prussian hauteur and authority. Old Dillon might have been going to the weekly meeting of Justice for Ulster at the committee rooms on Lower Broadway.

Crossing Manhattan in a southwest direction, Gruhl drove steadily but surprisingly fast (he was always lucky with the lights, Lombard had noticed). Then, unexpectedly, he stopped at the end of Fourteenth Street. Dillon got out, stood for a moment on the sidewalk, then raised his hand in dismissal.

Gruhl drove off. After a few seconds' frenzied discussion Lombard and Green-er both got out of the blue Oldsmobile in which they had been following, told their driver to go back to headquarters, and started after Dillon on foot.

Now he was entering the truck district underneath the West Side Highway, where the light was poor and big trucks were lined up in the narrow passages, casting huge shadows. Greener murmured, "You'd think he'd be scared to come down here alone."

Lombard said, "Do you think he doesn't know we're right behind him?"

The black shadows around them seemed to thrust at them menacingly. Drunks and derelicts would be sleeping here beneath the overhanging loading platforms of the warehouses, and often bodies would be discovered, victims of wino brawls or of neighborhood predators, killing for kicks.

Greener switched on his walkie-talkie, to be immediately overwhelmed by a burst of static. He switched it off again.

Lombard realized that the rest of the posse—as he derisively thought of it—weren't far away.

"Know what?" Lombard mused. "None of this is kosher."

"What?"

"It's too easy," Lombard said. "Everything is happening just like Benstead said." He shook his head. "Right in sequence. No way can this be genu-ine."

"Benstead—" Greener said. "What a prick!"

Neither spoke for some minutes. Ahead of them moved the erect, toylike figure of Seamus Dillon. Greener turned on his radio again; the static crackled away.

Now they were right on the waterfront where the piers stick out into the Hudson like ancient, malformed teeth. Dillon was walking along the huge beam which ran alongside a great shed as far as the dock. The dim lights shone on the dark water choked with scum and oil. Six or seven scows were moored here: they lay deep in the water like black logs floating, showing no sign of life.

Dillon had reached the steps at the end of the pier. He stood motionless, staring toward the Jersey shore.

"He's waiting for a signal," Greener said.

"For Christ's sake!" Lombard said.

They could hear someone coughing a few yards away. Must be Bullard or Le Mesurier; they had to be somewhere nearby. They went on waiting.

At first the sense of impending action made the time pass quickly. But then the minutes began to build up. Into a quarter. A half. It was 10:30 P.M. Watching Dillon, they began to feel hypnotized. The old man stood like a statue, the dim light catching his high cheekbones and straight nose.

Suddenly Lombard said, "C'mon, Ben—let's get to grips."

"What?"

"Let's you and me walk right up and shake Seamus Dillon by the hand."

"Benstead—"

"Fuck Benstead—"

They moved toward Dillon. They could see his lips moving. As they advanced toward him Lombard felt a sudden chill at the thought of Greener and himself marooned on this pier on the rim of Manhattan with a mad old man. Ridiculous, of course. What could he do to them? Anyway Lombard had a .38 under his armpit, and the dockside was crawling with his fellow agents.

To their amazement Dillon was singing.

And what color will they wear?
Says the Sean Bhean Bhoct:
What color will they wear?
Says the Sean Bhean Bhoct;
What color should be seen
Where our fathers' homes have been
But our own immortal green
Says the Sean Bhean Bhoct.

His voice was full of mocking glee. Lombard and Greener stared, bewildered.

And will Ireland then be free?
Says the Sean Bhean Bhoct.
From the center to the sea:
Then Hurrah for Liberty!
Says the Sean Bhean Bhoct.

No doubt Dillon had seen them. He turned toward them, openly jeering:

And all them big police
Monumentally obese,

Must I go on feeding these?
Says the Sean Bhean Bhoct.

He stopped suddenly; stared hard at them. Then he drew himself up, still an impressive block of a man, and snarled, "Crithim go bonn le Fonn do dhaortha!"

They stood goggling at him. He spat into their startled faces the single word "Scrios!" and then he was gone past them, striding away into the darkness.

And that was it. Dillon's bizarre antics would stay with Lombard forever as the final comment on the Big Boffola. This snitch of snitches had been a load of bullshit. Benstead had been the victim of a calculated humiliation, designed to demonstrate the power of the Irish republican movement in the States and the impotence of the FBI in the face of that power. Of course nothing had been shipped that night. The scows moored at pier 53 were empty. Old Dillon had taken a sadistic pleasure in setting himself up as a stalking-horse. Arms would continue to flow to Ireland through the proven, secret channels. And bit by bit, in the months that followed, Lombard and his colleagues had gotten the picture of a great reserve of arms being created in Ireland by Seamus Dillon and his associates. This was spoken of as "the foundation" or "the doomsday foundation" because it was created against a so-called doomsday situation in Ireland, North or South.

The night of the Big Boffola was several years in the past, but recalling it Lombard warmed toward Old Dillon. This carefully planned nonevent had been a real Irish bull: the essence of Celtic malice on Dillon's part.

Lombard grinned.

"Hey, Ben."

"Yeah?"

"The Big Boffola. Remember it?"

"Your fucking-A I remember it! So does Benstead, I bet."

He had stopped appraising the girls and was staring across toward Tom Dillon and Mary Ogham. "Hey—I think those two are about to make a move." He nodded. "They are. Here they come now. The ritual dances are over. They're gonna go and fuck at last."

"In about two minutes' time, all right?"

Angus McStay put the telephone down. Amusing how even at fifty-three the sound of a (presumably) attractive girl's voice set the adrenaline moving a little faster. *The Woman's Voice?* He'd never heard of it, but then why would he hear of it? There must be dozens of feminist magazines in New York: this was the very heartland of feminism.

"Tim!" McStay called.

Tim Malone stuck his head around the door. "Yes?"

"That girl. The journalist. She'll be up here in a minute."

Tim's heavy brows came together in a frown. He was the cliché policeman of legend. Muscular, authoritative, orotund of speech. Even his blue business suit sat like a uniform on his powerful shoulders.

Now he said. "That'll be difficult, so."

"Why?"

"The lady's sex will make a thorough check of her person rather a delicate matter."

"For God's sake, Tim. No need for that."

"In Belfast—"

"Tim—this is New York, not Belfast."

"Do you mind that one from Anderstown who had a wee bottle of acid hidden in her bra?" Tim's eyebrows were eloquent. "So what would you expect in New York? Fear city—that's what they call this place."

"The violence here—well, it's different."

"Is that so?" Tim asked. "Anyway I don't propose to let this lassie in to you without some wee bit of a search."

"Really, Tim!" McStay shrugged. "Look in her handbag or something."

"I will that," Tim said. "Of course if she wears a tight shirt and Levi's like most of the lassies, she won't be able to hide a nailfile, let alone a gun." He paused. "The whorish self-exposure of women!"

McStay laughed, but Tim's silence implied disapproval as he stumped into the other room.

He heard the buzzer go and then the burr of Tim's voice. Then a female voice. It had to be Ms. Nicholls, the girl who was going to interview him.

"Tim," he called. "I'll see Ms. Nicholls straightaway."

"Mr. McStay," she asked, "how has violence affected women in the Catholic ghettos of Northern Ireland?"

"Obviously," McStay said, "in every way. Socially, financially, sexually—it's affected them."

"Uh-huh . . ." She nodded. "Do you think it has diminished their sense of identity as women? This represents a retrogression to a fairly primitive situation—kind of a frontier-type situation where the man carries arms and goes out to protect the family. Could this not instill a feeling of inadequacy in a woman? Make her feel she's less able to play an active role than a man? Especially in some areas of Belfast and Derry, where most of the men are committed freedom fighters."

McStay asked carefully, "When you say 'freedom fighters,' do you mean the IRA?" He shook his head. "In no area of Belfast or Derry do members of the IRA form a majority. But your question. A woman in Northern Ireland may feel trapped. May despair. But she won't feel inadequate." He frowned. "Are you thinking of the small minority of women who join the IRA themselves?" His frown deepened. "I believe those women are being used—just as the IRA has even used children in the past."

He was beginning to find this girl's string of cliché-questions depressing. They were all delivered in the same mechanical tone: he had the odd feeling that she had learned them by heart.

The bright impression he'd gotten from her voice over the telephone had been erased by her physical presence. She was a plump, dolly-faced blonde with something zombielike about her. She stonewalled his polite questions about herself. Yes, she'd gotten into journalism straight after college. Which college? University of California at Berkeley.

She carried a holdall, and at the beginning of the interview she had unzipped it and taken out a small tape recorder which she placed on the table in front of her. She'd smiled—the one and only time—and said. "Your bodyguard was interested in my tape recorder, I guess. Maybe thought it was a bomb." But she had made no attempt to record her questions or McStay's replies. Nor had she written anything down, although she fiddled all the time with a gold-plated ballpoint.

It was nearly noon. Put the skids under this one, McStay thought. He said. "You must find all this pretty remote from your experience, Ms. Nicholls?"

"Really?"

"Yes. Considering how many Americans claim Irish descent, it's remarkable how little the history of Ireland is understood over here."

At that moment the telephone rang. McStay lifted the receiver. "Hullo."

Brenda Wilson stood up and moved over till she was standing right behind him. McStay didn't notice. "Hullo," he said again.

Brenda had the gold-plated ballpoint in her hand. As he said "Hullo" the second time, she pressed a button and the pen's retractable mechanism brought forward the end of a hair-thin hypodermic needle. "*Hullo*," McStay said yet again, irked by the silence at the other end of the line. Brenda had the illusion of slow-motion, of time stopping, as she brought the end of the needle up to a point just below McStay's left ear. She was so close to him that she could see an inflamed hair-follicle on his neck above the collar of his blue-and-white-striped shirt. She could hear him breathing.

She drove the needle in.

Harder than she need have, probably. Both Lang and Malachi had stressed that the lightest jab did it. Not that it mattered. The effect was instantaneous. The single injection carried in the needle point paralyzed the heart in a couple of seconds.

McStay slumped forward over the table. Quickly—for it was possible Big Mick Pig out there was listening for their voices and might notice a silence—she clicked the tape recorder on to playback. Immediately McStay's voice was heard, conducting a conversation on the telephone with someone whose voice had been edited out. (His office line had been taped and this recording made some weeks ago.) If Mick Pig was listening he would hear McStay apparently talking on the telephone.

It was 11:58. Malachi had been a little late making the call to McStay. Now she had to get her ass out of here. Some time should elapse before anyone realized that McStay had not died naturally. This method, an injection of shellfish toxin causing instant death, had been perfected by the CIA. Lang's group had used it once before, when Mark Durnan had killed the West German industrialist Gunter Wittels, jostling against him in the crowded lobby of the Festspielhaus in Salzburg. Everyone had thought it a heart attack until the autopsy had been carried out. Wittels had been supplying the Israelis with a variant of the Leopard tank: that was why a contract had been laid on him by the Baendlistrasse group of Zurich. In this present case the propaganda value of McStay's death to Loyalist Action lay in the stealthy, mysterious way it had been carried out—just as the Saint Patrick's Day killings had made their point through open shock and outrage.

Brenda was wiping her prints off everything. She glanced around once more, then walked into the other room, closing the door behind her with fussy, mustn't disturb deliberation.

"I'm through," she said. Mick Pig stared back at her, stolid, unsmiling. "He's taking a call," she said. "Long distance." She forced herself to smile. "But it's okay. I got all I wanted."

☘ ☘ ☘

Seamus Dillon lay in bed and watched the people on the TV screen arguing, laughing, threatening each other—all in perfect silence. He had asked his last

visitor, Martin Macowen, to turn off the sound while they talked, and when
Macowen left, Seamus said to leave it off. He couldn't help thinking it an
improvement. He hadn't caught a word of whatever was on now. The characters wore clothes roughly appropriate to a remake of *The Grapes of Wrath*, and
on one level of his mind Seamus had fun inventing a story and dialogue for
them.

On one level. The level he'd been functioning on when he was talking to
Macowen about the marketing of Penrith Pharmaceuticals (Ireland) products
in the States. Macowen was okay, good at his job. But he could never relax
with Seamus, and Seamus knew why. Not because they were in a boss-
employee situation, but because Macowen was fearful that Seamus was about
to use Penrith Ireland in some IRA plot. In fact the company had been very
useful when Seamus was building up the foundation, but that was before
Macowen got the job of general manager.

That was at one level. At a deeper level, Seamus kept thinking about Hogg
and the impending grand jury hearing. No good hoping that Hogg wouldn't
name names, wouldn't exploit to the full the value to the media of any "revelations" he might make. He was sure to mention both Wendell and Seamus—
what was it Costelloe had said? A prima donna?—and while Wendell was
beyond subpoenas forever, Seamus knew he would be called on to testify (or
forced to refuse to testify: more damaging still).

That was bad enough—but the question of Duane's succession as trustee of
the foundation really obsessed Seamus. That *had* to be solved. What could he
do? Go to Ireland and see Duane? Could he keep going long enough to do
that? Dr. Hernandez had actually said he could get up for a while today, but he
felt so tense that he'd crawled back to bed after a half hour. What guarantee
had he that if he went to Ireland he wouldn't collapse and die or at least be
hospitalized before he could see Duane?

And now of course the whole situation had probably been changed by what
Tom had told him this morning: how Tom had been approached by a girl who
claimed to be Peadar Mahoney's daughter. She had to see him, she said, and
Tom had quoted her words: "It concerns the foundation." Strange she had
given the name "Mary Ogham."

Seamus had never heard of a Mary Ogham. Was it a false name, a cover
name for Frankie McNagan, whom Seamus knew of course as Peadar's daughter? (He hadn't seen her, though, since he had held her in his arms when she
was three weeks old.) He knew her mother had taken her off to England, from
where she had returned a few years ago to marry Francis McNagan and
become the female half of the Two Frankies. He knew, too, that both Frankies
had joined Eireann Amhain and had worked with Duane. He had heard of

Francis McNagan's trial and imprisonment; presumably Frankie, the wife, Peadar's daughter, was still involved with Eireann Amhain.

But was it she? Was it Frankie McNagan, and if it was, what was she doing in New York?

This time Malachi called Associated Press from a pay telephone at Penn Station. When he asked for a news editor he half-expected to get the same arrogant-sounding bitch as before, but a man answered.

Malachi read:

"This is a statement from Loyalist Action. We repeat that name: Loyalist Action. We hereby claim responsibility for the execution yesterday of Angus William McStay, sitting member at the Westminster Parliament for the constituency of Belfast Southwest, at the Gotham Hotel. We note that reports in the media have not specified the cause of his death, and take this opportunity to point out that the method of execution used was an injection of shellfish toxin, humane and painless to the victim. Again—as in the bombing of the Fenian parade on Fifth Avenue—revenge is not our motive. The late Angus McStay was a traitor to his race, his religion, and his Ulster heritage. He had played a large part in preparing and arranging the so-called Initiative by the American president which represents a monstrous and unwarranted interference in the affairs of Ulster men and Ulster women. Let everyone concerned in this American aggrandizement take warning from the death of this corrupt politician. So will we serve all our enemies! Take heed that we, the loyal people of Ulster, will never yield up our allegiance—God save the queen!"

Kilbrangan House, near Kippure Mountain in County Wicklow, was long on history (in 1603 John Fitzpatrick, governor of Waterford, had been hanged before the main gate, and in 1789 Mary Fitzpatrick, a beautiful heiress, had gone mad for love and been kept a prisoner for forty years in the west wing), but was physically ugly: a barracklike building whose facade offered a bleak checkerboard of blocked-up and broken windows. Behind the house stood the old stables, making up one side of a half-square of decaying outbuildings, always overshadowed by the great bulk of the house itself.

As Mark Durnan took off the padlock and threw open the door of one of these stables, he heard a faint moaning sound. The smell of excreta made him want to throw up.

"Martin?" Durnan said.

Martin Leach was crouching in a corner of the stable, cowering away from the light. His face was fuzzy with beard: an impasto of dirt and sweat.

"Martin, baby—anything you want?" Durnan persisted.

He knew what Leach was suffering; he'd been through all this himself. Leach was past the early withdrawal symptoms now: the nose running and the eyes smarting. He was through with the fever too, the fever that had soaked him with sweat, convulsing him with spasms of hot-cold flashes. Now he was at the most acute state of withdrawal, his flesh sensitized as if electrically charged, his body jolting in agony at the stings of thousands of invisible insects.

Leach didn't seem aware that Durnan was there, but all the same Durnan was glad he had come down to him. In his present tortured, near-animal state Leach might get some instinctive comfort from his presence, although there was nothing anyone could do for him at the moment.

"Another day or two and he'll be down on his knees begging for a Hershey's bar."

Durnan turned. Lang stood there, looking cool and relaxed in silk shirt, London-tailored slacks, and Gucci loafers. He carried a duffelbag.

"That's right," Durnan said, and it was, of course. A lust for sweets begins the chucks—the tremendous appetite experienced by addicts during the last stage of withdrawal.

"Which he won't get," Lang added. "Bread and water for this dude then."

Durnan nodded; didn't answer. He'd suffered this too. Dry bread and water during the chucks was another trick of Lang's undertaken in the name of Sokatsu to make the process of withdrawal still more agonizing. "He's doing all right," Durnan said. "He's making it."

"He'd better make it," Lang said coldly. "I give him two days more."

"He'll be okay."

Lang smiled. "Looks like we'll have to hire us a bugler," He nodded toward the overweening bulk of the house. "Most of them are still asleep in there."

Durnan said, "The Irish air, right?"

Lang didn't answer. After a moment he said, "You're not Scottish, are you, Mark?"

"My family came to Virginia from Essex. About two hundred years ago."

"I was thinking," Lang said. "This Pan-Celtic Congress at Quimper. These nuts would love to think you were one of them. I don't think we should present you as Irish—but you could be Scots." Lang laughed boyishly. "Dance them a sword dance, cook them a haggis—"

He broke off abruptly. Leach had collapsed in the corner, moaning loudly.

"C'mon!" Lang said. "Let's get him out of here."

Slowly, laboriously—he was a dead weight—they dragged Leach out. To Durnan there was an air of medieval immolation about this tall young American, his thick black hair gummed to his scalp with sweat, his body caked with vomit, cowering in agony before a shower of unseen arrows.

He shrieked as he met the full glare of the sunlight. Then he fell forward onto his knees.

Lang grasped Leach by both wrists. With a great effort, he pulled him upward, then threw his inert body against the wall. He began to hit Leach. "Come–on–Martin–I–got–something–for–you." Each word was punctuated with a blow across the face with his clenched fist.

After a few moments Lang stopped. He picked up the duffelbag.

Leach's head, which had lolled from side to side as Lang hit him, seemed to straighten. His almost-closed eyes began to focus. He was looking at what Lang was taking out of the duffelbag. The eyedropper with the little rubber squeeze grape on it. A strip of nylon to tie off with. The spoon. And of course the needle. Everything but the one essential thing—the shit, the smack, the scag: the heroin itself.

Durnan knew it all. Once, Lang had done this to him, when he'd slipped, got addicted again, soon after he'd joined Lang's group. He had been at this same stage of withdrawal when Lang convinced him that he was about to give Durnan the fix he needed to save him, bring him unimaginable joy and release. He would never forget how Lang had carried through that agonizing pantomime. Cooking up plain water in the spoon and waiting for it to bubble; pinching Durnan's arm in search of a vein, tying him off, and then—the final mockery—letting him see the spurt of blood back into the dropper, sure sign of the hit that never was.

Leach was still shaking, drooling, but he was watching Durnan with a fevered intentness. Wait till he copped onto this as just another joke from Lang's dirty tricks department.

Weeks after Durnan had kicked the monkey again—Lang was making much of him, giving him a week at the Athens Hilton—Durnan had questioned the pointless cruelty of the gag. "Know any other way to run a commune, baby?" Lang had demanded. "Like with love, so with pain. One who kisses, one who gets kissed."

And of course, Durnan thought, when Lang had walked away, leaving him with the wretched Leach, trembling, writhing, still lacking his fix, he does this to all of us, one way or another.

Lang might call it Sokatsu, but it was really a kind of personal ascendancy based on the other person's need. Lang evoked—even demanded—a mixture of fear and dependency that had some element of gratitude in it too. Durnan didn't know how Martin Leach had first met Lang or the nature of Leach's dependence on him. Leach had been a chopper pilot in Nam (and of course sooner or later Lang would require him to fly a chopper in Ireland: that was why he was here). He had flown innumerable missions, and although Durnan had never served himself, he could well understand the self-destructive fever that drove Leach back to using shit from time to time. When he had attempted to defend Martin's latest lapse to Lang, Lang had said, "Excuses I don't need. Accuracy, audacity, discipline—those I need!" And he had Leach locked up in a stable, to sweat and shriek it out cold turkey. And yet when Leach would come out of it—clear-eyed and calm if a little shaky—no one would be more loyal to Lang than he was.

Durnan figured it would be the same with all the members of Lang's group. With Bud Rosen, a chemistry major who had belonged to tbe "Red" Mathematics Commune at Columbia in 1968, an expert on explosives and timing devices, whom Lang had rescued from the skid-row area of Detroit. With Mick Congar, an early member of the Black Panthers, who had gone to Algiers with Eldridge Cleaver. Later, Congar had quarreled with Cleaver and had to flee his villa. He had been starving in the Casbah when Lang found him. With Henri Barbier, a native of Constantine, a *pied noir* and OAS hardnose who refused to return to France. Barbier was an expert marksman; once, when de Gaulle was still paying lip service to a French Algeria, he had had the general in his cross-sights. "The big shit himself! But the OAS believed what he said and forbade me pull the trigger."

And so with all the members of Lang's basic cadre. Certainly with Durnan himself. The fact that Lang was dealing with both Loyalist Action and the Wednesday Committee bugged Durnan. Okay—as Lang said, they were bringing about a situation of revolutionary flux—but Durnan still didn't like it. It was an almost Faustian situation for a member of the old Weather underground, but shit, he had to go on. He could never face the prospect of creeping out into the cold light of today's America like some Weatherpeople had done (they must have felt a lot like those Jap soldiers who surrendered after holing up on Pacific atolls for thirty years). Even less could he go back to the blank limbo that was life on the lam. He had tried that already and Lang had rescued him.

Durnan came from a distinguished antebellum family from Richmond, Virginia. Rebelling against the "Southern Gentleman" persona, he had joined SDS. At first this had been part of a general reaction that included experimenting with dope—Seconal and amyl nitrate: no robust drugs to start with. Anything to kill the agony of being young. Ten more years and you'd be a cynical old hardnose of twenty-nine or thirty who didn't give a shit.

When he had joined the Weathermen, he felt he had an identity for the first time in his life: a tough stocky man in a biker's leathers and helmet and chains. Now he had a faith: live like Che! Live intensely when you are young and strong. Risk the waste of your life for an ideal. Kill or be killed. That is how to be a man.

Initiation? Self-discovery? In Chicago, Durnan had found himself trapped in an alley behind an upended Chevy. A cop had come straight at him, swinging a nightstick. Durnan bent forward—rage anesthetizing him against the flailing blows—and threw all his weight behind his helmeted head as he dived forward, smashing into the man's chest. The shock sent the air whistling out of the cop's lungs; he spun round and then crashed against the upturned front fender of the Chevy. Durnan stumbled back, recovered himself, to see the cop already coming at him again. Although the man was bigger and heavier than he was, Durnan started to pound at his face with his fists. He was wearing brass knuckles on his right hand, and with his first blow he could feel the bone crunching; soon the cop's nose was just a blob of gristle, dripping blood and snot. Durnan kept on hitting . . .

Now, years later, Durnan saw that fight with a pig as his induction into an army—an army without flags or uniforms or three-star generals. An army of men and women who had learned to kill in their war against a corrupt society. Just as Timothy Leary had once spoken of "Mutants"—those whose minds were fucked forever by acid—so there were thousands of other mutants: those committed to this struggle, their minds fucked forever by their experience of violent protest.

Well, whether he was in an army or not, he wouldn't have survived if he hadn't met Lang.

By then the Weathermen had long decayed into futility. Durnan had been on the lam for a long time: three times across North America and back again. He had taken job after job, always under false names—working in a hunters' camp in Maine, on a compost project in Rhode Island, as a busboy in a San Francisco hotel. Gradually he had drifted south, ending in New Orleans, where he haunted the twenty-four-hour saloons or hung around the Quarter, jostled by hordes of vagrant boys and girls. It was there, on Ash Wednesday, the day after Mardi Gras, that he met Lang in a crowded saloon on Decatur Street.

Durnan sometimes thought Lang was like one of those medieval kings around whom revolved a circle of satellites, any of whom might gain favor at a particular time. Durnan reckoned he had twice enjoyed that kind of closeness to Lang—when they'd first met and Lang had taken him via Cuba, to the Villa Ben Kalah—and again, briefly, a year ago. That psycho Malachi O'Farrell had enjoyed a turn too, and currently, of course, the favorite was Leni Reffenstab.

Durnan didn't like her—indeed, there was something snaky about her, something goddamn *evil*—but he wanted to fuck her. Not in some kinky group setup, but face-to-face, one-to-one, in the good old-fashioned way.

As he came out onto the gravel-surfaced square before Kilbrangan House, he wondered where she was now. With Lang probably. Durnan felt excluded, but he knew Leni must have her hour, along with all of the others. It would pass.

☘ ☘ ☘

Lang watched the red Ford Granada snake down the driveway, going fast, brake lights lurching on as it turned the corner through the birch wood and disappeared.

"Jesus," Lang said. "An Irishman and he drives like one."

"Rex—I think they must have the highest accident rate in Europe," Leni Reffenstab said.

Lang grinned. "The German rate is higher." She looked surprised and he added, "Like no one ever commits suicide in Ireland. The tourist image, right? The Land of Saints and Scholars. Leprechauns and stuff."

"Do you blame them for that?" Leni asked.

"Anyway," Lang said, "O'Flaherty is a nice guy. He'll write the kind of stuff we want to go with his pictures."

"Not like that bastard on *Der Spiegel*."

Lang grinned. "He was a crime reporter."

Leni was frowning. "Those pictures O'Flaherty took. Suppose someone in Germany sees them? Or"—her frown deepened—"say someone here recognizes them? There are a lot of Germans in Ireland."

"No chance!" Lang said. "Most people—German or Irish or anything else—absorb this publicity crap at a purely superficial level—"

"Rex, maybe they do but—"

"Look—they see this picture of voluptuous, raven-haired Gudrun Hebbel: lovely German actress who is to play a lead role in *Blood Scenario*." Lang shook his head. "No woman's gonna look at that picture for long—unless she's a dyke—you're too attractive. And the male reaction will be, 'Wow! That I would like to have!' " He shrugged. "No one is about to connect raven-haired Gudrun with Leni Reffenstab, the blond terrorist."

Now Leni smiled. "Maybe the same people who will recognize Rex Lang the film director as Rex Lang the—" She shrugged and laughed.

Lang laughed too. "Shit, the way O'Flaherty shot me—shades, leather cap, in profile—I could have been Fidel Castro at a distance. Or Gerald Ford on a fishing trip."

Leni reflected that Lang was probably right. Who would connect the coy stills O'Flaherty from the *Sunday World* had just taken—all creamy thigh and half-glimpsed boobs—with the brutal mug-shots published by *Der Spiegel*, captioned: "Seen Leni? Look out—she's a killer."

She hated to admit anyone could be as right as Lang was all of the time. Indeed, she accepted orders Lang gave with a readiness that would have seemed unthinkable a year ago. Even before joining Movement Second of June Leni had been politically active, but although she still called herself a Marxist, for years everything had been driving her toward a kind of autonomous nihilism. You could smell the bourgeois in most Marxists. Whether they knew it or not, they were dupes of the Spectacle; they'd chickened out before they had even begun. The test for Leni was: Would they kill? Did they accept Johann Most's dictum that there are no innocent bystanders (believing that innocent bystanders must be creeps, acquiescent to tyranny)? For instance, to achieve some truly revolutionary end, would they be prepared to leave a time-bomb in a bus full of children? No one wants to blow up a planeload of hostages, but it can be a necessary act. A military act. Confronted by such a necessity, Leni would kill a thousand "innocent bystanders" and herself along with them.

Lang said, "Nice of Marta Troy to arrange that session with O'Flaherty."

Leni nodded. "I suppose so."

"Good ole Marta. Ireland is a small country. I guess she knows people at all the right levels."

"Yes, Rex."

Ever since that first appearance on O Morain's "Weekend Show," they had been getting the right kind of media coverage: no doubt of that. Leni herself usually figured in a tits-'n'-ass presentation—as in the pictures O'Flaherty had just taken—but Lang himself evoked a buzz of flattering comment. Lang, they had it, was not the old-style American director—illiterate, cigar-chomping—but a transatlantic version of the Continental *auteur*. As the *Irish Times* said: "Mr. Lang must be the first of a new breed to arrive in Dublin from that

ancient wonderland called Hollywood, but—you better believe it—he will not
be the last."

And meanwhile Lang himself was delighting everyone: doing all the right
things. He had been on TV again several times, with Leni and without. On
O Dunnacha Duane's Irish-language show, "Daoine Ag Caint," Lang had naturally had to speak in English, but he assured viewers that he intended to learn
Irish "in such moments of leisure as I can muster while I'm visiting your lovely
country." In ten days' time, if an already tight schedule allowed, he would be
traveling to the Pan-Celtic Congress at Quimper: a festival of Irish, Welsh,
Manx, Cornish, Scottish, and Breton cultural activities. "Just to humbly watch
and listen, and—hopefully—learn," Lang said to applause from the studio
audience. Then, a few weeks later, he would be present at the Carrolton ceremonies, to be attended by the president of the United States before he went to
the Isle of Man Conference. "The Irish have always provided a leaven of wit
and poetry in that ethnic melting-pot we call America," Lang said. "As an
American not of Irish descent I shall be very happy to be there." Meanwhile—
dressed sometimes to suit the *auteur* image in knee-high leather boots, green
fatigues, and leather cap, and sometimes simply in a business suit—he was seen
around Dublin venues like Sachs, the Anna Livia Restaurant in Bloom's Hotel,
and Annabel's.

"Yeah," Lang said. "Good ole Marta. She'll see us right." He paused. "She's
given us that little special cachet we need." He nodded. "American moviemakers! The Irish know we're crazy already. We couldn't arouse suspicion if we
tried." He was smiling. " 'Paris is worth a mass . . .' Well, Marta was worth a
partouze, right?"

"That was what you wanted, Rex."

Leni didn't want to talk about it. She felt fairly indifferent about the
encounter Lang had arranged between her and Marta—with Lang himself performing what he described as "literally a backup role." Certainly she hadn't
been turned on by Marta's performance. Not that Leni claimed any right to be
turned on. It had been agreed when she first joined the group that if Lang
required her to make it with a man—any man—in order to further a specific
objective, then she would fuck like a machine, faking it brilliantly. It was
Marta being a woman that complicated things. Basically, Marta's demands
were more emotional than physical, and Leni couldn't respond to that. Not
without becoming involved herself—and she was resolved not to let that happen.

"Know what?" Lang said. "You gotta hurt Marta more the next time.
Pain—that's what that gal relates to." He paused. "Men she don't need, but

you know why she liked me being there? Because she has one fear—one tiny delicious little fear—that one day I'm gonna kill her." He was laughing. "That's the key to Marta. She wants everyone to fuck her—and then kill her. Kill her over and over . . ."

He looked serious as he went on, "And I'm about to dangle another cookie in front of her nose. A guest-star appearance in *Blood Scenario*. But I told her we have to change the script, write her in." He gestured. "I think the sun is coming out. Shall we walk round the demesne?"

The sun was indeed coming out, having lurked behind heavy clouds for the past hour. Even so, Leni didn't think the Irish climate so bad as Lang and Durnan made out.

They walked in silence. Looking over the tops of the trees, they could see Kippure, a mile or two away and a mountain by Irish standards—two thousand feet or more.

They reached the birch wood. Lang stood staring into the green, bosky darkness. Leni felt a momentary sense of peace and contentment. She became aware of the activity stirring in the secret world of the birds and insects and animals that were the real owners of the wood. A blackbird started to sing. A rare, pastoral moment. Leni wondered if Lang could respond to such a moment. She couldn't. More and more she was aware of a blankness at the heart of her: nothing responding to nothing.

Lang said, "I told O'Flaherty we'd start principal photography next week. So—we have to start going through the motions."

Leni nodded. This morning he had shown O'Flaherty an array of cameras and a wide variety of equipment, including the sound truck. Some of this gear wasn't functional, but there was a lot of it. As Lang had explained to her before they even arrived in Ireland, suggestion was everything. Shooting a movie—any movie—was such a tedious, fragmented process that no spectator, however idle, was going to watch it too long. Something more active was bound to beckon, even in Ireland. Just let them see an authoritative figure walking around with a bullhorn; a sound boom, and some lights on a scaffolding—and anyone would walk away impressed. Certainly O'Flaherty had swallowed the whole ball of wax. He had drooled on about how he'd already interviewed Kubrick and Boorman and how Lang obviously belonged in that company. No doubt O'Flaherty had gone back to Dublin a happy man, convinced that Lang was a nice fella as Yanks go; and no doubt the iced champagne and caviar sandwiches served in the long gallery above the banqueting hall of Kilbrangan House had helped that impression along.

"Not that we have to do much," Lang said. "Just get ourselves noticed odd places around Dublin and Wicklow." He paused. "Of course, Old Dillon releases the foundation and we have to do more."

He meant lifting the arms caches which had been laid down by Seamus Dillon when he was creating the foundation. That would be done under the cover of shooting exteriors on location throughout the twenty-six counties.

Leni said, "Rex—is there any news when we are getting the stuff from the foundation?"

"Not before we go to Quimper, I'd say. Old Dillon is an ornery old bastard, the word is." Lang paused. "But he'll come across. Ultimately."

"You think?"

"Frankie McNagan will be back from New York this week. She'll tell Duane what Old Dillon says. Duane will tell us."

"Suppose Dillon refuses? Finally?"

"A slight delay is all," Lang said. "We'll get our hands on his precious foundation—another two, three weeks . . ." He smiled. "Some pretty stylish frag there. Shillelagh missiles fired from a 152-millimeter gun, guided infrared. Some Dragon antitank missiles—thirty-one pounds and one man can handle them!" Lang was boyish in his enthusiasm. "Not that this kind of hardware is gonna be needed before the final phase of the operation. The stuff we need day-by-day we got already, and this we train with." He frowned. "Training— yeah! Right now we have to start organizing those animals back there." He tilted his head toward Kilbrangan House, morosely blocking the sky behind them. "They're settled in now, they're as comfortable as they can be in that goddamned gracious coldwater mansion." He paused. "Day or two more and they'll start serious drinking. Day after that—" He shrugged. "So. Training! The Mac 11 and the 180 particularly. Start tomorrow. Best have Mick Congar run it. He's a gun freak."

Lang's good mood seemed to have deteriorated. His tone curt and dismissive, he added, "We better go see what they're doing now."

🍀 🍀 🍀

"That's the situation," Frankie said, and her next words came softly as a sigh. "It's now or never."

Tom had brought Frankie into Seamus' hospital room a half hour ago. Somehow, Seamus had expected her to be tall, as striking as the young Junos who stride along the sidewalks of New York, but she was small and dark and now the intensity of her emotion sharpened her features into a kind of beauty. No doubt about this being Peadar's daughter!

Seamus himself hadn't said much this last half hour, as Frankie outlined the plan Duane and Rex Lang had conceived for a seizure of power in the South of Ireland. Lying back on his pillows, Seamus had listened intently, only occasionally interjecting a remark, resisting his natural inclination to play the Devil's advocate. But now he said gently, "It's a clever plan—and so bold that it's tempting to believe it might come off. Toujours l'audace, eh?"

Frankie was about to speak when he went on: "But depend on strangers, *mercenaries*—for that's what they are, aren't they?" He shook his head. "That worries me, Frankie. That really worries me. International guerrillas? Maybe I'm old-fashioned, but hijackers, guerrillas—they're all thugs in my book." He paused. "And this man Duane has met with. This Rex Lang. You tell me he's a former officer of the United States Army who is now an absentee? Forgive me, I take leave to worry about such a man. He has already betrayed one allegiance. How can you trust him not to betray you?"

"There are a lot of historical precedents," Frankie said. "Foreign help for the Irish cause. Wolfe Tone had to trust Humbert, right? But don't the advantages outweigh the risks? Why—the biggest risk of all is removed. Always in the past Irishmen seeking liberty have been betrayed by another Irishman. This time the executive action will be taken by strangers. Unknown to the government. Unknown to the Special Branch."

Seamus nodded. "That's a big plus all right. Everyone in the movement is on file at the Castle. Maybe they don't bother you too much while you're fighting for Ireland outside the bounds of the Republic. You can imitate Guy Fawkes and blow up the House of Commons and when you come home the Irish courts will never extradite you. But just make waves south of the border . . ."

"Well," Frankie said, "thank you for listening to me." She hesitated. "Now I have to ask you what Duane sent me all the way to New York to ask you. Will you release the resources of the foundation to the order of the Wednesday Committee?"

Seamus grinned, sank back on his pillows. "You're very like your Da, you know that? Except for the English accent. But you're just as persuasive."

"Mr. Dillon—"

"Call me Seamus, will you?"

"Can I add this?" Frankie said. "With the resources of the foundation behind us, we know our plan can succeed. Without the foundation—" She broke off.

Seamus didn't answer for a moment. Then he said quietly, "You know this isn't the first time I've been asked?"

"I didn't know, no."

"Michael McClymont, the TD [member of the Dail], the politician. He wanted me to make the foundation available to a group of Northern republicans a few years ago." Seamus paused. "After a lot of thought I declined."

"It wasn't Eireann Amhain."

"No, indeed it wasn't." Seamus grinned. "Duane would have told you, right?"

In fact McClymont had asked on behalf of a group even smaller than Eireann Amhain. They operated mostly in the very active border area around Crossmaglen in County Armagh. After a good deal of thought Seamus had decided that it would not be good policy to tap only a portion of the foundation's resources—lifting one or two of the caches put all the others at risk. And he was not convinced that anything like a doomsday situation existed, although he was sympathetic to the logistical needs of the group in question. But the foundation had been created—as he had told an angry McClymont—against a total, all-Ireland situation. It must be preserved for that.

Seamus had been sorry to rebuff McClymont, because the TD had helped him a great deal through the long haul of building up the foundation. Seamus had needed the cooperation of a man highly placed in the Irish political establishment, and McClymont had been that man. He and Seamus had not met since, although Seamus knew McClymont was a member of the Wednesday Committee.

Seamus went on: "You know I've been accused of having a proprietary attitude to the foundation? Behaving as if it's my personal possession, in fact. Well"—he gestured—"maybe there is a little truth in that. That would be human, I guess. But I'm always conscious that I'm just a trustee, representing thousands of ordinary men and women across these United States who happen to be proud of the Irish blood that runs in their veins. They built the foundation." He paused. "But of course I have to feel some personal pride. Those guns, that money—it took some putting together, you know it—and I'm not about to throw it away."

"I understand how you feel," Frankie said. "But sooner or later you have to let someone use those resources. Before the guns get rusty and obsolete and some informer tells the Special Branch where they're hidden."

Seamus nodded. "I've thought of that too."

He was silent for so long that Frankie wondered whether she should offer to leave and maybe come back tomorrow. At last he said, "Dublin? Why not Belfast?"

"The committee made that point to Duane," Frankie said. "He convinced them it should be Dublin." She paused. "For sixty years the chosen battle-ground has always been the same: British-occupied Ulster. Not since 1916 has anyone struck at the real target—Dublin."

"That's right," Seamus said. "And I would remind you that the 1916 Rising wasn't successful in purely military terms."

"Pearse and Connolly and the others took on the British Army head-on—magnificent, but it wasn't war! It was a miracle they held on as long as they did. A week! Facing the firepower they did, that represents unbelievable endur-ance." She shook her head. "The British were then the army of occupation—as they still are in the North. And the technique for overthrowing an army of occupation is quite different from a seizure of power in a sovereign state. The Irish Republic is a sovereign state—and at this moment it's wide open for a coup d'etat."

"That's the third time you've said that," Seamus murmured. "You must really believe it."

"Yes, I believe it," she said. "You, Seamus—you're a political animal if there ever was one—you must have studied the philosophy of the coup d'etat. The more centralized government is in a country, the easier that government is to overthrow. Ireland has the most centralized administration in Europe. Take Dublin and you lop off the head from the trunk!" She paused. "You fought in the Civil War. You know the IRA could have won against the Free Staters if they'd gone for Dublin in the beginning."

Seamus nodded; didn't comment. Then he said, "From what I have read about the coup d'etat, I understand that a purely military seizure of power can only last a few days. For a takeover to really succeed, there has to be a will towards acceptance of the new regime among the people of the state." He paused. "Would the people of Ireland accept the regime the Wednesday Com-mittee would impose?"

Frankie's eyes shone; her voice was steely with emotion. "Yes—if they got an Ireland that was new—and clean!" she cried. "It's sixty years since the British gave us that excuse for independence they called the Irish Free State. Sixty years—and now it isn't the British viceroy anymore—it's the EEC com-missioners in Brussels. Nothing really changes in Ireland: they just give things different names. But the sons and grandsons of the same exploiters are getting richer while the mass of the Irish people get poorer—and now they can't even emigrate because there's recession everywhere." Seamus could see she was fighting down her anger. "And now their EEC masters are ordering the Irish government to build a nuclear power station—to pollute the air, give children bone cancer, maybe kill everyone in a big explosion if one man forgets to turn off a heating system." She dropped her voice, but Seamus could still feel the steel behind her words. "I'm telling you: Ireland is a powderkeg if we lay the fuse right!"

🍀 🍀 🍀

"There you are!" The younger man who called himself Mr. Brown spoke in a rasping Belfast accent. "See them working in a club like this and you realize how they've infiltrated our society." He glared at the retreating back of the young Pakistani who had just brought them drinks.

"I don't know," the older man who called himself Mr. White said. "It's not as if this were the Travellers or even the Reform. I'd say the House Committee here are glad of anything they can get."

"A sign of decadence," Mr. Brown said. "Bloody nignogs wherever you turn in this town."

Mr. White smiled faintly but said nothing. Mr. Brown looked puzzled: his usual expression. Durnan wondered why they bothered to use these pseudonyms. Their real names wouldn't mean anything to him, and Lang probably knew them already.

Mr. White, Mr. Brown, Lang, and Durnan were sitting in the annex to the members' bar in Whig's Club in St. James's Street. When Lang had first told Durnan they were to meet with two representatives of Loyalist Action at Whig's, Durnan had relished the prospect of entering one of the older, crustier London clubs, but Lang had gone on to explain that this particular crust had gotten a bit soggy these last few years. The political heirs to the Whigs did not belong to Whig's Club. Today all that counted was the ability to pay the ever-mounting yearly dues. Lang quoted his faceless but omniscient adviser on English social mores: "Whig's tends to be the retreat of chaps with money but not much else. Captains of industry from Barrow and Belfast. That sort of chap."

"Are you sure this is your poison?" Mr. White inquired. He spoke with an uppercrust English accent.

"Just perfect," Lang said. The two Americans had asked for bourbon. The Ulstermen chose a Scotch malt whisky.

Mr. Brown said, "What about our loyal toast?"

Mr. White looked irked. "I suppose so," he sighed.

"We always begin any important discussion with our loyal toast," Mr. Brown explained. "And . . . er . . . we stand up."

When everyone had risen, Mr. Brown cleared his throat.

"Here's to the pious and immortal memory of King Billy, who saved us from knaves and knavery, slaves and slavery, popes and popery, brass money and wooden shoes. And if any man among us refuse to rise to this toast, may he be slammed, crammed, and jammed into the barrel of the great gun of Athlone. And may the gun be fired into the pope's belly and the pope into the Devil's belly and the Devil into the roasting pit of hell and may the door of hell be banged shut and the key kept in the pocket of a bold Orange boy. And may there never lack a good Protestant to beat hell out of a papish."

Mr. Brown paused. He looked across at Mr. White, who responded in a tone of ritual boredom, "And here's a fart for the bishop of Cork."

Mr. Brown smiled. "Well, that's it. Our loyal toast."

"Nice to see you here today," Mr. White said. He had a gracious, formal manner belied a little by his hard eyes and quick, empty smile. "You know it's hardly necessary for us to express our appreciation of your efforts on our behalf. Up to now," he added sharply.

Lang nodded.

"I saw your appearance on television the other night," Mr. White went on. "Must have been the first time we ever switched on to the Dublin station." He paused. "A stroke of genius, using the cover of a film director. That must represent carte blanche for any sort of lunacy, what?"

"Something like that," Lang said.

Durnan had asked Lang before they came here today if he didn't think it was dangerous being known as "Rex Lang" to both Loyalist Action and the Wednesday Committee. Lang pointed out that the two groups were at opposed poles: the chances against contact between them were astronomically high.

"We're very pleased about McStay," Mr. White said. "Of course we were absolutely delighted about Saint Patrick's Day too, but we've already told you that." He paused. "McStay was a special case. Wendell Dillon and the others killed in the parade were our enemies—ethnic, traditional enemies: Yankee Fenians who hated us, who gave their dollars to buy bombs and bullets to kill us—but Angus McStay was something worse."

"A fucking traitor, so he was!" Mr. Brown said.

Mr. White nodded gravely. "I'm afraid he was. A traitor to his race, to the religion of his fathers."

Feeling he had to speak sometime, Durnan said, "That's right."

"This so-called President's Initiative he helped engineer." Mr. White shook his head. "Sheer Yankee arrogance! An affront to Her Majesty's loyal subjects in the North."

"It's a well-known fact," Mr. Brown said, "that the White House takes its orders directly from the Vatican."

"Rather a pity, though," Mr. White continued, "that you haven't yet tracked down the old fox himself."

"The old fox?" Lang echoed.

"Old Seamus Dillon." Mr. White smiled. "He's the real godfather of the IRA in America. For half a century he's masterminded subversion and murder in Ireland—while he sits safely in New York."

"He'd have died if he'd been marching," Lang said. "Our information was, he always walked beside Wendell Dillon, with the other committee members." He shrugged. "Turns out he was in Doctors Hospital."

"Don't take my remark as a reproach, I beg!" Mr. White said. "I hear he has recently been visited in hospital by Frances McNagan, daughter of Peadar Mahoney, another Fenian murderer. That was for no good purpose, I suspect."

Lang said, "Of course the contract is still out on Old Dillon?"

"Of course," Mr. White answered. "The contract stands, and I have no doubt you will fulfill it in God's own good time."

There was a silence which Durnan broke by asking them if they would have another drink. Mr. White said they would, and Mr. Brown walked across the annex to tug at an archaic-looking bellpull. They waited, still in silence, till the Pakistani came in. They ordered and the Pakistani left.

"I have to pay him for these drinks," Mr. White said. "As a member." He gave his quick, empty smile. "You can pay me afterwards."

"It's an irony," Mr. White said, "to reflect that the extreme republicans and ourselves are at one in opposing your President's Initiative. They, because they see their criminal activities drowned with dollars. Danegeld in fact—bribes for the Roman Catholic community to behave themselves. If they're good little boys and don't put bombs in Protestant pubs, Yankee dollars will build factories for them to work in. And one or two Roman Catholics will become ministers in the cabinet of this ramshackle new state." Mr. White made a gesture of disgust. "Call it what you like—mini-Marshall Aid, anything you like. It's still a Pax Americana imposed on the people of Ulster by outsiders." He paused. "Naturally the IRA don't want any sort of pax, American or otherwise. They just want to go on burning and bombing and killing . . ."

He held his glass up to the light. In the last half hour they had progressed to a fine old Napoleon brandy: Mr. White's recommendation. Twirling the glass around, he continued, "Of course we're different, we Ulstermen. You have to realize that. And no one even tries to understand us. I sometimes think we are the most maligned ethnic group in the world, we Ulster Protestants. No one even knows who we are! In fact we are the descendants of the men who colonized Scotland from Ireland in the fifth century and who colonized Northern Ireland from Scotland in the seventeenth. For the last four hundred years we have known only strife, repression, and bloodshed. We have been loyal to Britain and Britain has repeatedly betrayed us. They resent having to keep an army in the North. The South hates us—and the Southern government in Dublin uses us to discharge the frustration engendered by their own repressive society. Worse, they give IRA gunmen comfort and refuge comparable only to that given by Lebanon to the PLO attacking Israel." He shrugged. "Gentlemen—I don't know why I'm generalizing like this. Probably because you are both Americans, and in America, above all, we have been treated most unjustly by the press. When we caused the Saint Patrick's Day Parade to be bombed, we were called monsters—but who ever saw behind the shamrocks and the shillelaghs and the green beer to the dollars collected for bombs that went off in Northern Ireland?" His pale eyes above the twirling brandy glass seemed to cloud. "I've seen the Irish march up Fifth Avenue. I've also stood in the bus station in Belfast on Bloody Friday and seen ambulance men shoveling up bits of human flesh and putting them into plastic bags."

Mr. White stopped as if cut off by a switch. No one spoke. Durnan admired Lang's ability to stay silent even more than he admired his occasional eloquence.

Now Mr. White leaned back in his chair. He seemed to relax, his eyes unfocused, almost sleepy-looking. Now you could visualize him chairing a board meeting of the family firm; addressing a long shot at golf; cosseting a grandchild.

"Well, gentlemen," he said. "You can of course take it that you are to prepare for item eight of your scheduled program for us—the Carrolton Inauguration."

"I hoped you'd say that, sir," Lang said.

"Payment for item seven of the program—McStay's execution—is already in course," Mr. White said. "As before, split between Philips International, Cayman Islands, and Fauberg AG in the proportion of one-third and two-thirds respectively."

"Right," Lang said. "Thank you."

"The advance payment for item eight will be conveyed through the same channels in the same proportions, if that is agreeable to you?"

"Right again," Lang said. "And thank you again."

"The vehicles. You've already taken delivery of the two Range Rovers. The jeeps we hope to deliver next week. In Dublin, I presume?"

"If you please," Lang said.

"There are two large trucks yet to be obtained," Mr. White said. "Ford Transits—they'd be large enough?"

"Sure," Lang said. "What about the dogs?"

"The dogs . . . Well, they'll take a little longer."

"Okay," Lang said. "They're only needed for the final sequence of item eight."

Mr. White stood up. "Grand. One thing—when we do get them, they won't attract much attention. In Ireland dogs and horses are part of the landscape." He looked keenly at Lang. "But I am relieved you're not asking us to supply you with arms, Mr. Lang."

☙ ☙ ☙

"Yes," Frankie whispered. "Yes . . ."

And then they were making love again, treading with abandon the path they had more impetuously—but still with tenderness—trodden the first time. Now they could be cool about it: dance their ballet of pleasure with self-conscious sensuality. Just before they fused together for a second time, Frankie's mind clicked like a camera shutter on a vision of Tom's face framed by a tousle of black hair, his expression abstracted, oddly sad.

After that they lay enlaced in each other's arms in a quiet conspiracy against the rest of the world. Time, Frankie thought, a moment like this—chopped off the roaring, unending flux of life as we live it, encapsulated, held—this is the only way to defeat time. Or rather, enjoy the illusion of defeating it.

Tom was asleep. She saw, with tender surprise, the streaks of gray in the black mop of his hair beside her on the pillow. Very lightly, she kissed his cheek, grazing her lips on the iron stubble already forcing through. A Black Irishman—she'd used the phrase earlier that evening, and he'd picked her up on it, even seemed pleased. That was what they'd always called him in the family, he said.

Frankie's left leg was trapped under Tom's right. Slowly, gingerly, so as not to wake him, she freed herself. As she did so, he sighed and rolled over onto his back. They were lying on top of the covers, both naked, and she admired his steel-taut physique, his Irish navvy's muscles.

She wondered where her guilt was: the guilt that so excited her, maddened her, degraded her whenever she fucked with Duane. It had been so different tonight with Tom—and yet it had been the same act. The quality of betrayal was the same. All the time she had been making love with Tom tonight—

knowing his thrusting flesh and writhing beneath him and crying out at their moment of greatest pleasure—all that time the Other Frankie had been locked up in a cell, perhaps a thousand miles away, less than a ghost in her mind. If he was sleeping—she accused herself—perhaps he would be dreaming of her; if waking, perhaps re-creating some shard of their long-ago loving in some muted, solitary act.

It was no good, though. She couldn't feel as bad lying here with Tom as she would have done with Duane. She couldn't feel for him the fierce antagonism that was part of her lustful excitement with Duane.

Tom was such a tender lover. Maybe that was why. And that had stemmed so naturally, so inevitably, from the gentleness—*gentlemanliness,* really—of his approach to her as a woman. If he hadn't actually bowed when he met her, a carnation in his buttonhole, presenting her with a spray of orchids as he swept her into a limousine—well, that was the kind of ambience he created and she was grateful for it. Weary and nerve-battered after months and years of conspiracy, of living under cover, she had been overwhelmed by Tom's simple friendliness, his politeness.

That must have been why. She was tired. Tired of the tightrope she was forced to tread all the time, traveling between Ireland and England and the European mainland. Tired of the responsibility Duane and the Wednesday Committee had imposed on her when they sent her here to see Seamus Dillon.

And she still didn't know if old Dillon was going to release the foundation to them or not. She'd spent herself trying to persuade him, but he wouldn't commit himself. Oh—he'd been friendly, charming even, but she sensed a certain steely arrogance in this old man. He was ill, she knew, but as he lay, leonine against his bunched pillows, she thought him full of power yet. Like one of Ibsen's formidable old men: Solness, or John Gabriel Borkman.

She didn't know how far she had carried him toward acceptance of the Wednesday Committee's plan. Toward the end of her visit she'd gotten the impression that he was dredging his mind for objections. "You talk of an Ireland that's new and clean," he said. "But what about a United Ireland? One Ireland—United, Gaelic, and Free! Suppose with the help of your Mr. Lang you do take Dublin. What about the North?"

"What about it?" she had retorted. "Throwing out the old gang in Dublin is the first step. Take Dublin and you're on the way to taking Belfast."

He'd been silent, pondering that. Then he had gravely thanked her. "Your father is a hero—you know that—and you're worthy to be his daughter." He paused. "If I were Peadar, I'd be proud." He frowned. "As for what you ask me—I have to consider . . . If, in a few days' time, I say no, then it will be an unqualified no and that will be the end of it. But if it's yes, then it will be a qualified yes. I should then want to see this man, this Rex Lang." He paused. "You said he would be at Quimper, at the Pan-Celtic Congress?"

"That's right," Frankie said. The congress was being held at Quimper in Brittany in early May. She said, "Lang will be there. So will Duane. And the rest of the committee."

Seamus said, "I don't know if I could go to Quimper. That depends on Dr. Hernandez of this hospital."

"If you *could* come—" Frankie said and broke off. Something drove her to make one final appeal: "You agreed that the president's so-called Initiative could freeze the status quo in Ireland, North and South—kill all our hopes. So—if we don't seize this moment, don't carry out this plan . . . Remember what Pitt said after Napoleon won at Austerlitz? 'Roll up that map of Europe; it will not be wanted these ten years.' Well, I say to you, Seamus Dillon: let this moment go and we can roll up the map of Ireland for a hundred years."

He smiled sweetly. "You're very eloquent, Frankie." Then he half closed his eyes; lay back further on his pillows.

"When shall we know your decision?" she asked.

"In a few days . . . a week," he said, apparently weary now. "Tell Duane I'll communicate in the usual way."

The usual way was through Penrith Pharmaceuticals (Ireland). Seamus usually communicated with Duane by telex. They had a repertoire of business messages like "regret this line no longer available" that served them as code signals. Penrith's manager, Martin Macowen, was a reluctant accomplice in all this.

"I'll telex," Seamus said. "In two or three days' time." There was no more to say. Frankie reached over and squeezed his hand, then left.

And so on to this evening just past. Tom had taken her to Pearl's, where they'd eaten the almost obligatory lemon chicken and stuffed iceburg lettuce. Tom had said, "You're not going back to Inwood tonight?" It was phrased as a question, but it seemed like an order. Frankie had shrugged, smiled, and gone with him to this apartment on Fifty-seventh Street near Columbus Circle.

She realized that he was awake and watching her. He raised himself on an elbow and reached over to kiss her, tenderly, inquiringly.

"Hi, mystery woman," he said.

She looked at him. "A mystery is what they used to call a girl who arrived in London from the country—or from Scotland or Ireland—hoping to meet her own personalized, gift-wrapped Sir Galahad in the big city."

"Really?"

"Unfortunately Sir Galahad usually turned out to be a pimp."

"Don't know nothing about no Limey pimps," he said. "Frankie—"

"Yes?"

"You're a mystery all right, but not that sort of mystery. Otherwise you'd never come here to see my uncle."

"You don't know anything about me—and I can't tell you anything."

"Only that you're young, you're married—and you're beautiful."

He kissed her again.

"Obviously," he said, "you're here on some kind of assignment. This time the IRA showed very good taste. They don't always." He grinned. "The emissaries they send to see my uncle are usually guys, either very old or pretty young. Never was one like you before!"

She didn't answer.

"Whatever assignment you're here on is completed—right?"

"You could say that."

"Then you don't have to go back too soon? You could stay a week. Maybe longer—?"

"No." The finality in her voice cut him short.

They lay in silence, holding each other so close that she could feel his heart beating.

"It's extraordinary," he said. "How I feel I know you. When really I know nothing."

"Enough," she said. "You know enough."

"When I came back from Nam—" he said and stopped. "How about that for an unfashionable statement? Boring, but relevant. I did three tours there—and three tours take you a long way from wherever you started . . ." He was silent. "What I'm really trying to say is, I came back to find that I was a stranger to my wife. Not just a stranger. A Martian. I looked human, but the issue was in doubt. I had eyes, a nose, a mouth—even other things Nancy wasn't interested in anymore—but I wasn't human. Liberation had done that. In this year, in this world, those gals have created a new racial tension, a new division, a new reason for hating—"

"Hey—I'm a feminist too!"

"Not in my book you're not."

"I am," Frankie said. "In Ireland you still have the conditions that create the kind of reactions you're talking about."

"Anyway, what I'm saying is, you're different."

He started to kiss her again, but this time she did not respond. Gently, she drew away. "Tell me," she said, "can I stay till morning?"

"Of course you'll stay till morning."

"I'm not going back to Inwood. I'll get a cab straight to the airport."

"You're going back to Ireland? Not tomorrow morning?"

"I have to."

"No," he said. "Not tomorrow. Stay a little longer. A day even—"

"Tomorrow. I must."

"When will you come back?"

"I don't know. Never—perhaps."

"You must come back. I must see you again."

"No," she said. "I'm not coming back. You won't see me again."

Two

Quimper

They said familiarity bred contempt, but not for this place. Superintendent Slowey visited Portlaoise Jail on the average once or twice a month and each time he found it more chilling and intimidating. This afternoon, waiting in his official car for the routine identification to be completed, he took in the rows of blank windows like dead men's eyes, the low walls that seemed to crouch behind a nimbus of barbed wire, the bored but uneasy-looking police and soldiers on guard, and thought for the hundredth time that this prison in Portlaoise was a huge wild-beast cage that barely contained the men inside it. He remembered the last big jailbreak here some years ago. Republican conspirators outside the prison had sent a truck loaded with gelignite crashing through the main gates, and one of the escaping prisoners had been shot by the army. That had been the worst break in the history of Irish prisons, and yet Slowey felt it had probably been only a ripple on the surface of the violence that was ready to burst forth from behind these walls. Every prison is a kind of microcosm of society, but by any criterion Portlaoise was unique. Its inmates were exclusively "politicals." Swindlers, burglars, or sex offenders may be intimidated by prison: not so political prisoners. Confinement only sharpened the will of these men. By sheer weight of numbers and intensity of belief they had imposed a kind of ascendancy on the governor and his officers. Explosives had been smuggled into the jail on a number of occasions—indeed, there were said to be caches of explosives hidden in the cells of certain prisoners which the warders were unable, or afraid, to find. Knives and pistols had often been brought in—no one knew how. No wonder some wit had scrawled on a wall outside the administration offices: "IRA rules here, OK?"

Not that these men were not divided among themselves. The largest category of prisoners was the Provisional IRA; the next largest, the "Stickies"—the Official IRA; then the IRSP—the Irish Republican Socialist Party; the rest, a variety of splinters and spin-offs from the Provisionals and Officials.

The man Slowey had come to see belonged in this last category. Frank Niles was a member of the Republican Freedom Fighters, a tiny splinter from the Provisionals that operated mostly in the border counties of Cavan and Monaghan. He had been arrested as a result of an anonymous tipoff made from a pay telephone in the area. Stopped on the road near Cootehill, County Cavan, Niles had been found to have a number of M16 Armalite rifles, a quantity of gelignite, and several detonators in the trunk of his car. Two days ago he had appeared in the Special Criminal Court in Dublin on the charges of being a member of the IRA ("IRA" being a blanket description that could cover several different and often mutually hostile organizations) and of having arms and explosives in his possession with intent to endanger life.

To have been caught red-handed like this meant that Niles had been set up. The tipoff was probably the result of some internecine feud in the RFF, but naturally this didn't bother the Special Branch. Niles wasn't important, though: they were on the lookout for bigger fish. Yesterday, however, Niles had managed to get a message through to Slowey at his office at C3 (Special Detective Unit, Dublin Castle), using one of the Portlaoise screws who had occasionally conveyed this kind of message in the past. Niles had valuable information which, under certain circumstances, he would be prepared to divulge. Information vital to the security of the State. He would only talk to a senior officer. Super or above. Oh—and had they heard of the Wednesday Committee? That was part of it.

Knowing Frank Niles as essentially small-time, Slowey would normally have discounted most—all—of these promised revelations. Except in the case of one member of an accused group turning state's evidence, this sort of deal rarely offered much for the police. Slowey had never heard of the Wednesday Committee till a week ago and then he hadn't been convinced that it really existed, although it had been referred to by one of his most reliable sources. But the fact that Niles also mentioned it, only a few days later, made Niles worth listening to. The effect was of two independent sightings sending two lines converging together on a chart. It could mean that the Wednesday Committee *did* exist and was a danger to the state.

They were waving his car through now. They performed these security checks meticulously each time Slowey came to the jail to see prisoners, although the police on the gate knew him well by this time. Quite right of course, but he always had the feeling that the tight external security at Port-laoise might mask doubt and even fear inside. He could be wrong—once or twice in his career his superiors had criticized him for "dramatizing" a situation—but his instinct as a detective had served him well for twenty years and this told him he was right. Once he entered those dingy corridors that suggested a Victorian workhouse he would feel uneasy. His every nerve would be alert. Not so much for physical attack as for treachery, betrayal.

Slowey wondered about Niles. The cover for his being brought out from his cell block to see Slowey was that he was being examined by a heart specialist from Dublin. Slowey wondered if the hard men on Niles' block would accept that story. Why not take Niles under escort to one of the Dublin hospitals?

Of course everything depended on why Niles was proposing to talk. He knew he had been snitched on; presumably he was talking to get back at someone and in the hope of getting a reduced sentence from the Special Criminal Court. This was most likely, but there was also the possibility that he was only carrying out orders conveyed to him in prison from some republican authority. That would mean that his information would be either false or hopelessly distorted; it meant too that this talk about the Wednesday Committee was an attempt to set up a stalking-horse to divert and confuse the Special Branch. God knows, the Branch had few friends and plenty of enemies, Slowey thought: even enemies among the government it was trying to protect.

His driver parked the big black Ford Granada near the administration block. Slowey got out. He stood quite still for a moment, seeking that moment of peace and psychic reappraisal that he had learned to seek in those far-off days when he was at the seminary in Carlow, studying for the priesthood. He had become a policeman, not a priest, but he liked to think he still carried some of the tender concern of that young seminarian within him.

The moment achieved, Slowey straightened his shoulders—a big man in his late forties with his thick black hair graying and the deep furrows in his cheeks indicating an inner tension controlled but never relaxed—and entered the administration office.

☘ ☘ ☘

"Slowey? Who the fuck is he?" Niles snarled. He was a hulk of a man with fair curly hair: a fairness transmuted to golden-red in his thick bushy beard. His accent was that of the submerged, republican areas of Belfast—Ballymurphy or the Ardoyne maybe—softened by some years in the South.

"Mind your dirty mouth when you're speaking to a police officer," the warder said.

"Police officer! Ass-licker!" Niles bared his teeth in a grin. "A shoneen ass-licker, what's more! Sure, lick hard enough and the shit comes off red-white-and-blue."

Slowey said, "All right. That's enough, Niles. You wanted to see me—"

"See *you?* On my fucking ass! I wanted to see a senior officer of the Special Branch of the Garda Siochana. Are you the best they can do?"

"Better than you deserve," Slowey said. "Now—what do you want to tell me?"

"I want to talk to you alone," Niles said. He glanced at the warder, standing blocklike, impassive, in the corner. "Get him out of here."

"You must know the regulations," Slowey said. "Remand prisoners don't even get to see their lawyers alone in here."

"That's because the screws don't trust lawyers," Niles said. "*I* don't trust screws. But just as you like," he added. "Tell him to take me back to the block then."

"Look, Niles," Slowey said. "Don't pretend to be stupid. You must have good reasons for wanting to talk."

"Take me back to the block, will you?"

Niles stayed silent, standing motionless, his head bowed. Slowey knew that to concede a point like this at the beginning was often to throw the game away in advance, but he sensed the bull-brute obstinacy of the man in front of him. An obstinacy that might, after all, stem from genuine distrust. "All right," he said after a moment. "Mr. Culshaw"—this was the warder—"you can leave us, if you don't mind."

"Well, Superintendent, I don't know—"

"I'll take full responsibility of course."

Niles nodded as soon as the door closed. "You don't know who *he* is, sure you don't! You don't know who anyone is. I'm taking a risk, talking to the likes of you." But he seemed more relaxed, now they were alone.

"What about the risk *I'm* taking?" Slowey demanded. "I could have traveled a hundred miles, from Dublin and back, to listen to a lot of ould cod!" He paused. "That's what worries me."

Niles didn't appear to have heard. "At least ten percent of the screws, they're in the movement—do you know that?" he said. "But you've no way of knowing who's bloody who!" He picked at his beard irritably. "But come the day, those boyos will be opening the doors and letting the hard men out. How does that grab you, Superintendent?"

Slowey exclaimed in disgust. "Aw—I've been listening to that kind of ould dreeders since I was a uniformed lad on the beat. You better do better than that."

"All right," Niles said with an air of decision. "But what do I get out of it?"

"You know we don't make bargains in the Branch," Slowey said.

"C'mon, Slowey! You know you could drop at least one of the charges. How about membership of the IRA? I don't even know what IRA stands for," he added mockingly. "As for the guns and the bangers, I'm an innocent victim. I was holding them for someone else. I had to do it or I'd get kneecapped. Intimidated, I was."

Kneecapping was a traditional IRA punishment: shooting at the accused's kneecap and crippling him, sometimes permanently.

"Who could intimidate you?" Slowey asked. Of course Niles was being facetious, but this might serve Slowey as a point of departure. "If anyone *did* intimidate you," he went on, "it was the same person you heard talking about the Wednesday Committee."

"Why should it be?"

"It's obvious," Slowey said. It wasn't obvious at all; he was shooting at random. But someone must have set Niles up—probably someone from within his own group—and that meant revenge or jealousy as a motive. Often a combination of the two. Someone informed out of a jealousy and then got informed on in turn for revenge. And so on: the chain of malice could go on for years, adding link after link. Slowey's opposite numbers in the Royal Ulster Constabulary had told him of more than one case where the commander of an IRA unit had been picked up and interned, and in his absence replaced by a younger, less experienced man. When internment ended, the original commander had returned—to find himself taking orders from the usurper. Later, the upstart commander had himself been shopped as the result of an anonymous informer. Wife or friend of the original commander? Slowey had noticed that in the submerged halfworld of republican conspiracy hatreds burgeoned and festered. And yet those people were idealists in their way. Their relentless scheming was not directed to a selfish end.

Driving down from Dublin, Slowey had remembered that another member of the Republican Freedom Fighters, Liam Bogan, had been arrested in circumstances similar to those of Niles five months before. Bogan was taken with two handguns in his possession; his explanation of their presence was accepted by the Special Criminal Court, but he had been given eighteen months for being a member of the IRA. Bogan, too, had been informed on: probably by someone within the RFF. At the time of his arrest he had called himself chief operations officer of the RFF while Niles was intelligence officer. After

Bogan's arrest Niles had become chief operations officer. It was possible that Bogan's friends within the RFF had suspected Niles and in due course taken appropriate action.

This was pure guesswork, but Slowey decided to go along with it. Given Niles' brutal obstinacy, there was little choice. You might cajole or bully another man, but not Niles.

Slowey said, "I suppose your friend Liam Bogan is on the same block with you?"

"Where else would they put him?"

"Good friend of yours, is he?"

Niles shrugged.

"You don't speak to him, do you?" Slowey said.

Niles grinned unexpectedly. "*We* don't speak but he talks plenty."

"Bit of a loudmouth, is he?"

Niles looked at him. "Takes one to know one."

Slowey said, "I put it to you that Bogan has been shooting his mouth off here in Portlaoise. You heard him doing it—or someone else did and told you—and now, just out of the goodness of your heart, you want to tell us."

Niles said, "I asked you before: what do I get out of it?"

"Depends on what the information is worth. Assuming it's worth anything at all."

Niles was staring straight in front of him. Slowey thought he looked like a sullen little boy ridiculously disguised with a red beard. "Someone else has talked already, right?" Niles demanded. "Else how did you know it was Bogan?"

Slowey didn't answer. He had to concentrate on not showing by so much as a twitch of an eyebrow the pleasure that surged through him. A shot in the dark—and right on target!

He had to sound impatient, almost bored. "Of course," he said. "But I don't have to tell you who it was. You're doing the talking, Niles."

"I'll expect something for talking."

"No!" Slowey said roughly. "No bloody bargains! Just you talk and I'll listen."

After a moment Niles said in a grumbling tone, "You know what a fucking snob Bogan is. He's got no education himself—so he likes to drink with those who have. The fucking so-called intellectuals."

"Like who, for example?" Slowey asked.

"Oh—I dunno," Niles flashed at him mockingly. "I'm so bad at names. But the élite of the movement. People who can tell you, in Irish, what Pearse had for breakfast the morning the Brits blew his head off." He paused. "Your bold Bogan likes to do his drinking with these ones. And then he spills his mouth with a lot of highbrow shit he's picked up from them." Now Niles spoke in a ludicrous, cod-English accent, "To impress members of the hoi polloi like poor Frank Niles!" He shook his head and went on in his usual voice, "And he's still plugged in to these ones in here, in this shithole. Don't ask me how, but he is." He paused; sighed; then said dramatically, "All right. This is it. I'll tell you what you came here to hear. You've heard of the Wednesday Committee?"

Slowey nodded. "Of course I have." He had heard of it first from Nora O Conaire, only a week ago, but he didn't have to tell Niles that.

"You know what it is?" Niles demanded. "It's like a coalition. There's people in it from every section of the republican movement. From the Stickies, the Provos, Saor Eire, the IRSP, Eireann Amhain—you name it." He smiled. "Don't worry, Superintendent—you'd know most of them. In fact you'll have a file on them, back at headquarters. You know where they all are. You could pick them up in the morning if you wanted to." His smile was almost a sneer now. "That's always been the great strength of the Branch, hasn't it? You always know who's who and who's where. So that if anyone shows any sign of stirring it up this side of the border, you can put them away fast." He pushed his face close to Slowey's. "*But not this time!* This time it isn't gonna be like that. Because the Wednesday Committee is hiring someone else to do the job."

"Someone else?" Slowey echoed. "One man?"

"Don't be so fucking literal, Slowey. One man, three men, ten men—whatever. The point is: strangers. People you don't know. Not the old faithfuls you've got pictured and fingerprinted on C3 files. Total strangers—and by the time you get on to them it will be too late. The job will be done."

Slowey still tried to sound bored. "Tell me something I don't know for a change."

"You're fucking bluffing! You don't know anything."

"What kind of a job is it?"

"A big job. The biggest ever. They're going to lift a taoiseach and the rest of his boys."

"Kidnap them?"

"Right, Superintendent! And once they've got them"—Niles was grinning demoniacally—"It's Ten Little Indians unless every demand is met. One"—he drew a finger across his throat—"then two. Then three ... . And then there were none! Next stop Mount Jerome Cemetery!" He stopped, his eyes burning, gloating at the prospect.

"You say these people are strangers?" Slowey asked. "Foreigners?"

"Never mind what they are. They'll do the job all right."

"Of course," Slowey said, "this could all be pure bullshit."

"Very probably, Superintendent," Niles said mockingly. "In that case let me go back to the block."

Slowey guessed that Niles had said all he was going to say, but he persisted. "You didn't hear the name of a certain American mentioned?"

"American?"

"Irish-American, really. Seamus Dillon."

"I'm so bad at names."

Slowey tried again. "You know the Pan-Celtic Congress that's being held at Quimper in Brittany? You didn't get any word of that?"

Niles shook his head; didn't speak. Slowey sensed a hostility in him. Perhaps he felt he'd said too much? He'd obviously been influenced by a mixture of motives. Spite against Bogan; the hope of buying leniency from the Special Criminal Court; above all by that feeling of power that often overcomes those in possession of secret information.

Slowey said, "All right, Niles. I'll call Mr. Culshaw."

"Superintendent."

"Yes?"

"You're not going to forget me when I come up again next Monday?"

"It's not a question of forgetting," Slowey said. "It's how much help you've given me." He shrugged. "I'm disappointed. I wonder, could your memory for names improve a little between now and Monday?"

Niles did not answer. Slowey went to the door to call the warder and then Niles said, "You know, Superintendent, I have the feeling that Bogan's highbrow buddies might go to that congress at Quimper. Could be their scene."

🍀 🍀 🍀

As they left Portlaoise, traveling north toward Dublin, Slowey tried to impose some kind of order onto his exchanges with Niles. He had got little enough hard information; nothing on which he could take positive action. What he had got was confirmation. The two lines had converged at a definite point on the chart. Niles had mentioned the Wednesday Committee; he had said they were planning something big; he had hinted that some of the plotters might be going to Quimper. He had not confirmed Seamus Dillon's involvement in whatever was being planned, but that proved nothing, either way. What Niles had contributed—and this was the biggest plus to emerge from Slowey's interview with him—was that a kidnap attempt was to be mounted against the taoiseach and the members of his cabinet. Assuming that the Wednesday Committee existed at all—and having heard it described in similar terms by two independent witnesses, Niles and Nora O Conaire, Slowey felt that it did—such a kidnap attempt seemed very likely. As a policeman concerned with what the news commentators called "international terror," Slowey had noticed that guerrilla groups throughout the world tended to use different methods at different times. For several years the hijacked plane with its passengers held hostages at gunpoint had been the dominant method. Planes were still hijacked, of course, but in Europe this last year or two kidnapping had come into favor. The Belgium millionaire Baron Bracht; the West German industrialist Dr. Schleyer; the former Italian premier Aldo Moro. When you remembered them, Niles' talk of Ten Little Indians struck home with chilling force.

His reference to "someone else" being hired to do the job was more worrying still. Niles was right when he said that the Special Branch knew all the republican activists in the country and could pull in most of them within a few hours. Indeed, the whole concept of security within the Irish state was rooted in this fact. Anyone who could threaten the status quo was known and catalogued. Before they could take any subversive action the Special Branch would arrest them.

But strangers? No good pressing Niles to say who these strangers were. He probably didn't know, anyway. Whoever they were, there was nothing to stop the Wednesday Committee hiring them to kidnap the taoiseach and his cabinet—just as the Mob hires hitmen in America. And what about the Japanese Red Army undertaking commissions for the PFLP?

Slowey's mind went spiraling off into horrible possibilities, but he checked himself. He was building on what were, after all, rumors emanating from two not wholly reliable sources: Niles and Nora O Conaire. Nora's report a few days ago had mentioned the Wednesday Committee and suggested that some kind of action was being planned which would probably be discussed at the Pan-Celtic Congress at Quimper.

Slowey knew he could rely on Nora O Conaire to a certain extent. She had never given him information that had been proved to be false. This time, both she and Niles had mentioned the Wednesday Committee and the fact that a "big job" was being planned. But Nora had mentioned Seamus Dillon too.

Nora was a small, sharp-tongued woman from Clifden in Connemara. She functioned as a stringer for several English Sunday papers, giving them the sexexploitation angle on subjects like Dublin massage parlors and English pimps running Irish girls, but her journalism was mainly a front. She probably also sold information to the British MI6 when she could.

Slowey felt frustrated that there was so little he could do till they got a more definite lead. They would have to send a man to Quimper, though. A relatively senior man—inspector or above—and, in view of this being the Pan-Celtic Congress, someone with good Irish.

Mickey Glinn was the obvious choice. He had all the qualifications, and was unlikely to protest at getting the assignment at such short notice. He was always eminently reasonable.

And yet . . . Slowey didn't feel altogether happy, sending Glinn. Slowey and he had been together in C3 (the section of the Garda Siochana concerned with subversion against the state) for over ten years. And during all that time there had been this slight tension—distrust would be too strong a word— between them. Maybe this was because Glinn had originally come from the coordinating and administrative headquarters in Phoenix Park, while Slowey had always been with the Special Detective Unit at Dublin Castle.

Whatever about it, Glinn it would have to be. Tomorrow Slowey would brief him on what Niles and Nora O Conaire had said. Tenuous as it was, Glinn was entitled to know.

Ballybrittas already. Slowey hunched his shoulders, shivered a little. The wind was buffeting the car, roaring over the grasslands and bunched trees like some bodeful mistral. To Slowey this would always be hostile territory: Injun country. Soon they would reach Monasterevin, where a few years ago two republicans had held the Dutch industrialist Dr. Tiede Herriman hostage for several days. Farther to the west, near Mountmellick, stood the ruin of the farmhouse where a booby-trap bomb had killed young Guard Clerkin and maimed some of his comrades. Yes, this was Injun country all right.

But whom was he kidding? It was all hostile country, this whole land of Ireland, for a man like him. Or so he sometimes felt. As an officer of the Special Branch, Slowey had to fight all the factions lumped together in the public mind as "the IRA." A game of cops and robbers, complicated by the fact that while only a small minority of Irish people approved of political violence themselves, a huge majority adored the romantic myth of the IRA. And every section of the establishment contained crypto-republicans, fellow-travelers who could betray you to the very men you were seeking. You never knew whom you were talking to.

Slowey slumped further in his seat and fumbled for a pack of cigarettes. Then he remembered: he had given up smoking a year ago. The old reflex operated whenever the pressure mounted—as it had, increasingly, this last year.

He sighed; wished he could be a bluff, not-for-me-to-reason-why type, but he lacked the temperament. Perhaps that was why he had flunked out of the seminary all those years ago. He suddenly remembered Robert Travers, the Anglo-Irish convert who'd been with him at the seminary. Travers had later run into Slowey when he was a young guard directing traffic at the end of O'Connell Street in Dublin. "Authority!" Travers had said. "Curiously, you evade it—and yet you really crave it!" And then he'd laughed and begun to hum "The Mountains of Mourne."

Maybe Travers, overclever as usual, had been right for once. Slowey worked for order in a cruel and anarchical situation. Worked, he hoped, with some of the compassion he might have displayed as a priest. Even now his lost vocation stood like a sunken reef in his mind. The spoiled priest thing didn't mean much anymore, but the first time he had come home to Galway wearing the blue uniform the neighbors had been shocked speechless. A spoiled priest was supposed to get himself off out of sight to England or the States, although one might occasionally creep in by the back-door as a National Teacher.

That was years ago. Slowey had never married, no more than if he had been a priest. If he had been ordained, he would have still been a curate, but promotion to parish priest would have been in sight by now.

Traveling back to Dublin this evening, his problems were perhaps more complex than those troubling a curate in an Irish country town. How much should he tell Glinn? Did he really trust Glinn—and if not, why not?

What was Seamus Dillon's role in this rumored kidnap of government ministers? What was his link with the Wednesday Committee? And—most delicate problem of all—how could Slowey get approval from his superiors for the kind of action that might become necessary without his colleagues in the Branch getting to know of it—any one of whom could be a spy for the Wednesday Committee.

Now they were into the very last leg of their journey: Miami. Tom reckoned it was something of a triumph—luck or judgment or both—to have gotten thus far during a gasoline famine of crisis proportions. Typically, his mother had not referred to the fact. Through all of her life father, husband, sons, had dealt with such problems without letting her know they existed.

Leaving Miami, of the vast overpass and shopping center, the new mansions of the Venezuelan oil barons, the geriatric hotels and the yellowed dying palm trees, Tom wondered what his mother found attractive in the place except perhaps Monsignor Bill's presence there. Anyway, there wasn't much farther to go now—the miles always seemed to go faster the more south you got.

His mother had always enjoyed this marathon drive down a continent, from New York to her home in Coral Gables, which was why Tom had suggested it this time, gas shortages notwithstanding. And of course he wanted to propitiate her: offer a sop for the fact that he'd agreed to go to Ireland with his Uncle Seamus.

Now, many hours and hundreds of miles later, he realized he'd made a rod for his own back in telling her at all. Better to have been sly about it and just *gone*, leaving Max Segal to tell her.

Characteristically, his mother had made little comment when he had broken the news to her in her room at the Drake Hotel. But no topic was ever finally closed with Kathleen Dillon. Not ever. Tom knew that from childhood experience. His mother was a monstrous repository of grievances. Her retrieval system for injuries, real or imagined, was totally effective, and could be activated in subtle and indirect ways years after the initial umbrage. No chance she wouldn't mention this again—she would consider his going to Ireland with Old Seamus an affront, coldly and callously inflicted. Nothing would convince her otherwise.

She had returned to the subject sooner than he had expected, at the very beginning of their journey, as they sat waiting, their car like a fly in glue in the logjam of traffic inching across the George Washington Bridge.

As he might have expected, she approached the topic obliquely. One of Monsignor Bill's friends was going over to Dublin for the Summer Show (she said). "She always goes. Except that in 1952 she had shingles and couldn't go."

"Really?"

Tom knew his mother didn't know the lady who had had shingles in 1952. She hardly met anyone now, but Monsignor Bill gave her a kind of vicarious social life with his endless, ongoing commentary on the doings of members of his flock.

After a moment his mother said, "I suppose it's possible you and your uncle might take in the Summer Show too? On this forthcoming trip?"

"We could at that." Tom nodded. "Sounds like a good idea."

"Would you be going to the Carrolton celebrations?"

"Why not?"

There had been silence then: a silence like a balloon gradually inflating with his mother's sense of grievance. Finally in a cold, tight voice she said, "What a strange perverse kind of man you are, Tom. You were well aware that I wanted you to go the Carrolton Inauguration to represent your poor brother Wendell—"

"Look, I—"

"You know how much that would mean to me."

"It's absurd," Tom said, "thinking I could 'represent' Wendell. A member of the United States Senate!"

"As far as I'm concerned," she said. "Wendell was going as a representative of our family. Of your father who worked so hard to make the Carrolton Institute a reality and never lived to see it. A representative of my forebears—the Quinlans and through them the FitzSimmons. We're actually kinsmen of the Carrolls of Carrolton!" She paused. "Doesn't that mean anything to you, Tom?"

"Of course it does," he said.

"Is it surprising, then, that I should wish you to take Wendell's place?" She paused. "That wish of mine was spurned—that's the hurting thing, Tom. And now you say quite casually you'll go to the inauguration with your uncle, a man who can only despise all Carrolton stands for."

"Really!" Tom said. "It's not like that—"

"Tom!" she cut in. "I can see right through you and do you know what I see? Selfishness. Just like when you were a little boy." She shook her head. "A boy who grew to be a man who joined the Marines and fought for his country in Vietnam. Don't think I don't admire you for that, that I'm not proud. And yet—spiritually"—she gestured with her hands—"I wonder if you ever grew up at all."

They drove on in silence. They were into New Jersey, cruising at an even sixty, before she spoke again. To Tom's relief, she didn't refer to his going to Ireland, but embarked on the kind of urbane chitchat he had heard her use with her friends in the East before she sequestered herself at Coral Gables. Soon she turned to a favorite theme: the moral decline of the United States of America. "You know what Monsignor Bill says? America will never heal its wounds until we stop worshiping false gods. Sure, we have an honest man in the White House now—but if we hadn't abandoned our ideals over the last twenty years, we should never have had anything else."

Tom nodded. His mother went on. "Was there ever a nation in history chased after false gods the way we do? And you know where most of those gods come from! Monsignor Bill always says there's more intellectual junk comes out California than good wholesome oranges." She shook her head. "You could go on listing them from here to Miami. Transcendental meditation. Erhard Sensitivity Training. Macrobiotic diet—"

"You're telling me they all come from there?"

"Everything unhealthy and cranky and bad you care to name. Including Richard Nixon. Of course I'm probably at least five years behind. Monsignor Bill says he can't keep up with all the crazy notions that keep pouring eastward."

She didn't attack the Irish issue again for many hours and miles after that. Then, crossing the Virginia state line, savoring what for Tom was always the first smell of the South with its greenery and laurel, she said, "You told me your uncle wants to see Ireland once again before he dies. Do you think I don't know the real reason he's going? Something to do with the IRA?"

"You know what his health is like," Tom said. "This really could be his last chance to go."

"His health! One thing I prophesy: he'll die in his bed. Not like the poor young men he's destroyed in the name of 'Irish liberty.' " She sighed and her next words came as a whisper: "I believe he even tried to involve Wendell in his scheming."

Later, when they were eating the routine honeybatter Southern fried chicken and collard greens at a huge motel complex off the highway, she said, "Tom— I'm going to tell you something you'll have cause to remember. Whatever your uncle has told you—whatever sentimental appeal he's made—once you get to Ireland, he'll try to involve you in whatever he's plotting—for he has to be plotting something. Well"—she paused and Tom had to respond to the fire in her eyes, the harsh-graven lines of her face—"let me tell you this. The plot will fail. As night follows day, it will fail. Irish plots always do."

He knew his mother would not detract from that prophecy by saying anything more, but now—with only a few miles to go before he delivered her into the womblike care of Mrs. McGuggin—he glanced again at her face: beautiful but set in implacable lines. It should have been easy to dismiss this as empty talk—the Bad Eye directed at Old Seamus, whom she'd always hated anyway— but in fact her words chilled Tom, struck at him with the force of a malignant curse.

🍀   🍀   🍀

Entering the courtyard of Trinity College, Dublin, Frankie emerged from reverie just in time to avoid colliding with a heavy young man who was running through the main gate into College Green.

She started to walk across the cobblestones toward the library. Since she returned from New York she had felt confused, bedeviled. Her relationship with Duane had been disorienting enough: now she had the image of Tom Dillon to set her senses spinning.

Frankie could have handled her emotions if it hadn't been for Duane. The night she got back to Dublin they had met at one of a series of venues: this one was in the Phoenix Park, ironically enough not far from the administrative headquarters of the Garda at the eastern end of the park. Frankie had told Duane that Seamus Dillon had not reached a decision; that, to agree, he must come to Quimper and meet with Lang, and that Dillon didn't know if he would be well enough to travel. Duane had taken the news calmly. "I'm sure he's genuinely undecided. And don't forget, he's an old man—he sees the world slipping away from him, it's not unnatural he wants to impose his will: make us wait." He paused. "I think it'll be yes."

When she had left Tom's apartment on Fifty-seventh Street she had promised herself that the sex with Duane was over, but of course the night of her return she had gone with Duane to Mick Lambert's scruffy pad near Trinity. She had told herself the thought of Tom would inhibit her with Duane, make Duane's coldly cerebral fucking distasteful to her, but it hadn't turned out like that. If anything it had been more exciting than ever. And with that fiendish sexual intuition of his, Duane had even known that she had been "unfaithful" to him: had whispered lewdly to her as he caressed her: Who was her New York lover? What was he like? Was he big? Did he satisfy her? How did he compare with Duane himself? With all her other lovers? (They didn't exist, of course.)

Only afterward did she reflect that she had not thought of the Other Frankie once. Of Tom, yes; but somehow, since New York, the image of her husband seemed dead, almost ossified in her mind.

Frankie's heart was thudding; there was a buzz in her ears; she didn't think she'd ever felt so tense. As she started up the steps of the library, she was afraid she might keel over in a faint. She wondered if the students who were thronging into the library noticed how pale she was. Usually she had a comforting sense of being invisible, in and around Trinity. The hundreds of students all dressed much as she did in jeans and casuals; she was older than most of them but that hardly showed. Anyway her protection was the fact that they were young and obsessed with their own concerns. They didn't have time for people-watching.

Frankie was in Trinity Library under another persona: her reader's ticket bore the name of Margaret Colebrook, a journalist from Hassocks, Sussex, England, engaged in researching a book on the Status of Women in Ireland (a working title). There were probably a hundred women engaged on similar projects at this moment, and yet, Frankie thought, a thousand books couldn't exhaust the subject. She had a kind of gentleman's agreement with Termagant Press (a gentleman's agreement with a feminist publisher?) and some time in the next three years she would deliver the book. One thing: the progress women's rights in Ireland had been making the last ten years, there was no risk of it being overtaken by events. This was a society where an elderly and ultra-montane bench of bishops denied young women the right to limit their fam-ilies—whether they were Catholic or Protestant. A society where there was no divorce, and where a husband could sue his wife's lover for "deprivation of services" (a view of a wife as a sexual chattel recently enthusiastically endorsed by the Irish judiciary), but where the wife of an unfaithful husband had no redress. A great portion of Irish matrimonial law was in fact the fossilized replica of its British equivalent prior to 1837.

Feminism was fine, more power to it, but Frankie had other things to do first. Meanwhile she had chosen this persona of Margaret Colebrook, which served her as a kind of magic cloak through all of her comings and goings in England and Ireland and, occasionally, Europe.

Margaret Colebrook had been created almost at random; only afterward had Frankie seen an unconscious, shaping rationale at work. Ms. Colebrook was the quintessential do-gooder, joining everything there was to be joined: Amnesty, the Howard League for Penal Reform, the National Council for Civil Liberties, and many more. Humorless, bespectacled, the living essence of Pro-test. And the irony lay in the fact that the British establishment would throw open doors to Margaret Colebrook, English Protestor, that would remain for-ever closed to the Irish-born Frances McNagan. Frankie went to see the Other Frankie in Parkhurst as Ms. Colebrook, member of the ELFPAPC [English League for Protest at Prison Conditions]. How fortunate that she spoke with the right kind of English accent. Any touch of Dublin and she'd have been finished before she started.

Neither the British nor the Irish police had ever bothered Frankie much, although she was still in their files. Margaret Colebrook's activities gave her a perfect cover for her real work for Eireann Amhain and, recently, for the Wednesday Committee. One irony she did not relish was the fact that she could function more or less undisturbed in the city of her birth as a visiting Englishwoman but not as Frankie McNagan. She dare not go and see her father at North Strand Road: that would have signaled her presence in Dublin to the Special Branch. Occasionally she would meet him on the drained, grass-covered Royal Canal bank at Phibsborough. Old Peadar would be sitting on a bench, a pensioner enjoying the sunshine. Frankie would pretend this was just a casual encounter, talking with him for perhaps half an hour, never quite at ease, always wondering if she was being watched.

She reached the top floor of the library. She actually seemed less out of breath after climbing three flights of stairs. She settled down at her usual place. The huge window in front of her gave her a view across the football field; she could see buses moving slowly up Nassau Street.

She liked Trinity library. It retained some of the genial, scholarly atmosphere elderly people would tell you the British Museum Reading Room had once possessed. And yet whenever she passed through the main gate on College Green into the cobbled square—a scene that immediately evoked the Anglo-Irish mythos that *was* Trinity in most people's minds—or sat in the dark-paneled chapel that had actually seen Swift and Berkeley, Frankie felt a slight unease. A suspicion that such gracious groves of academe were really refuges from a war that was being fought elsewhere. Fine to walk with the ghosts of Sheridan and Goldsmith, but what about the other Dublin a mile or two away? There you would find broken houses, rotting rooms where old folk cowered in silence, waiting for their door to be kicked in again, where boys of eleven and twelve sat on the steps of the Custom House every night, threatened by the winos and degenerates who prowled the city after midnight. There were said to be several thousand children sleeping rough in Dublin every night. Every time Frankie thought of *that* Dublin—the black pullulating core of the city—she seemed to hear a voice-over, pitched with just the right touch of blarney for the visiting Yanks, talking about Ireland of the Welcomes.

Frankie took a manila folder out of her carrier-bag. She didn't feel much like work this morning, but go through the motions, right?

Apart from her agonizing about Tom and Duane and the Other Frankie, she was worried about the possible failure of her mission. Four days now and Duane had heard nothing from Seamus Dillon. Suppose he decided to deny them the resources of the foundation? Duane and the committee were too committed to Lang and his plans not to go ahead now. They *had* to go ahead. And yet—if they acted without the resources of the foundation? The Rebellion of 1916 might have succeeded if the Irish had received the arms the Germans had shipped them in the *Aud*—which ended up on the bed of the ocean, scuttled near Cobh. If there was one lesson history had to teach the Irish, it was that they had never learned from their mistakes.

Tom Dillon and his uncle arrived too late to attend the official opening of the Pan-Celtic Congress at Quimper and thus missed Le Maire's speech. He welcomed the assembled Celts and then enlarged that welcome to include anyone possessing "the Celtic approach to life."

An agreeable speech, but some of those present would have preferred a more political orientation. Fine, to generalize about Celtic sensitivity, but what about devolution in Scotland and Wales? A lecturer in Cymric studies at Cardiff thought Le Maire should have spoken of the deadening pressures exerted by the EEC toward linguistic and cultural uniformity—so threatening to the Celtic minorities in the community.

But no one could deny the organizers had worked hard to make the congress a success. Sitting on the platform with Le Maire this morning were the professor of Welsh at Oxford University; a nonagenarian Scottish novelist who had been involved with the theft of the Scone Stone from Westminster Abbey many years before; the world's greatest authority on the Cornish language, from Princeton; an elderly Irish actress who had once broken a contract with Louis B. Mayer in order to play *Saint Joan* in Dublin in the Irish language.

On this, the first day of the congress, there would be a folk festival, chess and wrestling competitions, and the international hurling-shinty match between Ireland and Scotland. There would be a talk-ins with a panel of Breton, Welsh, Irish, Manx, Cornish, and Scottish representatives, on ways in which the use of the Celtic languages could be extended throughout Europe. Ceili were nearly continuous around the clock, and tomorrow there would be a song contest with each of the races represented putting forward a newly composed song in their own language. More talk-ins would discuss the problems of maintaining a Celtic identity in a hostile, increasingly uniform world. Thus O Dunnacha Duane would chair a discussion on what chance the Irish language had of getting accepted as an official language in the European Parliament. Finally, on the last day of the Congress, *The Three Queens of Cornwall* would be performed—the traditional pageant associated with Quimper for centuries.

Putting on the role of old-fashioned American in Europe—"A Henry James American," as he put it to Seamus—Tom had already walked around the town, taking in the sights. The Cathedral of Saint Corentin. The Museum of Breton Art. King Gradlon had given the land the name of Cornouaille in memory of the Cornwall he had fled. So the Cornish ought to be here in force, but so far as Tom could judge, the Irish outnumbered everyone else. Not that he'd have known a Cornish accent if he'd heard one. Already they'd gotten into conversation with a group of traditional musicians in a sidewalk café. Tom asked them if they were from Wales and—to Seamus' amusement—they said they were from Cork.

Indeed, Old Seamus was at the very top of his form. Any doubts Tom might have had about the rightness of his decision to accompany the old boy to Europe had been dissolved. He noticed the color in his uncle's cheeks, the glint in his eye. What had happened to the extinguished, lackluster figure slumped back against hospital pillows? Certainly Seamus was a man revived.

Tom was fond of his uncle. He always had related well to him and this had always irked his mother. He was delighted to be here in Europe with him. But if he were to be totally honest, he couldn't claim this as his only motivation: to be along to hold the old boy's hand while they went to Quimper and later to Ireland. That could have been, in a way, an excuse—though Tom certainly didn't need any excuse to take a trip to Europe. He had the time; he had the money; he had—as the old standard had it—a lull in his life.

He resisted the idea that his coming here had anything to do with Frankie McNagan. He liked her; he loved to talk with her—something unusual in his recent experience; the sex with her was marvelous. Above all she was *different*. But he mustn't let his delight in her difference drag him into some romantic fantasy.

He resisted, too, the thought that he knew very well Frankie was involved in whatever cloak-and-dagger drama his uncle had come to Europe to direct—or at least witness, and it might therefore be possible to make contact with her again. He wasn't about to chase any woman around Europe—even Frankie. In fact, certainly not Frankie, a professionally elusive character, a career conspirator.

Anyway here he was. He was going to enjoy himself. His uncle had gone back to their hotel to rest for a while. Tom would walk around a little longer before he met with his uncle for lunch. Already he had begun to swim in the pervasive ambience of the congress. A group of Breton folk-dancers brushed past him: the women in black dresses with satin aprons brilliantly embroidered in peacock colors and wearing high, starched lace headgear, the men in black suits and beribboned hats. Tom waved to them. They waved back, shouting greetings he did not understand.

This was the real face of the Pan-Celtic Congress: Tom knew that. But this wasn't what his uncle was here for. Old Seamus was using all this as a front. But whatever he *was* here for—whatever it was put the spring back into his step and the glint in his eye—he had to keep it to himself. Tom wanted no part of it.

☘ ☘ ☘

Frankie and Duane had arranged to meet at a bar called the Gradlon. Frankie had wondered if it was good security for the two of them to meet openly in a bar. Any of the hundreds of people attending the congress—which had to include someone from the Irish Special Branch—could stroll in and see them together. Duane had chuckled. "Odd you should mention security," he said. "We have our own security officer here at the congress. It's him I want you to meet."

Frankie wondered what he meant. She was still wondering as she sat here in the Gradlon. Its name might evoke King Gradlon's flight from Cornwall, but this long horseshoe-shaped bar was as French as a Dubonnet advertisement— all gilt mirrors and twinkling, exquisitely shaped bottles. To her surprise, the place was only a third full. Where were all the harpists and the ilen pipers, the *senachai* [storytellers] and shinty-players who thronged the town?

There he was, Duane, coming down the narrow stairs that led into the bar, buccaneerlike as ever with his black beard and flowing hair.

"Frankie! What are you drinking?"

"I have a drink, thank you. Duane—what's this about?"

"I'll get my drink first. Tell me—how's your book progressing? The Sexual Deprivation of Irish Women—that's it, isn't it?"

He always liked to counter a question with a question—especially when he knew you were bursting with curiosity.

"What's this about a 'security officer?' " she demanded.

"He'll be here in a moment. Excuse me."

He went over to the bar, was served and back to her in a few moments. He had a large whiskey for himself. It was a gift he had: commanding instant service in a bar.

"Slainte!" he said. "Prosit! Gesundheit! Skal!"

"All of those," she said.

She was wearing a green print dress with a petticoat. Duane leaned foward and lifted the flounce of the petticoat. She struck his hand away with pretended outrage. He sighed, a long mock-lecherous sigh. "What exquisite ankles!" he breathed. He stared at her, breathing with exaggerated heaviness, moistening his lips with the tip of his tongue. Frankie suddenly exploded into violent giggles. Duane puffed out his cheeks in pretended anger.

"Is your wife back at the hotel?" Frankie asked. "You brought her to Quimper of course?"

"That's a blow from a blunt instrument!"

In fact Frankie often wondered about his wife. How much she knew. How much she cared—or resented. "A shy creature emerging fearfully from the undergrowth." He'd described her thus to Frankie soon after they met, and Frankie had been furious on Mara Duane's behalf—even though she, Frankie, was technically the Other Woman. (One of many, she'd always suspected.) Only in Ireland, presumably, could a man indulge in such hoary Don Juanism.

None of this solved the mystery of Mara Duane, though, isolated in a big old house in Chapelizod on the outskirts of Dublin, caring for five children and married to Duane. Was she complaisant or merely long-suffering?

Duane was looking toward the stairs.

"There he is," he said.

He was grinning and nodding to someone. He half rose; then sat down again.

Frankie turned and saw the man making his way toward them through the now more crowded bar. A moment later he stood beside them: a small, red-haired man of forty in a rumpled business suit.

"Allow me to introduce . . ." Duane murmured, dropping his voice to a melodramatic whisper: "Inspector Michael Glinn of C3, Special Detective Branch, Dublin Castle."

"I knew Frankie would enjoy the irony of this," Duane said. "This is really— shall we say, *Irish?*" He grinned hugely. "The officer assigned by the Special Branch to track down the mysterious Wednesday Committee is himself a member of that committee."

Glinn didn't smile. "Amusing, isn't it?" he said. "What is not so amusing is that my immediate superior, Slowey, has been given some kind of lead. A tipoff."

"What sort of tipoff?"

"Not the right story exactly," Glinn said. "But some idea of it. Enough to be dangerous." He paused. "He got the information through two different channels, as I say. Nora O Conaire? Frank Niles?" Glinn shrugged. "Neither of them totally reliable, to put it mildly. Even so . . ."

Frankie said, "What rank is this . . . Slowey, is it?"

"Superintendent. My boss in C3. I've worked with him for years."

Duane asked, "What's he like? A dedicated bloodhound? A super-sleuth?"

Glinn said, "He's dogged. No whiz kid but stays with it." He frowned. "A little unpredictable. Some officers . . . I could tell you the way they'd go and plan accordingly. Not Slowey. Of course he's a spoiled priest. They call him Blessed Cormac Slowey in the Branch."

Glinn took a drink of his Vichy water. Frankie thought there was a vague, lost-dog sadness about him.

"This leak of information," Duane said. "How do we stand? Tell me the worst and the best aspects."

"The best aspect is the sources," Glinn said. "Forget O Conaire. Anything she gets is at random. Almost literally, she's an eavesdropper. Sits in pubs

where the boyos congregate and listens . . ." He frowned. "She could actually be killed one of these days. Niles—well, that is much more serious. He
apparently heard something from Liam Bogan, and Bogan just had to have
anything he knew from a member of the committee. That's the worst aspect: it
means there's a loosemouth on the committee."

"The oath," Duane said gravely. "The oath must be taken. This proves
it."

"I agree," Frankie said.

"What else?" Duane asked.

Glinn said, "I consider the most dangerous information Slowey has is what
Niles told him about the operation being performed by strangers, foreigners."

"But that's so vague!" Duane said. "What kind of foreigners? There are
thousands of foreign tourists in Ireland every summer. Who's Slowey going to
look for?"

Glinn nodded. "True enough."

"And, 'foreigners,' " Duane persisted. "I may be wrong, but to me that never
suggests Americans—always Frenchmen or Germans? Continentals of some
kind?"

Glinn nodded again.

"You said Niles mentioned Seamus Dillon?" Frankie said. "Surely that's the
worst aspect of all?"

"Not necessarily," Glinn said. "Old Dillon's been on file at the Castle so
long it kind of takes the curse off him, you know? He's been at the patriot
game for fifty years now. What can he do that's new?"

"I suppose that's true," Duane said. "Well—now we know the worst. What's
our strategy, Mick?"

"I have to bring Slowey back something from this congress," Glinn said. "If
I tell him there's absolutely nothing cooking here and everyone is just obsessed
with shinty matches and ilen pipes . . ." He shook his head. "He could begin
to wonder about me."

"Obviously," Duane said.

"You may not agree with this suggestion," Glinn went on, "it's based on the
fact that old Seamus Dillon *is* so well known at the Castle." He shrugged.
"Grounded in the argument that he's been plotting and planning for so long
that nothing he can come up with at this hour of his life can possibly succeed.
Ergo, that this plot can't be taken too seriously."

"Do you think Slowey would swallow that?" Frankie asked doubtfully.

"What I'm suggesting," Glinn said, "is that on my return I tell Slowey that I believe Seamus Dillon may be involved in something; that I've had a tail on him since he arrived in Quimper; that he has in fact met with representatives of some foreign activist group. Basque liberation maybe," Glinn added. "More plausible than the PFLP."

Duane said, "You mean set Seamus Dillon up as a stalking-horse for the Special Branch?"

"For Slowey, anyway," Glinn said. "Takes the heat off everyone else. And once he's given Lang the location of all the caches—which presumably he will do while he's here—his active involvement is over. No doubt he would endorse that himself."

Duane shook his head. "I see your argument, Mick, but I don't like it."

"Neither do I," Frankie said.

"All right," Glinn said. "The ball is in your court."

Frankie said, "What about me?"

"What?" Duane said.

"Why not tell Slowey that I've been in contact with ETA members here in Quimper? It's the same thing. And now I've been to New York and seen Seamus Dillon, my active function is over. Till the day of the coup, anyway."

Glinn looked doubtful. "Might work. After all, you never come to Ireland. You haven't been seen in Dublin for several years." He smiled for the first time since he had met them. "I don't think the Branch knows about Ms. Cole-brook."

Frankie felt a sudden chill. "But you do?"

"Don't worry. Private information," Glinn said.

Now they all three relaxed. The intensity of their low-voiced exchanges had made them oblivious of the other people in the bar. The Gradlon was very crowded now, but Frankie didn't mind. The babel of voices, the mass of people all around them was reassuring: made her feel anonymous.

She said, "How fortunate we are to have you, Inspector. God must be on our side."

Duane said, "You knew we had someone in the Branch."

"Tell me," Frankie said. "What will happen if someone sees Inspector Glinn of the Special Branch talking to two such subversive characters as Duane and me?"

"Easy," Glinn said. "I shall report your presence here at the congress; say I questioned you both in an informal manner. The difference was, Duane appeared to be clean; but something you said, Mrs. McNagan, aroused my suspicions and this led to my putting a tail on you."

"Fine," Frankie said.

"As a matter of interest," Duane said. "What other species of spooks are haunting this congress? There must be *some*. The DST?"

Glinn shook his head. "They are aware of our existence, I expect. But you know the French. They don't give a damn about Ireland or the IRA. If we were the Strollard Kommunour Breizh [a Breton nationalist group], then they'd be interested."

"The Brits then?" Frankie said.

"They've got someone here," Glinn said. "Sort of. Girl called Annabel Rayne. She's been in Dublin about a year now. She calls herself a journalist but she's really a bit of a whore." Glinn pronounced the word facetiously as "whoo-er." "Last few months she's been doing a line with Marta Troy—so now we call Annabel the Dyke's Delight up at the Castle."

"She doesn't sound very formidable," Duane said.

"She's almost a joke," Glinn replied.

"Anyway, she's here, in Quimper?" Frankie asked.

Glinn nodded. Duane offered him another drink but he declined. "I must leave you," he said. "Got to see how my sergeant's getting on."

He stood up, and just at that moment Frankie saw Tom Dillon at the other end of the bar. She stared at him over the sea of heads. She didn't know what to read in his face. Surprise? Pleasure? It looked like sadness.

He must have been watching her for several minutes. Frankie suddenly felt tense. What was the matter with her? She'd gone to bed with Tom Dillon: a one-night stand. Suddenly the phrase was repulsive to her.

Now Tom had reached their table. "Hi," he said.

"Hullo." Duane exuded friendliness.

"Tom!" Her greeting sounded hollow in her own ears. "Duane—this is Tom Dillon. Seamus Dillon's nephew."

"Of course!" Duane stood up; gripped Tom's hand. "Will you have a drink?"

"No, thank you," Tom said. "I have to meet my uncle and I'm late already."

"I think I'll have another," Duane said. "Frankie?"

She shook her head and he was off to the bar, leaving her with Tom.

"Frankie," he said. "What's this? A miracle? I see you again!"

She was silent for a moment. Then she said, "Tom—there's no future in us. There can't be. I'm married."

"Was that a problem in New York?"

"My husband is in prison. I didn't tell you that."

"What about Captain Bluebeard over there?" Tom nodded toward Duane at the bar.

"Someone I work with."

Tom nodded. "Of course." Now he sounded angry. "I suppose when you're not on some secret mission you live in a commune along with a lot of guys and dolls with beards and granny-glasses? And I suppose an asshole like Bluebeard gets to screw you on demand, like it's in the rules or something?" He paused. "Don't worry, Frankie. I won't bother you anymore."

The meeting of the Wednesday Committee with Lang was to take place not at Quimper but at Lorient, some miles away. Seamus felt doubtful about this. Why discard the automatic cover which the congress provided?

On his way to Lorient, Seamus wondered who would be present at the meeting. A few old friends probably, and one or two who might be a little less than friendly. Had Michael McClymont forgiven him for that rebuff over the foundation? Irishmen have long memories. But Duane had never mentioned that McClymont had quit, and now McClymont was even wealthier and more influential than he had been when Seamus turned down his request.

McClymont was that archetypal Irish figure, a "returned Yank" (in Ireland not a native-born American, but a returned emigrant). During thirty years in San Francisco he had made several million dollars, first in trucking and later in the manufacture of paints and dyes. Fifteen years ago he had sold out and returned to Ireland. He owned thousands of acres of prime land in County Meath and was on the boards of many companies, but his biggest investment had been in the war chest of the largest of the Irish political parties. During the last decade this had paid off, not in political office (which McClymont didn't want), but in backstairs power: something he relished above all else.

It was this political clout that had enabled McClymont to facilitate the building up of the foundation. When Seamus sold out to the huge Rossman Corporation, he had retained Penrith Pharmaceuticals Ireland as a personal stake in Irish industry: a gesture toward the country he loved. Thus, when he began establishing the foundation, Penrith represented a base on Irish soil. Their bank accounts in Ireland could be used for all financial transactions. A warehouse in the grounds of the Kenmare Plant served as a clearing center through which many of the arms shipments passed. (If the labor force or technical staff noticed anything unusual, they gave no sign.)

Mostly Seamus had used large freight containers. Thanks to Justice for Ulster supporters among the Teamsters and other waterfront unions, these had been gotten off safely from New York and other Eastern ports and routed to the port of Dublin. Since Penrith Ireland received most of its materials from the Rossman Corporation in New Jersey, many of the containers did in fact contain chemical supplies as their documentation indicated. But McClymont was warned of the impending arrival of a "red" container—holding arms or explosives for the foundation—and when it reached Dublin he swung into action. Exactly how, Seamus had never inquired; but McClymont had won some kind of customs immunity for these consignments, claiming no doubt that he was freeing an Irish enterprise from the stranglehold of bureaucracy. And while the Irish Government knew Seamus' reputation as a republican agitator, they had to propitiate him in his other role of American businessman who had had the vision to build a plant in Ireland.

Seamus had used other methods to get supplies in, of course. More direct methods: the consignment transferred from a freighter on the high seas to an Irish trawler which would then land them at some deserted place on the southwest coast.

He owed a lot to McClymont, though, and that made the coolness between them all the sadder. Seamus wondered whether McClymont had any role to play in the coup Lang and Duane were planning. Seamus felt intensely curious about Lang: at one level he wanted to be convinced by him, at another felt full of doubt. If he were honest with himself he knew he'd *had* to come to Quimper—he couldn't have kept away—and yet he was afraid Liam Costelloe and a lot of other people would regard his coming to Europe as a panic flight before Hogg's possible revelations at the grand jury.

Well, let them think that if they wished. A month or six weeks and he'd be back in the States: he'd face the music then. Meanwhile he had more important concerns.

Lang had chosen to meet with the committee at the Hôtel Vieux Colombier, which stood on a narrow street that had escaped the bombing and subsequent redevelopment of Lorient. Passing through the lobby, Seamus saw palms in pots and posters advertising a brand of vermouth no longer made.

A creaking elevator carried him to the top floor. There, two husky young men studied a file that held a recent photograph of Seamus. Then they asked, "An bhfuil to ag dul go dti an cuirt?" [Are you going to the court?] Seamus replied, "Ni cuirt gan acht, gan reacht, gan riail." [Not a court without law or statute or rule.] These code lines came from Merriman's *The Midnight Court*, that masterpiece of the hidden, proscribed world of the eighteenth-century Irish bards.

Meanwhile the elevator had brought up a tall, white-haired man, a priest. For a second Seamus wondered; then he remembered: Father Maurice Wenham—An tAthair Muiris [Father Maurice] to anyone in the movement. An tAthair's life had been devoted to two obsessions: medieval theology—he had written a definitive work *To Cut With Occam's Razor: Studies in the Minor Schoolmen*—and Irish republicanism. Seamus had met him first at Joe McGarrity's house in Philadelphia, not long before Joe's death.

The priest recognized Seamus too. They shook hands and the young men ushered them both into a large room that was already full of people.

The room held few surprises for Seamus. No Michael McClymont. No Peadar Mahoney either, but then age and ill health prevented him from traveling.

It was easy to pick out the active members of the committee from those who might be described as elders of the cause: those whose membership of the committee gave it authority among the thousands of submerged republicans throughout Ireland.

Oldest of the elders was Catherine Cudahy. Tiny, birdlike, and very deaf, she was a link with the Ireland of Yeats and Gogarty and Maud Gonne. Seamus noticed that she sat apart from everyone else, a half-smile on her face as if she were listening to music no one else could hear.

As assertive as Catherine Cudahy was withdrawn, Liam O Docartai was by now as inactive as she was. Seamus had served with him under Sean Gaynor in the Civil War. Like Seamus, O Docartai had escaped to the States after the defeat of the anti-Treaty forces, but returned to Ireland a few years later. With his red face and thick white eyebrows he looked like the cattle jobber from Kerry he had once been.

At O Docartai's elbow stood a tall, balding man in his early fifties. This was Philip Hurnan, who used the nom de guerre "Sean MacSaoirse." From the Anderstown district of Belfast, he had served a long term of imprisonment for shooting an RUC [Royal Ulster Constabulary] sergeant. Seamus supposed he would have to include MacSaoirse among the now inactive elders of the committee.

Certainly among the active were Maurice Slane and his wife, Maidred. In their forties, they ran a crafts and souvenir shop in Connemara, selling everything from a plastic leprechaun to a bolt of Donegal tweed. Slane had led a column during Sean Cronin's border campaign of 1957, but that was so long ago that Special Branch interest in him must have declined almost to zero. He would be one of six regional organizers briefing republicans throughout the twenty-six counties prior to the coup.

Seamus didn't see Duane or Frankie McNagan. Nor, of course, Dick Grogan. Seamus could never understand how a small outfit like Eireann Amhain could survive the antagonism that existed between Duane in Dublin and Grogan in Belfast. He knew Duane blamed Grogan for the Other Frankie's conviction and imprisonment. Seamus wondered what Grogan's attitude was to the plan they were here to discuss.

Seamus circled the room, greeting everyone. He didn't want to have much talk with any of them prior to hearing Lang's presentation. He knew he might still have to act the man from Missouri: a dissenting voice.

He was exchanging a few words with Austin Gaines, a lawyer and TD (he was a member of the same party as McClymont), spoken of as a future judge, when a tall man with blond hair and flowing mustaches stepped forward and grasped Seamus' hand. "Mr. Dillon—I've been waiting to meet you for twenty years."

Seamus realized that this was Colonel Blake Darrell. He looked what he was: a soldier, decorated for bravery while serving with the United Nations Peacekeeping Force in the Lebanon; an athlete, three times capped for Ireland in the Rugby Football game; and a horseman, who had represented Ireland at the Olympic Games as a show-jumper.

His presence in this room tonight showed how deeply the Wednesday Committee had infiltrated the Irish establishment at every level. People like O Docartai, McSaoirse, Frankie McNagan—and of course Seamus himself— were known to the Special Branch, on file at the Castle, but Colonel Darrell was thought to be apolitical: a simple soldier who would do his duty regardless. He didn't exist so far as the Branch was concerned—and yet there was no more fanatic member of the movement in this room tonight.

Suddenly there was a lull in the babel of talk. Seamus saw Duane and Frankie enter through the battered double doors at the end of the room. Duane stood to one side, with a slightly self-mocking air of ceremony. Then two men entered. The first, tall and fair, in a business suit. The second, older, with gray hair and a high-cheekboned, almost Egyptian-looking face.

The room had gone quite silent when Duane said, "Ladies and gentlemen, fellow members of this committee, may I introduce Mr. Lang?"

"Do you know what a Harvey Wallbanger is?" Tom asked.

"But naturally, sir! One Harvey Wallbanger coming up, sir."

This barman at the Gradlon was dark, ingratiating, saurian. Smashed as he was, Tom could still make with the ole mot juste. *Saurian* was sure as hell what this barman was.

He'd come straight back to the Gradlon after lunch with his uncle. He hadn't wanted to talk, but then neither had Seamus. Obviously this mysterious meeting tonight was casting its shadow.

Now Tom had reached a certain classic stage of being smashed, when self-pity is mitigated by detachment. He could still imagine Captain Bluebeard in bed with Frankie, but the keen edge of his jealousy was blunted.

"Harvey Wallbanger!" a voice beside him echoed. "Harvey Ballscrusher, more like! My dear sir, what kind of a drink is that?"

This was from a little elderly man perched on the next stool. Tom hadn't noticed him before. "Whatever it is, it's muck," the little man went on. "There is only one real drink." He indicated his own glass. "Uisce beatha—the water of life! Uisce beatha—the wine of my forefathers."

"I guess you mean Irish whiskey," Tom said.

The little man said accusingly, "You're an American!"

"Right," Tom said.

"Let me ask you one thing," the little man said. "Would you deny that in the last forty years the Americans have taken over from the British as the world's number one bullies, brainwashers, and general bastards?"

"I think I would deny that," Tom said mildly.

"No good denying it!" The little man goggled affrontedly through thick spectacles. "You're an obvious American. Got an American face. Only thing— you don't wear glasses. All Americans wear glasses."

"I'm not denying I'm American," Tom said. "I'm just denying what you said about Americans."

"Of course the Red Indians didn't wear glasses," the little man said. "Nor, I have to admit, did the Firbolgs."

"Firbolgs! How about that?" Tom said.

"No doubt, like most Americans, you claim Irish descent?" The little man shook his head. "Irish-Americans! I'm afraid Ireland has never exported the best of its citizens."

"Is that so?" Tom asked. Snobbishness took strange forms. Was this a variant of his mother pre-Famine Irish?

"Your ancestors now," the little man said. "Would I be right in saying they would be from Munster?"

"Right."

"Kerry?" the little man demanded. "God knows, haven't you the obstinate Caliban's cut of a Kerryman!"

"You're not far out," Tom said. "From the Cork-Kerry borders near Ballyvourney. That would be my father's family," he added.

"That's a Gaeltacht," the little man said. "But the West Cork Irish hasn't the fine blas of the Donegal or the Connacht Irish." Then he demanded, "Isn't your name O'Sullivan?"

Tom shook his head.

"Odd," the man said. "I had it firmly established in my mind that you were an O'Sullivan. You certainly don't look like a McCarthy."

"No," Tom said. Then after a moment he added, "My name is Dillon."

"Ah, of course!" the little man exclaimed, so keenly that he struck Tom with a note of unease. Who was this guy? Why was he asking these suddenly pointed questions? "I have you now," the little man went on. "You're one of the Dillons from the townland of Ballinmageery, just north of Ballyvourney, some of whom emigrated to America circa 1850."

"Yes," Tom murmured. "I'm sure you're right."

"Scratch an Irishman and you scratch a genealogist!" the man said. "I had to trace you out! Now let me buy you a drink."

Tom declined and levered himself off his stool. He had to get away. Here was this nut, encountered casually in a bar in Quimper, naming Tom's ancestors. That was the Irish for you, but somehow he wasn't crazy about it. When he came out of the men's room, he would just slip away.

He'd gotten to the bottom of the stairway when a female voice said, "Excuse me—"

He turned. He'd noticed her already when he'd come back to the Gradlon this afternoon. An English rose. In her late twenties or early thirties: long-legged, rangy, a genuine blonde.

"I'm terrible, but I can't remember your name," she said. "But I feel convinced we've met before."

A flagrant pickup, but why not? Tom remembered she'd been with a man when he noticed her earlier.

"Of course we have," Tom said.

"Can't think where, though. Have you been in London lately?"

Tom said, "Strange we should be vague about such a memorable occasion."

☘ ☘ ☘

After twenty minutes Seamus decided that Lang was probably just as good as everyone said he was. But he tried to keep a tiny skeptical corner open in his mind.

Lang had started off quietly, grinning boyishly as he said, "You all know *why* we've dreamed up this plan. Now let me show you how we can make it work."

He started by defining the conditions for a coup d'etat. An analysis of eighty coups in forty-five countries showed that certain factors were shared by all those that had succeeded.

"Success factor one," Lang said. "The target country must be independent politically." He grinned. "Maybe some of you are gonna tell me Ireland is not truly independent in economic terms. But militarily you are. No other country can intervene effectively to prevent this coup. Certainly not Britain. They're overextended, both in Northern Ireland and in NATO."

Success factor two, Lang said, demanded that administrative power in the target country be highly centralized. Nowhere in the developed world was government more concentrated geographically than it was in Dublin.

Success factor three: social and economic conditions had to be such as to confine political participation to a small section of the population. Lang grinned. "Nice one!" Even official statistics conceded that nowhere in Western Europe was a higher proportion of a country's wealth held in fewer hands. "The banks, the big farmers, one or two multinationals—they have the rest of you over the barrel," Lang continued. "And the two main political parties both effectively represent those interests—and no one else's! So you get a big population disillusioned, apathetic—particularly the young, the college kids. Parliamentary democracy is a crock of shit to them, right? Of course this is true all over Europe, but most of all in Ireland."

"Success factor four," Lang said, "I'm not about to spend much time on." An unsuccessful war or major defeat provided a favorable psychological climate for a coup d'etat. Lang shrugged. "Well—that's too obvious for comment. Don't tell me that the continued occupation of a part of Ireland by Britain hasn't left its scars."

"By God, yes—it has!" Colonel Darrell burst out. "Remember Bloody Sunday in Derry? I'll never forget the men under my command at that time. When they first heard the news they were stunned. And then angry. That they could do nothing."

"Thank you, Colonel," Lang said. "And that is also relevant to success factor five: widespread infiltration of the armed forces of the target country. You've just heard from Colonel Darrell, and you know that a senior member

of the Irish Special Branch is also one of us. In fact we have substantial support
in both the army and the police. And of course—this always happens in a coup
d'etat—they will be joined by most of their comrades once the coup is seen to
be successful."

Lang paused and then continued: "In Ireland every success factor exists.
Any modern state may seem solid, immovable—but that is an illusion. The
present Irish Government sits on a knife edge. To topple it we shall use the
technique of judo, by which a feather-light leverage can displace a vast boulder
and send it crashing down the mountain."

☘ ☘ ☘

"You know what Sheilah Graham said?" Annabel Rayne asked.

"What did Sheilah Graham say?" Tom demanded.

"That American men are the best lovers in the world. But American women
are the worst."

"Uh-huh? Wasn't Ms. Graham originally an English lady?" Tom said.
"Does she say English ladies are the best?"

But Annabel only smiled, reflecting that this pre-bed badinage was a bit
more civilized than usual. Such seduction-chat had a period charm, like a
pavane or gavotte. Mostly they just asked her to fuck. Tom must be one of
those old-fashioned Middle Americans you heard about.

"More important," Tom said, "you didn't order yet. Cautriade? Galettes?
Or both? I suppose you can have both."

"Tom, darling—I don't know anything about Breton food."

"Neither do I—except it's always fish. So why not simply have lobster?"

"What are galettes?"

"A kind of buckwheat pancake, I believe," Tom said.

"Then—cautriade? I'm always attracted by the element of chance."

"Right." Tom signaled the waiter.

They had come to this café after she had rescued him from that crazy little
man at the Gradlon. She had been tailing Dillon all day, and very tiring she'd
found it. She wasn't complaining, though. At least this was a real assignment:
following a man and picking him up and taking him back to bed in order to
get information out of him. Except that she only knew one line of conduct to
pursue with a man in bed—and that didn't include getting information out of
him. Afterward, she supposed. But what if he just wanted to go to sleep?

But at least it was some kind of action. Mostly in Dublin she just floated around like a dead goldfish in a bowl, getting herself involved with all kinds of repulsive people for no obvious purpose. Of course the SIS [Secret Intelligence Service] weren't paying her full time. For all what a former SIS director had called their "friendly, fatherly interest" in Ireland, they didn't believe in wasting money on their Irish operation. Not if Annabel was anything to go by. If all the British spooks in Ireland got as little money as she did and—she had to admit—provided as little information, the queen's messenger (or "bagman") who every week traveled from London to the British Embassy on Dublin's Merrion Road would have little worth carrying back on his return journey.

She'd been glad to get this assignment to Quimper. Her life in Dublin was dreary beyond words. Her control met her once a week, always somewhere like the Zoo in Phoenix Park or the center of St. Stephen's Green. Meeting him, she was always terrified of being observed by the Irish Special Branch or—worse again—the IRA. He was a meager, duck-footed man with a Belfast accent. Briefing her for Quimper, he had shown her photographs of Seamus Dillon and his nephew Tom, adding that the old man was one of the godfathers of the IRA in the States. Something was being planned at Quimper, and she was to try her best to latch on to the nephew, Tom Dillon. "He likes women," her control said, as if it were some special taste, esoteric and depraved.

Well, she was doing all right so far. Dillon had proposed a meal and, after that, bed must loom. But bed achieved, how did she wheedle any information out of him? "Listen!" her control had said. "Will you just listen to him? That's a moment when any man likes to boast a little. Ears and eyes, girl! Use them!"

Maybe. But if she didn't, what the hell? Sucks to MI6 anyway! The laugh was on them. Even the few quid they paid her was money down the drain. No one could be a worse agent than she was.

She glanced at Tom. She liked him. In fact she fancied him. He had sobered up a lot this last half hour. Bad for Ze Spy Annabel, but good for Ze Woman Annabel, no? She put her hand out to caress his cheek; then stopped. He was very dark, a Black Irishman: he would really need to shave twice a day. She thought with sudden excitement of that iron-black stubble rasping against her cheek. How good to have a man's hardness after the fevered, hysterical lovemaking of Marta Troy. Poor Marta. Of course, like everyone else, she hung around Marta for what she could get, but Marta was perfectly well aware of that. The ripoff was mutual—perhaps it always was, in all human relationships?—and Annabel had the feeling that Marta really wanted something else, which she did not choose to mention to Annabel.

The waiter came up. Tom started to give his order but the waiter interrupted him. "Pardon me. This man outside. There is a message. Mistaire Dillon? You are Mistaire Dillon?"

"That's right."

"It is for you, sir, then, that he asks."

Tom looked puzzled. "Excuse me," he said and followed the waiter out.

In the foyer a man stood with his back to the café entrance, staring out into the street.

"Yes?" Tom said. The man turned. It was the elderly nut from the Gradlon.

"Hullo, Mr. Dillon."

"They said there was a message—" Tom began.

"Quite right." The man came up close. "There is a message. Very urgent. Would you mind stepping inside?"

He indicated a telephone booth at the corner of the foyer.

"Why?" Tom demanded. "What message can there be?"

"Go on—get in there!" the man snarled. He took a gun out of his pocket. "Go on—move!"

There was hardly room in the booth for the two of them. Tom was forced back onto the swivel seat; the telephone receiver was digging into his back. The little elderly man stood in front of him, holding the door closed with one hand. His other hand held a big old-fashioned revolver pointing at Tom's chest.

"I wouldn't like to have to shoot Seamus Dillon's nephew," he said. "But I'd do it, if necessary." He smiled up at Tom. "This handgun should appeal to you as an American. A relic of the Old West. Hi Standard Longhorn revolver. Pure Buffalo Bill." He paused. "Much more effective than your nasty little automatics." He started to snicker unpleasantly. "You could blow someone's head off with this fella. Ever see that?" he demanded. "Like slicing off the top of an egg, with brains oozing out instead of the yoke! Brains—they look like snot, you know, all mixed up with the blood—"

"I was in Vietnam," Tom said. "In the Marines."

"Of course." The man quieted down. "Forgive me. Please don't think I want to be unpleasant at all. I'm only here to protect you. To guard you." He waved the gun barrel dangerously. "I was there in the Gradlon doing my humble best to entertain you—and then that whore descended on us. Of course I knew she would, sooner or later. She's been watching you all day."

"What whore? What do you mean?"

"That one. Calls herself Annabel Rayne. On Her Majesty's Sexual Service, she is." He shook his head. "Probably got electronic bugs on her nipples."

"The gun," Tom said. "Do you mind?"

"Pleasure," the little man said. "Just as long as you do exactly as I tell you." He lowered the revolver. "Accompany me back to your hotel. Don't go back into the restaurant. Just leave that whore where she is, sitting on the professional equipment she has, perforce, to leave unused." He lifted the gun again in a minatory gesture. "Your uncle is here on important business and it is my duty to ensure that nothing you do embarrasses him."

☘ ☘ ☘

Lang had held the floor for more than an hour. Questions multiplied, talk swirled around him, but he stayed cool and detached.

He had outlined his master plan in detail. Phase one would open on Saturday June 9 on the campus of University College, Dublin, at Bellfield, a few miles outside the city. At 11 A.M. on that day the Irish taoiseach and his cabinet, along with several hundred important personages from all over the world would attend the Carrolton Inauguration. The president of the United States would be present, together with such political figures as Speaker O'Neill and Governor Carey, and such dignitaries as the cardinal archbishops of Boston and New York, and many other eminent figures associated with the American-Irish Society and the Carrolton Committee. Not only the Irish and the Americans would be involved: hundreds of diplomats, academics, and religious dignitaries would be present from all over the world. The American president, of course, would attend Carrolton on his way to the Isle of Man Conference, at which his Initiative for Ireland would be debated and—it was hoped—some definite proposals would emerge.

The gathering together of all these key persons in a relatively small space— the interior of the Carrolton Institute—would give Lang his chance. Once everyone was assembled in the Aula Maxima, or great hall of the Institute, phase one could begin.

For operational purposes, Lang explained, his group would be divided into five task squads—A, B, C, D, and E—each with definite responsibilities. The ceremonies started at 11 A.M. and at 11.30 A.M. the five squads would move into action. Squad A, headed by Lang himself, would enter the Aula Maxima and take captive the president of Ireland, the taoiseach, and the members of the cabinet. All the other VIPs present, including the president of the United States and other distinguished Americans, would be detained, and token hostages might be taken from among them.

Meanwhile Squad B would have isolated the institute, circling it with a steel ring of machine guns, mortars, and rocket launchers. Squad C would take over the RTE television studios at Donnybrook (only a short distance from the university campus at Bellfield) and immediately proclaim the new regime, ordering everyone to remain at home and keep off the streets: a curfew broken only on pain of death.

Squad D would take what Lang called "diversionary action" throughout the city of Dublin. At the moment Lang preferred not to specify what this action would be.

Squad E might be described as an all-purposes unit. Its members would be responsible for bringing in government ministers not present at the Carrolton Inauguration and for disrupting supplies and communications throughout the country. They would destroy telephone installations, bomb banks and newspaper offices, uproot railroad tracks and burn buses, blow up gasoline dumps and tanker trucks.

By the time phase one ended (Lang said), the Irish people would be in the state of "anxious acquiescence" that was the usual mass reaction to a coup d'etat. "This is the time," Lang said, "when everyone is at their most vulnerable. Baffled. Confused." He paused. "That state of mind will have been created, blow by blow. Through surprise and terror. The bomb on the quiet sidestreet. The sniper picking off Dad as the kids play unsuspecting on the lawn. The Hitchcock touch—but for real! People clutching at any shred of normality—and not finding it. No mail. No telephone. No banks open—no money. No gas for cars or trucks. Soon, no food in the shops. Nothing but that face on the TV screen, ordering you what to do. You hate him, you fear him—and yet you get to love him in a strange kind of way. Because he's the only one who *knows*—who can tell you what to do." Lang grinned. "And when that stage is reached, victory is ours—yours!"

This was the nearest Lang had come to rhetoric. All he said increased one's confidence in him, and yet Seamus knew he owed it to himself to hold off from total acceptance.

Lang said that certain members of the committee would play an active part in phase one. "Intelligence is a vital function in the coup d'etat." One of their most important sources, he said, was a member of the committee who could not be here tonight. Seamus knew Lang must mean McClymont. This member of the committee who was in government would keep them informed about every detail of the inauguration: any change of arrangements. Another member of the committee who also had to be absent was a lawyer (he meant Austin Gaines, Seamus knew) who would keep them informed as to any changes in government and judicial policies on subversive activities within the state. And of course Inspector Glinn would warn them of any action the Special Branch might be planning.

Colonel Darrell would play the most active role of all. He would command the Honor Guard provided by the Irish Army for the inauguration. Ideally, all the soldiers comprising the Guard would be committed to the coup (if they were not, it would be necessary to substitute personnel who were). Then the Honor Guards, under Darrell, could cooperate fully with Squad A in the Aula Maxima.

On the morning of the coup Duane would arrive at the television studios at Donnybrook to prepare for the next edition of his Irish language program, "Daoine Ag Caint." He would be accompanied by several persons whom he would introduce at the studio as panelists on his forthcoming program. They would in fact be Lang's Task Squad C. At 11:30 A.M., at a time synchronized with Squad A's in the Aula Maxima, they would seize the studios.

Seamus knew that he would have to announce his decision on the foundation soon. If this were much longer delayed, he wouldn't feel up to it. The air in the room was heavy, vitiated with cigarette smoke. He was staring so hard at Lang that Lang's blond head appeared distorted, elongated. Seamus blinked and closed his eyes for a moment. No good interrupting Lang. Wait for the right moment.

"Any more questions?" Lang asked.

Seamus opened his eyes again.

"So far," Lang said, "we have discussed only the tactical aspect of the coup. But logistics are equally important. History is full of generals who lost battles because they neglected to ensure gas for their tanks or even food to feed their men." He shrugged. "We're gonna fight a war too—although it will be a short one. We shall need money and we shall need arms." He paused. "Leave the money aside for the moment. We shall need large quantities of small arms for the 10,000 republican sympathizers who will be joining us during phase one. The proclamation of the takeover on television will be their signal to arm themselves and report to their regional commander. These commanders will in turn make their personnel available to the six regional organizers headed by Maurice Slane. Mr. Slane estimates that seventy percent of these volunteers will need arms. Most of them have been trained in the use of the Armalite M16 and ideally these should be issued to them. If they can get M60 machine guns also, so much the better.

"But more immediately, at the very start of phase one Squad B will need heavier stuff to effectively isolate the Carrolton Institute. Mortars, rocket launchers, AK47 assault rifles. Stuff like that."

Lang paused. That's a cue for me, Seamus thought. But he waited for Lang to go on.

"Of course we could import this kind of hardware," Lang said. "We have, after all, an example before us. A vast quantity of arms have been brought into Ireland very successfully by a member of this committee." Lang smiled. "Of course he's here tonight and you all know who I mean"—he paused theatrically and then cried with the air of an emcee introducing a cabaret star: "Seamus Dillon!"

It only wanted a roll of drums. Duane started to clap and then there was a clamor of applause all around the room, rising steadily to a crescendo that was maintained for several minutes.

"Mr. Dillon," Lang said. "On behalf of the Wednesday Committee and of myself and my associates, may I ask that—subject to your approval of the plan just outlined—you will release the resources of the foundation of which you are the sole trustee."

Strangely—such was the ascendancy Lang had established over the last hour—Seamus felt on the defensive as he talked in the silent, smoke-filled room.

He didn't refer to the foundation immediately. Instead he trod water a little, alluding to the fact that the first blows in this coup had to be struck by foreigners. "I think Liam O Docartai spoke for all of us when he said, 'Why can't this be done by Irishmen?' Well," Seamus said, "we all know why. Because this is the only way we can achieve the element of surprise that is essential to our success. If we act alone, this plan of ours could go the way of most Irish plans from Ninety-Eight to the Fenian Rising to Nineteen Sixteen. We shall be betrayed before we start. So"—Seamus made a deprecatory gesture—"we have indeed to seek the aid of foreign allies." He paused. "Having listened to Mr. Lang outlining his plans to you tonight, I have no doubt that he will be a formidable ally, worthy of Ireland's cause."

There was dead silence in the room. They knew he had to mention the foundation now.

"Now," he said, "As to the foundation. I have no doubt its resources would offer the kind of logistic support Mr. Lang has just referred to—and I am prepared to offer those resources to this committee to be used by Mr. Lang."

The silence held for a moment. Then a kind of collective sigh: a susurration of breath that stirred the room like a tiny breeze.

"But first," Seamus went on, "I have something to explain. The foundation is not my personal property. I am not a free agent in this: to give or withhold at will." He shook his head. "I am the trustee for those ordinary men and women throughout the United States who built the foundation by their contributions. Hundreds, thousands of Irish-Americans whose names you will never know. Tonight I represent every one of those men and women, and I want to tell you that every dime and dollar they gave, they gave out of a burning love and care for Ireland."

He looked around the crescent of faces: all of them tense and expectant.

"So—I must be true to my stewardship. The full resources of the foundation are yours. I have said it. I will abide by it. Now," he continued, "those resources, arrived in Ireland, were concealed in various caches throughout the twenty-six counties. None of them has ever been betrayed to the Special Branch or been discovered by them in their routine searches." He paused. "As you are probably aware, while the location of individual caches may be known to local sympathizers, the location of all the caches is known only to me."

Lang leaned forward a little; nodded.

Seamus went on: "This was not because I claim any proprietary hold over the foundation. It was simply a matter of security." There was a note of defiance in his voice as he added, "And it is still in the interests of security that I propose to maintain that personal link."

Lang said, "How exactly do you wish to do that, sir?"

"Very simply," Seamus said. "When you, Mr. Lang, want to lift one of the caches, you tell me. I meet with you—I take you to it. That way I discharge my personal obligation as trustee."

Lang nodded. He said in a neutral voice, "I understand, sir."

Everyone still kept silence, but now Seamus sensed that their silence held a quality of surprise, even anger.

Duane said, "On behalf of us all I thank you for that decision, Seamus. Without your cooperation we could hardly go on. But this proviso you're making—how you have to be present when Lang lifts the arms—" He shook his head, gestured. "Well, you speak of security! Surely what you propose is suicide, security-wise? My God! Seamus—you are the Grand Old Man of Subversion as far as the Irish Special Branch are concerned." He was frowning. "Think of the opportunities you're giving them! The Branch have only to put a tail on you—"

O Docartai cut in a voice like thunder: " 'Tis bloody insanity, so it is!"

Colonel Darrell said unexpectedly, "Security aside, I understand how Mr. Dillon feels. The foundation was the great achievement of his life. He has to make sure it's handled right."

Seamus could feel an undertow of dissatisfaction swelling through the room. Maurice Slane was whispering angrily to his wife.

"Mr. Dillon," Lang said. He smiled, suddenly boyish. "Like the colonel says. I understand how you feel. I accept your proviso."

The mass was over. The members of the committee stood in line, waiting. One by one, each bared his or her arm so that Duane could prick them with a scalpel, letting their blood drip onto the Tricolor spread over the table that had served as an altar. Then An tAthair Muiris administered the words of the oath:

"I do solemnly swear in the presence of Almighty God that I will yield implicit obedience to the decisions of this committee, and I further solemnly swear on pain of death to preserve inviolable secrecy regarding all the plans of the committee discussed here tonight, and I do further swear that I shall not communicate with any other member of the committee about any matter, and if any such communication should become necessary, it will only be made through our comrade O Dunnacha Duane . . ."

Waiting in line behind Sean MacSaoirse, Seamus wondered if Duane wasn't going a little far in exacting this Oath of Blood—which was, of course, a shortened version of the original oath taken by the Fenian Brotherhood. But maybe it was necessary. As Duane had said, "Security is our Achilles' heel. We have to guard against some Judas Loudmouth in our midst. If the coup is to succeed, each of us has to stay in his own separate watertight compartment."

If he had felt the oath to be a little melodramatic, Seamus had to concede it would be inadvisable for him to attend the Carrolton celebrations in person (assuming the Special Branch would even admit him). It had been decided that those members of the committee not playing an active part in the coup would assemble at some appropriate venue to await the news of its success. These members—among were An tAthair Muiris, Catherine Cudahy, Liam O Docartai, and Sean MacSaoirse—of course included Seamus himself. Duane argued it would be most dangerous to have the bulk of the committee gathered together in Dublin in the hours immediately preceding the coup. But obviously they must remain together, awaiting the call to form a government once the coup was seen to have succeeded. What was needed was a retreat not too far from Dublin yet sufficiently obscure to avoid the scrutiny of the Special Branch.

It was MacSaoirse who suggested the island at the north end of Lough Ree, near Ballyclare, off the tourist track and fairly hard to reach; thus it should be outside of the ambit of routine police patrols. A friend of MacSaoirse's who lived at the loughside would ferry the committee members out to the island before dawn on the morning of the coup. The shell of a ruined Benedictine monastery would provide shelter and there was sufficient landing space for the helicopter that would finally bring the elders of the committee back to Dublin in triumph.

Yes, Duane was right, he supposed. And no doubt he was right about binding each one of them to all of the others with the mystic and ritual shedding of blood.

After they had made love Marta wanted to talk. She always wanted to talk.

"What were you thinking about?" She leaned over and kissed Leni on the mouth. But Leni looked away; didn't respond. "Please, honey! Talk to me."

Leni turned and looked at her. "What do you want me to say?" she demanded. "That you are beautiful? That you have a brilliant mind?" Leni's eyes were a deep blue that contrasted strongly with her black hair. "Or do you wish for the truth?" She rolled over onto her back with lazy, catlike grace. Marta thought again: How beautiful she is. "The truth," Leni said, "is that you are a stupid, aging woman living in fantasies of the past. Tolerated only for your money! I had not been in Dublin two days before people talk to me of you. As a joke—you know that?" Leni said fiercely. "You're flabby and ugly!" She grabbed Marta's nipples and started kneading and twisting them with such force that Marta cried out in pain. "Your boobs are disgusting. Cosmetic surgery, that's what you need."

Leni never looked lovelier than when she was tormenting Marta like this. Exquisite in her nakedness: cold and piercing as a sword with her chiseled profile, her hair blacker than the raven's wing.

Had Leni read Marta's nature from the beginning? Or had Lang programmed her? It didn't matter. Marta was sure that Lang's apparent domination of Leni was not of a sexual kind. Lang and Leni were both loveless freewheelers, coldly autonomous in sex as in everything else. The *partouze* with them had shown that. All the time Marta had felt that in some inside core of himself Lang had remained apart, coldly watching the three of them from outside of himself.

"Come on! Get out! Get off that bed!" Leni accompanied each command with a blow: slaps and cuffs that jolted and stung across Marta's face and head. Marta half-rolled, half-fell off the bed and lay crouched on the floor.

This was what Leni and she had to give each other: Marta knew that. Their relationship had defined itself from the first day they saw each other. One who kisses and who submits. Slapper and slapperat. A ritual preordained as the printout of a genetic code.

Later, when Leni had gone, and Marta was left as usual to contemplate the shabby surroundings against which she chose to conduct these encounters, Marta reflected that it *had* to be that good with Leni, for Leni had been born on March 22, which made her an Aries—strong, ardent, and impetuous, all of which qualities she was demonstrating in this relationship, to Marta's delight.

Marta didn't feel she exactly owed Lang, though. She was doing plenty for him, at that. Especially considering all the unanswered questions concerning this film *Blood Scenario* Lang was supposed to be making. This week Lang was said to be engaged on principal photography, but there was no more mention of the superstar who was going to take the male lead. Lang only referred to this mysterious figure when being interviewed on chat shows. And where was Bud Halsey? If he was really organizing the finances, really representing the front office in this project, it was strange he hadn't shown at all, however briefly.

Anyway, Marta figured she had done—was still doing—a splendid job on Lang's behalf. She had created for him that intangible called by PR men "a favorable climate of opinion." This summer in Dublin Lang was "Rex Lang, the film director," and he had Marta to thank for it. That luncheon with Conan O'Kelly, for instance, which Marta had hosted at the Anna Livia Restaurant in Bloom's Hotel. She had wondered how Lang would strike O'Kelly—that most culture-oriented of Irish politicians—but she needn't have worried. Lang and Marta had been able to flatter O'Kelly into feeling that they were, in a sense, all artists together. "Of course politics isn't a science—it's the most subtle of all the arts," Lang had pronounced by the time they'd gotten to the brandy.

The most tangible plus from this meeting with O'Kelly had been the minister's promise to get official cooperation for Lang's filming in Dublin streets and around the countryside. Lang had handled himself well with O'Kelly: Marta had to admit that. One moment an artist straight-shooting another artist. The next an earnest young American addressing a European statesman. He told O'Kelly he had most of the exteriors still to shoot (he'd already told O'Kelly what *Blood Scenario* was about: the IRA in Belfast impersonating a British Army unit and then holding the whole city at bay). "Before we actually came to Ireland," Lang said, "we were hoping to get the help of your Irish

Army in some of the combat sequences. Then we realized this wasn't on. Border security, your commitment to the UN peacekeeping forces . . ." O'Kelly agreed, and then Lang gave him some of the same zilch he'd given O Morain about Ireland being a moviemakers' paradise and Ireland replacing Spain as a venue. Lang continued: "I've most of the scenes still to shoot. Some in the country, some in busy Dublin streets—and some of these are scenes of violence, of confrontation that could alarm the passerby." He paused. "That's why we need official cooperation from your law-enforcement agencies. Just so that your police know we're simply a bunch of guys making a movie and not some kind of subversives."

"I understand your problem." O'Kelly had nodded in a magisterial way, still warmed by the food and the flattery. You could see he couldn't resist the idea of a movie that made the British Army look like assholes. "And we might arrange something through Interior Affairs. The commissioner of the Garda Siochana would have to be informed, and he could then alert local headquarters to give you cooperation."

"Why, thank you, sir! That's really tremendous!" Lang looked so much the clean-cut young college man that Marta nearly burst out laughing. He'd say "Gee whiz!" in a minute. But O'Kelly lapped it up, nodding sympathetically when Lang went on to say that he would want to hire a helicopter for the final scenes. "Funny thing is, I gather the IRA actually did hire a helicopter some years ago—and pretended they were making a film!" Lang shook his head. "Life imitating art, huh?" He frowned. "Thing is, when we try to hire our chopper, will they just call the cops?"

O'Kelly smiled at being reminded of the Provos' daring heist of several prisoners out of Mountjoy Jail in Dublin. He could smile because his party hadn't been in office at the time. He'd promised Lang he'd look into that too.

Yes, Marta had certainly done her best for Lang, and she was certainly enjoying Leni. But a vague unease remained. It was odd that neither Lang nor Leni ever invited her to Kilbrangan House, Lang's so-called headquarters in Wicklow. What could be there that was so secret? Marta's earlier feeling about Lang was reaffirmed. There was something unreal about him. Dealing with him was like shadow-boxing: you could never tell where he really was at.

☘ ☘ ☘

It was all so like the previous occasion in the Whig's Club that Durnan had a distinct feeling of déjà vu. Mr. Brown and Mr. White were there in the annex to the members' bar. The same Pakistani had served them with the same drinks: malt whiskey for the Ulstermen; bourbon for Durnan. The significant difference for Durnan was that this time he had to deal with the bosses of Loyalist Action on his own. Lang was in Paris, meeting with Camoumim, although he would be arriving in London in less than an hour's time. Durnan guessed that Lang could probably have made this meeting with Mr. White and Mr. Brown. It bothered Durnan that Lang had ordered him along as his deputy. Could be, it reflected Lang's confidence in him, but that didn't sound like Lang. Well-briefed as he was, Durnan felt uneasy. Suppose they asked him a question he couldn't answer? Lang had a great contempt for dumb bunnies who could take orders but were unable to function independently.

They were discussing item eight of Lang's program for Loyalist Action.

Mr. White had been exulting in the opportunity the Carrolton Inauguration presented. "Only consider! There in the institute we have all the people we want to snatch, there on one stage, confined within a few yards! Your American president." Mr. White paused. "Well, we don't want to harm him. We just want to teach him—and America—not to meddle in our affairs. To kidnap your mister president, the First Executive of the most powerful country in the world—that is not a negligible achievement in a propaganda war such as we are waging." His voice dropped. "The taoiseach and his cabinet are another matter. They are not going to get away so lightly . . ."

Durnan nodded. He knew what had been set out for Loyalist Action in the plan Lang had prepared, but the fate of the taoiseach and the other government ministers was a matter for Mr. White and his associates. Now Mr. White said that no money ransom could buy the release of the taoiseach and his cabinet. Loyalist Action would demand the return of twenty or more IRA prisoners, wanted for killings and bombings in Northern Ireland, whom the courts in the Irish Republic had refused to extradite. For each two republican prisoners delivered up, one member of the Irish Cabinet would be released. If this demand was not met within a specified time, Loyalist Action would start executing the members of the Irish Cabinet; by hanging, at intervals, one at a time. "Justice by reprisal," Mr. White explained. "Condign and summary justice administered to men who have consistently denied justice to others."

Durnan grinned. "This heist will be really something, wouldn't you say, sir?" He nodded. "This is the World Game all right."

It seemed that a momentary euphoria had gripped the three of them, even Durnan. But some doppelgänger outside of himself wondered what Mr. White and Mr. Brown would say if they knew that Lang was working for the Wednesday Committee as well, and had sold them an even more elaborately tailored scenario for the Carrolton Inauguration.

"You can inform Mr. Lang that payments to Philips International and Fauberg AG have now been finalized as regards the advance payment for item
eight," Mr. White said.

"Thank you, sir," Durnan said.

"We're sorry about the delay with the two Ford Transit trucks," Mr. Brown
said. "But we thought we could kill two birds at once, so to speak. Bring the
dogs down to Dublin in the trucks."

"Great," Durnan said.

"About the dogs," Mr. White said. "In the program Mr. Lang specified
German shepherds of average size, age around eighteen months old."

Durnan nodded. Lang had briefed him carefully on this. "Younger than
that, they're not fully developed. Older, and they could be into the wrong
routine."

"We have twenty-five German shepherds that fulfill those requirements.
Deliver next week."

Mr. Brown said harshly, "Police dogs! That's what you ought to get."

Durnan shook his head. "No. Monsieur Barbier, our trainer, says they get
too much training—of the wrong kind. We want guard dogs. Fear-biters. Nervous. Aggressive."

"These will be," Mr. White said.

"Deliver in Dublin. South Side. All right?" Durnan asked.

"All right," Mr. White agreed, and Mr. Brown walked across to tug at the
bellpull to summon the Pakistani.

Durnan had arranged to meet with Lang in St. James's Park. Emerging from
the Whig's Club, he felt an odd sense of unreality. He felt he had dealt with
Mr. White and Mr. Brown okay, and yet he wasn't eager to face again the
harsh laser of Lang's attention. If he *had* handled things badly, he figured Lang
would know. Lang always knew. Lang would not ask him how he had made
out but ask one, two, never more than three relevant questions about what had
been said. That would tell Lang all he needed to know.

He realized he was standing still on the sidewalk, lost in his thoughts like
some dazed old man. People kept brushing past him, nearly knocking him
over. St James's, in the heart of ancient, tradition-rich England, and yet this
could be Lexington Avenue—the same noise and bustle and gasoline fumes.
The people too. Obvious Latins, chattering Orientals, fellow Americans—he
could tell the women, particularly, by their distinctively square jawline and
their orthodontic perfection—and even a sprinkling of subdued-looking Brit-
ishers. Strangely, no Arabs, whose fief Olde England was now alleged to
be.

Durnan started to move off, but his progress was delayed by an American couple and their rather unisex-looking child, who had just been snapped by a street photographer on the sidewalk. The photographer was a tall, husky-looking man with a red beard. "Shall I do you next, sir? An authentic London clubman seen leaving his club?" he demanded of Durnan, who ignored him and began to walk away. Just then Mr. White brushed past him, immaculate in black overcoat and formal bowler, barely acknowledging Durnan's presence with a slight smile. Mr. Brown tagged along after him, carrying two bulging briefcases. At that moment the camera clicked.

"Lovely! Three genuine toffs discovered outside Whig's Club," the photographer roared in his unfamiliar accent. He was proffering a ticket to Durnan, who shook his head and walked on. Mr. White and Mr. Brown were getting into a chauffeur-driven Rolls which had just glided up.

Durnan was meeting Lang at the bridge in St. James's Park. "I'll be feeding the swans," Lang had said.

Entering Cleveland Row from St. James's Street, Durnan saw a building before him which the *ABC Street Guide* told him was St. James's Palace. He wished he and Lang were staying here a day or two longer so that he could really act out the role of American tourist. This square mile or so was soaked in the tradition millions of people came thousands of miles to savor. The queen. The household troops in busbies and bearskins. The changing of the guard at Buckingham Palace.

He wasn't really worried about the way he had handled Loyalist Action. And yet there was always worry when you were working for Lang. The shadow of Sokatsu. Of course he should be—was—flattered at being chosen as Lang's plenipotentiary. But Durnan disliked the assignment because these sachems of Loyalist Action were fascists in anyone's book. Right there along with the Klan and the John Birch Society. Selling guns to both sides indeed!

Although Lang never deigned to defend any course of action he was taking, he had mentioned that he considered they were merely carrying the policy of the Japanese Red Army to a logical conclusion. The JRA were always described as freelances, undertaking assignments all over the world on a contract basis. Of course Lang's real sphere of operations had been South America. The world of the *guerrilleros*, rather than the PFLP. Certainly he had been with the Monteneros and also a member of the Tupamaro-dominated Committee for International Affairs, whose function was to coordinate the strategy of various activist groups in Argentina, Brazil, Chile, Ecuador, and Peru. His last major task had been to lay down training and operational plans for the ERP [People's Revolutionary Army] in Argentina. He had told Durnan that, when he left, the ERP had a war chest of ninety million dollars. Perhaps some of Lang's financing came out of that? Durnan didn't know. There were so many questions one could ask about Lang.

Perhaps the oddest question had been asked by Malachi O'Farrell late one night at the Villa Ben Kalah in Algiers. They'd been drinking the heavy, cloying local red vino—stuff Lang would wave aside with contempt—and, for the first and only time, Durnan had come near to scratching the mask of scorn Malachi presented to the world. "Hey," Malachi had said suddenly. "Here's a thought. Where is Rex Lang's spiritual home?" Durnan shook his head stupidly, but Malachi persisted. "C'mon, man! No problem about *your* spiritual home, is there? A gracious mansion in Dear Ole Dixie. As for me," he added with a kind of savagery, "the Roman curia of course! Monsignor Malachi discourses on the Council of Trent." He scowled. "But Rex! I think there can be no doubt about his true background." Durnan was goggling foolishly at him. "Number Two Dzerzhinsky Square! Where else?" Durnan still did not understand. "The KGB, you prick! Surely only they could have created him? That relentless dialectic. That air of the sea-green incorruptible. That Grand Inquisitor style."

Durnan was sober enough to ask if Malachi had any proof of this. "Divil a bit!" Malachi said in a cod-Irish voice. " 'Tis idle speculation entirely. We must wait for a Sign."

Neither of them had mentioned it again. There was no reason to suppose Lang had anything to do with the Russians. Only his apparent ambivalence made Durnan wonder again now.

At least there was money at the end of the tunnel. Lang said so and he didn't make idle promises. Better than a million dollars each for what Malachi called the "hierarchy": Leni, Durnan, and Malachi himself. Less, of course, for the muscle and technicians. More—no one knew how much more—for Lang. All this when the present Irish operation was concluded: when the two conflicting, but from Lang's point of view complementary programs, pursued for Loyalist Action and the Wednesday Committee respectively, converged at the Carrolton Inauguration.

Lang was duly waiting on the bridge in St. James's Park. Below it, swans drifted with an elegiac grace only threatened when children tried to feed them crumbs out of paper bags. The park was quite crowded. Young couples sprawled on the grass. Old men sat and puffed at their pipes.

"I've been to Turnbull and Asser's," Lang said. "Bought some shirts. Only thing is," he added, pokerfaced, "I shall have to send them back to Turnbull's to get them cleaned. Wouldn't dream of having them laundered!"

Durnan stared across at the battlements of Whitehall. They looked like cardboard in the thin sunshine. "Don't you want to know what they said?" he asked.

"I got a good idea already," Lang said. "You didn't blow that one; you couldn't have blown it." He paused. "Harps are always predictable—and these are just orange harps instead of green."

"They said they were pleased with item eight."

"Of course they're pleased," Lang said. " 'Mr. White' would be a fool if he wasn't—and he's no fool."

"He calls the shots," Durnan said. "You can see that."

"Of course. He has the last word," Lang said. "Along with perhaps one other man." Lang paused. "I know his real name. He sits in the House of Lords. The queen's secretary invites him to garden parties at the Palace."

Lang was leaning against the rail of the bridge. He was wearing a tailored anorak and clean, pressed Levi's and trailed an expensive Leica over his shoulder. He looked like a tourist, but a young, informed tourist: all eager-beaver to observe and enjoy.

"They're sending us the two large trucks," Durnan said. "And the dogs. Twenty-five German shepherds."

Lang nodded. "Yes. It's time Barbier started training the dogs."

The park was filling up now. The lunchtime strollers had gone back to work, but they were replaced by the kind of people Durnan had noticed in St. James's Street: eager, noisy, and scarcely ever English.

"Did they mention Old Dillon?" Lang asked.

"Just to say that the contract was still on."

Lang nodded. "That could be fulfilled fairly soon," he said. "I had to agree to let him release the caches one by one. That's a nuisance. The Branch will probably put a tail on him." He shrugged. "We'll get the frag we want out first . . . They won't stop us."

Suddenly the bridge was overwhelmed by children—jostling, shouting, forcing Lang and Durnan back against the rails. Lang's face showed his distaste as he pressed himself back, trying to avoid physical contact. Durnan saw that there were adults on the bridge too: a young man and woman who looked like gypsies.

And now Durnan saw the red-bearded photographer of St. James's Street popping up genielike from the surge of screaming kids. He was grinning like a maniac: clicking away again and again.

"Hey—we gotta get out of this!" Lang said, but already some of the kids were off the bridge, fanning out in different directions as they ran, dodging around trees, leapfrogging over people reclining on the grass. The gypsy couple and the red-bearded photographer were going almost as fast, skirting the edge of the lake toward Duck Island.

"For Chrissake," Lang breathed.

"Rex!" Durnan said. "That guy with the red beard. The photographer."

"Yes?"

"That's the second time. He was outside Whig's Club when I came out."

"Outside Whig's?"

"Yeah." Durnan was frowning. He was trying to recall whether he'd noticed the man the moment he came out into the street. He didn't think so; only when he was photographing that American couple and their child. "Rex—I guess it's a coincidence, h'm?"

"Better not count on that," Lang said. "Why didn't you smash his camera?"

"Rex, I—"

Lang shrugged. "Too late to do anything now, anyway." He stared toward the lake. "Maybe you'll stay lucky. Maybe it was a coincidence."

"Rex—I'm sorry."

Lang looked at him and shook his head. Durnan was frightened by his restraint.

Lang leaned over and spat into the water, shooting neatly between two swans. A tweeded stereotype of an Englishwoman halted, mimed shock and outrage, and then—perhaps chilled by the steel in Lang's gaze—moved on. Lang said, "Know something? I don't think that was a coincidence."

❧ ❧ ❧

In all his years in the police Slowey had never quite accustomed himself to the sight of violent death. So—get it over with! He pulled the sheet back with a single sharp movement. There on a slab in the mortuary of Portlaoise Prison lay the body of Frank Niles. He had been found hanging in his cell.

Slowey forced himself to look, suppressing disgust and pity. Niles' face wore a surprised expression; the thick golden-red beard still looked curiously glossy and alive. He had not died by strangulation, but by a broken neck as in old-style judicial hanging.

"Mr. Culshaw came in with his breakfast and found him hanging?" Slowey asked the officer in charge of the mortuary.

"That was the way of it, sir."

"Niles just knotted the three towels together and hung himself from the bars of the air vent?" Slowey paused. "By the way, how did he come to have three towels at the same time? The issue is one, isn't it?"

"Sure no one knows how he got them, Superintendent."

Slowey drew the sheet over the body again, thanked the officer, and left the mortuary.

One thing, Slowey thought, sitting beside his driver on the way back to Dublin: murder or suicide—and who can say which in the circumstances?—it confirms what Niles told me. Or at least it confirms his sincerity. If he killed himself it was because he had said too much. If he had been murdered it was because others feared he might have said too much.

Murder was the most likely, although all the facts would fit suicide. Niles could have stood on the stool in his cell; could have made a noose from the knotted towels (he could easily have scrounged two extra ones); could have put the noose around his neck, adjusted the slipknot, and then kicked the stool away.

Could have, but probably didn't. Niles' passing had been achieved with the help of some of his fellow prisoners and at least one of the screws.

In fact Slowey dismissed the possibility of suicide. When he had visited Niles again three days ago—having received Mickey Glinn's report from Quimper—Niles had been obsessed with the fear that he had been betrayed. Indeed, he accused Slowey of betraying him. He'd had no business to pass on the information Niles had given him. Least of all to anyone in the Branch. That was putting his, Niles', head right on the block. Sure everyone knew the Branch was fucking infiltrated. "Of course the boyos are in the Castle—why wouldn't they be? Wasn't there a spy in the Castle in British days too—feeding out the shit to Michael Collins?"

It had been easy to brush aside these fears. Treachery was an occupational hazard for republican activists, and Slowey had to admit that the cover set up for his visits to Portlaoise—Niles being examined by a heart specialist from Dublin—was flimsy enough. Now that Niles was dead, Slowey felt full of guilt. His killer or killers had probably learned of his snitching from what Slowey had told Mickey Glinn. This didn't mean that Glinn could be blamed. What Slowey had told Glinn, Glinn had had to pass on to his subordinates— and that meant at least two or three people. Any one of these could represent the Wednesday Committee and have leaked the fact of Niles' informing back to Portlaoise: back to the men who had killed him.

Of course Slowey had always known that the Irish Special Branch was infiltrated by republican elements. There had been many instances, the most dramatic as recently as 1974 when the Special Branch were about to swoop on the secret peace negotiations between the Provisional IRA leaders and various clergymen being held at Feakle in County Clare. An IRA inside man at C3 Dublin Castle had called the Provo leaders, warning them that the Branch was on its way.

Yes, of course the boyos were there. You rubbed shoulders with them everywhere, at mass and everywhere else: why wouldn't they be in the Branch too? But it was something you had to forget if you wanted to go on working with the Branch: you had the choice of trusting your colleagues and hoping for the best or of yielding to paranoia and trusting no one.

Slowey had always steered a middle course between these two extremes, but Niles' murder had changed that. Paranoid or not, now he could trust no one.

☘ ☘ ☘

"He's not back yet?"

"Not yet, sir."

Tom thanked the receptionist and went back into the lounge. He sat down again in one of the big armchairs and stared out through the huge windows at the smooth expanse of Lough Ramor. A breeze was bending the reeds by the shore. Some ways, he preferred looking at a lake to looking at the sea. The sea was more exciting, more beautiful—but it was also treacherous: carried a threat. Easier to contemplate a lake and then dream . . .

Not, he reflected wryly, that he felt much like dreaming. Not at this moment. Dreamers had better eschew the company of his uncle Seamus Dillon.

They had been staying at this hotel for two days. It was set in wooded grounds on the southern shore of Lough Ramor. They had come here from Kenmare, where Seamus had visited his pharmaceuticals plant, Penrith Ireland, and also his house at Laragh on the north side of the Kenmare River (which is really an estuary). Tom had gotten the feeling that Seamus was settling accounts prior to taking a journey—and there were no prizes for guessing the nature of the journey Seamus would take. Penrith, the firm he had created, would go on: there was a board of directors to manage it; staff whose jobs had to be preserved. Tom had been particularly saddened by a visit to the house at Laragh. Despite the faithful surveillance of the Keanes, the couple who came in twice a week, the house was slipping into decay under dustcovers and behind drawn blinds. "There was a Dutchman in Dublin mad to buy that place," Seamus told Tom after they had left. "I suppose I'd let him have it if he still wants it."

They had driven up here to Virginia, County Cavan, in what Bord Failte called Lake Land. And now, on their second day here, Tom found himself half-amused and half-maddened to find that Seamus Dillon, the sick old man bidding farewell to the scenes of his youth, had given way to Seamus Dillon the dangerous anarchist, the cold, molelike conspirator. And—of course—the conspirator was the boss.

Tom was resolved not to be involved in whatever was being plotted, though. He had simply come along for the ride: a happy ostrich in his ignorance. He had remonstrated with his uncle about that old nut at Quimper who had pointed a Hi Standard Longhorn at him and thus (although he hadn't said this to Seamus) prevented him getting his rocks off with that English Rose. Seamus—again maddeningly—hadn't taken him too seriously. "You didn't get shot. Okay, a man pointed a gun at you. Could have happened in New York. Anywhere."

It was obvious at every turn that Seamus was involved in some labyrinth of his own creation. Tom had suggested laying out an itinerary in advance, before they began what Seamus had joshingly called The Great Hibernian Tour. But Seamus was cagey, awkward. He had many different people to see and places to visit. He had to stay "flexible." Only this way would he be able to see the men and women he had come all the way from the States to see—probably for the last time.

The evening of their arrival here Seamus had made a call from the pay phone in the foyer. Presumably long distance, for he had to get change from the desk clerk. The call made, he had gone up to bed at once—taciturn, unrelaxed, not saying much more than "Good night." In the morning he had been up early. Taking a hotel-packed lunch of smoked salmon, brown wholemeal bread, and fruit, he told Tom he was off to see an old friend in the district. Tom would have to excuse him for that day: he'd be back for dinner.

This surprised Tom a little. Ever since they had left Quimper, his uncle had seemed eager for his company: trying to make Tom see his beloved Ireland through his eyes, talking of all the changes he'd seen in fifty years of visiting the country. But that morning Seamus had walked out of the hotel with an air of purpose: poised but tense. He still appeared tense when he returned eight hours later. He usually relished his food, but he only picked at the trout baked in wine served that night. Again he soon went to bed, saying little.

The next morning he stayed in bed fairly late. At lunch he seemed anxious to talk—as if, indeed, he wanted to confide in Tom. At last he said, "You're the strange boy, all right."

"So they've always told me."

"When I was your age, if I'd come on a Great Hibernian Tour like this, I'd have been bustin' a gut wondering what it was all in aid of."

"So?"

"You don't want to know?"

"I think I know," Tom said slowly, "enough. Enough not to want to know any more."

Seamus shook his head. "Really?"

"You'd understand better if you'd been with me in Vietnam. Oh—we accusing ghosts are a bore, I know. But I was naive enough—old-fashioned enough—to believe we were fighting for a cause. Maybe not a wholly contemptible cause." He shook his head. "Three tours I had. Three circles in hell if you want to be dramatic about it. But when we came back—oh, boy! Metaphorically, it was Khesanh all over again! My own dear wife accusing me of machismo self-indulgence, sadism, you name it . . ."

"Your ex-wife is a bitch."

"Maybe, but what I'm saying is this: that was my cause and I'm not about to fight for another."

Seamus hadn't persisted. He asked Tom if he'd mind driving him somewhere that night. Tom said, "Of course."

Around dusk that evening Tom drove Seamus to a point near the western end of Lough Ramor. Seamus got out of the car, but continued walking till he disappeared around the next bend. Tom waited, parking lights on. After ten minutes a late-model pickup truck roared past, going in the same direction as his uncle had done. Tom didn't take much notice of the truck, but he did notice that as soon as it rounded the bend he couldn't hear its engine anymore. It must have stopped a few yards away, and he couldn't help connecting this with his uncle. Seamus was obviously meeting someone. Why not whoever was in the pickup?

Tom waited on. Half an hour, three-quarters. Then he heard the pickup start again. A moment later it swept past him, going north. A dark, scowling-looking man with gray hair was driving, with a blond woman beside him.

Five minutes later Seamus had appeared, walking slowly. He nodded to Tom and got into the car.

Back in the hotel Seamus thanked him. Then he asked, "I hope chauffeuring your wicked old uncle doesn't jibe with your ideals?"

"You were picking mushrooms near the lough, right? Dusk by a lake—that's the time to pick mushrooms, isn't it?"

And now, today, Seamus was still obviously playing the cloak-and-dagger game. He had hung around uneasily till nearly noon, glancing at the papers, drinking cups of coffee. Then the desk clerk announced that there was a call for him from Dublin. After that Seamus appeared relaxed, even jubilant. He told Tom they would be going back to Dublin that evening. At the moment he was out visiting his anonymous local friend.

Tom felt disturbed, even irked. What was happening? His only consolation was the thought that sooner or later at some twist or turn of Seamus' labyrinth, he would bump into Frankie McNagan again. Meanwhile he felt like someone riding a carousel which he had no power to control, or halt, or even get off.

🍀 🍀 🍀

Sitting at his big battered desk, hemmed in by the hideous, green-painted walls that, mercifully, he no longer noticed (familiarity anesthetizes), Slowey considered Glinn's report from Quimper.

He had to admit that logical, consistent, it met the old-fashioned criterion of a story in having a beginning, a middle, and an end. In fact it was almost too consistent. When Slowey had first read it, he'd been impressed. Now, a few days and two rereadings later, he found it less convincing. Too coherent. Too pat.

Glinn began by saying that the Wednesday Committee undoubtedly existed. They were a diverse group representing every shade of republican opinion, fanatically opposed to the President's Initiative. Glinn had not been able to penetrate any meetings of the committee, but he and Sergeant Quinlan had kept watch on a house in the older section of Quimper and on two different occasions he, Glinn, had seen Liam O Docartai enter the house. Later Philip Hurnan—who used the pseudonym "Sean MacSaoirse"—and Frances McNagan entered the house, accompanied by three men whom Glinn could not identify. But he had subsequently called at the DST [Direction de la surveillance du territoire] office in Brest and inspected mug shots of a large number of known members of urban guerrilla organizations. Finally he had identified two of the three men as Juan Hernadez and Fredrico Lorca (a pseudonym inspired by the murdered poet? Slowey wondered), members of the ETA, the Basque liberation movement. Glinn suggested that this indicated the ETA was the terrorist organization which was going to act for the Wednesday Committee. Niles had said that the initial action was going to be undertaken by "foreigners." The ETA activists would certainly fit this definition. They would come in as Spanish tourists: a useful cover in view of the traditional friendship between Spain and Ireland. And of course they wouldn't be known to the Irish Special Branch; they wouldn't be on C3 files; they would indeed be strangers who could function with impunity.

All this was theory, Glinn admitted, based on his own identification from photographs of two men he had seen once for two or three minutes. But it was a theory, he suggested, that fitted the facts. O Docartai, McNagan, and MacSaoirse were probably acting as liaison between the Wednesday Committee and the ETA—which, Slowey would recall, had been associated with the IRA in the past, notably when ETA and Breton Liberation Front members had trained with Saor Eire near Crosshaven in County Cork. It seemed plausible to assume that the ETA would figure they had a lot to gain by helping the Wednesday Committee. If they succeeded in a project as dramatic as this—kidnapping an entire government-in-office—then their status throughout the international terrorist network would be greatly enhanced.

To counter such a plan, Glinn suggested invoking the help of the Kommissar—the computerized information catalog maintained by the West German anti-terrorist authorities. The Kommissar had had some notable successes—as when the Germans grabbed terrorists hiding out in Bulgaria and Yugoslavia—and probably offered the best answer to this strategy of striking from a springboard of anonymity, of total surprise.

This was the essence of Glinn's report. Commenting on Nora O Conaire's mention of Seamus Dillon, Glinn said that while Dillon had predictably met with several known republicans at Quimper—including Liam O Docartai—these meetings had been at congress functions and were almost certainly merely social. It should not be forgotten that Dillon was known to have a genuine passion for traditional balladry and music: this must be his reason for going to Quimper.

Glinn added, almost as an afterthought, that Annabel Rayne, an agent of the British MI6, had also been in Quimper and had established some contact with Tom Dillon, Seamus Dillon's nephew—who was not known to be identified with the Irish republican cause in the United States.

Slowey stared around him. For a moment he *was* conscious of the hideous, green-painted walls. He was wondering why he had found Glinn's report impressive at first reading—and then, subsequently, less and less believable.

Glinn's theories were logical. They held together. Starting with evidence physically observed—but always by Glinn alone: Sergeant Quinlan had shared the watch on the house in Quimper but had never happened to be there when

anyone went in or out—Glinn had gone on to make his identification of the
ETA men on microfilm at Brest and on the basis of this presented his theory of
ETA collaboration with the Wednesday Committee.

It held together. And yet . . . Could it be this report had the carefully
wrought unity of fiction rather than the crude clout of fact? Slowey had
responded at once to Niles' disjointed testimony: he was distrustful of the
suave QED of Glinn's report.

He decided he wouldn't let Glinn know that but go along with him in all he
suggested: check out the ETA men with Kommissar and make Frances McNagan and Sean MacSaoirse alpha priority on the Branch's wanted list. In fact,
they had been wanted so long that no one in the Branch was really looking for
them anymore. O Docartai was easy. They knew where he was; could pick him
up any time—and this made Slowey think he couldn't be playing any very
important role.

But, however just he had to be to Glinn, he couldn't ignore the fact that
someone—someone to whom Glinn had in the course of duty passed on Niles'
information—had in turn passed on the fact of his informing to his killers. He
must check with Glinn exactly who had been told. Meanwhile Slowey knew he
had to do: proceed as if everyone in the Force—from the commissioner down
to the pleasant girl from Valentia Island who brought him morning coffee—
was working for the Wednesday Committee.

Three

An Oath Taken

"You won't forget, Ms. Colebrook?"

"You mean the book about prisoners' civil rights? I'll try and bring it on my next visit."

"Thank you, Ms. Colebrook."

"I'll be seeing you then, Frankie. Goodbye."

"Thank you, Ms. Colebrook. Goodbye."

So they had parted, an hour ago. A ridiculous scene. Or tragic, if you liked to give way to self-pity, which Frankie tried not to do. Or at least bizarre, between husband and wife. Frankie had been visiting the Other Frankie in the high-security wing at Parkhurst Prison, Isle of Wight. Talking to him not as herself, his wife, but in the persona of Margaret Colebrook, prison visitor, member of the English League for Protest at Prison Conditions. Now, in the train traveling back to London, Frankie couldn't help wondering if the whole Ms. Colebrook charade had any point. Oh, Duane and the Other Frankie himself had approved this role-playing, but she wondered if they weren't all of them—herself included—victims of what Duane had called the Cloak and Dagger Disease.

Of course, the awful truth was that today she'd been *glad* to be Margaret Colebrook. Pretending to be her, having the Other Frankie responding to Margaret Colebrook, Frankie had felt as if she were peering through the eye-holes of a mask. Today it would have been somehow terrible to have confronted him as herself. She was consumed with guilt at her adultery and yet—this was worst of all—she didn't regret anything she'd done.

Forcing herself away from these thoughts, she reflected that from the security aspect it *was* necessary to be Margaret Colebrook. If she had presented herself as Frankie McNagan, the British Special Branch would obviously have pulled her in under the Prevention of Terrorism Act and she would have soon found herself meeting Mr. Slowey at Dublin Castle.

But she couldn't stop herself thinking about Duane. She wasn't in love with him. If she were in love with anyone, it was Tom Dillon. And yet meeting Tom at Quimper had driven her straight into bed with Duane. Perhaps Duane cared more than he said? That last time, in Duane's hotel room in Quimper, their coming together had been like dying. Had that been sweat or tears on his cheek? Duane was more involved than he would admit.

She certainly wasn't in love with *him*. She admired him more than anyone in the world except the Other Frankie, but he touched no chord of tenderness in her. Not like Tom Dillon did.

Suddenly she was chilled to realize that the elderly man sitting opposite her was staring straight at her with a hot, bold look in his overbright but bleary eyes. Seeing her own mood mirrored in this old man disgusted her: it seemed like a final insult to the Other Frankie.

She forced herself to picture him as he had been at the moment of her leaving him. Pale, almost fevered, his look of suffering overlaid by a grin that wouldn't fool anyone. What had he been thinking?

She tried to keep his face before her. After all, she had something more important to think about than her despicable lust and guilt. This meeting he had set up for her with a representative of the Belfast cell of Eireann Amhain, who (she suspected) would certainly be Dick Grogan. If Belfast wanted to communicate with Dublin, why not directly with Duane? Grogan and Duane hated each other, of course—but if Grogan had to communicate through a prisoner serving a sentence in a high-security jail, then the breakdown between Dublin and Belfast was complete. The dangers in that were enormous. She wondered if it could have anything to do with the Oath of Blood. Grogan had no doubt taken that in Belfast—An tAthair Muiris had actually administered the oath to any member of the committee not physically present at Quimper— but it permitted him to communicate through Duane.

It must be something serious—and the Carrolton ceremonies were only five days away.

She would soon know, anyway. This train would get in to Waterloo Station in thirty minutes and she would be meeting Grogan at half past six on Shepherds Bush Green, across the road from the BBC's Union House. The arrangement was that he would show up at this rendezvous at this time for the next three evenings if she couldn't make it today. He would be walking a boxer bitch and wearing a cap.

She had forgotten the man opposite her. Now he caught her gaze and looked away: ashamed, diminished. It didn't prove anything, but at least she'd put him in his place.

"This is really the place?" Tom asked.

"I believe so," Seamus said. "In fact I'm sure so. I was on a visit here, maybe ten, fifteen years ago, and Canon Keenan, the parish priest—he's dead now but he was the greatest antiquarian in Munster—he and I went into it thoroughly. Baptismal registers, the rent rolls of the landlord's agent, you name it . . ." He nodded. "Yes, this is it."

They were standing beside a pathetic huddle of stones, now hardly identifiable as of human making, that was all that was left of the cottage of Michael Dillon, Seamus' grandfather and Tom's great-grandfather. One chill morning in November 1856 Michael Dillon had closed the door of his cottage behind him for the last time, loaded the few relics of his home that were portable onto a neighbor's cart, and then left with his wife and three children for the port of Queenstown [now Cobh], there to embark for America.

Tom tried to conjure up the ghosts of his forebears out of these poor grass-covered ruins, but they were obscured by the figures in a huge oil painting Tom had seen as a child. By some long-forgotten fellow of the Royal Hibernian Academy, it was called "Going into Exile" and was executed with a photographic eye for detail. It had shown a young couple standing on a quayside, obviously about to emigrate to America. They were surrounded by tearful, keening relatives, and in the background a black-painted brigantine awaited them, anchored on the gray waters of some nameless port. The husband was young but gaunt and hollow-cheeked; his wife pale and delicate. They had four children, ranging in age from the baby in his mother's arms to a tall, Byronic-looking youth who stared with a mixture of fear and fascination at the waiting brigantine. Certainly the artist had managed to convey some intensity of emotion—otherwise Tom wouldn't still see his picture so vividly in his mind—but hadn't he romanticized and therefore falsified the scene? Could any art convey the squalor, the stench, the fear and fact of death that had confronted people like these? From the time of the Famine onward there had been thousands of them, piling into the coffin ships: worse off, it has been suggested, than the black slaves being shipped from Africa some years earlier. The slaves had some commercial value that made them worth keeping alive: these poor Irish people had none.

Tom said, "Did the family all arrive safely?"

"Oh, yes. Perhaps conditions on the ships had improved by 1856. Or maybe they were just lucky." Seamus paused. "Of course Michael Dillon was only a small boy during the Famine. In Bangor-Erris in Mayo. His parents both died and a cousin brought him down here to County Cork. He was twenty-six when he decided to take his wife and family to America."

"His parents died?" Tom echoed.

"You didn't know that?" Seamus smiled wryly. "Of course your mother would never tell you a thing like that. She prefers to forget that people like Michael Dillon ever existed." He frowned. "The Famine-Irish. What an embarrassment!"

Tom didn't say anything. He was enjoying this pilgrimage, but he was a little afraid of the depth of emotion it evoked in his uncle. He had followed the old man up through heavy woodlands to the north of Ballyvourney to reach this townland of Ballinmageery. Always Seamus kept ahead of him, moving with surprising agility over the rocks and hummocks of grass that sustained the region's tough mountainy sheep. Michael Dillon's cottage had stood on a *roche moutonnée*, or sheepback, a rockmold rounded at the end, which faced the flow of a glacier. Seamus knew exactly where to go; he had made this pilgrimage many times before.

Now he went down on his knees, onto the stones and rough grass. He was fumbling for his rosary beads.

"For Michael Dillon," he said, "and his family."

He began: "Se do bheatha a Mhuire, ata lan de ghrasta, ta an tiarna leat . . ." Tom couldn't follow the Irish but he knelt too and mumbled a sympathetic "amen" at the end.

"Thank you," Seamus said as he stood up. "God looked after the Dillon family when they got to America, anyway. When you consider . . . The youngest son coadjutor bishop of Baltimore. The eldest, Old Daniel, my father, your grandfather." He smiled. "But you know about him."

Tom smiled too. "An Irish knight at the court of the Robber Barons, as Wendell put it."

Seamus nodded. He suddenly seemed abstracted, staring out across the wide valley that stretched out before them.

Tom took a deep breath. He wanted to enjoy this moment for itself. To clear his mind of everything but the vista of beauty before his eyes: to anesthetize his mounting unease about what his uncle was here in Ireland to do.

Ireland—this was the first time he'd been able to appreciate this land physically as a place of houses, fields, mountains, lakes—not just as an emotive
symbol or a state of mind. Always on previous visits—with his mother or,
once, with Nancy—he'd been dulled with the impedimenta of tourism: hotel
reservations, rented automobiles, obligatory sightseeing. These last three weeks
he'd had a chance to look and enjoy. How glad he was to be here rather than in
New York right now. He thought of kids bathing in the streams from fire
hydrants around 116th Street and of sweating, fanatic joggers beside the East
River. Ireland was every bit as beautiful as they said it was: green and sweet-
smelling, perpetually air-conditioned—he'd read that somewhere—even when
everything was about to be shrouded in that subtly phosphorescent haze of
rain.

Seamus said, "I never knew my grandfather, but you know what? I always
felt closer to him than I did to Old Daniel. Maybe his spirit has lived through
me in what I've tried to do for Ireland. Some recalcitrant rebel strain in me. Old
Daniel never understood that."

Tom nodded. Michael Dillon had never done anything rebellious—unless it
was emigrating to America—and he remembered his mother's comment that it
was only Old Daniel's hard-won fortune that had enabled his younger son to
devote his life to a cause his father would have despised. Ireland had hardly
existed for Old Daniel. So far as Tom knew, he had never returned to the
country he had left as a small boy that November morning in 1856.

Tom stood motionless, captured by the sense of history perpetuated
through three generations. From these tumbled stones that had once been a
home had come a child that had become the father of his, Tom's, own father.
Because both Old Daniel and his father had been nearly fifty when they married, Tom could span nearly a century and a half of his own heritage as he
stood here looking southward toward Ballyvourney.

Suddenly he could sense his uncle's mood change. He looked grim: com-
minatory as an Old Testament prophet. "The Famine!" he said harshly. "And
the cholera that followed it. Did you know there was a mass grave not far from
here?" he demanded. "They buried them in pits, as quickly as they could,
terrified that they would catch the plague themselves. Hundreds, thousands, of
men, women, and children—nameless, faceless—crushed together in a deep
pit, rotting away together into the ultimate corruption . . ."

Seamus was silent. "Are you wondering who was to blame? Not for the
failure of the potato, but for the unmerciful savagery with which starving,
dying people were treated?" He paused. "I'll give you a clue, Tom. A coroner's
jury in Connaught held an inquest on a woman who'd died of starvation. They
brought in a verdict of willful murder against the English prime minister.

Remember the woman who wrote that book on the Famine—she wrote under some English name but she was really a Fitzgerald. She said that the English had to pay a price for the Irish Famine—the undying hatred of all Irish-Americans!"

He was still staring out across the valley. He added, "I sometimes think there are two kinds of Irishmen, Tom. Those that remember and those that don't."

Tom didn't answer. Obviously at this moment his uncle was in thrall to the passion that had shaped his life. And whatever the ramifications of his present plotting, things had clearly gone well since they arrived in Ireland.

From Cavan they had gone back to Dublin, where Seamus had booked a suite in the Royal Dublin on O'Connell Street. They had stayed there two days, with Seamus resting most of the time. Then they had taken off in their rented Ford Capri on the next stage of The Great Hibernian Tour. This time they had gone to an extreme Southwestern location: Bantry in County Cork. They stayed four days there, at Cantys Hotel. The pattern of their stay in County Cavan was almost exactly repeated. Again Seamus telephoned long distance. Again he went off on a picnic lunch, alone and on foot. Again he asked Tom to drive him to an isolated venue just as the light was fading—in this case to the neighborhood of a half-ruined Martello tower close to the ocean. And to clinch all these similarities, Tom saw the same pickup truck—it had Northern Ireland plates, he noticed—this time closely followed by a Range Rover.

But his uncle's mood was different. He seemed more relaxed, and in Bantry he actually met some friends and introduced Tom to some of them: a retired schoolmaster who had fought in the International Brigade in the Spanish Civil War and had been excommunicated for it when he came back to Ireland; a "returned Yank" who had organized a branch of the Gaelic League in a remote corner of Origen; a Scotswoman who collected and taped ballads and folklore. Tom could believe in these people because he saw them and drank with them, and they gave him a new and warming sense of his uncle as a man and a friend.

Back to Dublin again and then off to Carna, in the heart of the Connemara Gaeltacht. Tom got a sense of more urgency this trip. They only stayed two instead of their usual three days, but Seamus found time to show Tom Padriac Pearse's cottage near Rosmuc. There was no local socializing here, except on their first evening when they went into a bar and Seamus talked Irish with the men drinking there (the local National Teacher complimented him on his "blas"—pronunciation). By this time Tom had accepted the oddly ritualized, cloak-and-dagger atmosphere of The Great Hibernian Tour. He had begun to enjoy himself. If his uncle wanted his company—fine. But if he wanted to go

off on his own mysterious business—fine again. He could usually find someone interesting to talk with. Preferably someone local and Irish, but sometimes
American. He often got a whiff of pathos off these American tourists, most of
whom were elderly and working hard at enjoying themselves; halfheartedly
trying to trace relatives who had died a century earlier.

After Carna they had not returned to Dublin but had driven south from
Galway into Clare, traversing the paleozoic grandeurs of the Burren and crossing the Shannon by the ferry at Tarbert. Once in Kerry, they drove through
Listowel and Tralee on their way to Dunquin on the Dingle Peninsular. There
they stayed at the inn once run by the famous "Kreuger" Kavanagh. Exchanging reminiscences of Kreuger with the locals, Seamus brought the old man
alive before Tom's eyes.

They went through the usual ritual in Dingle, but Seamus dispensed with his
usual preliminary sortie. On the evening of their first day he had Tom drive
him to a point on the coast just south of Clogher Head. Tom stopped the car
and watched the old man pick his way up a stony lane to where a tall chimney
rose from a cluster of half-ruined buildings. Tom made himself dizzy staring at
the gulls wheeling around the chimney that had once served the smelter of a
now-abandoned copper mine and wondered again what his uncle was really up
to.

That night he realized that Seamus must be under some kind of police
surveillance. Goddamn it, the FBI had been watching the old boy for years, so
the Irish Special Branch had to have tags on him too! As they were leaving a
bar in the main street of Dunquin that night, a man jostled them, mumbling an
apology. Tom realized he'd seen him around the village: a big husky fellow
with bull-like shoulders incongruously masked by a business suit. The man
stood out like a sore thumb among the guitar-toting, blue-jeaned young
people who thronged Dunquin. As they parted to go to bed that night Seamus
said, confirming Tom's intuition: "Ray McGuffin was never the brightest, even
when he was directing traffic in Limerick twenty years ago. God help the
Special Branch if they have to hire the like of him."

Seamus didn't seem worried. In fact he began to act like someone on holiday. They went from Dunquin to Killarney, where Seamus had brought his
bride, Magda, in 1928 (the first time he'd ventured into the Free State after the
Civil War). He had never spoken to Tom about his marriage, but the sight of
every jaunting-car clipclopping out to Muckross must have stirred bittersweet
memories.

And now they had come here to this townland of Ballinmageery to the
ruined home of their forefathers. Tom knew his uncle must have planned this
as the crown and climax of their visit to Ireland.

Still staring out across the valley Seamus said, "Only one more to play now. That's at a place called Kilhassig near Courtown in County Wexford. Then—well, mission accomplished! My part of it, anyway." His gaze, alert as ever, challenged Tom. "Sure you still don't want to know what I'm doing?"

Tom shook his head.

"That's up to you," Seamus said. "All the same, I have to say this: you've helped me a lot. Helping me, you have helped Ireland."

"The Irish cause?" Tom grinned. "I told you: I've already had my cause. The Last Great Cause—where did I hear that phrase?" He shrugged. "What did I do, for God's sake? Drive you a few places. If I did, it's only because I'm dumb enough to like you, you hardnosed old bastard!"

Seamus was silent. Then he said, "There is something else. This really is a farewell visit. This time I'm really looking my last at this green land of my forefathers." He hesitated. "I'm going to die, Tom."

Embarrassed, Tom countered, "We're all going to die."

"There's a term on this, Tom. You know how they change my blood every couple of months? Well—soon that won't work anymore." He paused. "That's—well, I guess that's why I'm so glad you came with me this trip."

"Look," Tom said. "Let's get back to the car and we'll make it to Dublin as fast as we can. You can go into the hospital immediately—"

"No," Seamus said. "I've got this other . . . business first. And aside from that, I can't go into the hospital for another week at least."

"Why not?"

"The Carrolton Inauguration."

"You're not going to *that?*" Tom demanded.

"No—but I can't be in the hospital when it takes place."

"You surprise me. I wouldn't have thought that kind of shindig was your style."

"I'm not going to be physically present, but the event itself is still important to me."

"I'm only going out of a kind of left-handed loyalty to my mother," Tom said. "It means something to her, all right—but to you?"

Seamus smiled and shook his head enigmatically. Then he slowly circled the ruins of Michael Dillon's house. "The last time I shall see this place," he said. "But don't grieve for me, Tom. What I have done these last few weeks is more important than anything I have done in all of my life before. And you helped me." He was silent for a long moment. "Ireland," he said. "We're going to make a new Ireland, Tom. The Ireland men have dreamed of and died for. One Ireland—United, Gaelic, and Free."

❧ ❧ ❧

"Now," Dick Grogan said. "Exhibit A."

He handed Frankie a large colored photograph, blown up from an original of snapshot size. It showed a short red-haired man standing on a street corner. Close to him, apparently exchanging some kind of friendly greeting, stood an elderly man in an overcoat and bowler hat. In the background hovered another man, holding two briefcases and obviously surprised and resentful at being photographed.

"Well?" Grogan asked.

Frankie shook her head. "No, I don't know them. Any of them."

Grogan smiled. Frankie had never met him before, although Duane had described him as a cold-hearted schemer under his mask of dandyism. "And why would you know them?" he demanded. He had the kind of soft Belfast accent you'd enjoy listening to. "Yon is only the first link in the chain. Keep your eye on your man, though—the foxy fella—and I'll promise you a wee surprise!"

They were on their second time around Shepherds Bush Green. Wearing a check cap and expensive tweeds, with his white boxer bitch walking beside him, Grogan created a stylized and very English impression. Frankie had played up to his security obsession by pretending to admire the boxer before she actually spoke to Grogan himself—thus suggesting the old routine of man-picking-up-girl-through-girl-patting-dog—which was presumably what he had in mind.

"Look here upon this picture, and on this," Grogan quoted. He handed Frankie a second photograph. This showed the same red-haired young man standing on a bridge spanning an artificial lake in a public park. The bridge was crowded with children—swarming with them—but all Frankie's attention was grabbed by the other man in the photograph, who stood talking to the red-haired young man. She recognized him at once of course. The photographer had got him full-face, front-on. It was Rex Lang.

"You know *him*, don't you?"

"I do of course!"

Grogan nodded in a satisfied way. "The man you know as Rex Lang. I recognize him too—seen him on the TV up in Belfast! The man your friend Duane sold to the Wednesday Committee in a big way." He paused. "He's equally big with Loyalist Action."

"Loyalist Action!" Frankie cried.

"Aye!" Grogan nodded. "Keep walking," he added, for at his last words she had come to a dead stop. "All things to all men, Mr. Lang is."

"I don't understand," Frankie said. "What have those two photographs got to do with Loyalist Action?"

"I'm sorry," Grogan said. "Let me explain. The red-haired man is called Durnan. He's one of Lang's aides, but Lang has never let him meet the Wednesday Committee. You'll understand why when I tell you that Durnan represents Lang in dealing with Loyalist Action. That imposing-looking fella in the bowler he's talking to in the first photograph is top dog in Loyalist Action. One of its founders. A peer of the realm whose ancestors built half of Belfast's shipyards. He uses the pseudonym Mr. White. The fella holding the bags is just a shit-shoveler for the old guy. He calls himself Mr. Brown. Some days ago White and Brown traveled from Belfast to London. We had a tail on them. They met with Durnan at Whig's Club in St. James's Street. Now," he continued, "that first photograph shows Durnan with them just after they left the club. Now"—he gave Frankie the second photograph again—"you can see Durnan in the company of his boss, Rex Lang."

Frankie didn't say anything. "Keep walking," Grogan warned her. "Come on, Maisie! Step out a bit sharper!" It was the first time he had addressed the boxer by name. "I might add," he said, "that these two photographs were taken within twenty minutes of each other. The second shows Durnan consulting with Lang on the bridge in St. James's Park after he'd met with Loyalist Action."

Frankie was still silent. She felt dazed, poleaxed by what Grogan had said.

Grogan's voice went on, gentle, relentless: "We've had our suspicions for a long time. We haven't voiced them hitherto—partly because we had no proof and partly because Duane and the rest of you seemed so starry-eyed about Lang. But we've always known Loyalist Action didn't have the heft or the know-how to mount the Saint Patrick's Day killings alone. That had to be a contract job." He paused. "We only got a definite lead by chance, though. In fact it was a million to one against. Fella called McVeagh. Used to be with the UFF [Ulster Freedom Fighters]. Some kind of executioner. Anyway, McVeagh went to New York just before Saint Patrick's Day. Used a false name—a taig [Catholic] name, of course—and posed as an IRA man. Of course the Yanks didn't know the difference!" Grogan grinned delightedly. "After he got back to Belfast he got careless. Got pissed in a pub on the Ormeau Road one night and our lads took him in." Grogan was smiling, but his voice took on a new, cold note. "We convinced him to talk. After a time. Eventually he talked quite a lot. He didn't know much about Lang, but he told us who were behind Loyalist Action." He paused and then added, "They were right on our doorstep and we didn't know it. It was only a question of keeping a tail on them after that."

They had completed their third circuit of the Green. A little West Indian girl of five or six blocked their path as they came level with Union House again. She wore a minuscule bridesmaid's dress and she stared at them with huge incredulous eyes.

"For once," Grogan said with a flicker of bitterness, "we poor taigs are one up on you sophisticated Dubliners." He was deliberately thickening his Belfast accent. "Sure, your Mr. O Dunnacha Duane was quite infatuated with the great Mr. Lang!"

But all Frankie could think was: Lang is a fake, a traitor; he's playing a double game.

The Carrolton Inauguration was only twelve days away.

The telephone was ringing in Marta's suite in Jury's Hotel. She came running out of the bedroom to answer it, thinking it might be Leni Reffenstab— and despising herself for running at the same time.

But it wasn't Leni. It was Bud Halsey.

"Hi, Marta."

"Bud . . ."

It was extraordinary—almost supernatural—that he should have called at this particular moment. She'd been thinking bitterly that her relationship with Leni was definitely on the down—the bitch hadn't called her for a couple of days—and regretting how she'd busted her ass trying to get Lang favorable publicity in Ireland. And now Halsey. The only person in the world who could confirm or deny all her suspicions about Lang.

He joshed her a bit about all the signs being propitious for both of them— but that irked Marta always, because she knew Halsey didn't believe in astrology, and anything he said about it was just bullshit.

Halsey said he was calling from Dublin Airport. No, they couldn't meet. He was going straight on a TWA flight via Shannon to New York.

For a minute or two Marta didn't mention Lang: she found she didn't want to; she had a bad feeling about it. Halsey rapped on about mutual acquaintances—they got less mutual each time she spoke with him, she thought. Who was doing what. What—and who—was bankable these days.

Halsey said he had been in Rome (she knew that already), looking in on the making of a thriller about the theft of a Michelangelo from the Sistine Chapel.

Quite deliberately, Marta said, "I suppose you'll be coming back to take a look at your investment here?"

He paused for a moment, then said, "Nothing in Ireland right now, sweetheart. In the fall—well, maybe."

"Rex Lang's production. *Blood Scenario.*"

Now Halsey's silence was dumb bafflement—she could sense that. She guessed he'd even forgotten Lang's name.

"Yeah—I remember. Rex Lang," he said finally. "I didn't know he had anything to do with the industry. I thought . . . well, never mind what I thought."

"You don't know anything about this?"

"Some mistake, I guess. Maybe some other Halsey."

"There is no other Halsey."

"It's probably all quite kosher," Halsey said. "Our friend just doesn't want people to know who's really behind him."

Halsey didn't linger long after that. Marta asked him, was he still hosting those Jacuzzi soirees? He said, sure and did she want the franchise to import Jacuzzi into Ireland? Could do big things for Irish sensory awareness . . .

Afterward Marta sat thinking. Despite her suspicions, she was chilled by this certainty that Lang was a fake. He wasn't making a film at all. It was all a cover-up for something else.

What chilled her still more was the knowledge that if Leni chose to call, this newfound certainty would count for nothing. She still wanted Leni.

True to his military background, Lang undertook a daily inspection, getting an as-now report from each section. In the best army tradition of catching the enlisted men with their pants down, no one ever knew exactly when he would be making the rounds. He was usually accompanied by one of the "hierarchy"—Malachi O'Farrell or Mark Durnan and, most often, Leni Reffenstab. She was with him this morning.

"Come on," Lang said, "let's start with the Herr Doktor."

Even in summer the outbuildings behind Kilbrangan House were blocked from the sun, and this morning the air struck dank and chill. Leni shivered. She was wearing Levi's and a bikini top, and now Lang surprised her by laying his hand on her bare midriff and then sliding it down to cup the cheeks of her buttocks.

He pushed open the door. A naked electric light bulb swung like a pendulum, throwing long shadows on the walls. In his persona of Mad Scientist, Bud Rosen was working as usual in a jumble of dirty testtubes, pestles and mortars, and dismembered clocks. Anyone else and Lang would have blasted his ass off for working in such chaos, but he considered Rosen the best.

"The Great Rosen!" Lang cried.

Rosen leaned forward, bursting with pleasure at the greeting. "Hi!" he said.

"Well, Herr Doktor," Lang said, "zere are only ten days to go to ze Carrolton Inauguration. How is it—how you say it?—coming?"

"Okay, Rex." Rosen pushed back the lank twist of hair that kept falling over his eyes. "Okay. We'll be there on the day."

Why are some American men so immature? Leni wondered. This Rosen. He was over thirty. He had been a political activist for years. He had made bombs that had killed people. And yet, to Leni, he had the personality of a schoolboy.

"Don't worry," Rosen went on. "You'll get the material." A note of authority entered his voice. "One thing. The car bombs don't have to be quite as large as you specified."

Lang gestured in mock deference. "Herr Doktor!"

"About two hundred grams of Old Faithful—Composition B—with the usual timing device."

"Casualty zone?" Lang asked.

Rosen shrugged. "Sixty, seventy feet."

"Okay, Herr Doktor," Lang said. "At your discretion. Matter of fact," he added, "car bombs have actually gotten unfashionable the last two or three years. The Provos in Belfast have been using sophisticated incendiary devices. The Dublin police are going to be as surprised as hell when these start going off."

"Right, Rex!" Rosen was nodding eagerly, once more the gangling college kid.

"How many are you making?" Lang asked.

"You suggested ten. I'm doing twelve."

Lang looked at the wooden boxes stacked against the wall and nodded. "Fine."

Leni felt she had to say something. She hated just tagging along beside Lang: a dumb symbol of female assent. She said, "Those must be easy for you,

Bud. You have made car bombs before. What about the bombs for the dogs?"

"Right!" Rosen went on nodding in his exaggerated way. "Problems there, Leni!"

"Problems which you, Herr Doktor, will certainly solve," Lang said.

"Of course, Rex—I appreciate the challenge," Rosen said. "The gear for the dogs is something else again. The main danger of any impact device is that it will explode prematurely. Either when you fit it on the dog's back or later, with his jumping and twisting around. Trouble is, these are wild bastards. Angry. Ferocious. They've got to be. Of course," he added, "I could fit a straightforward timing device but that wouldn't jibe with the strategy of the operation."

Lang nodded. "Right."

"So it has to be a trembler, an impact device. You ask a lot, Rex, but I have to deliver." He indicated a complex interaction of springs and wires on the bench in front of him. "A sensitive vibrator fitted to a trigger. The vibrator reacts when a certain ceiling of movement—of disturbance—is reached. The contact claw completes the circuit and activates the detonator." Rosen was frowning. "But it's difficult. The appropriate degree of sensitivity can only be guessed at. Rex—I tell you: this time you got me on the horns of a dilemma."

Lang leaned forward; grinned; patted Rosen on the shoulder. "I know you, Herr Doktor. You won't let me down."

They went straight from Rosen and his bombs to Henri Barbier and his twenty-five German shepherds. As Lang and Leni entered, a frenzied anger seized the dogs and they began to snarl and bark and rattle the chains that held them in their stalls.

Barbier shrugged and said in a surly tone, "See? Those dogs are like athletes who train too long. They are—what is it?—gone stale!"

"Only ten days more, Barbier."

"Ten days and they ought to be used now. They're ready for action *now*. And when does Rosen have the devices ready? So that I can fit them to the dogs' backs?" He had to shout to make himself heard above the barking and rattle of chains. "The dogs have to get used to the gear. Know what it feels like. I must—rehearse them."

"That is surely very dangerous," Leni said.

"You think I mean rehearse with live explosive on their backs?" Barbier showed his yellowed teeth in a snarl of contempt. "What kind of crazy shit is that? No—Rosen has to make me dummy gear so that they can get used to the feel of it on their backs." His snarl turned to a grin. "Come here," he said. "Watch this."

They moved a little closer, Leni with reluctance.

Barbier leaned forward, extending his arm over the nearest stall. A huge German shepherd bounded forward, snapping his jaws, but Barbier was too quick for him, snatching his arm out of range. The dog howled with rage as the chain pulled taut.

"See what I mean?" Barbier demanded. "Even before I got them, these dogs were nasty customers."

"That's what we need," Lang said.

"Pain," Barbier said. "All the time." He moved on to the next stall, where an even larger dog lay dozing. He picked up a cattle prod and lunged at the dog's genitals. The dog squealed in pain and anger, starting up a new clamor from the others. "Pain," Barbier repeated. "So that they get kind of crazy." He let the prod fall to the ground. "Or you can use this. Strictly for the males." He picked up a loop of wire. "Twist this around his scrotum and then hook it to the wall. He learns pretty fast he has to stay still or tear his balls off!"

"Wow," Lang said. "We can use that as a Sokatsu discipline next time someone steps out of line. How about that?"

Barbier said, "You think I overdo this training? They're mad, dangerous bastards—but that's what they have to be. How do you fit bombs onto those dogs' backs without blowing yourself to fuck? Tell me that, fräulein?"

Lang was grinning. "Barbier, I think you're trying to get me worried."

Barbier grinned too. "Rex—I am working at it."

Serious again, Lang said, "You know something, Barbier? I think you have the answer to this all the time. Yes," Lang went on, "I know you, Barbier. I also know the spirit of France—the true France, the France of the OAS." He was smiling now. "So I know that somehow you have the answer."

Suddenly Barbier looked shy, pleased. Leni thought: Lang treats these men like children.

"Maybe." Barbier nodded. "Maybe if after their last meal the night before, we feed them a strong sedative. Then we get the gear onto their backs while they're sleeping."

"Just so long as they don't wake up too soon," Leni said.

"Or don't wake up in time," Lang added.

"They'll wake up," Barbier said. "In the vans. Hungry. Thirsty." He paused. "They'll feel plenty mean by the time you let them loose."

Lang nodded. "Great. But have you thought of this? When they wake, they'll be jumping around, knocking against each other in the vans—they'd be certain to detonate the bombs, right?"

Barbier nodded.

"So we need a safety catch, only released the very moment you turn them loose."

"That's it, Rex," Barbier said. "That's the answer."

"Good. Rosen can organize that."

Leni couldn't wait to get out of here. The heavy animal fug made her want to throw up, and she hated Barbier. Naive, brutish peasant, at one with the dogs he tortured. Although she had to admit that he had come up with a good idea when he suggested booby-trapped dogs. He had reminded Lang that the OAS had first thought of this at Vesoulin in 1962 (although there was some doubt at the time as to whether this wasn't just a canard put out by the Gaullists). Lang had gone for the idea at once and so had Leni, but she still detested Barbier.

"Uh-huh," Lang murmured as they left the stables. "All our pots are simmering nicely." He shrugged. "Any problems so far have been incidentals. I'd be more worried if we *hadn't* got them, know what I mean?"

He grinned at Leni, suddenly at his most boyish. "Good thing I don't listen to you goddamned gloomy Europeans or morbid Celtic-Americans like Malachi."

She pouted. "Ever hear of hubris, Rex?"

He laughed and didn't say any more.

They were more than a hundred yards from the house now. Ahead of them stood the huge barn that housed the arms from the caches so far taken up. The caches had been listed alphabetically by Seamus Dillon—A, B, C, D, E, and F—but they didn't necessarily have to be lifted in that order. Cache C had in fact been the first to be taken up, from a cave on the shore of Lough Reamor in County Cavan. C had consisted entirely of explosives: several tons of gelignite and a quantity of the TNT-base explosive known as Composition B (a favorite with Bud Rosen). Cache A, located beneath the haybarn of a farmhouse on the south side of Bantry Bay, had contained grenade-type missiles, ranging from the heavyweight Soviet-made RKG3 antitank grenade to the featherweight Dutch-made V40. Cache D, in a disused copper mine on the Dingle Peninsular, had contained machine guns, not only the American M60 but also Stirlings and a number of machine pistols, including the Czech-made Skorpion.

Dillon had also given Lang the location of Cache E, at Carna in Connemara, but since this consisted entirely of Armalite rifles—intended to be distributed to republican sympathizers who would declare themselves in the first twenty-four hours after the coup—Lang had told Malachi not to bother to lift this cache at all. They both knew that the first twenty-four hours weren't going to go quite the way the Wednesday Committee thought they were.

In the main, Lang had been pleased with the matériel. He commented that at least no one could accuse old Dillon of being prejudiced. "Russian or American or whatever—he bought it, he shipped it."

Leni and indeed all of the hierarchy had been amazed that Lang had agreed to the ridiculous conditions Dillon had laid down at Quimper for lifting the caches. The ritual telephone call to announce where Dillon was; the dangerous obligatory meeting between Dillon and Malachi O'Farrell when the old man told Malachi the exact location of the cache—all this was sheer kamikaze from the security aspect, especially as the Irish Special Branch must have surveillance on Dillon. But when Malachi had protested (hence Lang's reference to "morbid Celtic-Americans") Lang had stonewalled. "Ridiculous? I know. But what's the alternative? Dillon is the only man alive who knows the location of all of the caches. Other people may know individual ones—but how do we get on to those others? Even working through the Wednesday Committee, how do we make them tell us?" Lang shook his head. "Take us months and we've only got days! Easier to go along with him and get our hands on the stuff. Anyway," he had added, "as Inspector Glinn says, old Dillon has been at the patriot game so long that no one takes him seriously anymore." Seeing Malachi unconvinced, Lang said joshingly, "I'm relying on you, Malachi. Just regard these dangers as a challenge."

But everything had gone perfectly so far. Too perfectly—which was why Leni had gibed about hubris. Only two more caches remained to be lifted: B—which Lang had told Dillon they didn't need to bother with till after the coup, since it only contained more M16 rifles—and F, perhaps the most important of all, as it contained the mortars and rocket launchers that were to throw a ring of steel around the Carrolton Institute. Cache F was located near Courtown in County Wexford, and Malachi had left about an hour ago to lift it.

Lang paused at the door of the barn. "Okay, Leni. I'd better let you go now."

She had to get changed and then drive into Dublin for a lunch date with Marta Troy. It was probably the last time she would meet with her, although Marta didn't know that. But there was clearly no further point in her and Marta. They had gotten all they needeed out of Marta's influence on what might laughingly be called The Irish Cultural Scene. As a longtime friend and associate of Marta's, Lang had been accepted without question as an American moviemaker—with all the clout of wealth and eccentricity that implied. Thanks to this, Malachi O'Farrell—as assistant director in charge of Lang's second unit—had been able to traverse the length and breadth of Ireland, lifting the arms caches as Seamus Dillon identified them. Thanks to Marta's introducing Lang to Conan O'Kelly, the Irish police would give the okay to the hiring of a helicopter by Lang—would, in fact, be able to reassure the once-bitten helicopter company about the propriety of hiring them to a "film producer." Similarly, the police would clear several "action scenes" that would take place on the streets of Dublin on the morning of the coup. Marta had certainly served her purpose.

"That's right. This can be the last time," Lang said, as if he'd read her thoughts. "Kiss her goodbye for me. No bitterness. No regrets. Just lovely fragrant memories. Marta's just another loose end to tie up." He sounded exultant. "We're in the home stretch now, baby. Into phase one in just a week from now."

"What about Loyalist Action?" Leni asked. "What are you doing about them?"

"Durnan's going up to Belfast to meet with Mr. White and give them a final briefing. After all"—he shrugged—"the plan we are selling them is a basic, embryonic version of what we're selling the Wednesday Committee." He paused. "And then of course there's the question of Old Dillon. After Malachi lifts the last cache today, we can fulfill the contract Loyalist Action laid on him last year." He smiled. "So—we give them the old man's head. That'll please Mr. White."

☘ ☘ ☘

"Yes, of course. You look marvelous," Marjella said. "It gives me a kind of inner peace just to look at you."

Frankie stepped back and regarded herself in the long mirror. Disguising oneself as a nun had familiar and melodramatic overtones—going back as far as Nazi fifth columnists dressed as nuns in the invasion of Holland in 1940. Not that this was really a disguise. A brown-colored gown plus a modified headdress: a long way from the black robes and distinctive wimple of the nuns Frankie remembered. Unfortunately, Marjella's cousin—whose spare uniform this was—belonged to a nursing order functioning in San Francisco who were very much "in the world" and dressed accordingly. At the moment Sister Attracta was visiting other relatives in Donegal; she would be away a week at least.

"Yes," Frankie said, "I think your cousin's habit suits me."

It didn't, of course. With a total absence of makeup and old-fashioned shell-rimmed spectacles, the effect was merely prim and spinsterish. Ms. Colebrook had followed her into the religious life.

"Yes—you look marvelous," Marjella said again. "And absolutely invisible to the fuzz of course. No detective is going to look twice at a nun."

"Let's hope you're right," Frankie said doubtfully. Ireland had changed a lot. Was the garb of a religious still the powerful totem it would have been a few years ago?

Marjella said, "What a pity you can't just stay here. I'm all on my own. Attracta won't be back till Thursday week and Mummy and Daddy are away in the Algarve for three weeks. No one would ever know you were here."

Frankie smiled. Marjella was obviously enjoying all this enormously. Frankie had never met the girl before today. Grogan had given her a name and telephone number and commented: "A family with a republican tradition that amounts to a bit more than the usual self-seeking bullshit." Were they active in the movement? Frankie had asked. Only the brother, Grogan said. He lived in Philadelphia; he'd been involved with Seamus Dillon in setting up the foundation—if only in some minor capacity. The parents? They were stick-in-the-muds. Ossified into conservatism, they probably voted Fianna Fail. But this girl, this Marjella, had the real stuff in her.

Indeed she had. Frankie knew that now. Telephoning from Dublin Airport the moment she'd arrived, on Grogan's instructions Frankie had said she was a "friend of Kevin's" (the brother in Philadelphia) unexpectedly in Dublin. Marjella hadn't hesitated. "Twenty minutes. I'll be out there in twenty minutes," she had said and hung up. It had been fifteen minutes. Without asking a single question, she had driven Frankie straight to this house overlooking Dublin Bay.

"No one would have a clue you were here," Marjella reiterated. "This would be a real safe-house."

"What a pity Sister Frances doesn't belong to a contemplative order," Frankie said. "Unfortunately hers is a very active vocation."

🍀 🍀 🍀

The old graveyard was triangular in shape, with the base of the triangle turned toward the ocean. Ancient cypresses drooped in the wind; two massive oak trees had split and straddled the broken headstones. The tide was on the turn and a light spray beaded everything with moisture.

"Know something?" Malachi demanded. "You want the real Ireland? Okay—you got it. This is it."

"That so?" Congar asked.

"The analogy is really heavy. Your true Gael feels most at home in a graveyard. He's worshiped failure all his life—well, death is the ultimate failure, right?" He shrugged. "That's why I tell you that this burial ground enshrines everything that Ireland is about."

Congar stared at him. "Yeah," he said in a bored voice. "Yeah."

They had already opened the gates and driven the pickup truck and one of the Transit trucks up the overgrown drive that ran through the old burial-ground. At the end of the drive, backing onto the ocean, stood a square, ivy-encrusted building, the mausoleum of the Bagenal family, although a Bagenal hadn't been buried here in the last forty years. To the north swept away the long crescent of Kilhassig Bay. Farther north beyond that lay Courtown and Ardamine. This part of the Wexford coast was distinguished by thatched cottages, sanddunes, and insistent, ever-eroding tides.

Malachi shivered a little in the damp wind. He felt tense and anxious: more so than when lifting any of the previous caches. But not only was this Cache F the most important, it was also the most risky to lift. This time they were really laying their ass on the line. Set high on a ridge and visible from a considerable distance, the Bagenal mausoleum would be easy to peg out and then surround as Malachi and the others were bringing out the stuff. That was why Malachi had wanted to lift this one by night, under cover of darkness. But Lang had argued that a night operation would attract more attention. Malachi had also protested at leaving the lifting of this, the most important cache, till last—only four days before the coup. To this, Lang retorted that he had postponed lifting Cache F precisely because it *was* the most important: he didn't want the hazard of storing the stuff longer than he had to. In fact the contents of this last cache would be taken not to Kilbrangan House but straight to Lang's final advance-post in a disused bottling plant on the south side of Dublin. The whole group would be moving there tomorrow, leaving Kilbrangan House deserted.

Today Malachi's "second unit" consisted of Congar, Bud Willard, Brenda Wilson, and Martin Leach. At the beginning, lifting the earlier caches, they had really worked at shitting people that they really were making a movie. Now, although they still brought a couple of cameras and some sound gear along, they didn't bother that much. Mostly, the caches had been located in such desolate and lonely venues that they hadn't seen anyone. And those persons they had seen had been too stupid or too uninterested to care what they were doing.

The gates of the mausoleum were fastened by a rusty padlock, which Malachi now attacked with a hacksaw.

"That Dillon!" Malachi said. "Cute old bastard didn't put on a new padlock after he stowed the stuff because that might be noticed."

"He's an Irishman," Leach said, winking at Congar. "They're all cute bastards."

The padlock disposed of, Malachi paused for a moment to study the coat-of-arms on the arch above the gates. Through the obscuring moss he could pick out a shield depicting some mythical creature—a wyvern? a griffin?—and a date, 1793.

He muttered, "Ascendancy shit!" and plunged into the fetor of the vault.

"Come on—move it!" Malachi said. "Let's have some logical sequence in this operation, right? Get the rest of the hundred and twenties aboard before you touch anything else."

The Transit truck had been backed up right to the gates of the mausoleum. Now Leach and Willard were loading the cases that contained the French-made 120 mm light mortars. The more important Soviet-made Katyusha rocket launchers were already stowed in the truck. Only some Dragon antitank missiles remained to be brought up.

"One thing," Malachi said. "You gotta hand it to Old Dillon. He brought all this stuff in on a Breton trawler, unloaded it out in the bay there, and then ferried it across the sandbar in a flat-bottomed boat. All by night, of course."

"Where was the Irish Navy?" Leach asked.

"They got a long coastline to patrol." Malachi grinned. "But that Dillon—I just have to admire him."

And indeed he was genuinely impressed with the way Dillon had laid down this cache just over two years ago, thus completing the foundation's resources in Ireland. A week before Dillon arrived, local republicans had entered the mausoleum and, lifting the flagstones, had excavated a deep pit, large enough to accommodate the bulky cases holding the mortars and rocket launchers but not threatening the foundations of the building. Then the flagstones had been replaced, now resting on newly inserted wooden joists. When Dillon and his party arrived, it had taken them just under an hour and a half to lift the flagstones, stow the arms, and make it back to the trawler.

Dillon had described all this to Malachi the previous night when they had met briefly to go through the usual ritual of Seamus Dillon notifying Malachi of the exact location of the cache. That ritual of meeting was crazy, Malachi thought. With each repetition it got more crazy. Just as well last night had been the last time.

But that thought didn't comfort him this morning. This morning he couldn't think of anything but the danger they were in: how naked they were to discovery and capture. Normally he would have gotten exquisite pleasure from the irony of lifting these magnificent modern instruments of death out of the ancient, rat-infested tomb of the Bagenals, but not now, not at this moment.

All the 120s had been stored now. Leach and Willard had got the ten

Dragon missiles stacked against the inner wall of the mausoleum: they only had to be loaded onto the Transit truck. Another ten minutes and they all could be out of here, on the road to Dublin.

"Willard," Malachi said. "Leave the rest. Leach will handle those. You come outside with me."

The Transit truck was parked in front of the gates of the mausoleum, effectively masking what was happening inside. Now Malachi and Willard emerged, squeezing themselves past the back of the truck. A few yards to the left, using the cover provided by a clump of ragged, overgrown rhododendron bushes, stood Congar. Armed with a 180 submachine gun, he was acting as guard while the others lifted the cache. Farther down the drive Brenda Wilson sat at the wheel of the now fully loaded pickup. She had a view of the road in both directions. If she saw anyone coming, she was to flash the lights once and Congar would alert Malachi.

"Willard," Malachi said. "You and Brenda can split. Immediately. You know where to go." He paused and then added, "We won't be long after you."

He watched Willard start down the drive toward the pickup. Willard had a long, oddly shaped skull which made him look birdlike from the back.

Malachi looked around uneasily. The tide was fully turned now and the gray, sullen-looking sea was seeping, flooding in all along the shallow crescent of the bay. It was quite calm but Malachi didn't like the look of it. He'd always hated the sea. There was treachery implicit in the sea—just as there was in Malachi's present situation. They had to get out of here fast.

About to turn back into the mausoleum, Malachi caught the flicker of brightness as Brenda flashed her headlights.

"Okay," he said before Congar could speak. "I saw that. Come on," he added. Let's get the show on the road!"

He ran inside and began to bring out some of the props they used in their charade of filmmaking. He handed out a forty-pound Panaflex camera and a microphone and other sound gear, but already they could see why Brenda had signaled them. A police car had stopped at the bottom of the drive. Two uniformed Garda got out and approached the pickup truck. Malachi could see one of them leaning forward, his hand resting on the hood, talking to Brenda.

Leach came out. Seeing the patrol car, he was about to duck inside again, but Malachi stopped him.

"Stay out here," he ordered. "Congar—get inside and wait."

In silence Congar picked up his 180 and went into the building.

The man who was talking to Brenda nodded and turned away. He exchanged a word with his comrade. For a moment Malachi thought they were going to get into their patrol car and drive away again.

They didn't, though. They must be sitting inside the car debating whether to investigate further, he thought.

"I guess Brenda gave the right answers," Leach said.

"You better believe it!" Malachi said. "Otherwise . . ."

The two men got out of the patrol car and started to walk up the drive toward the mausoleum.

"All right. You know the story," Malachi said. "We're Rex Lang's second unit and we're just setting up to shoot a scene."

"Yeah," Leach said sarcastically. "Next time let's have lights and a dolly track and grips to work it—the whole schmear!" He paused. "What'll they think? Shooting a scene in a boneyard!"

"The pigs won't question it," Malachi said, "because they're Catholic pigs and the bones buried here are Protestant bones."

He didn't feel as happy as he sounded. This could be the one, unique time when Lang had miscalculated.

The two policemen kept coming. Malachi stopped tinkering with the Panaflex and acknowledged them by smiling and nodding. If he'd been in the States he would have considered this might arouse suspicion, but here he wanted to act the lovable Yank.

The older of the two men smiled back. He was white-haired, heavyset. The younger of them—not thirty, thin, and dark—did not smile.

"Hullo, sir!" The older one spoke so thick that it was almost a cod accent. Kerry? Malachi wondered.

"Top of the morning to you, gentlemen!" he said jauntily. "I'm Malachi O'Farrell, second unit director for Mr. Rex Lang of Omega Films, Sunset Boulevard, Hollywood, California!" He waved toward Leach. "This is Martin Leach. I guess you met my other colleagues already."

The older Garda nodded but Leach didn't respond. Goddamned zombie! Malachi thought. Leach might be a hotshot at the controls of a gunship over Laos, a tower of strength during an elephant zap, but in every visible aspect he was still the redneck from Parkersburg, West Virginia.

"Films, is it?" the older man asked. The younger one still didn't speak. "You'd be getting ready to shoot a bit of film?" He pronounced it "fil-lum," as Malachi remembered his father's folks visiting from County Longford had done.

"Late, aren't you?" the younger man demanded sharply. "I thought you people started at first light?"

Malachi smiled—genially, admiringly. "Gee—I can see you've read the books! Get those cameras rolling at dawn, right?" He frowned. "In fact, you got a lot of imponderables in this business." He paused. "Like the capricious temperament of certain beautiful actresses."

"Is that a fact?" the old Garda asked.

"Like the particular lady who's playing lead in the scene we're shooting this morning."

"That would be what you would call the artistic temperament?" the older man inquired in a grave, wondering tone.

But the younger man wasn't listening. He circled the truck: restless, eager—like a man who doesn't quite know what he's looking for, almost scowling in his frustration at not finding it. He said, "Do you have permission of the Church of Ireland Governing Body to use this burial ground for filming?"

"Well, now . . ." Malachi was still smiling broadly. "That would be something to ask Mr. Lang himself. He'll be along later—"

"But currently he's not here. And you are!" the young man cut in.

"Sure, didn't the man tell you? Mr. Lang will know," the older man said.

His comrade ignored him. "I see you've actually opened the vault," he said in a cold, accusing tone. "Do you tell me that Mr. Lang would ever have got permission to do that?"

Malachi countered that question with another. "I suppose," he said, "you're here to give us official clearance?"

"Pardon?" the older man said.

"I mean, I know Mr. Lang arranged with Mr. O'Kelly, minister for internal affairs, for us to clear some external scenes with you people. Scenes that have a certain element of violence," he added, "that might alarm onlookers who saw them being made." He grinned. "Not that the scene we're doing this morning is of that nature."

"Conan O'Kelly, the minister?" the older man echoed respectfully.

But the young guard seemed not to have heard. "Why did you open up the mausoleum?" he demanded. And then harsh, urgent: *"What have you got in there?"*

Malachi said, "It's kind of embarrassing . . . I guess we shouldn't have done it, at that."

"Done what?" asked the older man.

Malachi was almost pleading. "You know how it is. We needed some place to put our gear—"

"What's wrong with the truck you brought it in?" the younger man interrupted.

Malachi was silent. Then he burst out: "Okay. Okay. I didn't like to admit it, knowing the respect we Irish have for the dead." He paused. "There's a broad in there! She's getting ready to play this scene and—this is the embarrassing part—it's a nude scene, right? So—you see—"

"Do you believe him?" the younger Garda demanded, and started toward the half-open gates of the mausoleum.

🍀 🍀 🍀

Keeping her head well down, Frankie pretended to riffle through a directory while she looked out through the glass door of the telephone booth. This was just inside the main entrance of the General Post Office in O'Connell Street in Dublin and she was watching out for a man she thought might be following her. She'd seen him twice already this morning. That could be pure coincidence. Equally well, he could be from the Special Branch. They could have been on to her from the moment she arrived at Dublin Airport.

How she regretted offering herself as a stalking-horse to Inspector Glinn! Glinn had told her how he intended to create a diversion for his boss, Superintendent Slowey. In his report Glinn would suggest that the Basque ETA were going to collaborate with the Wednesday Committee. He would say that Frankie, along with Sean MacSaoirse and Philip Hurnan, appeared to be the liaison between the ETA and the committee.

She had agreed to this at the time because it seemed then that she had nothing to lose and that her name would add credibility to Glinn's tactic. Anyway she'd played her part in acting as courier between the committee in Dublin and Old Dillon in New York: there would be little for her to do now until the day of the coup itself.

Now that she was back in Dublin trying to alert the members of the committee to Lang's treachery, she realized how her situation had changed from the old days of Margaret Colebrook. To be in the files of the Branch was one thing; it was quite another to have your details run through the computer and to know that Branchmen at every port and airfield would be scanning the faces of incoming passengers in the hope of recognizing you. She realized how clever Lang had been. Using the Irish phobia about treachery and betrayal, he had bound them all by an Oath of Blood that kept them isolated, separated, in the watertight compartments Duane had spoken of.

Frankie still couldn't wholly accept the fact that Lang was corrupt and treacherous: that he was in the process of betraying them all. The shock had been too big to contain, immediately.

Meanwhile she had to go on telephoning. She had to warn as many members of the committee as she could, and it was only logical to start with those who lived in Dublin. Of course it was crazy to go into a telephone booth and start calling them on an open line—but what choice had she?

The oath, of course, had bound each member of the committee to make communications only through Duane. But Grogan's revelation made the oath irrelevant—obtained, indeed, by fraud. She just had to blunder on: speak to whom she could, when she could.

She'd tried to call Duane first, but the number had been busy. Then she called Colonel Darrell's office at Collins Barracks. A personal matter, Frankie explained, and his aide told her that the colonel was visiting the Curragh today. No, it would not be possible to reach him by telephone. The best he could do was take a message so the colonel could call her tomorrow.

Frankie paused to consider. Even allowing for the desperate situation, was blundering on like this the answer? Would it be safer to get in touch with Duane first, rather than feverishly trying to contact someone like Colonel Darrell, whom she hardly knew? And then there was the obstacle of the oath. She knew what tremendous force that would have.

She got through to Duane's house at the third attempt. It was strange to be telephoning like this. She had never called his home before.

A woman answered. It had to be his wife, Mara. The woman whose husband she slept with, but whom she had never met. The voice was pleasant, low-pitched, so gentle as to suggest an abnormal passivity. Mara didn't even ask who was calling. No, Duane wasn't there at the moment. When would he be there? He was in Galway today and Mara didn't know where he was staying, but he was returning tomorrow at two o'clock to open a seminar on the sixteenth- and seventeenth-century Gaelic poets Fearflatha O Gnive, Gerald Nugent, and Geoffrey Keating that was being held at the Dublin Institute for Advanced Studies on the Burlington Road. Mara sounded as impersonal as an answering machine. Frankie thanked her and hung up.

Two o'clock tomorrow? Impossible to go to Galway and find Duane—and waiting till tomorrow meant a whole day lost.

It was now 11:20 A.M. on Thursday. The Carrolton Inauguration ceremonies began at 11 A.M on Saturday. Just under forty-eight hours to go. Say forty-five hours to convince all of the committee that everything Lang had projected so brilliantly and convincingly at Quimper was false. A lie—a fraud—with them, the members of the Wednesday Committee, the victims.

How could she ever convince them? Not so much the bald fact that Grogan had brought home to her—that Lang was playing the Wednesday Committee off against Loyalist Action, using them both against some ultimate end of his own. No, it was worse than that—worse even than asking Irish men and women to breach their oath—she would be asking these people: Colonel Darrell, An tAthair Muiris, Maurice and Maidred Slane, Michael McClymont, Seamus Dillon, Duane himself, to give up a dream. A dream that most of them had lived with, suffered for, through most of their lives. She thought of what Seamus called the elders on that island in Lough Ree, waiting for the dawn they believed would signal their day of triumph. She thought of Seamus Dillon—how tell *him* that Lang was a fake?

But someone had to tell him. Someone had to tell all of them—and who was there but her? No good waiting for Duane now, with less than forty-eight hours to go! She had to contact the other members of the committee—all and any of them—as and how she could.

An tAthair Muiris. Try him next. He didn't figure in the actual mechanics of the coup, but his academic fame and priestly status set him aside from the others. If anyone could breach Lang's watertight compartments, he could.

She didn't know where he lived. She would telephone the Department of Philosophy at University College, Dublin, and find out.

Something made her look up—and then look down again. The man she thought might be following her passed the telephone booth, his face only inches from hers through the glass. She hadn't seen him so close before. He was a fat man who swaggered as if flaunting his fatness, and he was walking up and down inside the Post Office with the self-conscious impatience of a man waiting for someone who is already late: a favorite pose with agents conducting surveillance in a public place.

Sitting in the Land-Rover, Slowey enjoyed a clear view of the old burial ground and the Bagenal mausoleum. This natural observation post had been suggested to him by Sergeant Frawley, who came from Wicklow and knew this terrain.

A mass of tangled whitethorn bushes growing on the lip of this cavelike hollow enabled Slowey and his two subordinates to keep the burial ground under observation while they themselves remained unobserved. (The smallness of the team reflected Slowey's doubts about security in the Branch itself.) This hollowed-out bluff of land ended the ridge which the old graveyard began: some fifty yards separated Slowey from the men he had been watching intently for the last fifty minutes.

And everything had gone perfectly, like well-oiled clockwork, until five minutes ago. Then Slowey had seen the Garda patrol car arrive and the two uniformed men get out.

Up to that moment it had seemed as if his patient surveillance of Seamus Dillon was going to pay off. Last evening he had watched a tall, gray-haired man talk with Dillon outside the gates of the mausoleum. This morning he had seen a late-model pickup and a Transit truck arrive at the burial ground. The same gray-haired man had opened the mausoleum and then begun to superintend the loading of various boxes and cases first onto the pickup and then onto the other truck. The pattern they had observed at Dingle, at the old copper mine near Clogher Head, was being exactly repeated, except that this time they were going to catch the bastards red-handed, driving away with the arms—for Slowey had no doubt that he was watching the liquidation of the doomsday foundation by the man who had created it—Seamus Dillon.

When the gray-haired man and his cohorts had finished loading, Slowey had intended to pounce on them. To surprise them from behind by taking the Land-Rover along the rough narrow track that twisted its tortuous way across the top of the ridge. They wouldn't expect an attack from that quarter: they would be watching the road. Slowey would take them at the crucial moment. The timing would be perfect, the surprise complete.

But it didn't look as if it was going to work out like that, thanks to the intervention of these Garda. That a routine police patrol would notice the unusual activity at the old graveyard had been the one unpredictable X-factor and, maddeningly, Slowey had even foreseen it. He'd said to Frawley, half-jokingly, "Let's hope the law don't arrive and put their big feet into it before we catch those bastards with their pants down."

Slowey's powerful binoculars framed the little group in front of the mausoleum as if they were feet instead of yards away. The two Garda—an old one and a young one—were talking to the gray-haired man. One of his henchmen stood behind him. Another man was with the girl in the pickup; a third must be inside the mausoleum. Slowey prayed that the uniformed men would be thick enough to be satisfied with whatever explanations the gray-haired man was giving them. Otherwise—

Suddenly the younger of the two Garda broke away from the group and started toward the mausoleum. For a moment Slowey lost sight of him as he passed behind the parked truck. Then he reappeared at the gates of the mausoleum, the sun behind him striking him into an angular silhouette against the skyline. For a moment he stood there. Then he seemed to crumple. He swayed, half-turned, with the blind groping movement of someone dazzled by the sun. His legs bent beneath him; his body jerked forward—and he fell to the ground.

The old policeman moved forward, his face distorted with anger and fear, and at that moment the third man emerged from the mausoleum: a huge black man holding a submachine gun.

Slowey saw him raise the gun; saw the old man's head disintegrate into blood and snot like a bursting paper bag; saw him slump to the ground beside his comrade.

All this in a single frozen moment of silence—the machine gun made no noise at all—and then Slowey was out of the Land-Rover, running toward the mausoleum, shouting for Frawley and McGuffin to give him covering fire. He started along the ridge, drawing his .38 as he ran, although he wouldn't be able to hit anything at that range.

He didn't think they'd seen him, but then he was blinded by a searing scarlet ball of light in his face. He threw himself down and was aware of the bullets scything only inches above his head. So that was it. The legendary laser 180, the silent killer.

The track was uneven, twisting its way along the top of the ridge, full of humps and holes and rocky knolls, and this made it hard for the man with the 180 to draw a bead on him. Crouching face downward in a rut dried iron-hard by the summer sun, Slowey wondered why Frawley and McGuffin weren't giving him covering fire.

Then he heard the roar and rattle of the Land-Rover as it laboriously turned up and out of the hollow and onto the track. Sergeant Frawley must have judged that they couldn't fire effectively from this distance and so had decided to bring the Land-Rover along the track.

The 180 had stopped firing. Slowey didn't dare raise his head far enough to see what they were doing, but they were still there by the mausoleum. They must be: he would have heard the Transit truck starting up.

Meanwhile he could hear the Land-Rover thumping and grinding along the track. Did Frawley know where he was, or did he think the 180 had got him with that first burst?

Cautiously and laboriously, he started a slow, crablike movement to the left, off the track, still not raising his body more than an inch or two. He would try to drop into a ditch that ran roughly parallel with the track. It would be wet and full of briars and thorns, but through it he might be able to crawl most of the way up to the mausoleum.

He hadn't got as far as the ditch when he heard the Land-Rover stop a few yards away from him. They probably couldn't make it any farther. The rest of this track would be impossible even for a vehicle with four-wheel drive. He hoped Frawley had radioed to the Castle for support. No point in getting unarmed uniformed men from Wicklow town. They'd only be slaughtered.

And now, closer, within effective range, Frawley and McGuffin opened up. They were shooting wide at first and Slowey heard the bullets hitting rocks with a harsh, plangent sound.

Slowey raised his head a few inches. He couldn't see anyone around the mausoleum, but they were probably using the van as cover, sheltering behind it until the Branchmen got nearer. What did surprise him was that they had stopped shooting.

Now his own men had the range and Slowey guessed they were hitting the Transit truck. He was a little worried by the lack of response. That had to be a trap of some kind. He hoped Frawley wouldn't attempt to get any nearer. Let him stay here and keep up enough offensive action to prevent these bastards from getting away. Plenty of time to close in when they'd got their backup from the Castle. If that meant a siege, what harm? This burial ground was easily surrounded; it was a long way from any dwelling houses; there were no hostages. For once, all the advantages lay with the police.

Suddenly he heard a sound that made him crouch down, spreadeagled against the iron ruts of the path. A cumulative, metallic *thwock* like a great stone being hurled against the bottom of an empty boiler. He saw a huge globe of fire swell up and rise over the mausoleum in front of him. Then, as he pressed his face downward, he heard the explosion behind him, heard its echoing roar hit at him from all the surrounding hills, and felt a white glare of light sear through his tight-closed eyelids.

For what seemed like minutes, stones and clods of earth fell from the sky. Raising himself at last, Slowey saw that a cloud of black smoke so dense as to seem solid hung where the Land-Rover had been. Red tongues of flame licked in and out of the smoke, consuming what twisted shards of body or chassis remained. There was no sign of Frawley or McGuffin.

This had to be a missile of some kind. A rocket or bazooka, perhaps a mortar shell.

Only now did he realize that his own clothes had been scorched and blackened by the heat of the explosion. In fact the back of his coat was still smoldering. Roll into the ditch, he thought. There'd be water there to put it out.

As the hours passed, the water got colder. And, as the cold began to pierce like needles of ice into the very marrow of Marta's bones, anger and humiliation turned into fear. If she stayed here in this bath long enough, motionless, immersed in cold water, could she die of exposure? What was "exposure" exactly? The fact that she could hardly move at all must surely affect her circulation? And what would that mean? Frostbite? Gangrene?

Amazing to think this had all started as a sexy romp. When Leni had suggested taking a bath together, Marta had protested that the water wouldn't be hot enough to bathe in this time of day (the supply of hot water was always erratic in this crummy apartment). But Leni shook her head. "That does not matter. You are dirty, Marta. And before I touch you again you must wash the crabs from under your armpits and between the cheeks of your ass!"

Marta had liked that: she had whimpered and protested. Leni was splendid tonight: strutting, arrogant, piercingly beautiful in her nakedness. Punishing, authoritative: totally a Nazi. Although she could not admit this to Leni, Marta's fantasy centered around Leni as a Gauleiter in a death camp, thrashing and tormenting other women till they consented to function in one of the brothels provided for the SS guards.

How could she—how dare she?—refuse anything to Leni at such a moment? Especially when Leni produced a pair of steel grips shaped like a figure eight, one ring of which went around Marta's wrist while Leni held the other. If Leni twisted the grips one way, Marta fell on her face; the other, and she fell on her back.

And Leni twisted them now, suddenly, savagely, so that Marta fell forward, shouting with pain and nearly climaxing with pleasure and excitement.

"Okay—then you come into the bathroom and let me wash you, you dirty old bitch!" Leni twisted the grips the other way, jerking Marta onto her back. "Up!" She jerked them again and Marta struggled to her feet. "Come with me."

Then, while the rust-speckled, grime-encrusted bath gradually filled with cold water, Leni had made Marta lie face downward while she manacled her ankles and then expertly tied her wrists to the faucets at the end of the tub. Marta hardly noticed how cold the water was, she was too deeply into the impotence and humiliation of her situation. And Leni kept up a constant storm of abuse. "One word more out of you and I'll hold your head under till you drown, you filthy old dyke! . . . You're hot now but I'm going to leave you there till you get ice in your cunt . . . In a minute I'm going to drop that electric heater into the water and then switch on and kill you, you know that?"

Gradually Leni's rhetorical threats grew fewer. By the time the bath was full she had stopped uttering them altogether. Marta became aware that the water was really very cold, that her wrists were hurting, that the fetters on her ankles weighed her down like lead. And then she heard Leni saying in a cold, matter-of-fact voice: "Okay, that's all of it. This is the last time, so I give you your money's worth, right? You wanted me to play the whore for you, so I did, okay? I did it because Lang told me in case you think any different." There was hatred in Leni's voice as she went on: "You American women, you're all bourgeois cunts, you know that? You with your talk of liberation! You castrate your own men and then you think you can do it to the rest of the world with your money and all the shit you write and talk. But you, you're not quite the perfect American libber, are you, with your tastes? You wouldn't want your friends Millet or Steinem or Fonda to know you're into SM, would you?" Leni paused and then added in a quieter voice, "You can just stay there, tied up in the water, and good luck to you! You told me no one comes by this apartment; that's why you chose it. So you can stay there for the next two days—or two hundred days—but two will be enough."

She had gone away then and Marta had heard her moving around in the bedroom, dressing. Then she had left, closing the front door quietly behind her.

Now, an hour later, trying desperately to hold a tiny corner of her mind against the fear and horror that kept flooding in on her, Marta thought: She's not quite right about no one ever coming to this place. Someone else does know it: Annabel Rayne. She was coming here before I ever met Leni. (And since Annabel had come back from Quimper, she'd been here again, a couple of times.) She'll come here, she must, when she calls me at Jury's and they tell her they don't know where I am.

When, though? How long would Annabel take to decide something was wrong? When would she come here?

Hardly tonight. She might even be out of town tonight. She had friends and activities Marta didn't know much about—and naturally she'd given more time to them since Marta had taken up with Leni.

But maybe she would come in the morning? The thought of Annabel was a little island of hope in Marta's mind. Hold on to it! It was perfectly possible that Annabel would come in the morning. She almost certainly would come if—and it was *if*—she called Jury's and was told Marta hadn't returned to her suite. If she didn't call—but don't think of that! Pray that she did call. Pray somehow, even though Marta didn't usually pray: didn't know how to, really—and she felt a gust of anger toward her nut of a mother with her token Christian Science membership and then the series of expensive physicians when the going got rough. Yoga? The Third Eye? She didn't know much about that, either. But somehow she would find the blind mindless faith to hold on till morning. It had to be morning: no hope of Annabel coming before that. She couldn't freeze to death, could she? Not in summer surely; even an Irish summer.

She wondered where Leni was now. Back with Lang, of course. Back at Kilbrangan House. Now she saw with perfect clarity how Lang had used Leni in manipulating Marta. "You would play upon me; you would seem to know my stops." The line came to her from the rather diminished days when her grandfather had been carrying his *Hamlet* around the boondocks. She hadn't been born then, so how could she have heard him say that? Some atavistic memory, or had her father simply quoted it to her?

Anyway, that was it. Lang had plucked out the heart of her mystery all right. This time fantasy had betrayed reality with a vengeance. Leni wasn't just the hyped-up German guttersnipe Marta had thought she was; she offered the glamour of true evil, and so of course did Lang himself.

In her heart (Marta supposed) she had known that all along. Known too, even before that call from Halsey, that all this flimflam of moviemaking was merely a cover for some monstrous crime.

The evening news on TV was in Irish—as the name "Nuacht" indicated. Tom could hardly understand a word, but he could tell from the newscasters's subdued voice and solemn expression that he was describing alarming events. Even aside from that, Seamus Dillon's sudden shocked alertness a moment ago when this newscast came on would have told Tom something was wrong.

They'd been on their way back from Old Peadar's when Seamus had suggested stopping by for a drink before they returned to the hotel. This wasn't quite in character for him but of course Tom had agreed. They had gone to a bar at the back of the General Post Office. Tom was drinking a glass of Guinness and his uncle the usual John Jamieson on the rocks when Nuacht had come on.

The newscaster had to utter the name "Kilhassig" several times before Tom realized why his uncle sat motionless, his eyes riveted on the television set high above the bar.

From the newscaster's quickly flowing Irish it was possible for Tom to pick out other phrases: "Garda Siochana"—"Special Branch"—"IRA." Then came a film clip showing police sifting through the remains of some kind of vehicle. One could identify a wheel, a shattered headlight, and, incongruously, a leather briefcase that was quite undamaged. The camera moved on to show what were obviously four dead bodies covered with white sheets.

Now it was for Tom to sit shocked, incredulous. Behind the hurrying police and ambulance men he recognized the old burial ground at Kilhassig. He had driven his uncle there at dusk the previous evening. As usual, he had left

Seamus alone there and returned later to pick him up and take him back to Dublin.

Now the newscaster was obviously talking about something else. The Common Agricultural Policy of the EEC. Seamus leaned forward and began to speak to Tom in a low voice. He looked all of his seventy-nine years. The bone-mask behind his face was apparent now, mocking the fullness that sometimes made him look younger. He said hoarsely, "You know what happened? You know what he was saying?"

"Something about the graveyard at Kilhassig? Where we were last night?"

"Right." Seamus nodded. "We were there last night—and this morning four policemen were killed there. Two Special Branch men and two uniformed guards. Some kind of a shoot-out." He shook his head. "I don't quite get it. Apparently the two lots of police weren't working together . . ."

Tom realized from what his uncle told him that the police weren't releasing more information than they could help. On information received, the Special Branch had decided to stake out the old burial ground. Certain subversive elements intended to lift a cache of arms that were hidden there. And, whatever its source, this information was correct: this morning these so far unidentified subversives had started to lift the arms. The Special Branch men had been keeping the burial ground under observation, without revealing themselves, when two uniformed guards on a routine patrol of the area had arrived. When they sought to investigate, they had been shot. In the course of a subsequent gun battle with the Branch men, the subversives fired a bazooka or mortar shell into a police Land-Rover, killing two officers. Now the police and the army had set up roadblocks and special checkpoints throughout a thirty-mile radius of Kilhassig.

Tom had never seen his uncle so shaken. For once the cool conspirator had been overthrown by the warmhearted Irishman, grieving for the men who had been killed.

"It's an informer," Seamus said. "It has to be an informer. You know what they say—'Put ten Irishmen around a table and one of them will play Judas.' " He paused. "It goes right back through history. Always there has been one of our own to betray us."

Tom said, "We all of us rationalize something. Something that's important to us."

Seamus shook his head. "Vanity! The vanity of an old man who sees reality slipping from his grasp . . ." He paused. "The danger was spelled out to me—and I still insisted on doing it my way."

Tom nodded; didn't speak.

Seamus went on, "Now, of course, this makes nonsense of our plans. And those four men are dead."

They sat on in silence. Trying to detach himself from the noise and bustle that swirled around them, Tom studied his uncle's face, now rearranging itself into the familiar, genial mask. And yet the man behind this mask had unwittingly caused the deaths of four innocent men. Four men who had left their homes this morning, making the usual everyday commitments to wives and children who would never see them alive again. Smiling, easygoing, his uncle's face mirrored the paradox of Ireland itself: smiling, on the verge of laughter—and then that laughter blowing up in your face, spattering you with the blood and brains of the innocent.

Seamus might have guessed what he was thinking. "All right," he said, "your dear mother's words are ringing in my ears too. But this particular Irish plot hasn't failed yet."

"No," Tom said. "I wasn't thinking about that."

"I am," Seamus said. "It's obvious that I led the Special Branch straight to Kilhassig, so they're no doubt waiting for me back at the hotel. No need for you to get involved, though—"

"I'm involved already," Tom said. "Driving you there."

"Not necessarily," Seamus said. "That's why I want you to take the car and go straight to the airport. There's a TWA flight to Kennedy at eleven o'clock. You might just get on that. If you don't, drive to Shannon. You'll get onto one there."

"What about you?"

"Me?" The smile on Seamus' face was perhaps self-mocking; certainly there was a weariness behind it. "Don't worry about me. My holiday in Ireland"—he enclosed the words in derisive quotes—"is nearly over anyway. I've done what I had to do. As I told you in Ballinmageery, I'm overdue for the hospital, and this time there's a chance I won't come out." He grinned suddenly. "I don't think even the Special Branch can do much to a man of seventy-nine who's stuck in a hospital bed having his blood changed."

"Listen," Tom said. "I'm not leaving."

"Even remembering what your mother said?"

Tom didn't answer. Seamus sat staring in front of him. There had been silence in the bar while the newscaster was describing the shoot-out, but now the roar of voices seemed to batter at Tom's brain.

Suddenly Seamus tapped himself sharply on the chest—as a pious Catholic beats his breast in token self-mortification at mass—but the intensity of his gesture made it compelling. "Who am I fooling?" he demanded. "Refusing to face the fact of my own stupidity!"

"What do you mean?"

"There doesn't have to be an informer," Seamus said. "They only had to watch me, right?" He frowned. "You knew the Branch were tailing me?"

"I knew"—Tom shrugged—"*someone* had to be."

"I suppose," Seamus said, "I knew it too. You saw McGuffin hanging around in Dunquin—he got it this morning, poor dumb bastard!" He shrugged. "If I hadn't been so convinced of my own cleverness—so goddamned full of shit!"

Tom didn't say anything. Better to let his uncle play out this mood of self-accusation to the end.

"Yes, I should have known," Seamus said bitterly. "It was obvious enough. Look at me! Do I strike you as senile?"

Seamus didn't answer, but he was smiling back at Tom with all his old charm and brio. Tom suddenly felt irked. "Hear this, Seamus Dillon," he said. "I'm staying with you for purely personal reasons. Because I *want* to stay with you: bigoted, intractable old bastard that you are! Also because I don't like running away." He paused. "Ideals—'causes'—don't enter into it."

His uncle nodded.

Tom said, "This Irish cause is still a load of horseshit. To me. Personally. Right?"

Seamus nodded again, still with the half-smile on his face.

"Question is," Tom went on, "do we go back to the Royal Dublin? Are the Special Branch going to be sitting there waiting for us?"

"Probably," Seamus said.

"Why don't we both do what you suggested a moment ago? Drive to Dublin Airport and if we can't get onto a flight go straight on to Shannon."

"Uh-huh." Seamus shook his head. "I'm not running away either."

Neither spoke for a moment. The bar was emptying fast. Suddenly Tom felt naked, exposed. At this very moment the police were probably looking for his uncle—and maybe for him too. And even in tourist-thronged Dublin they might attract the attention of some alert cop.

"Tell you what you do," Seamus said. "Call the Royal Dublin. Ask if there's any message. Anyone looking for us."

"Suppose the police are there already?"

"Don't call from here," Seamus said. "There's a pay phone along the street. Call the desk clerk. You'll be able to tell if the Special Branch is breathing down his neck."

🍀　🍀　🍀

"You're sure," Seamus said, "that there's no hope of contacting Duane before tomorrow?"

"No," Frankie said. "I called the Department of Celtic Studies at University College, Galway. They say he took part in a students' debate there last night, but where he is today . . ." She shrugged. "But he'll be at the Institute for Advanced Studies tomorrow afternoon."

"Tomorrow afternoon is a long time away," Seamus said. "In the circumstances."

Frankie said, "It must be possible to reach some of the others on the committee before then."

"We have to keep on trying." Seamus nodded grimly. " 'Watertight compartments!' That bastard Lang sure knew what he was doing."

Frankie noticed that Tom said nothing. He was noncommittal, detached. But his coolness and disinterest might be to help sustain his uncle through the old man's shock and horror at the news of Lang's perfidy. It was no doubt a measure of that shock and horror that Seamus was now talking openly before Tom of the Wednesday Committee and their plans, apparently not caring what Tom made of it all. Frankie hadn't protested either. All of those plans lay in ruins anyway. What they had to do now was stop Lang.

"At least I found *you*," Frankie said.

"You were lucky at that," Seamus said. "We nearly decided to stay over in Kerry another day."

And indeed Seamus Dillon had been the last committee member she'd tried. She'd admitted defeat with Duane early on. Assuming that Colonel Darrell would have returned from the Curragh and gone home by six or seven in the evening, she had called him at home, but the phone had gone unanswered. University College, Dublin, had given her An tAthair Muiris' telephone number. In addition to his lectureship, he was chaplain to a community of enclosed nuns and lived in their convent at Swords, County Dublin. When Frankie called, a sister said that An tAthair was away in Killarney, conducting a retreat for some visiting American religious. No: it was obviously impossible to make contact with him during the retreat. The sister appeared shocked at the thought. The retreat would end, she added, at midnight on the following day (Friday) with An tAthair celebrating mass in the historic Muckross Abbey outside Killarney.

Who else was there? Michael McClymont, the TD, the rising politician and businessman, the "returned Yank" and self-made millionaire, who was still prepared to destroy the establishment he adorned. After Duane and Colonel Darrell, McClymont would be the member of the committee with the most important connections: the man most able to halt the machinery that Lang had duped them all into setting in motion.

She had called McClymont's offices in Westmoreland Street. Progressing through three secretaries—as symbolic of power and success in Dublin as anywhere else—Frankie had finally been told that Mr. McClymont was not available. Not away, not in conference. Simply: not available. And the most senior of his secretaries could make absolutely no prophecy as to when he would be available. Her cold voice was like a steel shutter rolling down.

Of course Frankie had been forced to ignore security and give her real name. If she had been able to meet McClymont face to face, she could have explained everything. As it was, this attempt to communicate with him must appear to him a gross breach of the rule laid down at Quimper—Lang's policy of watertight compartments.

Frankie encountered the same difficulty when she called the lawyer, Austin Gaines. No, his clerk said, he wasn't in court today. Who did she say was speaking? The clerk was away for several minutes. Frankie was afraid she would be cut off: she was using a pay phone of course. Finally the clerk returned. He explained in a careful voice that Mr. Gaines was sorry but this particular matter was sub judice and therefore he was unable to discuss it with Ms. McNagan.

After that there had only been Seamus Dillon to go to. (There were Maurice and Maidred Slane in Connemara, of course, and several other committee members scattered throughout the country, but all of these were comparatively small fry and anyway she didn't have time to go outside Dublin.) So it had to be old Seamus, and she knew that meant seeing Tom again. Did she want that?

This time she didn't telephone. She went straight to the Royal Dublin in O'Connell Street, where she knew the Dillons were staying. She was still in her nun's uniform, still "Sister Attracta" (Marjella's cousin would never know the patriotic use to which her name in religion had been put), and she noticed that there were several other nuns sitting in the foyer. She went up to the crescent-shaped reception desk and asked if Mr. Seamus Dillon was still staying at the hotel.

He was, but the clerk wasn't sure if Mr. Dillon was in just now. They would have him paged. Frankie sat sweating with anxiety while they did so. She couldn't decline to have Dillon paged—that would look funny—but suppose she was still being tailed and the spook heard that name booming over the intercom? After several attempts, she'd finally shaken off the fat man by the old trick of going into the women's room in Trinity College library (familiar terrain to her but not, presumably, to the fat man), locking herself in a toilet, and then squeezing out of the window. But of course the fat man knew she was dressed as a nun and she had no opportunity of changing. So she was a sitting duck for him or any other agent who guessed she might go to the Royal Dublin to look for old Dillon.

Dillon hadn't responded to the paging, but the clerk said he must be back soon: he never stayed out late. So after a second's indecision Frankie had sat down to wait in the foyer, near—but not next to—the other nuns. She hoped they wouldn't start to chat with her in a spirit of sisterly friendliness. Or if they did, that they would prove to be Irish nuns living in Ireland. She might be able to put herself over then as an English Dominican visiting Ireland, but if they were from England themselves, no chance!

The nuns didn't speak, though, and it hadn't been long before one of the desk clerks beckoned her over. Mr. Tom Dillon was on the telephone asking if there were any messages for his uncle. Would she perhaps like to speak with him? There had been a brief, oddly numbed exchange between her and Tom; he'd gone away to consult the old man, to come back with the request that she meet with them at McDara's Hotel in about ten minutes' time. Did she know it?

She did. McDara's stood at the corner of Parnell Square, across from the Gate Theater. It was a cavernous, meticulously preserved chunk of old literary Dublin. Brendan Behan had been ejected from here, spewing curses in Gaelic; Patrick Kavanagh had held court here; the protean Myles had done most of his drinking here during his last tragic days. McDara's was only about five minutes from the Royal Dublin, and Frankie had been here for the last half hour with the Dillons, discussing how they could thwart Lang even at this eleventh hour.

"There are two factors we must consider," Seamus said. "First, the security barrier Lang was clever enough to set up between committee members. We have to surmount that barrier: actually speak with the person in question face to face." He paused. "The second factor is the relative importance of each committee member. Even if we succeed in getting over Lang's treachery to him, is he influential enough to make it worth while? Does he have enough clout in the republican movement to sway events? To put the machinery into reverse?"

Frankie said, "Obviously we should consider the second factor first. To decide priority."

Seamus nodded. "I agree."

Frankie said, "Then Duane of course. He's the most important in every way."

Seamus nodded again. "Of course. But we can't see him before two tomorrow afternoon, which is dangerously late. What about Colonel Darrell?"

"He's certainly important," Frankie said. "In fact, as commander of the Honor Guard at the Inauguration he's the only member of the committee who's playing any active part in phase one of the coup. If he only knew what Lang is planning—"

"Hold that a minute!" Tom cut in unexpectedly. "Do any of us know what Lang is planning?"

Seamus said impatiently, "Tom, you've been sitting there this last half hour. Listening to Frankie. You saw those photographs. You know Lang was behind the Saint Patrick's Day Massacre. That he's working for Loyalist Action—"

"Sure." Tom nodded. "He's getting something out of both sides. He's gotten money and arms out of the foundation; who knows what Loyalist Action gave him?" Tom paused. "But why should he favor Loyaltist Action more than the committee? I'll bet he's shitting both with a fine impartiality. Lang is working for Lang."

"Of course he is!" Frankie said. "We don't know what he's going to do, but surely you agree we have to stop him, whatever it is?"

"Of course." Tom shrugged; sat silent again.

"One man you haven't mentioned," Seamus said. "Mickey Glinn. His function in phase one is just as important as Darrell's. He monitors the Special Branch throughout the coup. In fact," he added, "he's more important than Darrell. Get through to him and you could really do something to stop Lang."

Frankie said slowly, "I don't know. He's a funny, distrustful kind of a guy— although I suppose that figures. Can you imagine what it's like, playing that kind of double game inside the Special Branch?"

"But if the Branch could move against Lang—"

"We'd be picked up and in the slammer before we could ever get near him," Frankie said. "You just try telling Glinn. He'd probably think you were chickening out—even trying to inform in some way. No," she said. "Glinn has to be our last resort."

Seamus nodded. "All right. Is there anyone else? O Docartai?"

"The Castle have him under constant surveillance."

"MacSaoirse?"

"Goes from one safe house to another. By the time we'd found him . . ." She shrugged. "Anyway, by your criterion—which I agree with—they're neither of them important."

"It's Darrell then," Seamus said. "Try to see him tonight."

No one spoke for a moment. They were sitting in a small, black-paneled room on the ground floor of McDara's, although the noisy main bar, the dimly lit saloon, and these four private chambers were in fact all on different levels, fused together by twisted rickety bits of stairway.

Frankie marveled at the calm way Seamus had taken the news that must have destroyed all his hopes. As she told him what she had learned about Lang, his lips had tightened a little as if he'd been bracing himself against a sudden stab of pain. That was all. (And she didn't forget that he had heard about the debacle at Kilhassig only minutes before.) Now he sat calmly considering and planning: one of Ibsen's formidable old men again.

What was Tom thinking? Whatever his reaction to what he had just learned of his uncle's plotting, he wasn't showing any emotion. Of course he couldn't have traveled thus far and thus long with the old man without guessing that he was involved in a republican plot of some kind, but from their time together in New York, Frankie knew that Tom had long turned his back on all political causes and regarded his uncle's gut-and-soul dedication to Ireland as a romantic dream: half enviable, half pitiable.

Like own feeling for him? Frankie wondered. Romantic, it was—unlike the cold, cerebral lech she had going with Duane. Enviable, or pitiable, it was not. When she had decided to contact old Seamus, she'd wondered if seeing Tom would upset her, turn her stomach over the way it had in the bar in Quimper. In the event, she felt too numbed by the collapse of all their plans. Tom was there and she was glad to see him there: that would have to do for now.

"How much longer is there?" Tom asked.

"It's past eleven," Seamus said.

"Eleven o'clock Thursday night," Frankie said. "The inauguration begins at eleven on Saturday morning."

"Say thirty-six hours," Tom said.

"Shall we get a little more specific?" Frankie said. "We can't just go on sitting here till the Branch comes and collects us."

"Right," Seamus said. "Let you, Frankie, go to Colonel Darrell's home—I think he's got an apartment on Pembroke Road. If you don't get him, go on to McClymont's house—it's on Ailesbury Road, where all the embassies are. If *he's* not there, go on to Mount Merrion, where Gaines lives." He paused. "This time of night you must get one or other of them in."

"Suppose I'm unlucky?" Frankie asked.

"With all three?" Seamus demanded. "Okay—when you've tried Gaines and he isn't in, go right back to Darrell's and start all over. Eventually one of them *has* to be in. Pembroke Road, Ailesbury Road, Mount Merrion—that's roughly a circle. Any luck and you might get two out of the three."

"They're the only ones on the committee worth a damn," Frankie said. "Except for Duane of course."

"Aside from Duane and Darrell there is one important man," Seamus said. "I'm going to try to get to see him."

"An tAthair Muiris?" Frankie asked.

"Right," Seamus said. "He knows everyone. Everyone respects him. Not only in the republican movement—right through the thirty-two counties of Ireland. Yes, sir!" he nodded. "That man can pass through doors that stay bolted to everyone else. If anyone can turn the tide against Lang, An tAthair Muiris can."

"You're going to Killarney to see him?" Tom asked.

Seamus nodded. "By train, in the morning. They won't expect that—they'll expect to see you and me together, in a car." He paused. "So—this is where we split, boy. The parting of the ways, Tom. I don't want you to get any further involved. You're too late for that TWA flight, but take the car and go to Shannon. You'll get something going out around dawn. Doesn't necessarily have to be New York. Anywhere in the States. Just as long as you get out of this green and lovely land before they pick me up and involve you too." He fumbled inside his jacket. "Here . . ." He produced two thousand dollars in new bills. "You'll need that maybe. You, Frankie—you'll need money too—"

"No." Tom handed back the bills. "I told you before: I'm not going. And certainly not now that I'm needed,"

"Tom, I don't want—"

"Not you. I mean Frankie. She needs someone to drive her, don't you, Frankie?"

She smiled; nodded.

"See? I'm hired. As chauffeur. I'll drive her wherever she wants."

Seamus was smiling. "I thought Mr. Machismo America was dead?"

"It seems he's been drafted again."

☘ ☘ ☘

Frankie had decided to go back to Marjella's, where she could change out of her now incriminating nun's uniform. She would take a cab a mile or two out of the city center and then bus or walk the rest of the way. Tom had arranged to meet her at the end of Pembroke Road, about fifty yards from Darrell's apartment.

Meanwhile his uncle was insisting that they have one farewell drink and then split. Why? Tom wanted to know. If they weren't going back to the Royal Dublin because it was the first place where the Special Branch would look for them, why wouldn't they drive around and find Seamus some lesser-known, smaller hotel, preferably in the suburbs? There'd be time if they left now. But his uncle kept insisting that they had come to the parting of the ways. Tom was puzzled. Old Seamus was warm, even emotional, but never sentimental in quite this way. Frankie's extraordinary, terminal news about Lang must have struck deep. It had challenged, stimulated at first, but now that the decisions had been made and Frankie had gone, the old man seemed to crumble a little.

"Come on, Tom. One last jar and then we'll go our separate ways."

"I keep telling you. Not till we've found somewhere else for you to sleep tonight."

"Okay—let's have that drink and talk about it."

There didn't seem any point in arguing further. Agree and maybe he could get his uncle out of here all the quicker. If the police were looking for them— and they had to be, if they linked Seamus with the Kilhassig incident—then they would be combing city-center venues like McDara's. Anyway Tom could use a drink himself.

Neither of them had figured on the main bar being so crowded. New drinkers kept entering as if to discredit forever some axiom of physics or mechanics that states a given space can only accommodate an amount of matter equal to that space. Such a rule was being fast disproved, right here in McDara's. Sixty or more people were drinking in an area that might have comfortably held six—and others kept coming. Tom remembered reports of certain pub bombings in Belfast and thought how a few pounds of gelignite would mash and mangle this sweating thirsty mass of propinquant flesh.

It was hard to get a foot inside, let alone get to the bar, even if he'd been able to see where it was. But Tom started to work his way forward, muttering "Excuse me" at intervals although no one could hear him in the general uproar.

He had only achieved a few inches—he could still touch his uncle on the shoulder—when the bar was suddenly plunged into darkness. There were squeals and shouts and then the lights came on—only to go off again a second later. Tom recognized a familiar trick in Dublin pubs to harass drinkers who are reluctant to leave after closing time. But it wasn't closing time yet.

Then a voice blasted through the shouts and yelps; brassy, authoritative: "Ladies and gentlemen—a little hush, please! We're asking for your cooperation for a few moments. The police are here." The word "police" reduced the ceiling of noise immediately. "But you don't have to worry. This is not a raid.

These officers are conducting inquires in the city-center area and they must include these premises as a matter of routine. So the more you cooperate the sooner we can get back to enjoying ourselves . . ."

Silence now. Then a buzz of surprised voices. Then striking through them another voice, quieter than the landlord's but just as authoritative: "Thank you! We apologize for this intrusion but we won't keep you long. Could everyone just stay where they are and then gradually start filing out through this door, two at a time, so that we can establish your identities as quickly as possible. Thank you!"

Tom felt his uncle's hand on his shoulder: squeezing, signaling. He had to heave himself past a girl with glasses, dragging at her plump buttocks as he did so, and then he was face to face with Seamus again, only inches away from him.

Seamus muttered something. Tom bent his ear down so that Seamus could whisper: "Get out. Go. Up those stairs and past the room where we were before. "I'm going to create a diversion. When I shout out and keel over, you beat it, right?"

Tom didn't speak but stared at Seamus for a long moment. He realized that he was fixing forever in memory the fine features set like stone, the blue eyes blazing.

The police voice was giving instructions: "That's right. Two at a time. Not more. That's right, Thank you . . ."

Already the crowd was thinning. You could move now. Seamus held Tom with a steady gaze for a second longer; then his whole body grew rigid; he swayed from side to side; he seemed to be trying to speak but only a horrible gurgling shout emerged. Then he lurched forward, his whole weight crashing onto a small table covered with glasses and empty beer bottles. Several women cried out in shock and alarm. Seamus lay groaning, spreadeagled on the floor amid shattered wood and glass. Tom could hear the police voice saying: "Excuse me, excuse me . . . please stand back there . . ." and as he started up the rickety stairs a shrill female voice began an act of contrition: "Oh, my God, I am heartily sorry for having offended Thee. I detest my sins . . ."

By 5 P.M. this Thursday the whole of Lang's operation had been transferred from Kilbrangan House to the disused bottling-plant on the Stillorgan Road. Lang had located the place about two weeks ago, realizing at once that it

would make an ideal springboard for phase one. Huge in extent, with nearly an acre covered by straggling buildings, the premises included a vast glass-covered area which had once housed a fleet of trucks bringing the morning milk to thousands of Dubliners. The name "Leinster Dairy Products" was still spelled out along the plant's frontage in letters twelve feet high.

From an operational point of view the place was perfectly situated, being almost equidistant between the RTE television center at Donnybrook and the campus of University College, about a hundred yards from where Nutley Lane enters the Stillorgan Road. It was a natural from the security aspect too. A line of big old sycamores masked the plant from the road, and the covered assembly-area was large enough for Lang to marshal his vehicles and heavy armament there without risk of discovery from the air.

It was important that the new occupant of the plant not be identified with Rex Lang, the American film producer, so Mark Durnan had dealt with the realtor, posing as a scout for a Milwaukee-based babyfood manufacturer attracted by the tax concessions offered by the Irish Government. Of course it was all still in the process of negotiation, but Durnan had parlayed the realtor into letting them have full access to the plant for a couple of days. Technical experts, he said, would be flying in from Milwaukee this weekend to assess the potential of the plant.

Now it was nearly midnight and in the huge marshaling area, under the glare of arc lamps, Lang's cohorts were being drawn up in line of battle against the morning of the coup.

Task Squad A, made up of Lang, Leni Reffenstab, and Malachi O'Farrell, would enter the Carrolton Institute with everyone else, a holiday delegation of Swedish students who, presumably, would not be searched for arms. An arms check was unlikely, but any bulky weaponry was obviously ruled out. The inauguration would begin at 11 A.M. after the VIPs present had earlier attended a variety of religious services organized by every denomination in Dublin. When the ceremonies were well under way—around 11:20 A.M.—Lang would give the signal to Colonel Darrell. In fact, although designated at Quimper for the capture of the American president, the taoiseach, the cardinal archbishop of New York, and other hostages, Squad A was only a spearhead for the task to be carried out by the Honor Guard under Colonel Darrell. It was for them to effectively take over the hall and subdue any resistance within a few minutes.

There was obviously no need for Squad A to muster in advance. But for the last hour Squad B had been marshaled in the assembly area. This comprised Mick Congar and ten others. They would be carrying five 152 mm guns firing

Shillelagh missiles (guided infrared), Dragon missiles, and long-range mortars in four large trucks shrouded in tarpaulin in the manner of the old covered wagons. As Lang had said at Quimper, their task was to throw a ring of steel around the Carrolton Institute, effectively sealing it off from the outside world. Timing would be of vital importance. The guns had to be deployed outside the institute no more than a minute or two before Lang signaled to Colonel Darrell. That meant the trucks had to enter the university grounds between seven and eight minutes earlier, around 11:10 A.M. Congar would tell the gatekeeper and any other official he met that they were delivering catering stores to the institute. Hopefully, that would be believed—but no time was to be wasted. Anyone obstructing Congar was to be killed immediately. Congar would have to gauge the time factor according to the opposition he encountered. Obviously no dry run would be possible, although Lang had driven from the university lodge to the institute, roughly simulating the speed of Congar's trucks. Once his guns ringed the institute, Congar would establish radio contact with Lang.

This afternoon Squad C—four men and three women headed by Ken Chandler and Brenda Wilson—had visited the RTE television studios in nearby Donnybrook. The men had worn jeans and combat jackets; the women, jeans and ponchos. They had claimed to be students from the University of Denver, majoring in television direction. They would enter the center at 11 A.M. on the morning of the coup, introducing themselves as panelists on O Dunnacha Duane's Irish language program, "Daoine Ag Caint," that was scheduled to go on tape that day. Around 11:20 A.M. they would go into action. (Here again timing was vital: their initiative had to be synchronized with Lang's a mile or two away.) Duane was familiar with the layout of the station; under his guidance they would seize all the technical key points, taking hostages to ensure the necessary acquiescence among RTE staffers. (Of course a number of these were republican sympathizers who would be waiting in readiness to cooperate with the squad.) At first Lang had considered establishing a direct visual link between Donnybrook and the Carrolton Institute, but had decided against it. An RTE newsteam would be filming the ceremonies: they could record any significant happening that Lang wanted the public to see. It would be easier for him to return to Donnybrook in his command helicopter, bringing his hostages with him. Then at about twelve noon he would make his initial television statement to Ireland and the world. "Urbi et orbi," as he put it.

Squad D was, of course, not an operational unit at all but a grouping of different individuals, each working towards a common end; that end being to shatter morale and create a mood of fear and apprehension throughout the city and county of Dublin—a mood that would engulf the whole country within an hour.

One of the garages at the rear of the plant had been allotted to Henri Barbier and his German shepherds. Tonight and tomorrow the dogs would stay in improvised pens while he fed them a minimum amount of food and harassed them to frenzy with the wire leash and the cattle prod. The more aggressive they were when he turned them onto the streets, the better. At 10:15 A.M. on the morning of the coup they would be fed with a sedative that would knock them out while the explosive devices were being strapped onto their backs. Then they would gradually regain consciousness as they were driven into central Dublin: to spring into sudden snarling life when Barbier and his handlers released the safety catch on the bombs and let the dogs jump out of the trucks.

Another, smaller garage was given over to Bud Rosen. His bombs, his trembler devices and timing mechanisms, were ranged in readiness around this shabby whitewashed cave. He had spent the afternoon studying the parking arrangements for central Dublin. His car bombs would all go off within ten minutes of each other; the last a few seconds before Barbier unleashed his dogs. Today Rosen had drawn a rough circle—taking in such places as the Bank of Ireland, Trinity College, the General Post Office—within which his bombs would explode with the maximum shock effect. The cars to be used would not be stolen till early on the morning of the coup, but Rosen had already worked out the location of each one of them. Car bombs were old hat to him, but he wasn't looking forward to helping Barbier fit the gear onto the dogs—even though the brutes were supposed to be drugged.

Mark Durnan would head what Lang called the mobile destruction section of Squad D. By 10:15 A.M. they would have planted bombs at the offices of *The Irish Press*, the *Irish Independent*, and *The Irish Times*. (One of the Cork detachment would be performing a similar duty at the *Cork Examiner*.) Then, mounted on powerful Honda 1200s, they would range through the Dublin area performing a wide variety of tasks that included cutting telephone wires and electric cables, wrecking ESB transformer stations, and blowing up gasoline tanks.

And so, at two minutes to midnight, they were all assembled in the echoing, battered emptiness of the old milk plant. In his best five-star-general manner Lang had given orders that everyone was to hold themselves in readiness for his inspection. And while they might be impatient, they were far from resentful. They knew that Lang would instantly tease out any doubtful aspect of the projected action, and would proceed to resolve it by discussion and, if possible, by rehearsal, getting as near as was practicable to the conditions they would face on the morning of the coup. They all knew they could rely on Lang.

☘ ☘ ☘

Frankie knew she was climbing the wide steps leading up to McClymont's front door so slowly because she was nervous. Tense. Even apprehensive. More so than she had been in quite dangerous situations. Probably she'd been more confident then because she was functioning within an accepted framework: the cautious, almost paranoid, look-twice-behind-you rituals of the undercover activist. Now Lang's treachery had flushed her out of cover; forced her to make this blundering approach to McClymont that, by its very directness, must arouse suspicion.

She was glad to have shed Sister Attracta anyway; to be anonymous in Levi's again. She'd gotten to Marjella's house and changed without incident. Tom had met her as promised at the end of Pembroke Road. He'd told her how the police had raided McDara's soon after she had left; how old Seamus had staged a collapse as a diversion to enable Tom to get away.

"I don't know if I did the right thing," Tom said. "I don't know about 'staged' either. He's pretty near a real collapse. He must be in the hospital now."

"What about the Branch?"

Tom shrugged. "They'll probably have a detective at his bedside. Isn't that the form? He won't be able to go to Killarney now."

"I wouldn't be too sure. Knowing him."

Tom hadn't said any more. The fact that he had done what his uncle had wanted and got out—thus ensuring that the Special Branch would be chasing *him* now—seemed to indicate that he had finally committed himself to this cause he didn't believe in. Why? Some kind of quixotic loyalty to his uncle? It could never be because of her: that was certain.

Of course, she reflected with a touch of bitterness, now that it was a matter of stopping Lang, not working with him, Tom was fighting with the Good Guys: Order against Subversion. She supposed that if she hadn't learned about Lang, Tom might have continued supporting and chauffering his uncle—but still aloof, contemptuous of involvement. Or would the deaths at Kilhassig have made any difference?

Anyway, he was involved now. Getting no answer at Colonel Darrell's apartment, they had come to try their luck at McClymont's house on Ailesbury

Road. Tom was sitting down there in the car, a few yards away, waiting for her. Whether it was for her or his uncle or whatever, there he was. And she was glad he was there. Suddenly the fact of it touched her heart, investing her with a feeling of warmth and security—yes, even happiness!—that was quite ridiculous in the circumstances

There was no entryphone but a doorbell set in a circle of glittering brass. Frankie pushed it.

The door was answered immediately by a housemaid in the traditional uniform of black dress with starched white cuffs.

"Mr. McClymont?" Frankie asked.

"May I ask who wants him?" the maid said. She was unmistakably, fruitily, English. Wow! Hiring the daughters of the Raj as domestics? Was this the latest in High Dublin chic?

"I'm Frances McNagan. I called Mr. McClymont at his office this morning. I'm afraid there may have been some confusion. I don't think he was too clear who I was . . ."

"You want to see him?" the maid asked. She was about thirty: a brisk, depersonalized blonde. "Wait here, please."

Frankie turned her back to the half-open front door and stared down the steps to where Tom sat in his rented Ford Capri. She could see the parking light like a tiny beacon. What was he thinking about as he waited there? What did he really think of her, anyway? What did he want from her?

The maid was back. She said, "I gave Mr. McClymont your message. And he said to tell you there was no question of a misunderstanding. His secretary told him who you were and it was a clear-cut decision not to see you." She paused. "He says you should understand very well why."

Frankie didn't answer for a second. Then she said, "Thank you. I do understand. But circumstances have changed from what Mr. McClymont thinks they are. Could you perhaps tell him that?"

The maid had a hard, blank look. "Something else he told me to mention," she said. " 'Watertight compartments.' " She snickered a little as she said this. "I was to tell you that."

"I understand," Frankie said, "but maybe I could ask you to give him this?" She fumbled in the pocket of her Levi's, found a used envelope, and, smoothing it against the surface of her handbag wrote: "Screadaim go h-ard le gáir na tíre/Agus leagaim id lathair cas na ndaoine." [I shout aloud the country's report/And lay in your presence the people's woe], the lines from *The Midnight Court* used as a password at Quimper. Surely McClymont would realize that these lines had a particular significance now?

The maid looked at the envelope. "This *Irish?*" she demanded.

Frankie nodded. "Would you mind giving it to him?"

The woman pouted, openly sneering. "All right."

She went off again, closing the front door behind her. She was away longer this time. Again Frankie looked down at the car, parked directly outside McClymont's house. This was ridiculous. They were making themselves sitting ducks. What had become of the training she'd gotten from the Other Frankie and, later, from Duane? If the Branch hadn't checked with the rental companies yet, they soon would have, and Avis was such an obvious choice for an American they'd probably go there first.

The door flew open. Now it was McClymont himself: thick gray hair, red face furiously topping a great barrel-shaped belly hoisted on thin legs. He wore a tuxedo and smoked a panatella. "What's this?" he shouted, waving Frankie's envelope. "This . . . this *shit!*" As he leaned toward her, Frankie was sickened by the reek of cigar smoke and brandy. "I don't understand a word of it. I don't know you, anyway. You're an imposter, pretending to be Frankie McNagan's wife . . ." He sounded as if his rage was draining away inside him—and he wanted to keep it alive. "I only know we have a lot of crime in this district. The guards have been alerted. They're mounting special patrols."

McClymont knew she was no imposter. He remembered her all right. He knew those lines from *The Midnight Court* too—and that meant he must know why she was here. But this man was frightened. She could see that in the brandy-poached eyes in the bull's face.

"I'll put the fucking dogs on you, so I will," he muttered and turned, slamming the door behind him.

☘   ☘   ☘

"No," Seamus said. "I have absolutely nothing to add, Superintendent."

"You still won't say where your nephew is?"

"I don't *know* where he is," Seamus answered. "Tom is an adult. Over thirty years of age. When last seen, fully dressed and in his right mind." He paused and then added, "You know he's a citizen of the United States? Holds an American passport."

Slowey nodded. "As you do."

"Right."

"You might just be forgetting something, Mr. Dillon," Slowey said. "An American passport is a nice thing to have. But it doesn't confer diplomatic immunity. An American citizen commits a crime here in Ireland—he can be tried in our courts." Slowey shrugged. "He can even be found guilty—with infinite regret all round of course!—and even sent to jail—with still more regrets . . ."

Seamus was smiling. "Superintendent—I'm sure you're a great detective, but you've still got a smack of the seminary about you. A certain ex cathedra eloquence. You'd be a powerful man conducting a mission."

Slowey didn't smile. This ancient republican godfather was offering a face of stone to all Slowey's probing. When he'd collapsed in McDara's, Slowey had thought the old man was faking: possibly to enable his nephew to escape through the cat's cradle of stairs and landings that was the ground floor of McDara's. Now, two hours later, in St. Vincent's Private Nursing Home, the interns told him that Dillon's condition was serious, even critical. He was suffering from aplastic anemia of long standing. He'd probably been on the verge of collapse for days—and tonight he had collapsed. The senior intern was irked at Slowey's hint that Dillon could have been malingering. "He's on the way out," the doctor said. "Sure and why wouldn't he be? You can't go on changing the oil in a car forever, let alone an old man's blood."

Seamus closed his eyes. His face was paper-white; he could have been dead. But, for Slowey, Dillon's passivity held an armored, brooding quality—like an old crusader lying on his tomb waiting for the last trump.

He opened his eyes and said, "Look, Slowey—am I under arrest or am I not?"

Slowey was deadpan. "Let's say you're helping us with our inquiries into the murders at Kilhassig. No question of arrest—yet!"

"Arrest? Horseshit!" There was an unexpected vigor in the old man's voice. "The most of it is that you saw me visit the burial ground the evening before."

"I also saw you talking with a man who I later identified leading the attack on the police this morning." Slowey paused. "A man whom you choose not to name."

"I always knew cops led sheltered lives," Seamus said. "Did you never chat with a total stranger? When you were on vacation? That tall, gray-haired guy just happened to be around. I never knew his name. I was asking him a few questions on the history of the place—not that he knew much." He added: "As for Tom—he just drove me there. You've got nothing on him. Anyway, he doesn't care about politics."

"Really?" Slowey said. "Then why did he accompany you to Ireland?"

"Friendship. Simple kindness to me. Don't worry," Seamus said, "he was in Vietnam. He rejects all political solutions."

"Including the violently imposed ones *you* advocate?"

Seamus did not answer. He closed his eyes again; lay impassive, immobile, apparently indifferent to Slowey's gnatlike persistence. Slowey wondered whether to take a chance. He decided he would. He said, "If your nephew is such a political innocent, how come that we've got a report that he was seen an hour ago in the company of Mrs. McNagan?"

"So?"

"So he's involved with the same kind of subversives you've been involved with all your life."

"Where is he supposed to have been seen with her?" Seamus asked.

"Why do you want to know?"

Slowey had been back at his office in the Castle when Glinn had called him with this information about McNagan and Tom Dillon. Glinn had got it from one of his snitches, he said. Slowey didn't press to know which one. But while Slowey didn't doubt the truth of this report, exactly, his reaction to it was colored by his distrust of Glinn—something which he couldn't logically justify. And yet that distrust had caused him to impose a full surveillance on old Dillon while at the same time letting Glinn think it was merely a routine check (rather unprofessional between one senior officer and another). Well, his surveillance on Dillon had paid off—suddenly and bloodily—this morning. Dillon had been proved to be the associate of a group concerned with the illegal importation of arms: a group that had not hesitated to kill four police officers to effect their escape. Whoever they were, Dillon's claim that he did not know them was manifestly false: he must have been collaborating with them since he arrived in Ireland. Glinn knew all about the arms lift at Kilhassig by now and yet—Slowey knew—he would never refer to it. In the same circumstances any of Slowey's other colleagues would have been furious: would have demanded to know why they had been excluded from an important aspect of the investigation. Not Glinn. He hadn't said a word.

Or was this distrust Slowey felt quite irrational? A projection of his own frustration onto the most convenient target? Because Slowey knew he wasn't getting anywhere with any of this. It was all loose ends. Blind alleys. Pieces from different jigsaws that none of them fitted together. Nothing jelled, nothing made sense.

He still believed that misfortunate bastard Niles had been sincere when he told about the Wednesday Committee planning something against the Irish Government. The fact that Niles had been murdered so soon afterward made that all the more likely. And Niles had been killed by someone who knew he had talked to Slowey. That information could have come from a fellow prisoner on his cell block but equally well from someone in the Castle.

And then there was Glinn's flanneling line on Old Dillon, whom he had discounted as an active agent in any impending coup against the government. And what about Glinn's theory of ETA involvement and his suggestion that the Branch should invoke the help of the West German antiterrorist unit known as the Kommissar? Slowey had called Hans Glauber of Kommissar (called him from his home, not from his office at the Castle) and asked him what he thought of the chances of Basque participation in an Irish plot. Glauber had reminded him that the Basque separatists were now divided into two factions—an activist one that operated in small units of two or three and a politically orientated Marxist one. This internal feuding, Glauber thought, would make any involvement in Irish affairs unlikely, however much lip service the Basques paid to the idea of Irish freedom.

So what about Glinn's identification of mug shots of ETA activists on the DST files in Brest? An error?—the sort too-zealous officers sometimes make—or something else?

Slowey was standing at the end of the bed, looking down on Seamus Dillon. The old man had his eyes closed; he was breathing lightly; his hands were folded across his chest. Slowey thought of the crusader on his tomb again. The intern had told him they'd already taken blood samples: Dillon would get his first transfusion in the morning. Slowey had had to press hard to get to see the old man tonight, but if necessary he'd have obtained a court order to do so. Time was running out, and here he was still stumbling, foostering in the dark. Tomorrow the president of the United States would arrive in Dublin. He would enjoy an unprecedented civic welcome; he would ride through the streets to the music of the Garda Band and the Number One Army Band and the pirouetting of several groups of majorettes—Irish-trained exponents of an American art. The president would meet the taoiseach at Leinster House; then, having attended an Anglican service at St. Patrick's Cathedral, he would go to a reception hosted by the lord mayor of Dublin at the Mansion House, ending the day by dining with the president of Ireland at Aras an Uachtaran. The following morning, having been present at a special mass at the Pro-Cathedral, he would attend the Carrolton Inauguration ceremonies at University College, Dublin. Then on Sunday morning he would leave for the Isle of Man for the conference on Northern Ireland—a meeting that promised to be even tougher turkey than the Begin-Sadat talks at Camp David had been.

And somehow, somewhere in that chain of official appearances, formal meetings, and public celebrations must occur the moment of weakness, of maximum vulnerability, that someone, the Wednesday Committee or Loyalist Action or whatever faceless group lurked behind those titles, intended to seize. Of course nothing in Slowey's ragbag of rumors, hints, lies, and half-truths pointed directly to the American president—but there had to be *something*. The president's coming to Ireland was an event of such importance that in the present political climate in this country someone had to exploit it.

That was why Slowey couldn't let up on the Dillons. They were his only link with whatever was being planned. Old Dillon was safe enough for the moment—although Slowey was taking no chances and was posting a man, Will Crane, outside this room. It wouldn't prove too difficult to bring in the nephew within the next few hours, although the woman, Frankie McNagan, was a slippery dangerous bitch. But the police had the license number of the car young Dillon had rented from Avis and an all stations had gone out for the two of them. Although Tom Dillon was compromised only by association—with his uncle and now with Frankie NcNagan—there would be no problem about holding him for two or three days under the Offenses Against the State Act.

Suddenly Seamus opened his eyes and regarded Slowey. "Aren't you going to give me absolution, Father?"

Funny how the spoiled priest thing always bugged these old men. Slowey said, "Oh, I don't think that would be within my powers at all, at all! I don't have to remind you that certain grievous crimes are reserved for the bishop alone."

Seamus said, "How can you do it, Slowey? Your job, I mean."

"Because that's what it is," Slowey said. "A job—and I do it."

"Like the RIC did theirs pre-1920? Or the RUC in the North today?"

Slowey said carefully, "I serve the democratically elected government of the Irish Republic."

Seamus mocked him: "I like your carefully sanitized language, Slowey. 'Democratically elected government.' Beautiful!"

Slowey nodded. "Yes. The most feeble, the most corrupt democracy *is* beautiful—when you consider the alternative."

"Who are you kidding?" Seamus demanded. "You've never had true democracy in Ireland. When the British left the South they were succeeded by the men they *wanted* to succeed them." He grinned demoniacally as he quoted: " 'The Freestate Huns who bought the English Guns!' Jackals who moved in when the British lion stopped feeding." He smiled grimly. "Don't talk to me about the other crowd either. Judas de Valera, the man who founded the Broy Harriers to hunt down his old comrades."

Slowey said, "You oversimplify. You know what I think about you old Irish-Americans? You got stuck. History stopped for you—when? The end of the Irish civil war? The death of Parnell?"

Seamus shook his head. "The Irish in Ireland often say that. It's just an excuse for chickening out." His voice grew harsh. "Don't forget we Yanks practically invented the cause of Irish liberty. Stephens founded the Fenian Brotherhood in the States in 1858; it didn't reach Ireland till 1865. We've always been ahead of you. Where would the IRA have been without Clan na Gael? Don't waste your time on me, Slowey. I'm an old Fenian. Not a dime for blatherskite, every dollar for dynamite!"

It was 12:40 A.M. and Squads B, C, and D were still yawning under the arc lamps, waiting for Lang. If he hadn't returned to the milk plant by 2 A.M., Mark Durnan had the authority to dismiss all personnel, to reassemble at 8 A.M. the next morning.

Durnan knew where Lang was. At an empty warehouse off Leeson Street Upper. When the group had moved from Kilbrangan House to this last base at Leinster Dairy Products, two other smaller premises had been taken: this warehouse and a two-room apartment in Coleraine Street near Kings Inns.

The warehouse was to serve as a reception area for the volunteers drawn from a number of republican cells who were to function in the hall of the Carrolton Institute during phase one of the coup. There were forty-five of them, all young men between eighteen and thirty. They had been selected by the cell commanders represented on the Wednesday Committee by Duane in Dublin and by Maurice Slane and the other regional organizers in the rest of the country.

These volunteers had been brought here tonight by an advertisement in the three Dublin dailies:

> Extras required for film being made in Dublin center area. Young men of good physique and appearance under thirty. Apply Gribben's Warehouse, Upper Leeson Street next Thursday between 10 and 11 P.M.

This advertisement avoided any problems of communication between Duane and the republican cells. Four hundred and fifty-six young men turned up at the warehouse in response, including the preselected forty-five (who had naturally been briefed as to when and where the advertisement would appear). The forty-five identified themselves by whispering to Malachi O'Farrell the key lines from *The Midnight Court:* "Screadaim go h-ard le gáir na tíre . . ." The other four hundred and eleven who'd applied were dismissed as unsuitable, and by 11:30 P.M. Malachi had the forty-five assembled to await Lang's coming.

They were all hardcore republicans, cleared by the Wednesday Committee, but true to his policy of watertight compartments, Lang thought it better that they not go to Leinster Dairy Products but remain isolated in Gribben's Warehouse till the morning of the coup, just under thirty-six hours from now.

He was explaining this to the volunteers now (he had finally arrived at 12:20 A.M.). "I must apologize," he said. "But you must remain here incommunicado until we take you out of here on Saturday morning. I think it's obvious why. We are involved in a very large and very complex operation—an operation in which you men are to play a vital role. I wouldn't exaggerate if I said your function made you the most important single factor in phase one." He paused. "Therefore we can't risk anything happening to any of you during the next thirty-six hours. The committee informs me that none of you have a file at the Castle. Okay, great—but we still can't risk having any one of you picked up."

Lang went on to say that they would be provided with sleeping bags, and hot meals would be brought in as required. Tomorrow (Friday) would be spent in special training and in making sure that their uniforms fitted and looked right. "Most important!" Lang said. "That advertisement asked for extras, but what you've got to be on Saturday morning is *actors* and don't you forget it. You just better be convincing."

At 8 A.M. tomorrow Sergeant Gover would take over. A former drill instructor in both the British Army's Irish Guards and the Irish Army's First Infantry Battalion (one of the few men alive to have served in both forces), he would put the forty-five through their paces. Perfection in formal drill was important because the Honor Guard would be made up of highly trained soldiers and any shortcomings in drill or demeanor would stand out. Fortunately a few of the volunteers had already seen service in the Irish Army and several more in the FCA (Fórsa Cosanta Aitiuil: a part-time auxiliary force) and Gover would have time to put a sufficient polish on them all. The committee had guaranteed that all the men were fully trained in the M16 Armalite rifle and the M60 machine gun.

"We'd hoped to give you a dry run over the actual territory tomorrow," Lang explained. "Not the Carrolton Institute of course—but the rest of it." He shook his head. "We decided it was too risky. We dare not risk attracting any sort of attention." They would however get a full briefing tomorrow evening from Colonel Darrell himself. It might just be possible to set up some kind of rehearsal exercise within the very limited confines of the warehouse. "Colonel Darrell can decide," Lang said. "He knows this aspect of the operation better than I do. He'll think of angles I can't think of . . ."

He let his gaze sweep the faces in front of him—some eager, some stolid, some smiling, some grim—but all of them reflecting their awareness of the task that was to be theirs.

"All right," Lang said. "Now Mr. O'Farrell will answer any questions you wish to ask."

❧ ❧ ❧

As the blue BMC 500 drew away from the curb—0 to 60 mph in 4.4 seconds—Leni Reffenstab said, "Rex, there is something I do not understand."

"Uh-huh?"

"Why are we doing so much all at the same time? All at once? Tonight, these forty-five men who have to be drilled and taught all in the course of a few hours. Tomorrow the mortician's firm and the helicopters."

"Yes."

"With one day still before us? Only one day? So much—so late?"

Lang said, "But not too late. That is important. And the opposite of too late is too early."

"I still do not understand."

"Like I always say: security. That governs me in this and in everything else. Things we had to start on early we did—like lifting Old Dillon's arms caches or having Barbier train his dogs. But anything you can leave late, you leave late, because that's better security. Usually, the later you initiate action, the more successful it's likely to be."

"Yes, Rex."

He was looking straight in front of him, not smiling like he usually was when he laid the law down on any subject. She had asked the question she had not because she hadn't known the answer—more or less the one he had just given—but because she felt tense and uneasy tonight and Lang talking was less menacing than Lang silent.

Now they were driving down Morehampton Road on the way back to the milk plant. The night was soft and warm, the air damp with rain just fallen and slightly tacky with gasoline fumes. There was a lot of fast traffic still, although not as much or as fast as in Paris or Berlin at this time of night. Leni noticed Lang was driving more slowly than usual, presumably lest he be stopped for speeding and attract unwelcome attention.

They drove for two or three minutes in silence and then Lang said, "The physical preparations for an operation like this is the least part of it. The important thing is to create a climate of acceptance in which you can work. And to do that you have to create an image. It's like advertising. In this case the image is Rex Lang, American movie producer in Ireland. Once establish that image and you can do anything you like."

They were into the Donnybrook Road now, covering the ground that the chosen forty-five back in the warehouse would cover on Saturday morning. Leni felt more uneasy than ever. She sensed in Lang's manner a coiled-spring menace that could mean he was looking for a scapegoat.

"Why," Lang said, "the police are even giving us clearance for anything we do on the streets. Now that's really something." He paused. "Preparation! Like," he added softly, "the way we worked on Marta Troy . . ."

"Yes, Rex."

"Yeah. Good ole Marta. She really did a lot for us. Introducing us to members of the government and all. Getting us onto TV. Only thing is—she knows a few things about us. Or thinks she does. So"—the steel softly unsheathed itself in his voice—"if you had to put her into that goddamned bathtub, why didn't you hold her head under till the bubbles stopped coming?"

"Rex, I—"

"You didn't see it? In the *Evening Herald*? Just two or three lines. 'Actress found unconscious in flat.' "

"Rex, I didn't think they would find her so quickly."

"Of course they found her. With her kind of money, Marta must have a whole corps of sycophants—asshole experts you don't know anything about. Of course they'd go looking for her."

"Rex—"

"Why did you do it?" he asked quietly. "Self-indulgence?"

"I hated her," Leni said. "Okay, Rex—you will admit that I did what you asked me to do?"

"And I suspect you enjoyed it."

"Rex—American women are such *cunts*. And Marta Troy is the biggest cunt of them all. She's—Supercunt!" Leni gestured in the darkness. "You're an American, Rex—you're supposed to be an American—you know what they're like, what she's like."

"Self-indulgence," Lang said again.

"I wish I'd killed her."

"You should have. That way it wouldn't matter. Do you think she won't talk about this? About you? About me?"

"What are you going to do, Rex?"

He didn't answer. They had stopped beside a sprawl of buildings that lurked behind a row of trees that stood like black, menacing sentinels. It was still light enough to read the tall, skeletal letters LEINSTER DAIRY PRODUCTS.

"What you think I'm going to do?" he demanded. "Do you think I care what you did to a fucked-up old dyke like Marta Troy? I'm only concerned with the security aspect." He paused. "You think I should punish you, Leni? No doubt your behavior merits the discipline of Sokatsu. Maybe you even want that?"

"No, Rex, no—"

"You should be punished. But with thirty hours to blast-off I should waste time on punishing you? That would be more self-indulgence—on my part! No"—he shook his head—"I think I'll give you a task to perform. With Mark Durnan. *Under* Mark Durnan. This run you're his subordinate. Do exactly as he tells you."

"With Mark? I do what Mark tells me?"

"Right! You can regard that as your punishment."

His tone was almost joshing again, but she was frightened. He would never be content with that as a punishment. Soon, some time when she least expected it, he would come up with something else. She said, "What is it I have to do?"

"Frances McNagan. Glinn called me about her tonight. She's in Dublin, back from London, and she spent the day trying to reach different members of the committee. She was trying to tell them that we burned the Saint Patrick's Day Parade." He shrugged. "Don't know where she got that. Probably some Eireann Amhain snitch in Belfast. That doesn't matter now." He paused. "Most of the committee members wouldn't see her, and of course some of them were out of town. But old Dillon listened to her, and it seems he believed her because when the Special Branch came to pick him up about the killings at Kilhassig, his nephew went off with McNagan."

Lang seemed to expect some comment, so Leni nodded. "Yes, Rex?"

"You go out with Mark and whoever else he wants and get this bitch. I mean, kill her. Nothing subtle, no angles, any way you like just as long as she's dead."

"Sure, Rex."

"Before she gets to talk with Duane. He screws her; he'd listen to her."

"Right."

"And young Dillon too, of course," Lang said. "He'll be with her, he'd be a witness. One thing," he added, "we don't have to worry about that contract on the old man anymore. He's in the hospital and Glinn figures he won't come out."

Leni said, "Rex . . ."

"Yes?"

"Why did Inspector Glinn tell you this?"

She felt sure he was grinning in the darkness. "He tells me everything. McClymont called *him* as soon as McNagan left."

"But, Rex—how strange that McClymont didn't believe her. And why didn't Glinn believe her? She's Irish—like they are. Why do they trust you—a foreigner—and not her?"

Lang said, "You don't understand these people, do you? They're not programmed to a logical sequence, like you boring Germans. Glinn and McClymont are Irish; so is Frankie McNagan Irish. And that makes them distrust her!"

"No, I don't understand that."

"It's something to do with religion. They love to talk about informers. Betrayal turns them on. The shittiest Irishman wants to be Jesus Christ, but the one he really identifies with is Judas Iscariot."

☘ ☘ ☘

The figures in Tom's dream were thin, empty wraiths—thin and fevered as the sleep that gave birth to them—but there was enough reality in them to make him wake with the taste of fear on him. Curiously enough the dream hadn't been about Nam, but there'd been death in it all the same. "The Pale Heads of the Dead." Where had he heard that phrase?

He felt a movement beside him. Frankie. She had gone to sleep beside him in the back of the car.

Tom was fully awake now: stiff-legged, dry-mouthed, unshaven, bleary-eyed—in that particularly grubby state of discomfort only achieved on very long journeys. But it was essentially a civilized, *civilian* feeling. In the army, in Nam, you sank so much lower in the scale of discomfort that personal itch and filth became the norm.

He put his hand out and touched Frankie's shoulder.

She opened her eyes at once—so quickly that he wondered if she'd been alseep at all. "Hullo," she said. She certainly didn't look frowzy and beat-up like he felt. A bit tousled and windswept maybe. She had exchanged Sister Attracta's prim uniform for an Aran-knit sweater and Levi's and he was more sexually aware of her than ever, but when he had parked the car here less than three hours ago they had exchanged only a single, decidedly sisterly kiss before sliding into thin, uneasy sleep. What did that mean? Chaste comrades till their mission was achieved?

Maybe that was how it had to be with her. Was the night they'd had together at Max's apartment on West Fifty-seventh a once-off, single fragrant episode in the grimy murderous life of an urban guerrilla? Which, after all, was what she was—although he could never really accept her as that. Ever since he'd first met her, ever since they had walked together in Carl Schurz Park, he'd been tormented by that menacing image of her. Was she really like that?

Suddenly in the intense weariness of this dry-mouthed 5:30 A.M. waking— there were red blush-marks showing through the clouds over the Dublin Mountains: it would soon be light—Tom longed to say, "Let's forget Lang, Seamus, the Carrolton Inauguration, America, Ireland: all of it—and just take off, baby!" Where, did not matter at all.

Of course it was all nonsense. They had to keep on. Having once entered his uncle's and Frankie's world, he could not cop out. It was a shadowless, low-profile world; a paranoid world where you trod out elaborate rituals of disguise and recognition. A gameplayer's world where you played with life and death for forfeits.

It wasn't his world, though. Tom felt he was being programmed to play the kind of hero he'd often seen during the early days in Indochina—and resolved never to be. Not then—and not now if he could help it. His mother was right about Irish plots and plotters. This looked like being the hairiest fiasco since the Fenian attempt to invade Canada in 1866.

Hindsight always presents everything as simple—black and white, right or wrong—but Tom wondered about the obstinacy that had made his uncle insist on personally identifying all the arms caches for Lang. And why had Duane accepted Lang's package almost without question, selling it to the rest of the committee practically sight unseen. Why had Duane's former comrades of Eireann Amhain in Belfast been able to unmask Lang when Duane couldn't? Were political activists merely romantic incompetents, lurching from one self-imposed disaster to another, only saved by the still greater incompetence of the agents who were chasing them? But then Tom remembered the four policemen murdered at Kilhassig . . .

One question still nagged him: why could not Frankie, once she was convinced of Lang's treachery, make immediate contact with Duane and Darrell and the others? All right to talk about Lang's watertight compartments, but this went beyond that. It revealed the unsuspected depths of distrust that yawned between different members of the committee.

No point in asking these questions now, though. No point in looking beyond the immediate facts of the situation. So far all their attempts to halt the ongoing machinery of the coup had proved futile. Duane was apparently unreachable for another seven or eight hours. Till two this afternoon in fact, when he would be at the Dublin Institute for Advanced Studies, talking about the Gaelic poets of the sixteenth and seventeenth centuries.

Last night, after their hostile reception by McClymont, Tom and Frankie had driven to Duane's house in Chapelizod. They had parked opposite a gloomy, tree-masked Victorian villa and at once Frankie had said, "He's not there. His car's not there."

"Whose is the Fiat 127?"

"His wife's. He drives a Renault 4."

Tom realized that Frankie disliked the thought of the wife's physical presence inside that house—and he in turn was obscurely hurt by that, because he knew it had to do with her screwing Duane.

They drove in silence. By now it was nearly two in the morning and they had tried all the Dublin-based members of the committee with one exception. "Inspector Glinn?" Tom had asked.

Frankie shook her head. "I still think that's too dangerous. We have to see Duane first."

"Try Darrell again, if you like. He must be home by now."

And so they had driven back to Pembroke Road to climb again the massive flight of steps up to Darrell's apartment. And this time, when they spoke through the entryphone, they got an answer: a huskily muttered question that could have come from either a man or a woman.

"Who?"

Tom figured it was a woman.

"Francis McNagan," Frankie repeated.

There was a grumbling murmur that was quite unintelligible. Then laughter like hiccups and a whispered comment: "Why not? If you want to rape me, what have I to lose?"

After a moment they realized they were being admitted: the front door was open.

Darrell's apartment was number four. They passed one, two and three on their way up. Then they heard a woman shouting: "Come on, you fuckers! What are you waiting for?"

She was standing on the next landing, at the open door of the apartment. A tiny woman, dark and haggard, she wore a man's white shirt—frayed at the collar and black with dirt—and the stained pants of what had once been a modish trouser suit.

"You're fucking slow, aren't you?" she demanded. "I hope it doesn't reflect the pace of your actual fucking or you're in the height of trouble!"

She addressed them not as strangers but as if the three of them were continuing a conversation already begun.

"I know you didn't really want to see *him*. You knew he wasn't here, didn't you?" she said and winked. "But I was onto you. You bet your fucking gonads! From the moment you spoke into that tube. 'Francis McNagan.' That has to be a pseudonym, I said. A fucking *nom de guerre!*"

Frankie shook her head. "My real name."

Ignoring her, the woman went on, "There's a suggestion of fate in all this. Because I've been out all night and I've only just come home. Not five minutes ago. Just before you chose to arrive." She paused and then added triumphantly, "But don't think I don't know who you are."

Tom said, "Mrs. Darrell, isn't it? It's very important that we speak with your husband."

"Don't try to cod me," she said. "I know who you are."

"It's most urgent," Frankie said.

"I'd say it is," Mrs. Darrell agreed. "A fucking urgent matter! Or, more accurately, a matter of urgent fucking."

Tom realized the woman was smashed. And not just normal smashed, but so soaked and sodden that she had passed through all the stages—aggressive-drunk, stupid-drunk and the rest—and straight out again into a world of her own.

"Mrs. Darrell," he said, "I wouldn't try to fool you. Maybe you do know who we are."

She nodded. "Come inside."

The room was dark and airless, obstructed by heavy mahogany furniture. In its Victorian heaviness it seemed to cry out for tusks and antlers and stuffed birds.

Mrs. Darrell held on to the edge of a huge sideboard while she fumbled with a cigarette. She was quite emaciated: at once childlike and haglike under her filthy clothes. Tom remembered old Seamus pointing out her husband to him outside the Gradlon in Quimper. Tall and lean, whipcord-muscled and gray-mustached, Darrell was so much the stereotype of "The Colonel" that he might have been an actor playing the role.

"You're detectives, aren't you?" Mrs. Darrell said. "Gathering information for a nice filthy crim. con. case against Darrell with nice fat damages. 'Criminal conversation,'" she said gloatingly. "Makes the poor old English divorce sound tame, doesn't it?"

"This is very important," Tom said. "But it's nothing to do with Colonel Darrell's private life."

"Private? It's all he can do not to screw that fat whore Sheila Borrett in *public!* Fucking the wife of his adjutant and brother officer, dear little Diurmid Borrett—who doesn't *mind!* Who actually welcomes it if it helps his chance of promotion." Her tone grew solemn, self-pitying. "And you both know he's there in the bungalow with her, getting it up for maybe the second or third

time tonight—and you're cruel enough to come here and talk to me like this."
Two huge teardrops gathered glistening at the corner of her eyes and rolled
down.

"Can you tell us where he is?" Frankie asked.

"You'd like to go up there and catch them at it, wouldn't you?" Mrs.
Darrell demanded. "You'd enjoy *watching* wouldn't you? And it's a bungalow
so you wouldn't need to go up a ladder to take photographs."

"I assure you—" Tom began.

"No!" Mrs. Darrell shouted. "I've been dragged face downwards in the shit
for long enough! There are limits . . ." She came forward and stared up at
Tom. "It's blackmail. A put-up job. Diurmid is a contemptible pimp. I'd be a
fool to help you take money out of Darrell's pocket and put it into Diurmid's."

Instinctively, in unisin, Tom and Frankie both moved toward the door. As
they passed through it, they heard Mrs. Darrell say in a musing tone: "Maybe
Diurmid *does* care after all."

"Wow," Tom said as they reached the ground floor.

"How about that?" Frankie exclaimed.

"That's it for Darrell then," Tom said as they were getting into the car.

"Unless we try him again at Collins Barracks tomorrow," Frankie said. But
she didn't sound very hopeful.

"That makes Duane the last hope of the side."

After that they had agreed that there was nothing more they could do that
night—or rather, that morning, for it was approaching three o'clock. Soon
afterward Tom had parked in a cul-de-sac near the Royal Dublin Society
grounds at Ballsbridge, and they huddled together to grab an hour or two of
fretful sleep.

And now it was light again. Another day beginning. The last full day before
the coup. The last day on which Lang could be defeated.

"I suppose there's one other thing we could do," Frankie said.

"Yes?"

"Go to Killarney and see An tAthair Muiris," she said. "I suppose one could
get to see him? Even when he's conducting a retreat?"

Tom shook his head. "It's nearly two hundred miles from Dublin to Killarney. Get there and back by two this afternoon? Anyway," he went on, "the
police have got to have details of this car by now. In fact it's amazing they
didn't get us when we were sleeping. Maybe the Special Branch don't work a
night shift?" He paused. "But we should sure as hell ditch it now it's
light."

"Don't forget the president's coming to Dublin today," Frankie said. "That will divert a lot of police energy. Lang is counting on that."

"The president is going to have a nice day for his visit," Tom said.

Indeed it was a beautiful summer morning with the promise of later heat tempered by that unique softness in the air that keeps Ireland green. A morning to be happy on. Not a morning to be killed on—or to kill anyone else. Although, strangely, the prospect of violent action didn't sicken Tom as much as it should have done. This morning he felt an athlete's relaxed alertness, the sharpened sense of observation that seems to make the seconds tick slower. He hadn't felt this way since his first days in Nam.

Shit, he should know enough by this time to resist that kind of adrenaline boost. And surely he ought to share the anger and disappointment Frankie and his uncle felt at the collapse of all their plans. But somehow he couldn't. After all, they had never been *his* plans: he had never known what was happening. If he had, he would never have gone along with it. This plot to create a single united Gaelic Ireland by taking over the Irish Republic on the eve of the Isle of Man Conference and then, in the chaos that followed, grabbing the strife-torn Six Counties as well—this was the stuff of fantasy. But the kind of fantasy that, acted out, represents a scenario for bloodshed. *Blood Scenario*—wasn't that the title for Lang's film that would never be made?

The irony was, he had gotten himself drafted only to *prevent* something his uncle had worked so hard to bring about. A further irony lay in the fact that while he, Tom, was certainly on the side of the good guys, fighting to maintain law and order, he now found himself for the first time in his life outside the law, on the run from the police.

No good theorizing, though. During the next few hours Frankie and he had to hang on somehow. By some means or other alert Duane and Darrell and Glinn so that the vital army and police would be withdrawn from Lang on the morning of the coup. Eleven A.M. on Saturday—only just over twenty-four hours away.

Tom said, "I hate to do it, but we have to dump the car. This is crazy, just sitting here waiting for them to take us."

Frankie nodded. "Right." She smiled suddenly. "I guess you don't think much of me as an urban guerrilla? Yet I've worked undercover for three years." She frowned. "It's funny. To be a revolutionary is like being an athlete. You spend your life in training, in preparation, a year's practice against a minute's performance and then quite often the event itself is canceled." She paused. "That's why I've felt . . . well—a bit lost since I found out about Lang."

"I know," Tom said. "Like the army. No one ever trains you to really act alone. Only to obey orders."

Frankie smiled and touched him on the cheek.

"Ten after six," Tom said. "Roughly an hour before this city begins to get going, right? Maybe a little longer. We'd better decide how to use the time before we see Duane at his lecture."

Frankie nodded. "First thing," she said, "we better arrange against emergencies. If we get split up? If one of us is taken?"

"Rendezvous at Duane's lecture then?" Tom said. "And each of us, lacking the other, acts quite independently?"

"Right."

"Look," he said, getting out of the car, "we have to lift our ass out of here—fast! Take the minimum—just your handbag if you can manage with that."

He suddenly felt intensely vulnerable. Suddenly the peace and quiet all around them seemed deceptive. Except for an occasional rumble of traffic from the Merrion Road or the rattle of a horse-drawn cart, all was quiet. Dublin lay embalmed in its early-morning death. And yet Tom couldn't help feeling he was under some kind of hostile surveillance.

He looked across the road, but the sun was in his eyes and he couldn't see anything. There was a Mercedes 280 parked directly opposite. Tom thought for a second there was a man sitting in the driver's seat, then decided there wasn't. But someone could be sitting in one of those cars over there, watching Frankie and himself. A sniper? He could draw a bead on them, kill them, and be halfway across Dublin before anyone knew it.

Tom forced himself to move. He and Frankie were nearly to the end of Simmonscourt Road, walking toward the Merrion Road, when they heard a car behind them.

It was a blue BMW and it turned into Simmonscourt Road out of Anglesea Road. It was coming slowly enough for Tom to see a red-haired, freckle-faced man at the wheel and a dark attractive girl beside him. Two men sat in the back of the car.

The BMW moved slowly along Simmonscourt Road. Tom was reminded of a driver cruising, looking for a parking place, but there was plenty of room to park here. The BMW drew level with Tom's discarded Ford Capri; slowed; almost stopped. Then started coming again; faster now.

It was pure instinct made Tom grab Frankie and pull her down beside him onto the sidewalk just as the dark girl leaned out the car window and opened up with an automatic rifle. Tom could feel the slipstream of her bullets through the air above his head; one of them hit a metal trashcan and struck off it with a fierce *yang!* to ricochet away onto a parked car.

Tom kept holding on to Frankie, forcing her head down. He could feel the damp of the flagstones seeping up into his clothes.

Now the BMW stopped a few yards farther on. They were going to attack again.

"Come on!" Tom said, grabbing Frankie's hand and pulling her across the sidewalk and into the front garden of a house.

The garden wall was about four feet high. They crouched behind it, kneeling in a flowerbed. "Keep your head down," Tom commanded. Then, very slowly, he raised his own head so he could see over the wall.

The red-haired man and the dark girl were out of the car and were working their way towards where Tom and Frankie knelt. They moved slowly, flattening themselves against the garden walls, utilizing every scrap of cover like advancing soldiers who expect to be fired on.

"Christ!" Tom exclaimed. "Don't let's just wait for them."

Frankie shook her head. Tom saw she held a Walther automatic and was pressing in a clip. She spoke in a whisper: "People will have heard the shots and they'll have called the police. So you go—I'll hold them here for the moment."

The freckled man and the girl were very near now. Suddenly the girl fired a burst, striking chips off the top of the garden wall. Frankie fired back. There was a moment's pause before the girl let off another burst, firing from under the branches of a tree that overlapped the sidewalk.

"That's the German girl with Lang," Frankie said. "I've seen her before." Then, urgently: "You go! Beat it before the police come."

As the shooting began again, Tom started off running, jumping the dividing fences of adjoining gardens. He saw no one. If they had heard the shots, people probably figured it was safer to stay indoors.

Still running, he crossed the road and found himself on the southern edge of the Royal Dublin Society showgrounds. He decided not to enter them—safer to stick to the streets—so he turned left toward Anglesea Road.

He came out into Anglesea Road and stood hesitating on the curb. Six-thirty A.M. There was a little more traffic now, although nothing like the amount coming into any American city at this time of the morning. Tom wasn't sure which way to go. Obviously the whole area would soon be full of police: someone was sure to have called them when the shooting started. And Lang's cohorts in the BMW would have split by now. Tom wondered if Frankie had got away all right.

Meanwhile, how was he to use the morning that stretched ahead of him? Was there any way he could find out where old Seamus was and how he was?

Telephone all the Dublin hospitals? But that was exactly what the Special Branch expected him to do. To fall into a trap like that would be unforgivable in his uncle's eyes.

He had started to cross the road before he noticed a tall man standing on the other side—almost as if he were waiting for him. Tom knew that to start back now would look suspicious, so he kept going.

He reached the farther curb at a point a few feet from the man who stood motionless, not looking at him. Tom started to walk away. Then the man called out: "Hey! Excuse me . . ."

Tom turned. "Yes?"

"I am an officer of the Garda Siochana—" the man began and moved toward Tom, who immediately wheeled round and started off in the opposite direction.

He had run about twenty yards—tearing along blindly with the man's heavy feet pounding closer and closer behind him—when he saw the car. A police car? A man got out and stood on the sidewalk, blocking his path.

Tom hunched his shoulders, drew in his elbows, and kept going, hoping to cannon into the man with sufficient force to knock him out of the way.

For a second Tom wondered if that would happen—and then he crashed into him. The impact was considerable, but the detective was big, built like a football player, and it only sent him spinning sideways while he stayed on his feet. Dazed by the crash himself, Tom tried to dodge past, but the man grabbed him in a powerful bear hug. As they grappled together, Tom could smell the damp tweed of his opponent's jacket, almost taste the stale cigarette smoke off his breath.

The detective was the stronger. He was forcing Tom backward. Then Tom managed to get a knee up into his crotch. The big man yowled with pain and—unexpectedly—went right over. Tom went lurching backward; didn't fall though. Standing, trying to recover himself, he saw the detective down on all fours on the sidewalk. Turning, he saw the first man who had been chasing him come right up behind him. He too was big—but no bigger than Tom. Tom hit him: the direct classic straight left to the jaw.

The second detective was struggling to his feet, but Tom grabbed one of his ankles and pulled, sending him sprawling again.

Then Tom was running away. He heard shouts behind him and what must be the squad car starting up.

He came to a side road and turned down it. He could hear the police behind him and he wondered how long he could keep on running like this.

He saw a gap in a garden wall and instinctively dodged into it, to find himself falling through a kind of gully choked with broken bricks and booby trapped with jagged thorns. He couldn't stop his fall, but did manage to slow it down, at the cost of some extra wounds from the thorns. Then he was standing on a long, ragged lawn. Stumbling across it, he heard the clatter of bricks falling down the gully. The Branch men were coming after him. He saw an open window in an ivory-covered wall. He ran toward it; then climbed through it, pushing past closed drapes into a darkened room. He heard a gasp: the beginning of a scream, stifled. Climbing in blindly, he'd expected to feel his feet touch the floor, but he was sprawled on a bed and there was someone in the bed who had awoken in terror at feeling Tom's body land.

He whispered, "Don't say anything. Don't call out."

The response was a tiny breathy sound: half moan, half sigh. Very slowly and gently Tom slid himself under the covers. "Don't worry," he whispered. "I won't hurt you. It's all right."

Now he knew that the body underneath him was that of a woman. She was young and attractive and she was naked. However fear and embarrassment might freeze his responses, he had to be aware of her velvety skin, her taut nipples, and her firm flesh tense and motionless beneath him.

Everything was quiet. They must be still outside, searching the garden. But sooner or later they would guess he was hiding inside the house.

They arrived sooner than he'd expected, with a tap on the door and a throaty voice asking, "Hullo, miss? Sorry to disturb you. Special Branch!"

The girl underneath him didn't say anything for a moment. Then when she spoke, the words came out soft, bewildered, blurred with sleep: "What is it? . . . What do you want?"

"We're very sorry to disturb you, miss."

Tom could see that the door had been opened: the room was lighter. They stayed outside the door, though.

"Special Detective Unit, Dublin Castle," the voice went on. "We're looking for a man who was seen entering the garden of this house."

Would they come any farther into the room? Tom hoped their Irish Catholic modesty would deter them from violating a lady's darkened bedroom.

"I'm just after coming off night duty and I was asleep." Precisely the right note of impatience in her voice. "I didn't hear anything."

A long pause. Too long? Then: "Didn't realize you'd been on night duty, miss, and sorry to be disturbing you. God bless!"

They had closed the door.

Now Tom could feel the girl trembling uncontrollably beneath him.

"Thank you," he whispered.

"Who are you?"

"That doesn't matter. But I'm very grateful."

Suddenly he kissed her—boldly, sexually, their bodies pressed together breast to breast and thigh to thigh, his tongue exploring her mouth. As she responded, her trembling ceased.

She said, "I thought you were going to rape me."

He levered himself gently off the bed.

"You'd better not put the light on," she said. "You wouldn't want me to recognize you if I saw you again." She paused. "What's all this about, anyway?"

"Republican politics," Tom said and the girl gave a sigh of instant understanding and sympathy.

☘ ☘ ☘

It was 7:00 A.M. and Seamus lay in his bed in St. Vincent's Private Nursing Home trying to decide what to do. Every minute that passed reduced his area of choice. Now, lying in bed, holding himself motionless with the self-conscious fragility of a very old, very sick man, he still had one or two options. Let him lie here a little longer—till the nurses came with the apparatus to set up a blood drip—and he would have none.

Their arrival couldn't be long delayed. St. Vincent's was the most exclusive private clinic in Ireland and this fact was reflected not only in the luxurious rooms but in the fact that time schedules here were more in line with those in the outside world. Patients weren't jolted from sleep at 6 A.M. as they would be in a public hospital. Even so, they'd have to set the drip up before 8 A.M.

Options? There were really only two. The first and most obvious was to simply lie here and let things take their course. Every bone, every nerve in his body demanded he do that. Lying here with his eyes closed, he just wanted to curl up against these crisp, fresh-feeling sheets and sleep. Forever. Drift away on a dark, swift-flowing river . . .

With an effort of will that was almost physical he made himself reject that. To give up now, to lie back and accept, as an unworthy surrender: a betrayal of himself as a Catholic and as a man. His second option was the only possible one. Somehow—however slowly and laboriously, at whatever cost in pain and anguish—he had to climb out of this bed, dress, and walk out. And he had to do it *now*—before the nurses came and set the needle for the drip in his arm. Once the transfusion started he was caught: pinioned in this bed for a week at least. By then everything would be over: won or lost.

If he could somehow manage to get up and get out of here, he could still go to Killarney and see An tAthair Muiris. As he'd told Tom and Frankie, An tAthair was unique among the members of the committee in the influence he wielded through the whole of the country. He could command the ear of the primate of All Ireland in Armagh as easily as he could that of an taoiseach in Dublin. An tAthair Muiris would know some way to reach the republican grassroots. He would have a contact in the army who could get through to Colonel Darrell; someone in the Special Branch who could talk to Mickey Glinn without fear of betrayal.

Of course Tom and Frankie might have succeeded in getting through to Darrell and even to Duane. There was no way to know if they had or not. At the worst, Slowey could have arrested them, or—worse still—Lang could have gone after them.

He had to move. Get up and get out of here.

Slowly, as if a too hasty movement might break his fragile bones, Seamus raised himself in the bed. He glanced at his watch: ten after seven. A nurse had looked in on him about fifteen minutes ago; he had appeared to be sleeping so she had glided away without disturbing him. Any luck and she might not be in again for another ten minutes.

Poised on the side of the bed, Seamus extended first one leg to the floor, then the other. Then slowly, with infinite care, he heaved himself up off the bed, gradually letting his legs take the whole weight of his body.

He'd done it! He hadn't been sure he had the strength. His collapse in McDara's had been a tactical diversion, but the intern who'd admitted him last night had told him he was amazed Seamus was still on his feet—so low was his blood count. Giving his medical history to this black-jowled intern (a Galwayman by the sound of him), Seamus had mentioned what he had been told in New York Hospital: that he might have reached the point where these massive blood transfusions would no longer be effective. The intern had nodded gravely but made no comment.

Seamus went over to a closet the other side of the room. Thank God they hadn't taken his clothes away. He wasn't quite a prisoner. Of course Slowey hadn't actually arrested him—it wouldn't be the best of timing to grab a United States citizen the morning the president arrived in Dublin—but it would be surprising if there wasn't some kind of surveillance mounted on this place.

Dressing was an exercise in willpower. Seamus took it slowly, item by item. Shirt first; then pants; then socks—extra difficult because he had to lean forward, dragging them on, making himself dizzy.

He was dressed at last. It had taken longer than he could possibly have imagined. He slipped on his dressing gown, pulling it around him so that it concealed the fact that he was fully dressed underneath it. His trouser ends showed, but he hoped that would not be noticed or would be considered some senile quirk.

He looked around the room. One whole wall was given over to a single huge window that overlooked Elm Park golf course. With its fine trees and velvet-smooth grass, it was a vision of pastoral delight this summer morning. In the distance could be seen the RTE mast at Donnybrook, reminding Seamus of what Lang had planned for the television center there tomorrow morning.

He considered for a moment, then hid his discarded pajamas under the mattress. He had kept his slippers on. Now he took a towel and bundled it around his shoes. Tucking the towel under his arm, he went to the door.

The room Seamus occupied was on the second floor, the last room on a short corridor. At the other end of this corridor was an office used by the nursing staff, and past that lay Seamus' immediate objective—the elevator.

Or so he hoped. After all, he had only passed along this corridor once before, last night, and then he'd been lying on a stretcher, pretending to be unconscious. But he'd tried to memorize the layout.

Last night the office had been empty, but it could hardly be empty this morning. The day staff would come on soon—if they weren't on already—and they would be bustling in and out, getting their routine under way. If anyone challenged him, he would act a bit gaga and say he was going to the bathroom. In fact there was a private bathroom opening out of his own room, but Seamus hoped to give the impression he was too old and muddled to realize this. With luck they might humor him. Equally well, they could decide to shepherd him back to his room.

He was lucky so far. There was no one in the corridor. He moved along it with controlled haste. If he pushed himself too hard he could collapse.

Two, three, four doors: each opening onto other rooms. Out of each one could appear a patient—or worse still—a nurse.

Four, three, two—only one to go and he would be out of the corridor and facing the office, a half-rectangle of glass that commanded both this corridor and a shorter one leading to the elevator and the stairs.

There he was—and the office was empty! Or, no—it wasn't. At first glance he'd missed the white headdress of a nurse sitting writing in a report book. She was leaning foward over the book—he couldn't see her face—and yet he had a crazy desire to speak to her, to excuse his presence there in the corridor.

She would hear him. She would look up and see him . . .

But she didn't. Now he was past the office and facing the door of the elevator.

The indicator light told him that the elevator was at rest on the top floor. Seamus was about to press the button to summon it when the light changed, indicating that the elevator was now at the third floor, coming down.

It would be full of nurses or interns on their way to this floor. He dare not wait and see.

He started down the stairway, walking carefully, making the taking of each step a separate enterprise because it would be so easy to slip.

He passed the first floor. No one in sight. A few more steps and he would be down into the entrance lobby. That would be the point of maximum danger. All the medical staffers had to pass through there on their way in and out.

Seamus stopped on the stairway. He took off his dressing gown and slippers and put on his shoes. Fully dressed, he had some chance of walking out of the main door of this hospital; none if he was obviously a patient still in his pajamas.

The entrance lobby resounded with the laughter of five young nurses. They ignored Seamus completely and after a moment, still laughing and joshing each other, they crowded into the elevator. Seamus was moving toward the wide entrance doors when he felt a hand touch his arm.

"Mr. Dillon!"

Dazzled by the exuberance of the nurses, Seamus hadn't noticed this man sidle up. Tough, leathery-looking, he could have been a farmer.

"The last time I saw you, Mr. Dillon, you were lying flat on the bed up there. You didn't look to know what was happening, any more than the bed!"

Seamus shook his head; didn't speak.

"Going out?" the man asked. "Sure, and isn't it a grand morning for it? I'll sample the air with you."

He half pushed, half guided Seamus out through the doors and on to a covered area with seats and tables where convalescent patients sometimes sat with their visitors.

"Begor, the super would be pleased at your rapid recovery, but would he be so pleased to see you out here?" the man demanded.

"The super?"

"The Blessed Cormac Slowey, who else? 'Tis he has me posted on the corridor outside your door. Will Crane. Special Detective Unit, Dublin Castle."

Seamus said carefully, "As you know, I'm not under arrest. You can't hold me. Unless you have a warrant?"

"Divil a warrant!" Crane said. "Sure we could hold the pope himself under the Offenses Against the State! No bother with you, Mr. Dillon." He paused. "Blessed Cormac has it all figured out. You just try to get away."

"And suppose I just do that?"

"Well"—Crane grinned unexpectedly—" 'tis a little late in the day for me to stop you."

He was looking hard at Seamus and a sardonic note entered his voice as he quoted: "Screadaim go h-ard le gáir na tíre . . ."

☘ ☘ ☘

The offices of Hibernian Helicopters (1977) Limited, at Dublin Airport, stood only a few yards from those of their longer-established rival, Irish Helicopters (owned by Aer Lingus, the national airline).

Although still a small outfit, Hibernian prided themselves on displaying a transatlantic drive and gusto. Already at a few minutes before eight this Friday morning their general manager, Fergus Daimon, was involved in discussion with Lang and his aid, Martin Leach.

"What kind of aircraft did you have in mind, Mr. Lang?" Daimon asked in his clipped British tones.

Lang shrugged. "That's a question for my technical adviser here. Martin?"

Leach said, "A Bell 212."

Daimon smiled. "Foolish question. Of course you want a 212. Only thing is . . ." He frowned. "Can we provide one at this sort of notice?" Now he sounded as if he were making a prepared statement: "We're actually more and more into a long-term leasing situation and more and more out of the short-term charter situation. We've got 212s—certainly we've got them—but they're out on lease. To the Irish Lights commissioners among others. And to Zenith Exploration. You know they're prospecting west of Gweebarra Bay in Donegal for natural gas—"

Leach interrupted: "Shit, Colonel, have you got a ship for us or not?"

Daimon protested, "Really, Mr. Leach—"

Lang grinned. "Well, have you, Mr. Daimon?"

"Of course I've got a 'ship' for you," Daimon said. "But not a 212."

"What have you got?" Leach asked.

"Sikorsky 61. Beautiful job."

"It's a question of the range," Lang said.

Daimon gestured. "No problem! The Sikorsky I'm offering you can cover above a hundred miles—thanks to extra fuel tanks we recently installed." He paused. "Or we could give you a Bolkow—"

"The Sikorsky will be okay," Leach said.

"Really?" Daimon said. "Does that suit you also, Mr. Lang?"

"I told you"—Lang smiled—"Martin is our expert." He stood up. "Now— the money. Get your girl out there to prepare the invoice and I'll pay you cash." He indicated the black leather case beside him.

Daimon said, "Just as you like. But I can assure you, your check—"

"Mr. Daimon," Lang said, "here I am walking in off the street and hiring a ship worth . . . what? A million dollars?" He shrugged. "What do you know about me?"

"Mr. Lang," Daimon said, "your reputation as a filmmaker preceded you to Ireland." He paused. "And of course I've seen you on television with Miss Troy."

"Really?"

"To recap," Daimon continued. "One Sikorsky 61. To be hired from 10:30 A.M. tomorrow, Saturday. To be used for filming exteriors and action sequences.

"Right."

"Where will you take delivery? Here, at the airport?"

Lang shook his head. "No. You know what's happening tomorrow?"

"You mean your president coming to Dublin? In fact he's already here."

"He's opening the Carrolton Institute at University College, Dublin," Lang said.

"Well?"

"We want that ship landed at a point on the extreme southwest perimeter of the UCD campus. At 11:30 A.M. tomorrow."

"Right," Daimon agreed. "Will do."

Lang smiled. "I'm asking you to land that helicopter a half mile from the president, the Irish taoiseach and his cabinet, and VIPs from all over the world. How does that grab you, security-wise?"

Daimon said, "Point taken, Mr. Lang. But you and Mr. Leach are Americans. You hardly realize . . . this is Ireland, where thugs rob a bank every day and the government lets them because they're too scared or too stupid to do anything about it. In England or the States there would be tremendous concern over the security aspects of this kind of event." He shook his head. "Not here, Mr. Lang."

"You surprise me," Lang said. "Anyway I wanted to reassure you that we have police clearance on this production. From the commissioner of the Garda Siochana. Obtained through Mr. Conan O'Kelly, minister for internal affairs."

"Congratulations," Daimon said, "but I can assure you it couldn't matter less." He paused. "The Irish are an anarchic race. That's part of their charm." He smiled as he added, "Law and order doesn't mean a thing to them."

☘ ☘ ☘

"Yes," Slowey said, "I think I'd better see her. Just on the off chance. No, not before the weekend, old man. I couldn't, not with all that's cooking. Well . . . thanks, anyway, Liam."

He put down the telephone receiver. He had been talking to Liam Garvin, a detective inspector in C4, the section of the Garda that dealt with straightforward, nonpolitical crime (when they could find any: as Garvin said, these days it was a matter of honor with any self-respecting bank robber to claim that his heist was undertaken for the IRA). The person Slowey intended to interview was Marta Troy. She had been found tied up in a cold bath in the apartment she rented under a false name. When discovered, she had been half dead with shock and exhaustion. Slowey had seen the headline "Actress found unconscious in flat," but hadn't given it much thought.

Now, however, Garvin had called him, saying that there were aspects of the incident that might—just might—interest the Branch. Garvin was one of the few sleuths in C4 who didn't regard the Special Branch with distrust born of a feeling of inferiority. He often fed Slowey tidbits of information and Slowey reciprocated when he could.

Garvin had told Slowey what had not been in the *Evening Herald*: that Marta Troy had been found by a woman known to both C4 and the Branch as a British agent—Annabel Rayne. She had been carrying on an on-and-off affair with Marta Troy for some months past. "But this SM bondage caper in a cold tub isn't Rayne's style at all," Garvin said. He went on to explain that Annabel Rayne had been away for a few days and, on her return, not finding Marta Troy at her suite at Jury's, had gone to the anonymous apartment Marta kept for sexual encounters. "Troy claims it was a German woman tied her up in the bath," Garvin said. "One Leni Reffenstab. Supposed to be an actress. We're checking with the Kommissar for terrorist associations."

"How is this relevant?" Slowey had asked.

"Kinky stuff between dykey ladies," Garvin agreed. "Of no interest to us. But this Leni Reffenstab came to Ireland with a Yank called Rex Lang—"

"Film producer? Been on TV?"

"Right. Now Marta Troy says he's no moviemaker but merely a con artist. Who has lied to her about the backing his film is getting in Hollywood. Who has lied about everything."

"Woman scorned?" Slowey asked.

"Stranger than that," Garvin said. "Troy was sleeping with Reffenstab and she did all she could to boost Lang. Cozy little triangle."

"Yes," Slowey agreed.

"Of course Troy is hardly in a normal state of mind," Garvin went on. "After this experience. She keeps saying Reffenstab tried to murder her. Maybe she did. Of course there's no question of Troy proffering charges. But we could just get a lead on to something . . . Troy says Lang was an officer in the U.S. Army in Vietnam and deserted through Laos to Cuba. Anyway," Garvin continued, "we've asked the FBI for anything they might have on him. Tell you one thing that might interest you: Lang was at the Pan-Celtic Congress at Quimper. And apparently Annabel Rayne told Marta Troy—of course this is hearsay—that Lang met with old Seamus Dillon at a hotel in Lorient."

"Seamus Dillon!" Slowey exclaimed.

"You didn't get any report about that?" Garvin inquired.

Slowey didn't answer. There was no reason for anyone in C4 to know Mickey Glinn had gone to Quimper for Slowey—and yet Slowey felt that Garvin did know.

"Where is Lang now?" Slowey asked.

"Gone! Vanished! He was out at Kilbrangan House in the Wicklow Mountains—that was in the Sunday papers, how he'd taken over this rotting stately home, rats and all—but now he's vanished. With all his technicians, all his gear—"

"Anyone see them go?" Slowey demanded.

"A kid cycling home from school saw Lang's vehicles coming out of the lane and onto the main Dublin road. That was Thursday midday."

"Interesting," Slowey said "but, I don't see what it all proves, do you?"

"Have to wait till we hear from the FBI, eh?"

A moment later Slowey excused himself and ended the conversation. He wanted to think. He had to work out all the implications of what Garvin had told him.

Today the familiar walls of his office seemed like cell walls: he was the prisoner of what in the last analysis must be his own slow-wittedness, his own lack of imagination.

For he wasn't making any progress. He was still getting pieces of different jigsaws and they weren't fitting together. One thing: each disparate piece was indelibly stamped "Michael Glinn."

Now he had solid reason to be suspicious of Glinn. If the likes of Annabel Rayne could come up with a link between this man Lang and Seamus Dillon, what had Glinn been doing in Quimper? Glinn had tried to fob him off with phantom ETA plotters, linking them for the sake of credibility with Frankie McNagan. Slowey wondered why the hard facts always had to reach him casually, almost by chance, always from an outsider, never from anyone here in the Castle. Had poor Frank Niles been right? Was the whole of the Branch really infiltrated?

He stared at the telephone on his desk. It was black and ugly and functional. He put his hand out to lift the receiver, then decided against it. Why call Glinn? What did he expect Glinn to tell him?

Slowey had been hoping all morning to hear that Tom Dillon and Frankie McNagan had been picked up. When the phone rang a second later he grabbed it hopefully.

It was Glinn. He'd been trying to call Slowey for some time but Slowey's extension had been busy.

"It's old Dillon," Glinn said. "I'm afraid he pulled a fast one on Will Crane this morning."

☘ ☘ ☘

"So we Irish always return to the theme of the Heart in Exile," Duane said. (The Heart in Exile was the title of his lecture.) "Crushed, dispossessed by the invader, always the Gael holds something to himself the Saxon cannot steal."

Duane could have been a great actor, Frankie thought, rediscovering for a moment the proprietary pride of a lover. Not a modern actor, exuding sullen machismo, but perhaps a Hamlet in the classic mold, infusing old words with his heart, his fire.

Of course she couldn't concentrate on the lecture. All of her attention was focused on the members of Lang's hit team. There was Leni Reffenstab, with her long black tresses and the sullen, brooding look that cheated her of real beauty, and beside her the freckle-faced man who had been driving when they fired on Tom and Frankie. At the other side of her sat Malachi O'Farrell.

This was an old-fashioned lecture room with descending rows of seats set in a half-circle facing the podium. Leni and the two men had been sitting at the back, on the top row. When they saw Tom and Frankie enter they had moved down two rows, positioning themselves directly in front of Tom and Frankie. They continued to sit there, apparently absorbed in what Duane was saying.

What were they going to do? Frankie tried to put herself in their place. Their orders had to be to stop her talking with Duane. Duane was the only liaison between Lang and the Wednesday Committee; he was the linchpin connecting Lang's cadre with all the people in Ireland whose cooperation was essential to the success of the coup. The republican sympathizers in the army; Glinn and his fellow conspirators in the police; the Dail deputies and civil servants who would ensure the smooth transfer of administrative power—and of course hundreds of secret republicans up and down the country who would be awaiting the call to arms on the morning of the Carrolton ceremonies. Only Duane would be able to dismantle the massive snarl of this conspiracy.

So of course Lang had to keep Frankie from talking with Duane. At all costs. If that meant killing Frankie—and Tom as well—Leni and her comrades wouldn't hesitate. You better believe it, Frankie thought—but how to warn Duane? How get through to him in this crowded lecture room? Would Leni be prepared to kill Tom and Frankie in front of witnesses? And if there was confusion, a panic, would she be concerned about killing innocent bystanders? Frankie knew there were no innocent bystanders in Leni's scheme of things.

"Take Geoffrey Keating," Duane said. "He represents another key figure in the Irish mythos. The priest on the run from the English invader."

He knew he was beginning to repeat himself. The cardinal sin, but Duane found it hard to hold on to his theme. He kept wondering what Frankie and Tom Dillon were doing here. Frankie's presence denied everything agreed on at Quimper: broke the Oath of Blood.

"The invader," Duane continued, "not content with seizing the Irishman's land, must also seek to destroy his faith . . ."

It wasn't just Frankie and Dillon. It was Leni Reffenstab and Malachi O'Farrell too, sitting up there with a ginger-haired guy Duane didn't know. What were *they* doing here? Whatever emergency brought Frankie to him could not possibly touch them. They didn't even know Frankie. Only Duane himself and, briefly, old Seamus Dillon had ever dealt directly with Lang or his cohorts. So what were Leni and the others doing here now? Their presence was worse than unexpected: it was sinister, almost frightening.

But he had to press on and he did, using every actor's trick to keep his performance going. He'd always been able to lift an audience with O Gnive's "The Downfall of the Gael." So, with all the emotion he could muster, he quoted:

My heart is in woe,
And my soul deep in trouble—
For the mighty are low,
And abased are the noble.

He was still holding their attention—the German couple in the front row, their jaws clamped together in owlish concentration; the cluster of Dominican nuns; the two earnest-looking ladies who kept nodding appreciatively; the various priests dotted around the room. But he saw that Frankie and Tom Dillon had moved from the fifth row to the third, while Leni and her comrades had abandoned their pretense of listening to the lecture and were staring aggressively at Frankie and Tom.

Duane noticed that Leni was nursing some bulky object in a canvas case. A submachine gun? An automatic rifle?

He started onto the second verse:

The Sons of the Gael,
Are in exile and mourning,
Worn, weary, and pale,
As spent as pilgrims returning.

Even as he spoke he saw Leni, Malachi, and the other man move down to the row in front of Frankie and Tom, stumbling over peoples' toes as they did so. It was obvious that Frankie and Tom were quietly working their way toward the podium—and that every move they made was being matched by Leni.

Whatever Frankie had to say must be so urgent that it overrode all questions of security, shattered Lang's watertight compartments, made the oath void. And, whatever it was, Lang had sent Leni and the two men to block Frankie getting at him, Duane.

Now they were sitting at the end of the second row, directly behind the German couple. Even if they'd been strangers, Duane would have read the menace in Leni's sullen stare; sensed a hunter's ferocity in Malachi, lounging beside her.

It seemed best to him to go on talking, weaving his frail spell of words against the violence these three could unleash.

"So," he said, "you get this theme of alienation running through Irish poetry for five centuries; this sense of the Gael as a stranger in his own land."

His words sounded stilted, dead. He was watching Leni, but she looked as bored as ever. The ginger-haired man suddenly yawned. Malachi O'Farrell pursed his lips impatiently.

"Excuse me! Mr. Lecturer!"

Frankie. Standing up. Smiling, arm upraised like a child interrupting the teacher.

"I'm afraid I can't pronounce your name correctly, Mr. Lecturer. Since it's in the Irish language. And do forgive the interruption. But there is something I very much want to ask you."

She was into her persona of Margaret Colebrook: garrulous, irrepressible, full of bumbling benevolence.

"It just that it's frightfully relevant to what you've just said," she added.

As she spoke Frankie had left her seat and had moved down onto the center aisle. Now she stood level with Leni and her companions.

Duane responded in his suavest platform manner: "Dear lady—I appreciate such an interruption. At least it doesn't spell indifference."

Leni moved suddenly. For a second he thought she was going to take out a gun, but she just continued to stare at Frankie, who was now approaching the podium.

"Betrayal, Mr. Lecturer!" Frankie cried. "Betrayal! The Gael a stranger in his own land—of course!" She paused dramatically. "But what of betrayal? Every time the Gael moves to shake off his chains, he is betrayed. You don't mention that."

Betrayal? What, exactly, was Frankie trying to say? Clearly that now, on the very brink of the coup, they had been betrayed. But how? By whom? And where did Lang come into it?

Keep her talking. Get as much as he could.

He nodded. "Yes, indeed! All through our sad history we've never lacked a Judas waiting in the wings."

Leni was sitting quite still, the two men blank as zombies at each side of her. Tom Dillon had followed Frankie out onto the aisle.

"That's a strange thing, isn't it?" Frankie said. "Always a betrayal—"

"Right!"

Leni and the two men had left their seats and now stood only a few feet away.

"Right," Leni said again. She held an automatic rifle, which she leveled at Frankie. "Enough talking! Mr. Duane—this you will understand later." Then she snarled at Frankie, "Go on—go over there!"

Frankie hesitated and then moved toward the blackboard on the wall behind the podium.

"Go on—move it!" Leni shouted. "Hurry up. And you"—indicating Tom Dillon—"you too."

Slowly and reluctantly Frankie went toward the blackboard, with Tom following her.

"What's all this about?" Duane demanded.

"They are traitors—that's what it's about."

"No!" Duane said.

"Now," Leni said. "Both of you—turn around and put out your arms beside you—like you were being crucified, right?"

All at once Duane was aware of the audience, important a moment ago but now existing only through their silence. Everyone in the crowded lecture room appeared frozen, paralyzed, literally holding their breath.

Tom and Frankie stood in front of the blackboard. Leni continued to cover them. Malachi O'Farrell moved away toward the entrance. The freckle-faced man remained at Leni's side.

Angrily, Duane protested again, "I tell you, you're mistaken—"

Suddenly Tom Dillon dropped to his knees, jerking Frankie down in front of him like a player tackling an opponent in the Rugby football game. Instantly, instinctively, Duane sprang forward, catching hold of the barrel of Leni's rifle, forcing it upward so that the burst she unleashed went wide, shattering the transom above them.

While Duane grappled blindly with Leni she kept shouting at him to let her go, that he was a dupe, a fool, that he would wreck all their plans . . .

The shots thrust the whole room into uproar. A nun was screaming uncontrollably; an old man was shouting, "For Christ's sake fetch the Guards!" Students from the back of the room were pouring down the aisles, to form a seething, shouting mass around the podium. Keeping their heads down, Tom and Frankie fought their way toward the entrance, although Frankie kept protesting that they mustn't desert Duane.

Falling, slithering, jostling, they got to within a few feet of the door. There they came face to face with Malachi O'Farrell. Tom saw the gleaming, upraised blade of a bowie knife. He struck upward, trying to knock the knife out of Malachi's hand, but missed and fell forward. Struggling to his feet, he expected to get the knife in his back, but instead saw O'Farrell collapsed against the wall, groaning. Seeing the upraised knife, one of the students had knee-kicked him at the base of the spine. Against Frankie's last protests, Tom dragged her through the door and into the street.

Still grappling desperately with Leni—he was a lot bigger than she was, but she was very strong and he was getting out of breath—Duane felt himself gripped around the neck and jerked savagely back so that his hold on Leni was broken. The red-haired guy! The hands that gripped him seemed strong as steel—wrestler's, strangler's hands—and Duane was forced backward over a chair. He saw Leni level her rifle at his chest.

Gazing into her eyes and noting their unyielding gray-blue color, he was aware that a question was being posed in Leni's mind, a choice considered, and now a decision arrived at. He realized that she was going to kill him.

With an extraordinary sense of detachment, he reflected on the irony implicit in this, his own death. He, O Dunnacha Duane, the man a hundred women had called a cynic, throwing his life away in a gesture of romantic self-sacrifice. The cause? Ireland? Wouldn't he have served Ireland better by staying alive? If he hadn't jumped forward when he saw Frankie threatened? How could anyone halt Lang now?

He didn't know how long it was before Leni fired. The shock was so great that it seemed to lift him up, disassociate him from his body, set him spinning off into the darkness of infinite space. And yet he wasn't sure he was dead: some shard of consciousness floated somewhere, plucked from his shattered body, high above anything as earthly as pain.

Tom and Frankie were coming into that part of the South Circular Road that becomes Suir Road, passing Old Kilmainham. They were driving in Duane's shabby Renault 4L, and now Tom had to give it all the gas he could because the blue BMW that was following them was increasing speed, having overtaken three intervening cars.

They drove in silence. Neither had much doubt that Duane was dead. As the door of the lecture room finally closed behind them, they'd heard a burst of automatic fire. It had to have come from Leni. Even then Frankie had wanted to go back, but Tom had forced her to keep going. She'd recovered sufficiently to point out Duane's car parked a few yards on. He always kept the keys hidden in the glove compartment: she knew where.

The blue BMW was coming up fast. Tom tried to force a little more from the Renault, but the BMW kept gaining. He glanced back and saw that the freckle-faced man was driving and Malachi O'Farrell and Leni Reffenstab were crowded in beside him.

Now they had reached the intersection of St. John's Road and Bothar Coilbeard. "Left!" Frankie said and Tom turned into Coilbeard. Just as he had completed the turn, the BMW drew parallel with him, forcing him against the curb and causing him to nearly crash against a pickup truck parked outside the Rowntree-Mackintosh plant.

The BMW stopped, double-parked, representing a dangerous obstruction on a busy corner. Tom realized that with the BMW outside them and the pickup in front, they were hemmed in on two sides.

Leni and the gray-haired man got out of the BMW and two men got out of the pickup. Tom immediately put the Renault into reverse, frantically trying to get out of the trap.

But before he could move the car more than a few feet, one of the men from the pickup hurled a huge wrench at the Renault's windshield. It crashed through, missing both Tom and Frankie, clanging onto the car floor.

By now Tom had gotten the left-hand door open. He lurched through it, Frankie following him. They emerged to see the freckle-faced man coming at them with the still bloodstained bowie knife. Close behind him came Leni Reffenstab. The man's arm swung up; he lunged at Tom with the knife. Frankie dived forward, slamming her knee into his crotch. The man yowled with pain; the knife went skittering away, clinking on the flagstones.

Now Frankie was holding the knife, circling it in front of her in a wide defensive arc. The two men from the pickup stood behind Leni, eyeing Frankie cautiously. The freckle-faced man was on his knees, struggling to his feet.

"Across the road and into the park!" Frankie called.

She whirled around, darting into the road, skipping dangerously through two streams of traffic. Dodging the speeding cars and trucks, Tom followed her.

She ran along the sidewalk that skirted the edge of Islandbridge Memorial Park. After covering about a hundred yards she swerved right and into the park.

Tom risked a look backward. The BMW was straddled over both traffic lanes, forcing across the road.

The ground dipped down into the park. Keeping a few yards ahead of Tom, Frankie ran down several flights of stone steps, past fake-Grecian pillars and ornamental water sluggish with lilies into the main park, a grassy expanse dotted with trees that sloped down toward the River Liffey.

Frankie was making straight for the river. Keeping close after her, Tom saw three people running, coming toward him through the trees. Leni and the others must have entered the park higher up, hoping to cut Tom and Frankie off while the BMW covered the road.

Now the distance between them and their pursuers suddenly seemed much reduced. The three advancing black dots became people. Tom identified Leni Reffenstab's pale face and black hair—and then he saw her go down on one knee, lift her automatic rifle, and fire.

The two men were also firing. One of them was using a submachine gun, and bursts of automatic fire hit the trees, scything down the foliage with a sharp chopping sound. Tom was glad there were so few people in the park. An old man threw himself flat on the ground; two girls ran screaming toward the Hurling Grounds.

Tom couldn't understand why Frankie kept running toward the river. Lang's team would be able to take potshots at them as they clambered out onto the other bank.

But Frankie kept going, crashing through a field of daffodils that bordered the water's edge. Leni and the others were only shooting occasionally now. Tom wondered if they were closing in for the kill.

Here the Liffey ran high and full, almost level with the bank. Tom had an instant, second-long vision of idyllic summer peace: a kingfisher alighting, a sculler flashing by on the smooth, suavely flowing water—and then Frankie had crashed in ahead of him, blundering through the reeds and into the river. Tom followed her.

At first the strength of the current surprised him. And the coldness of the water, considering the bright sunlight above. Tom struck out with a strong breaststroke, following Frankie.

It seemed a long time before Leni and the others opened up, but before Tom was halfway across they were shooting: the bullets hissing and plopping into the water.

Frankie wasn't swimming straight across the river; she had swung to the right, toward the weir Tom had noticed from the bank. A minute or so more and she'd reached it, with Tom a yard behind her. There she rested, her arms stretched out above her, grasping the balks of timber that topped the edge of the weir. That way, with only her head above the surface of the water, she didn't present much of a target.

Tom swam up beside her and held onto the slime-encrusted rotten timber that seemed to slip and almost crumble under his fingers. He realized why Frankie had swum toward the weir. If they could once get over it and into the deep, enclosed pool the other side, they would be safely out of sight and range of Lang's team.

But how get over it? Climbing over, teetering clumsily on the edge of the weir, they would be sitting ducks for the poorest marksman. Lang's squad had stopped shooting now: this had to be what they were waiting for.

He had to think of something. Impossible to hold on much longer. His fingers were aching; soon they'd go numb.

"Frankie," he called loudly, above the gentle roar of the rushing water. "Along there to the left, behind that white rail . . ."

"Yes?"

This was a wooden rail, once white painted, that formed an apparently useless barrier in the water at a point beyond where the edge of the weir ended.

Tom said, "As far as I can see there isn't anything very solid behind that rail. Just bushes growing in the water."

"I'll look."

"If you could find a way through—" he said.

"Right."

"And I might create a diversion . . ."

She didn't say any more but slithered away toward the clumps of sodden foliage behind the white rail. At that moment three bursts of automatic fire came from the bank, striking with a dull pludding sound into the rotten wood Tom was clinging to.

They stopped firing. A minute or two passed. No sight or sound of Frankie. Had she got through? Somehow penetrated those waterlogged bushes and made it over the weir?

Probably. And now was the time to create a diversion.

The balk he was clinging to was loose—or rather, the log supporting it was loose. It moved a little when he put his weight on it. Very carefully, maintaining a precarious foothold, he tried to lever it free. At first it seemed firmly anchored; then suddenly it came away, nearly knocking him over. Holding on to the balk with one hand, he cradled the log with the other, working it backward and forward to make sure it was free of mud and slime. He stayed like that for several minutes, trying to define what exactly he intended to do. He knew it was a pure gamble. Win or lose, however the dice fell, he just had to go ahead and do it.

He groped for a better foothold. Now he was standing on a natural ledge of stone: too narrow to be the perfect springboard he wanted, but firm enough.

He flexed his leg and thigh muscles, thinking how out of condition he was. But decision should equal action: releasing his hold of the balk, he gripped the log with both hands and then heaved it away from him. As it splashed forward he shouted loudly—and then jumped. Jumped with a precision he'd never achieved before, using the tensile strength of legs and thighs to catapult himself forward as a cat does, clearing the top of the weir while Lang's squad was still firing at the log, splitting and splintering it as it sank out of sight.

🍀　🍀　🍀

The Connolly-Coughlin Funeral Home was situated in the part of Dublin still known as The Liberties. A small mortician's firm, established in 1914, its premises had been brought up to date with thick carpets and glossy paneling. It was still run by the two grandsons of the original founders, who had been antithetical physical types: fat and lean respectively. Their successors maintained the same equation. Des Connolly was fat and easygoing; Fergus Coughlin was a leathery sprat of a man.

Before the Yank had come in, Fergus Coughlin had been wondering if Des Connolly intended to relieve him for tea at all. They had a removal of remains from a house in Harolds Cross to the Pro-Cathedral in an hour's time. You could imagine what a bitch it would be getting a hearse and four carloads of mourners across Dublin at the peak of the rush hour. Especially after the morning's parades in honor of the American president. That would have given the city fathers an alibi for every traffic snarl-up for the next week. Coughlin looked at the clock on the wall and muttered, "Shag you, Des Connolly!"

But now this Yank held all of Coughlin's attention. Coughlin thought him a bit odd—but when did you ever meet a Yank that wasn't as odd as two left shoes? At least this guy didn't claim to be Irish, blah-blahing about the little gray home in the West his ancestors left in eighteen-forty-something. No: this fella was different. Although he was here on the usual business he wasn't exactly dressed for it: he wore a leather jacket and thigh boots. He simply gave his name, with no smile, no handshake.

Coughlin was writing down the details. "Would the deceased be a relative, Mr. Lang?"

"A friend."

"You said his name was O'Sullivan, Mr. Lang?"

"Lawrence O'Sullivan. Aged fifty-two."

"He was from the United States, like yourself?"

Lang nodded. "Right. Native of Providence, Rhode Island. Engineer by profession. Leading member of the O'Sullivan Sept and as such a frequent visitor to this country." He paused. "This time he was here for the same reason as our president: the Carrolton Inauguration."

Coughlin cleared his throat and asked, "Was the end sudden, Mr. Lang?"

"Heart attack. Larry opened his mouth like he was about to say something— then he just keeled over. I saw it. I was there."

"Where are the . . . er—remains?"

"At an apartment on Coleraine Street, near the Kings Inns."

Coughlin was writing busily. "I see. I presume you have a death certificate, Mr. Lang?"

"Not right here I haven't. But Larry's own first cousin attended him. Dr. Aloysius O'Sullivan of Schenectady, New York."

Coughlin said, "As long as the certificate is produced before the interment. Or do I misunderstand you, Mr. Lang? You're not taking him back to the United States?"

Lang shook his head. "No, sir. Larry wanted to be buried right here in Dublin. Mount Jerome Cemetery: next grave to his grandmother. We promised him."

Coughlin gave a professional smile. " 'Tis great you have it so cut-and-dried. Irish people—so vague, you wouldn't believe!" He paused and added, "When is the removal to be, sir?"

"Removal means you take the casket to the church ahead of the funeral itself, right?"

Coughlin nodded.

"I'm afraid we don't have time for that," Lang said. "My friends and I are on a flight out of Shannon to New York tomorrow night. So we gotta have the ceremony all in one."

"Was Mr. O'Sullivan a Catholic?" Coughlin asked.

"With a name like that? His brother, Father Magnus O'Sullivan of the Church of the Sacred Blood in Far Rockaway, is arranging things with your archbishop right now."

"I see . . ." It was all distinctly odd and Coughlin figured this man Lang could be troublesome, but what harm? Yanks were usually troublesome, but they were often loaded too.

Lang said, "We want the funeral real early tomorrow. Maybe have a requiem mass at the Pro-Cathedral first. Father Magnus will be fixing that."

"Early?" Coughlin shook his head. "If I may mention it, sir—we shall have to . . . prepare Mr. O'Sullivan."

"You be at Coleraine Street sometime tonight, right?"

Coughlin didn't answer. He felt more and more uneasy about this funeral, but if they produced a valid death certificate, what the hell?

"Naturally," Lang said, "you might be wondering about the financial side . . ." He laid a billfold on the table. Coughlin could see there was plenty in it. Fivers, tenners . . . "Payment will be in cash. In advance."

"No problem, Mr. Lang!" Coughlin protested. "My partner, Mr. Connolly, and I will be there to do the necessary for your poor friend. Could be midnight before we get there, though."

Lang nodded. "Another thing. There will be at least forty-five mourners."

"Forty-five?" Coughlin echoed.

"Yeah. Say—nine cars?"

"Very well, Mr. Lang." Coughlin figured he'd have to borrow four of the cars from another mortician.

"Old Larry had a lot of friends in Dublin," Lang said. "Could you arrange for the cars to pick up the mourners at Upper Leeson Street? Nine tomorrow morning."

"Right, Mr. Lang," Coughlin said. He was distinctly puzzled now.

"We aim to have the funeral around nine-thirty," Lang said. "That way we maybe dodge the traffic from the Carrolton celebrations."

☘ ☘ ☘

Once he was safely aboard the Killarney train, Seamus allowed himself to relax. Only it wasn't a genuine feeling of relaxation: it was a strange numbness, a conviction that everything was slipping away from him. And he didn't care. It was as if all his resolution, his sense of the dangers ahead, was blurred, muffled.

He kept going over things in his mind. How had Tom and Frankie made out? They must have established contact with Duane hours ago. How had Duane reacted? Had he already begun to send the machinery of the coup into reverse? And what about Darrell? Had they succeeded in getting through to him today?

Try as he would, he couldn't keep these things in focus in his mind. He kept telling himself everything would be all right when he got to Killarney. An tAthair Muiris would put things right. But although An tAthair was a man of great courage and intelligence, he was no magician. Certainly he had great influence in the republican movement, but it might already be too late to halt the machinery Lang had set in motion. And yet Seamus knew that he had to see An tAthair Muiris and get his blessing before his time ran out altogether.

☘ ☘ ☘

"Thanks!" Slowey said. "Sure, Philomena, you're the darlin' girl."

She left the coffee on the table in front of him and went out. Slowey sipped the coffee and wished he could smoke a cigarette. Then the thought struck him: what was Philomena Keane doing here at the office this late? He certainly hadn't asked her to stay late this evening.

There could be a number of reasons, of course. She was a civilian employed at the Castle: her services weren't exclusive to him. She could be doing a photocopying job for someone else. All the same, he couldn't help wondering . . .

He was getting more paranoid than ever. That must be because of Mickey Glinn. And of course today had been tense and traumatic. This morning there had been a parade in honor of the American president's visit—and Slowey supposed he should be on his knees now, thanking God it had passed off without incident. Banners had stretched across O'Connell Street saying WELCOME TO THE PRESIDENT, but Slowey didn't fool himself that security would be any better here than on Fifth Avenue. This morning, as he stood outside the General Post Office, admiring the swing and brio of the marching bands, the graceful cavorting of the majorettes, the huge Mardi Gras masks that depicted both Irish and Irish-American politicians, his fears had re-created the blood and terror of Saint Patrick's Day in New York.

Thank God the parade was safely over—but then had come news of O Dunnacha Duane's murder. That was worrying enough. There had always been disagreement in the Branch as to how far Duane was really involved in IRA plotting. Slowey believed Duane to be a typical intellectual—a talker rather than a doer—but he had certainly been associated with Eireann Amhain, and recently the snitch Nora O Conaire had suggested he might be a member of the Wednesday Committee.

And now he was dead. Murdered. Did his death have any bearing on Slowey's present concerns? The testimony of various eyewitnesses was being collated, but no totally coherent picture had yet emerged. Apparently a woman (the witnesses said she was a foreigner: Dutch or German) had held Duane and a young man and woman at gunpoint. Duane had been shot; the young couple had escaped. Their description *could* fit Tom Dillon and Frankie McNagan, but it could also fit hundreds of other young men and women in Dublin at this present time.

Slowey continued to brood uneasily. Of course the visit of the American president could serve as a focus for all kinds of subversive acts. Tonight the president was dining with the president of Ireland at Aras an Uachtaran. Security would be tight, but somehow Slowey didn't think anything would happen.

The Carrolton Inauguration tomorrow could be a different matter; pose a different kind of threat. Today Dublin had worn the devil-may-care Luck of the Irish smile that Yanks believe to be the true face of Erin, and it was easy for even a policeman to feel euphoric. The Carrolton ceremonies tomorrow would present a much bigger challenge.

The phone rang. Garvin of C.4. He wasted no time getting to the point.

"Your friend Mr. Lang," he said.

"Yes?"

"The FBI came back on that one. Nothing firm at all. There *was* a Rex Lang, a captain in the army in Vietnam—and he certainly disappeared. Could have deserted, could be dead. But there's no evidence to link him with the man Marta Troy knows."

"The name!" Slowey protested.

Garvin repeated that the FBI would make no positive identification. A few years back Marta Troy's Lang had been known in radical chic circles around Malibu and Beverly Hills. He had posed as an authority on the then burgeoning guerrilla movement throughout Latin America, but the FBI had not considered him worth investigating further.

None of this helped. But then Garvin said, "One other thing . . . But I suppose you know?"

"What?"

"This film Lang is supposed to be making. He got special clearance from the commissioner. For certain action scenes he wanted to shoot in the streets of Dublin." Garvin paused. "The commissioner granted it on the say of the minister, Conan O'Kelly—and of course that was really thanks to Marta Troy."

"No," Slowey said, "I didn't know that."

"As a matter of routine we had to inform the Castle."

"Who was told?" Slowey asked.

"Mickey Glinn."

Slowey stayed silent so long that Garvin said, "Hullo! Hullo!" thinking he'd gone.

That had been forty minutes ago. Slowey was still brooding on the dilemma that confronted him. If he took steps to have Glinn taken off the Carrolton assignment at this late hour, Glinn would no doubt protest, and Slowey might have to justify his decision to higher authority. Could he so justify it? And—of course—to take Glinn off this detail would be to warn him that Slowey suspected him. That risk surely outweighed all others? Ideally, Slowey thought, he would himself be present at Carrolton—but unofficially, pretending to be off-duty, perhaps with one or two men he could trust. But he could see no way of doing this. His dilemma persisted.

It was strange, but Tom and Frankie found themselves making love again in this dusty storage hut in the Phoenix Park. They had found a haven here when they emerged on the other side of the Liffey after escaping from Lang's hit team at the Salmon Weir. Covered in mud, dripping with water, they knew they must attract attention—and sooner or later that meant police attention. So when they saw this hut and found it open, it seemed like sanctuary.

They had managed to fasten the door from inside and for the last two hours had lain cradled in each other's arms, creating for themselves a tiny cave of refuge. Finding more comfort than provocation in their enlaced bodies, they made love and then Frankie slept—with the total abandon of a child—and now they had made love again.

Frankie said, "You must think I'm awful. A monster."

He kissed her. "My favorite of all monsters!"

She turned her head away. "No. Please—not charm! Not at this moment . . . Do you think I'm heartless—after what happened to *him?*"

This was the first time either of them had mentioned Duane.

"No, love," Tom said gently. "What happened was quite natural. Physiological, really."

She stared at him; shook her head.

"Truly," he said. "There's an old priest my mother dotes on. Lives in Miami. Monsignor Bill. When we were kids we used to go confess to him." He paused. "Sometimes we made a good confession, sometimes not."

"I know," Frankie said.

"Who am I telling?" he demanded. "I always forget you're a Catholic. Anyway, one time I told my sins—dirty thoughts, something like that—and he said that when he was a chaplain in the Pacific in the Second World War—Iwo Jima, Guadalcanal, all that—after the guys had been in action, killing Japs and seeing their own buddies killed, they got as horny as hell." He paused. "Monsignor Bill put it more elegantly: 'The concupiscence rose in you like a sword!' "

After a moment she said, "My relationship with Duane—I used to think it was entirely lustful and sordid." She shook her head. "But it wasn't just the total of what we did in bed."

"It never is," Tom murmured.

"Oh—I suppose you think this is the liberated woman letting down her guard and talking like some fluffy little thing in some soppy magazine?" She paused. "Duane seduced me—that's a nice old-fashioned word, isn't it?—and I think there was some kind of innocence in him that enjoyed that. And I think I pitied that innocence in him." Tom could feel the tears trickling down her cheek.

A minute or two later he said, "What are we going to do now?"

"I don't know," she said. "Duane stood at the center. He was the only liaison between Lang and the committee. Lang used him to set up the coup—and now he's killed him." She was frowning. "Maybe Lang planned to kill him all along."

"Back to the beginning then," Tom said.

"I suppose so," she said wearily. "Aside from Duane, Darrell is still the most important—but how do we get to him?"

"We keep trying," Tom said. "Say—our clothes should be nearly dry by now."

She pulled herself away suddenly and stood up. Stretching her arms, matter-of-fact in her nakedness, she said, "Glinn! He's our last hope."

🍀   🍀   🍀

Fergus Coughlin had known there was something wrong the moment he entered the place. This ground-floor apartment on Coleraine Street was dirty and sordid-looking. The windows hadn't been cleaned for years. This room held only a crude kitchen table and a single chair. It was certainly not the place that would be rented by a well-heeled Yank, even for the briefest vacation in Ireland.

Fergus Coughlin and Des Connolly arrived at 11:40 P.M. Lang had said that the late Larry O'Sullivan was a tall man, so the two morticians had brought along a black oak job with brass handles—chaste-looking but expensive—that would comfortably accommodate a six-foot-six corpse.

The man that opened the door was gray-haired and gaunt-faced. He spoke like a Yank. "Put the casket down there," he ordered. "Mr. Lang isn't here right now. My name is O'Farrell. Wait here till I come back."

They had waited in the desolate room for ten minutes. Predictably Des Connolly got restless. "What the shaggin' hell is your man up to?" he grumbled. "I'm giving you notice, Fergus—I hold you responsible. They're your clients."

At that moment O'Farrell came back. With an authority that quietened even Connolly, he started to question them about the arrangements for the funeral tomorrow. Where was the hearse? Parked in the street. Was the driver waiting? No. This was Sean Quigley's night off, so Des Connolly had driven it himself. Who would be at the funeral, of the Coughlin-Connolly staff? The two of themselves; Quigley, driving the hearse; and of course the drivers of the nine mourning cars. Were those cars definitely arranged for Upper Leeson Street in the morning? Certainly. They would be there at 9 A.M. as arranged.

O'Farrell kept nodding grimly as he got these answers. Coughlin could see

Connolly gradually inching up to the boiling point. What harm? Des was the boy to straighten out this arrogant fellow.

"Excuse me, sir," Connolly burst out at last, "but this is Hamlet without the friggin' Prince of Denmark! The deceased, sir. The dear departed. The poor mortal remains of Mr. Larry O'Sullivan that we have to prepare for his long day's journey into night."

O'Farrell smiled coldly. "He isn't here," he said.

"Isn't here?" Coughlin echoed.

"No."

"Look—we came here to prepare a cadaver for a funeral," Connolly said. "It's bloody midnight already. Let us do a job on him and then go home to our beds."

"Go home is one thing you won't do," O'Farrell said. "You'll both come with me and remain with me till after the funeral tomorrow."

"That's bloody ridiculous—" Connolly began. His protest trailed away as an enormous black man entered the room. He carried a submachine gun.

"One of you will drive the hearse to where I direct you," O'Farrell said. "The other will go in the car with Mr. Congar here."

☘   ☘   ☘

Walking slowly down the High Street in Killarney, Seamus noticed how quiet the town seemed. A few kids lounged in front of cafés that were mostly closed. A Garda passed along a line of parked cars, shining his flashlight on their license plates, doing his job with ritual boredom. Occasionally a girl would scurry by with a clack-clacking of heels. Sure, it was almost midnight, but this was the tourist season for God's sake. If the tourists were here, they certainly went to bed early. Seamus half expected to see the ubiquitous little horse-drawn jaunting cars, but even the eager, hustling drivers must be asleep.

He wished he could have gotten here earlier. He had already called at the Franciscan Friary on Fair Hill, to be told that An tAthair Muiris had left for Muckross Abbey, where he would celebrate mass in Irish to mark the end of the retreat he had been conducting.

Seamus managed to pick up a taxi at the corner of Countess Road and Muckross Road. The man could hardly believe that Seamus wished to be dropped near Muckross Abbey at this hour of the night. Surely it was a private house he wanted?

The man accepted his eccentricity after a moment and they started off. It was a grand night: the moon had risen by now. For the thousandth time Seamus regretted the high wall that blocked any glimpse of Lough Leane from the road.

The ruined Abbey of Muckross was about three miles from Killarney town, and stood some distance off the road. Seamus knew the nearest point; he would get the cabdriver to stop there and then walk the rest of the way. He would try to hear mass discreetly, without making his presence known. A layman, he wasn't going to butt in to a retreat for members of a religious order. Only when the mass was over and the monks dispersing would he go up to An tAthair Muiris and talk with him. He would suggest they travel back to Dublin together. They could be there by 4 A.M., which would give them several hours to get a strategy going against Lang.

"You *know* who I am!" Frankie protested. "I met you at Quimper. At the Gradlon. I was with Duane. You *must* remember."

Inspector Glinn said, "What are you trying to tell me? What is all this about?"

Looking at Glinn's pudgy face and cloudy, lost dog's eyes, Tom was seized by that oppressive sense of repetition common in dreams. Indeed, this whole long day and night of trauma and rejection was like a nightmare from which he strove, vainly, to wake.

They were sitting in Glinn's car, which was parked near the southern gate of the Phoenix Park on Conyngham Road. It was now 2:55 A.M. on Saturday morning.

After a good deal of discussion they still had not risked calling Glinn at his office at the Castle. They had waited to call him at his home in Blackrock. They hadn't gotten to speak with him till 1 A.M. Then he had been deadpan, nonreactive, although he had finally agreed to meet them in Phoenix Park. Now Frankie was sitting beside him in the front seat of his Fiat Ritmo, while Tom sat in the back. They both of them felt strangely isolated talking to Glinn in this tiny lighted cabin carved out of the enveloping silence and blackness of the park.

Frankie said, "You're the third member of the Wednesday Committee who's gone through this farce of pretending not to know me."

Glinn said, "An oath taken is an oath taken."

"Why don't Irish people ever trust each other?" Tom asked.

Frankie said, "Poor Duane used to say it. Get enough Irishmen around a table and one of them has to be Judas. Only this time Judas is the host."

"You're talking about Lang," Glinn said.

"Of course," Frankie replied, and added bitterly, "I suppose I can't make you believe me. It all goes back to the founding of Eireann Amhain, doesn't it? When my father and the others followed Saor Eire out of Sinn Fein and then founded their own group."

Glinn smiled unexpectedly. "Irish republicans are a bit like medieval theologians. I have to apologize to you, Frankie. What McClymont told me led me to call Lang and tell him you were in Dublin, trying to stop the coup." He shrugged. "McClymont is hostile to Seamus Dillon and, to some extent, to you. I let him influence me. I'm sorry."

"You mean—" Frankie hesitated. "You've changed your mind?"

"When Duane was killed," Glinn said, "then I knew you must be telling the truth about Lang. You had to be."

☘ ☘ ☘

The tall figure of An tAthair Muiris stood at a rough-hewn table on which reposed a silver crucifix and attendant candles that flickered slightly in the night wind. Seamus could hear An tAthair's "In ainm an Athar agus an Mhic agus an Spioraid Naoimh" and the monks' intoned "Amen."

Seamus loved the familiar Latin prayers, the Tridentine mass he had known for so much of his life, but these words in Irish struck deeper. Here in this Abbey of Muckross—founded in 1448 for the Observantine Franciscans by Donal MacCarthy, the chieftain of Desmond, and burned down nearly two hundred years later—was being enacted the mass his forebears had known. These words in these surroundings, in this ruin, between these ancient walls, stirred the folk memory of faith and persecution all of the Irish carry with them through all of their lives. These sacred words had been spoken, in this same Gaelic tongue, in Penal Times at mass rock, in deep forest and secret cave.

"Glan mo chroí agus mo bheola, a Dhia uilechumhactaigh, chun go mbeidh mé in ann do Shoiscéal a fhógairt go fiúntach."

Seamus closed his eyes, let the words flow over him, tried to pray. When he opened his eyes again he realized he must have dozed off, for now An tAthair Muiris was passing down the long line of brown-clad monks, giving them holy communion. Seamus wished he could receive communion too, but he was sitting at an aperture high in the wall, a natural vantage-point reached through a gallery above the cloisters that had surrounded the monks' garden. No one could see him; no one knew he was here.

He closed his eyes. A great weariness had overtaken him. He just wanted to lie back, relax, abandon himself to the spirit of this ancient place.

Later he heard the monks chanting:

Ag Criost an siol,
Ag Criost an fomhar,
In iothlainn De
Go dtugtar sinn.

Ag Criost an mhuir,
Ag Criost an t-iasc,
I lionta De
Go gcastar sinn . . .

The chanting went on for a long time. At last Seamus opened his eyes—and, looking down, saw that the chapel was empty. No monks, no An tAthair Muiris—no one. The moonlight, stronger now, emphasized the emptiness. An tAthair and the monks could have been so many vanished ghosts.

Seamus struggled to his feet. He must keep calm. Nothing had really been lost. An tAthair and the monks couldn't have been gone long. He looked at his watch: 1:10 A.M.

He started down the gallery. Halfway along it, a narrow stairway built into the thickness of the wall led down into the cloisters. When he first traversed this gallery, Seamus had moved carefully, testing each foot of the way. Now, in his eagerness and anxiety, he moved too fast and contrived to miss the entrance to the stairway. He found himself at the end of the gallery. He turned back, careful again, feeling before him like a blind man, his right hand extended in front of him caressing the rough stonework of the wall. A few feet on he found what he was looking for: a gap in the stonework about half the width of a normal doorway. He stepped forward.

But this wasn't the stairway. His feet, feeling for steps, found only rubble that went slithering away beneath him, so that he was sliding downward at ever-increasing speed.

By 9 A.M. every section was in readiness at Lang's final headquarters at Leinster Dairy Products on the Stillorgan Road. Intensive preparations had been in progress there since before dawn. Lang had to personally inspect every item of

equipment that was to be used, and give a last, definitive briefing to the leaders of the various operational units. Squad B: Congar with his 152 mm guns and Shillelagh and Dragon missiles mounted on trucks that would hold the Carrolton Institute in a grip of fire and steel. Squad C: Ken Chandler's and Brenda Wilson's group, whose duty it was to take over the RTE television studios at Donnybrook (their operation would be modified but not essentially altered by Duane's death). Squad D: that loosely linked nucleus of experts, each answerable only to Lang himself—Rosen with his car bombs; Barbier with his booby-trapped German shepherds; Leach, who would take over the Sikorsky 61 hired from Hibernian Helicopters when it landed on University College Dublin campus this morning; Durnan, heading his mobile destruction squad that would plant bombs at the major newspaper offices and wreak havoc throughout the whole Dublin area.

Since the group had moved to Leinster Dairy Products from Kilbrangan House every aspect of the forthcoming coup had been subjected to searching scrutiny by Lang. "A chain is as strong as its weakest link, right?" he demanded. "A cliché, but it has to be true." And so every conceivable weakness in their strategy had to be projected and in some cases rehearsed so that an answer could be found. "I don't play chess," Lang remarked once, "but I sure as hell have the temperament."

Now Lang and Leni Reffenstab sat in the dusty, glass-fronted office near the main gate of the bottling plant. Leni was using the retrieval system on the small computer Lang had brought here from Kilbrangan House to run a final check on all relevant facts. All the task squads had been dealt with. Lang said, "Don't touch them now; don't even breathe on them! They're at concert pitch."

So, in the few minutes that remained, they were clearing up some loose ends.

"What else?" Lang asked.

Leni's fingers were busy. She'd gotten quite adept at handling this machine. "Leeson Street?"

Lang said, "Malachi will leave here shortly with the two morticians to rendezvous at Leeson Street at 0900. The forty-five volunteers are ready now. I just checked. The cars for the mourners will be there on schedule. I checked on that too."

Leni paused, her fingers on the keys. "Seamus Dillon? He is reported to have left St. Vincent's Nursing Home."

"Doesn't matter what he's done or where he is," Lang said. "He's lost all power to influence events. The same goes for his nephew—and for Frances McNagan."

"What about Duane?" Leni asked. "If the police get on to some-thing?"

"They don't even know whether the killing was political," Lang said. "Duane had a name as a cocksman, you know? You could have been a woman spurned, right?" He frowned. "Of course . . ."

"Yes?"

"They just *could* have latched on to something—thanks to your joke on Ms. Troy." The steel was there under the velvet in his voice and Leni felt afraid. Lang hadn't forgotten.

He was smiling. "But again," he said, "any inquiries will take them some time."

This morning Lang hardly looked thirty. His cheeks seemed to glow with health; the harsh strip lighting above them caught the gold in his thick, dust-colored hair. He vibrated confidence. Leni wouldn't mention hubris to him now.

☘ ☘ ☘

The bluish-gray light came filtering down into this narrow fissure in the thick, ancient wall. Dawn. Seamus looked at his watch but it had stopped at twenty after two.

He tried to move, but the sense of weakness, of feeling himself drifting away on a dark tide, came over him again. He was too weak to move. When he'd entered St. Vincent's twenty-four hours ago the intern had said his blood change was overdue. But aside from that he knew that the prophecy uttered in New York Hospital on Saint Patrick's Eve must sooner or later be fulfilled. Sooner or later those damned white leucocytes were going to win—and it looked like sooner.

He didn't think he'd hurt himself in the fall. He hadn't landed at the bottom of this hole with any great force. Or *had* he hurt himself? Were his senses anesthetized by weakness? He could have broken his hip, his spine. Old men had brittle bones. Suddenly he had an image of ivory-white, Belsen-feeble bones cracking horribly.

He was thirsty. He'd had nothing since that cup of tea on the train. God, for a sup of water . . .

No, he told himself. You can hang on. (Not much choice was there?) Offer it up, as his mother would have said. An hour or two more and people would be around. Caretakers or whatever. He would hear their voices, their footsteps, and then he would shout aloud and they would haul him up, out of this damned hole.

But could he shout? Loud enough for them to hear him? Panic gripped him. Could he talk at all?

"Seamus Dillon," he said. "Seamus Aloysius Patrick Dillon. Born New York City, twenty-sixth of August nineteen hundred and one."

He sounded strange, but at least he could hear himself.

The light that was filtering down now was whiter, more luminous. In Killarney on his honeymoon with his hoosier bride Seamus had known the magic of such dawns across the lakes; the sky striped with red over Sheey Mountain, then whitening over the higher Purple Mountain beyond. The magic owed something to the peculiar softness of the air—that hint of rain that an Irish sky holds on the brightest day.

He would try a decade of the rosary. Like his mother always said, a decade of the rosary never did anyone any harm.

☘ ☘ ☘

The Guard of Honor for the Carrolton Inauguration left Cathal Brugha Barracks at 10:10 A.M. Saturday morning. Headed by Colonel Blake Darrell with Lieutenant Marcus Beale as second-in-command, it consisted of thirty NCOs and men picked from various units of Eastern Command. More than one officer had remarked to Beale how unusual it was to have someone of Darrell's rank commanding the Guard—trust Darrell to grab the limelight!—but Beale shrugged that off as jealousy. Darrell's critics were only plodding behind him in efficiency, popularity with their men, and hopes of promotion.

Indeed, looking at Darrell now, with his finely tailored uniform, his dazzling boots and Sam Browne belt—six foot two inches of ramrod authority—Beale wondered if his colonel wouldn't steal the show.

But Darrell wasn't in the best of form this morning. He hardly spoke a word as the small convoy—the two officers in a staff car, the troops in three jeeps—passed down the Morehampton Road, the Donnybrook Road, and finally entered the Stillorgan Road. Traffic was light. They were overtaken by a few cars, probably taking people to the Carrolton celebrations, but the usual Saturday rush wouldn't start till around eleven or even later.

They were approaching the RTE television studios in Donnybrook when Beale noticed some kind of hassle in front of them. Getting nearer, he saw a hearse and what was apparently a line of funeral cars halted at the corner of Airfield Park and the Stillorgan Road. As the convoy got nearer still, the hearse started to move, making a right turn from Airfield Park into the Stillorgan Road. Beale wondered if the hearse was out of control, for instead of completing its turn into the left-hand lane, it careered forward, fetching up just short of the sidewalk on the other side of the road. The first two funeral cars had followed the hearse into the turn and when it went out of control the second car cannoned into the rear of the first with sufficient force to lock their fenders together. With a hearse and two big cars slewed across it, the Stillorgan Road was totally blocked, and the driver of the staff car had to brake sharply, bringing them to a spine-jarring halt with the first jeep only inches behind them.

Beale could see that the driver of the hearse had got out and had the hood up, looking at the engine.

"Couldn't have blocked us more effectively if they'd done it on purpose," Darrell murmured.

"Shall I turn around, sir?" their driver asked.

"And drive where, Madigan?" Darrell demanded. "I suppose we could go through Eglinton Road and get onto the campus by the back way, but by the time we've done that . . ." He shrugged.

Now a gray-haired man had stepped out of the first funeral car and was talking to the driver of the hearse.

"Madigan," Darrell said, "go see if you can give them a hand."

Corporal Madigan alighted and went over to the hearse.

Already the block had caused some buildup of traffic in both directions. Frustrated drivers were honking angrily.

"What's happened to our traditional reverence for funerals?" Darrell asked sardonically, and then surprised Beale by getting out of the car himself. He walked over to where Madigan was investigating the engine of the hearse, exchanged a few words with him, and then returned to Beale.

"All four wheels are locked—something to do with the driveshaft," he said. "Only one thing to do," he added. "Manhandle the bloody thing off the road."

"Sir?"

"Get the men out here and have them lift that hearse out of the way!"

"But, sir—"

"Tell them to get their tunics and belts off and get crackin'!" Darrell glanced at his watch. "We're due at the Carrolton Institute at 1050."

Beale passed the order on to his sergeant-major. The men got out of the jeeps, minus tunics, belts, and arms and, formed into two squads, were soon sweating and heaving as they tried to move the hearse.

Suddenly Beale realized that the mourners were getting out of the cars.

Pouring out, dozens of them it seemed, all wearing long black raincoats. They surrounded the hearse, massing around it, forming a circle that masked what was going on inside it, though Beale was close enough to see that the mourners—all young men—were closing in on the Honor Guards, holding them at gunpoint. The soldiers were outnumbered and taken totally by surprise. Handcuffed together in threes, they were herded into the undamaged funeral cars.

Beale watched fascinated as the mourners took off their long black raincoats and revealed Irish Army uniforms identical with those worn by the Guard of Honor. They formed up in three squads and began to move toward the empty jeeps.

Only then did Beale come to his senses. He got out of the car; looked around him; started to run.

But Colonel Darrell was there in front of him, holding a Webley automatic to his head. "Sorry about this Marcus, but you'll have to go along with the others."

Once the new Honor Guards had taken their places in the jeeps, the hearse and the two funeral cars were moved and Colonel Darrell and his men took off again for the Carrolton Inauguration. Lieutenant Beale, all of the original Honor Guards (except for one NCO and two enlisted men who were associated with the Wednesday Committee), and a Garda motorcycle patrolman (who had happened along immediately after the switch and had started to ask questions) were taken to the Leinster Dairy Products plant and locked up in a large storeroom, guarded by the volunteers from Leeson Street who had not been required for the new Guard of Honor.

As Malachi O'Farrell remarked as he drove off to join Lang at the Carrolton Institute, "That's the changing of the guard—Irish style."

"Frankie—tell me something."

She glanced at him. "Yes, Tom?"

"Do you think Glinn was sincere? Meant what he said?"

She shrugged; said in a tired voice, "I hope so."

They were walking along the newly made road on the UCD campus that led to the Carrolton Institute. It stood a hundred yards ahead of them: a dazzling artifact of steel and concrete surmounted by a glass dome that glittered in the sun. It was twenty before eleven, and one could feel the promise of future heat, although as usual the Dublin air retained an edge, a bite.

"Glinn implied he could get through to Darrell. Maybe convince him," Frankie said.

"Unless Darrell distrusts *him*, in turn," Tom said.

She shrugged; didn't answer.

Tom went on, "I keep thinking—could we have done any more than we did? Last night—after we'd seen Glinn."

"Last night? It was this morning . . ." She smiled and shook her head. "What could we have done?"

After Glinn had dropped them off outside the Phoenix Park, they had spent the hours before dawn in a house on the North Circular Road, which struck Tom as the Dublin equivalent of those hotels in the West Forties where Welfare used to lodge old people. There in a sleazy room with torn wallpaper they had made love with a kind of desperate, for-tomorrow-we-die tenderness.

"I wonder how your uncle got on," Frankie said.

Tom grinned. "I bet he got to see An tAthair Muiris. That old guy has got a way of getting what he wants."

"Where do you think they are, then?"

"That depends on what An tAthair was able to do, doesn't it?" Tom said. "Presumably they haven't gone to the island."

The so-called elders of the committee had been due to rendezvous at the town of Ballyclare in the early hours of this morning. Then, when they had all assembled, they would be ferried over to the island to begin a vigil that could last a few hours or several days. An tAthair Muiris was to have gone to Ballyclare straight from Killarney.

"Of course," Frankie said, "Seamus and An tAthair could be in Dublin now."

"Tell me," Tom said. "What do you think the An tAthair can do?"

Frankie shrugged. "I don't know."

"What can *we* do, really?"

"I don't know," she said again.

"Only thing to do is keep going, right?"

She nodded. Then she said, "I think we'd better split up here."

"Yes," he said. "Wouldn't do to have them see us kissing each other good-bye in the foyer."

They had decided that they had to enter the Carrolton Institute separately, allowing a few minutes between them. This doubled their chances: if one of them was detained, the other still had a chance of making it. There would certainly be a Special Branch check at the door—primarily for arms, but possibly for identification as well. The invitation cards had not been issued in the names of their holders, although of course the serial numbers provided a rough indication of each holder's category. Tom held the invitation that would have gone to Wendell Dillon; Frankie had one obtained by An tAthair Muiris for the ever-useful Mary Ogham. Of course if the Branch men at the door had their pictures as well as their descriptions, they could both be arrested and that would be an end of it. That was a chance they had to take.

Four

The Carrolton Ceremonies

Marta hadn't intended to come to the inauguration at all. It wasn't that she was still suffering physically from her recent ordeal. As poor old Rudi always used to say, she was about as indestructible as a Model T. But this went deeper than physical hurt. She'd never, at the basic core of herself—the part that really counted—been afraid of anyone. Ever since she was a little girl she'd hugged to herself a precious sense of her total uniqueness. She was Marta Troy. And of course when she grew up and became Marta Troy Superstar, this feeling had been reinforced. The really bad things always happened to other people. Other people got mugged, robbed, raped, humiliated, even murdered. Not her.

Now she'd lost that immunity at the hands of that Nazi guttersnipe. That was why she was here this morning. Fliers took up a plane immediately after a crash, right? So here she was playing the superstar up to the hilt: smiling, waving to friends, nodding to the photographers, making sure she was in range of the TV cameras.

She was early, but a lot of people had gotten here earlier. Her eyes ranged around the hall. Some United Statesmen were already in their seats. On the edge of the platform, among the most honored guests, sat Governor Hugh Carey. Next to him Daniel Moynihan. Speaker Tip O'Neill was placed a few seats away—nearer, no doubt, to where the president would sit when he entered. Since events had made the Carrolton Inauguration a kind of prelude to the Isle of Man Conference, it seemed right that these three men should be here. If the American Initiative succeeded, it would be in some measure thanks to their appeals reiterated over the years, that Britain should end the murderous deadlock in Northern Ireland. If after a thousand years the Irish Question was about to be solved, these Irish-Americans had helped solve it.

The hall was filling up quickly. Developed from a motif of concentric circles, it had ascending rows of seats ringing a central area in which stood a raised platform. Inspired perhaps by a Roman amphitheater, it reminded Marta of a boxing arena. RTE and NBC television crews were politely jousting for the best position in the narrow areas between the platform and the first row of seats. BBC and Télévision Française 1 teams were already established on top of the wide tunnel (leading from the foyer to a point just in front of the central stage) that was the public entrance to the hall. There was also a private entrance: a high causeway, so narrow as to be almost a catwalk, that led straight onto the platform from the administrative offices. (One architectural commentator had already condemned this as ugly, and elitist in purpose, designed solely to save VIPs from having to rub shoulders with the hoi polloi.)

Marta went on watching the people come in. Lots of churchmen: jovial, ascetic, rubicund, austere—all kinds and conditions. The papal nuncio. The Irish bench of bishops. The cardinal archbishops of New York and Boston. The Anglican archbishops of Dublin and Armagh, and of course the Catholic cardinal archbishop of Armagh. Members of the judiciary: hungrier, more anxious-looking than the ecclesiastics. Academics, from the university colleges of Cork, Galway, and Maynooth, and of course from this, the host institution, University College, Dublin. Politicians: Dail deputies who were preparing to relax at an occasion at which they were not required to speak. Members of the Senate.

Now the Guard of Honor entered: immaculate automata in their gleaming white belts. At their head Colonel Darrell. You just have to hand it to him, Marta thought. West Point. Sandhurst. Saint-Cyr. If they'd all collaborated they couldn't have produced a more elegant incarnation of the military caste.

What about security? Those beefy-looking guys dotted around the hall were presumably plainclothes spooks from the Irish Special Branch. The president would no doubt have his entourage of secret service men. The Company had their operatives in Dublin: Marta even knew a couple of them. Surely they'd send someone along this morning? And the British must have fielded a spook or two for an occasion like this. Annabel! Marta had more than once had the rumor that she was in British Intelligence. Annabel—that birdbrain with a memorable body? Well, maybe—but Marta felt that if this were true she ought somehow to have divined the fact sometime they were in bed together.

❧ ❧ ❧

Seamus was quite clear in his mind now: calm and composed. For the last half hour his brain had been chill as ice, seeing exactly how things were going to be. He was going to die. Die grotesquely, even ridiculously, trapped in a bloody hole in a wall. But it didn't matter: his time had run out anyway. The very blood in his viens was rotten, useless. So accept it. Say an act of contrition. Death was here.

But then the clarity was gone and he was going down, down dipping into sleep as insidiously as one nods off on a hot afternoon. And indeed that was what this was: one of those hot, brilliant summer days that only seem to happen in childhood. And he was a child and there was his mother coming toward him, smiling and young in a flowered print dress—younger than he remembered her. He ran toward her, burying his face in the soft, vaguely scented folds of her dress . . .

He had to move. Get himself out of this somehow. He was coldly conscious again. The sun was getting up; he could feel its heat, baking its way through these ancient stones. He tried to think of Magda, his wife, dead these several years. How good she had been, how kind, how tolerant. And yet he couldn't remember what she looked like, how her voice sounded . . . How unfair that was, both to him and to Magda, the wife of his heart for thirty years. His eyes filled with tears.

He tried to speak her name; heard nothing. Tried to count—one, two, three, four . . . He thought he heard himself counting, but couldn't be certain anymore.

❧ ❧ ❧

Slowey stared at the familiar objects that surrounded him—the calendar from Allied Irish Banks, the small brass monkey given him by his uncle, who had been with the Society of African Missions in Nigeria, the silver cigarette box that now held paperclips—and dumbly sought inspiration from them, as if one of them might prove to be the manta that would bring him enlightenment.

His dilemma persisted, and now it was a matter not of hours but of minutes before he made a decision. He had never wavered like this before; indeed, he had always gained a tonic force from the very act of making up his mind, but never before, in all his time in the Force, had so much hung on a single decision.

Should he let Glinn proceed to Carrolton or should he not? Ever since Garvin had brought him face to face with this dilemma, Slowey had been tortured by the thought that if he removed Glinn from his detail on suspicion alone, he could do Glinn's career great damage—even if those suspicions afterward proved to be unfounded. But if Slowey were right—then letting Glinn go to Carrolton could have hideous, almost unimaginable consequences. If he were a traitor, in cahoots with Lang—

In his frustration Slowey cursed the destiny that had made him a policeman and not—as God had perhaps intended—a priest. Although he had stopped short of being ordained, Slowey had for many years known an intense inner life comparable with that of a priest. Now the distrust he felt toward Glinn gnawed at him inwardly. All human life is based on trust: deny that, Slowey felt, and you become a machine, fueled by duty alone.

Ten-thirty A.M. Time had run out. Indeed, Glinn could have already left for Carrolton. If Slowey wanted to go there, he would have to leave immediately to get to Bellfield before the ceremonies began.

He stood up. He had come to a decision.

He walked across the room. As he put his hand on the doorknob, the door swung open, nearly knocking him over.

Mick Glinn stood there.

Slowey cried out in surprise: "You? I thought you'd have left for Carrolton by now?"

Glinn didn't answer; stared back with an aggressive air that Slowey didn't recognize. Gone was Glinn's usual restraint, the slightly doggish melancholy.

He spoke with the theatrical, topheavy irony of a drunk. "The Blessed Cormac Slowey! Our Saint in the Castle. Mea culpa, Father! Mea maxima culpa!"

"Glinn!" Slowey protested. "For God's sake—"

Glinn nodded. "For God's sake, indeed. Because I have to make a confession to you. A good and general confession."

Slowey grabbed Glinn's arm. Glinn stepped back angrily; shook him off.

"Let me speak!" He was almost snarling. "Know what, Slowey? You've never understood any of us—the men you work with. You're still half a priest, aren't you? And so you're the right man to hear my confession." He paused. "I have to tell you, Slowey: I have been at the center of a conspiracy. I have planned the overthrow of the legally constituted government of the Irish Republic. All these months you've been sniffing around the likes of poor Frank Niles—here I was, right at your elbow, the man you really wanted."

Slowey wanted to speak, but held himself back.

Glinn went on: "Of course, since this is Ireland and we are Irishmen, the conspiracy was a failure." His voice was mocking. "I thought I was working for Ireland—the Ireland the true Gael has dreamed of for a thousand years." He shook his head. "We were betrayed. As usual. In my heart I suppose I always knew we would be. But not by an Irishman. That's one consolation," he added bitterly. "A man called Lang. He's supposed to be an American—"

"Lang!" Slowey cried. "So it was Lang—"

"Yes, Slowey, it was. Lang has made fools of us all—you, me—and the Wednesday Committee. Another hour or so and he'll have made fools of the whole world!"

Slowey grabbed Glinn's arm and this time he did not let go. "Go on, tell me!"

"Too late." Glinn sounded as if the drink he had taken was overwhelming him at last. "Can't do anything. He's fooled us. Frankie McNagan it was opened our eyes—she's on the committee too, you know that? I tried to stop him, but it's too late. He made us swear an oath—you understand me, Slowey, he played on our weakness, our distrust, our fear of an informer . . ."

"You say you tried to stop him?"

Glinn nodded. He seemed to grow more haggard and wild-eyed each moment. "Yes . . . I sat at that telephone in my office for the last four hours, but I couldn't do anything. Couldn't reach anyone who mattered." He gestured. "That oath—it was a noose, Slowey, a noose he's drawn tight . . ."

"Come on—pull yourself together—"

"I'm drunk, Slowey, and that's typical too. When I found I wasn't getting anywhere I started on a bottle of gin—"

Slowey began to drag him toward the door. "Start talking!" he said. "We might still be able to stop him."

❧ ❧ ❧

The president was coming. Marta recognized that familiar figure at once. As a matter of protocol—he was their guest—he preceded the taoiseach and his cabinet.

There he was, coming down the narrow causeway onto the platform. The president of the United States of America, still the most powerful country on earth. A man—with a man's fallibility and self-doubt—but invested with something like the mythic burden of a god.

The applause started; rose quickly to a deafening level which was maintained for several minutes. The president of Ireland should have come next, but he had developed a chill. So next came the taoiseach, with his battered tragedian's face, a cleanshaven Lear making a comeback. Then the minister of economic affairs, followed by several other ministers. And, almost last, Marta's friend Conan O'Kelly, bless him! No mistaking that short-paced penguin's strut.

When the applause died down, Marta wondered if they would start by playing "The Soldier's Song" [the Irish national anthem], like they did before a performance at a theater or movie house. She was looking around to see if there was any kind of band in evidence when she found herself looking into the oddly transparent, empty eyes of Rex Lang.

Lang had devised a complex pattern of diversionary action to accompany the main coup at the Carrolton Institute. He had originally intended to coordinate and oversee operations from a command helicopter which would circle the city throughout the action. When he decided he had to head the squad in the Carrolton Institute himself, he had the choice of delegating command to Mark Durnan or Malachi O'Farrell or of trying to program events so that his executive presence was not required.

He chose the second alternative. Marrying the talents of Rosen, Barbier, and his other specialists, Lang evolved a coordinated strategy. He decided that during the first half hour of phase one, Barbier's dogs should precede Rosen's car bombs. Now Barbier's arduous training of his twenty-five German shepherds was to pay off. Nervous and aggressive—"fear-biters"—when they were first delivered to him at Kilbrangan House, he had brought them to a hair-trigger savagery through teasing, starvation, and the systematic infliction of pain.

They were first unleashed when one of Lang's trucks turned out of Parnell Street and stopped at the end of Moore Street, full of fruit and vegetable stalls. This Saturday morning it was thronged with women doing their weekend marketing. They were too busy stocking their bags with bargain-priced apples and potatoes to notice Barbier and another man get out of the truck. Swiftly, they led four German shepherds through Moore Street, to release them in Henry Street, a pedestrianized area crowded with shoppers moving in and out of stores like Roches, Arnotts, and Woolworth's. Then they went back to the truck and got four more dogs that would be released in the busy shopping arcade behind the General Post Office. Finally Barbier's aide ran back to the truck for the last two German shepherds, to be set free in Liffey Street. Then he and Barbier got into the truck and drove off. In the space of a few minutes ten booby-trapped dogs had been released among the thickest crowds to be found in Dublin that morning.

"Sure, aren't I telling you—my name is Mary Ogham. O-G-H-A-M—" she spelled it out, letter by letter. "And I work for Mayo County Council." Frankie wondered how she was making out with the Limerick accent, since Mary had been born in Newcastle West. This man from the Special Branch sounded as if he came from Kerry, which was a bit too close for comfort. And horticulture— she was a horticultural adviser, for God's sake! She wished poor Duane had given her the identity of someone she'd actually *met*.

"I know, miss, I know." The Special Branch man was young and affected a ponderous manner which accorded badly with his babyish features and apple-red cheeks. "And I'm not doubting you exactly. But the fact remains you can produce no positive proof of identification." The uniformed policewoman beside him nodded agreement. (Presumably she was there to search ladies suspected of carrying arms.) "Frankly, miss, you could fit the description of this lassie we're looking for, this Frances McNagan."

"But if you keep me waiting here I'll miss the inauguration," Frankie wailed. "I do *so* want to see the American president!"

"Sure, the inspector will be along in a minute. He might decide to let you in. But I can't, miss—not on my own bat."

The foyer was nearly empty now. The ceremonies would be starting any moment. Tom had obviously got in all right. That was something. But what could Tom, what could anyone, do against Lang?

Slowey glanced at Glinn, sitting beside him in the big black Granada. Now Glinn's face was perpetually trembling, dissolving, as a small child's does just before it bursts into tears. But Glinn didn't cry. His despair went too deep for that.

He had grown increasingly silent as the stream of fresh air blowing through the car window sobered him up, but even in the fifteen minutes they had been traveling between the Castle and Bellfield, he had told Slowey a great deal. The basic nature of the coup. The composition of the Wednesday Committee—

Slowey had been amazed, even shocked, to learn of Darrell's involvement; and disconcerted, but far from amazed, to hear of McClymont's. Some of this information was almost academic, though, considering what was about to happen at the Carrolton Inauguration. Slowey had heard of the switching of the Honor Guard with despair; he had been almost as appalled to learn that (on Glinn's instructions) Lang and some twenty-four of his group had been granted admission to the institute en bloc as a holiday delegation from the Swedish university of Uppsala. "No arms check?" Slowey demanded. "A distinguished foreign academic and his students?" Glinn echoed. "No way!" He had gone on to say that although the Branch men on the arms check outside the institute were not privy to the coup—"I couldn't fix that"—those inside were. Would they be baffled that Glinn hadn't turned up to take charge? Slowey had wanted to know. Glinn had told him it wouldn't matter.

So, with the Honor Guard, Glinn's subverted Special Branch men, and Lang's Tontons Macoute (Lang's jovial name for the twenty-odd members of his group who had gained entry along with him), the odds inside the hall were overwhelmingly in Lang's favor. He had it made before the ceremonies began.

Now they came to the university lodge and turned onto the road that led across the campus to the Carrolton Institute. Glinn could be asleep. His face had stopped trembling, but in repose still mirrored anguish and bewilderment. Slowey wondered what his driver, the rocklike Garda McLintock, had made of Glinn's ramblings—he must have heard them. What harm? McLintock was too good a policeman to ever blab anything.

Slowey was looking in his briefcase, checking its contents. Glinn opened his eyes suddenly; he saw that Slowey had a submachine gun and a hand gun, a small Walther automatic. "That's not official issue," he said, indicating the Walther. Slowey nodded; didn't answer. "David and Goliath," Glinn said. "You going in there with those! Worse—it's a kid taking on a tank with a water pistol!"

Slowey nodded again. "McLintock will take you back to the Castle," he said. "I suggest you go into your office and stay there. Better still, go into my office. Keep out of the way till I get back," he added. "Whenever that is."

Slowey saw the Granada turn and drive away. Then he entered the Carrolton foyer.

He recognized Frankie McNagan at once. She was talking to a Ban Garda and to a very recent recruit to the Branch called Keane. As soon as Keane saw Slowey his stance was transformed: you could see him in uniform again, pounding a beat.

"Keane."

"Superintendent, sir. I was expecting Inspector Glinn—"

"He won't be here," Slowey said. "But I am." He indicated Frankie McNagan. "Some problem?"

"Superintendent—this officer is keeping me here because he says I look like some criminal they're looking for."

"Not exactly a criminal," Slowey said. "More like a terrorist."

"Is that so?" Frankie asked, wide-eyed.

You have to hand it to her, Slowey thought. A real pro. Her air of outraged innocence wasn't overdone. But even if he hadn't been sure of the face, that touch of an English accent would have given her away.

She kept trying: "I've told this officer I'm prepared to produce my passport and other identification at a Garda station. But the inauguration is going to start any moment—"

"That's all right," Slowey cut in. "You can let the lady in, Keane. I know Frankie McNagan—and this isn't her."

Frankie was smiling and thanking the both of them. Then, as she hurried toward the doors, Slowey caught up with her.

"Better stay with me," he said. "I might be able to get you a better seat."

The taoiseach was speaking: ". . . and so I will repeat at the end what I said at the beginning. We stand here at the meeting place of two cultures, one belonging to the new world, the other to the old. One, the ancient culture of Ireland, the other, the less ancient but equally dignified culture of the United States of America. We are met together today to celebrate and"—he inclined his head toward the cardinal archbishop of Armagh—"to consecrate this beautiful building, to be called the Carrolton Institute, for which we have to thank American generosity and indeed the American passion for all things Irish— Irish legends, Irish art, Irish culture in general . . . Indeed, you might ask: where would we Irish be without the Americans?—but then you might ask too: where would they be without us?" A ripple of polite laughter greeted that.

Okay, just okay, Tom thought, but then you didn't expect eloquence from politicians but a predictable style. Anyway, at this moment Tom was too tense to pay much attention to what anyone said. He was wondering what had happened to Frankie. Had she been nabbed by the cops at the door? He didn't see her—but in this huge assemblage that didn't mean much. He didn't see Glinn either: had he been able to do anything?

☘ ☘ ☘

For the first few moments no one took much notice of the big German shepherds with the odd equipment on their backs. There were so many dogs nosing around Dublin, with or without their owners. And the dogs themselves did little to attract attention. Maybe they were puzzled—finding themselves roaming free after their cruel captivity under Barbier.

Then, in the most crowded part of Moore Street, a little girl patted one of the dogs on the head. He snarled and jumped at her, knocking her down between two stalls. Holding her prostrate with his front paws, he started to savage her as she screamed horribly, the blood from her wounds running into the gutter. One of the stallholders—a husky, redhaired woman, went for the dog, swinging an iron bar at his head. She missed his head, but caught him across the back, activating the trembler device of the bomb he was carrying. It went off with a roar, smashing and searing through the close-packed human flesh all around, killing six people.

Panic gripped the whole block. Trapped in the Post Office Arcade, a man tried to fight off one of the dogs and in the struggle set off the bomb. The walls of the arcade collapsed, burying everyone who was inside it.

By now the happy crowd of marketers had become a hysterical mob. As the dogs roamed the web of sidestreets behind the General Post Office, everyone fled from them, shrieking in terror. Many escaped into stores and offices, but old people and children were particularly vulnerable. An elderly woman tripped and fell in the now deserted Henry Street. A German shepherd was onto her at once, tearing her face to pieces. No one interfered with him as he savaged her and his bomb remained unexploded.

Meanwhile the other fifteen dogs had been unleashed in different parts of the city center. Seven were roaming the triangle made by Westmoreland and D'olier streets with College Green as its apex. A dog wandered into the crowded Sealink tourist office on Westmoreland Street. His bomb went off and in the confined space killed eighteen people. On College Green a Trinity student tackled a dog rugby-football fashion and was blown to pieces.

Another of Lang's trucks had put the last eight dogs into the Grafton Street district. A group of young people coming out of The Baily on Duke Street stumbled onto a dog and set off a bomb that killed them all.

Within a few minutes the center of Dublin was deserted, with a number of the dogs still alive, roaming the empty streets with their deadly gear strapped to their backs.

☘ ☘ ☘

There was considerable applause when the taoiseach sat down. Then silence, tinged by expectancy. Would the president speak next?

He stood up. The First Executive. Still the most powerful man in the world. Still the holder—despite all the follies of Vietnam, all the shit of a Watergate—of a moral mandate from the American people. Of that at least I can be proud, Tom thought.

The president said, "I guess you all expect a text from me, so I'll give you one, just to get it over with." A flash of humor, dipping into earnestness. "Romans, the ninth chapter, the twenty-first verse. 'Hath not the potter power over the clay, of the same lump to make one vessel unto honor and another unto dishonor?' "

Style, he has, Tom thought. Hard to define it. If you wanted to praise him you could say he had the ability to make earnestness—moral endeavor—not only credible but attractive.

"Let us hold before this concept of honor and dishonor," the president went on. "Let's consider this man, this Irishman, Charles Carroll, whose name is perpetuated in this Carrolton Institution." The president looked up; smiled at the hundreds of faces around him. "In 1830 Charles Carroll was an old man. Today we should call him an elder statesman. He was the sole surviving signatory of the Declaration of Independence . . ."

Lulled by rhetoric, looking up at the president, surrounded as he was by representatives of the whole establishment of the West, Tom found it hard to believe in the threat that lurked so close.

☘ ☘ ☘

If it was true that you saw all of your past life pass before you when you were dying, then he wasn't dying, Seamus thought. But of course he knew he was.

He felt quite clear in his mind now, although he still couldn't conjure up any vision of Magda. He wondered what was happening at the Carrolton Inauguration. Had Tom and Frankie been able to influence anyone at all? Tom was okay, he had the kind of gut-courage that counted, and Frankie was Peadar's daughter, but what could they do?

He wondered about An tAthair Muiris too. Still in ignorance of Lang's treachery, he would have gone straight to the island. He would be there now, waiting along with Catherine Cudahy, Liam O Docartai, MacSaoirse, and the others. No doubt he would celebrate mass there as dawn came to Lough Ree.

He would never get An tAthair's blessing now. And then the thought struck Seamus like a sword of ice: he was going to die without a priest. He was going to die here, in this hole, unshriven, lacking all the comfort and salvation a priest can bring to the dying.

Seamus reflected that they must find him eventually. There would be a search for him. Indeed, the Special Branch were already looking although they wouldn't expect to find him dead. They had to find him sometime. If they didn't, then he supposed it would be like a man whose body has been lost at sea.

Ireland. Would they say he'd died for Ireland? He truly had, in a sense. Sure, they'd say it anyway. With a drink to wash the words down and a ballad to speed him along. One of his favorites—"The Fenians' Escape" or "Come to the Bower." Hadn't he done it himself, totting up the score of a man's life with the aid of a ball of malt? There wouldn't be too many to do it for him. The world turns swiftly, and he was an old man: you need contemporaries to mourn you and most of his were dead.

Ireland. Kathleen ni Houlihan. Roisin Dubh. The Old Bitch. Ireland is important but there are things more important. Think of the cross. Pray. Oh my God, I am heartily sorry . . . Fair play, man! In Irish! . . . Gur chuir me fearg ort, agus ta fuath firinneach agam do mo pheacai agus gach olc eile . . .

He could hear himself praying, although he'd thought his voice was gone. Strangely now, other voices seemed to take up his prayer, but he couldn't make out the words.

He was blind now and he was aware, in some little remaining islet of consciousness, that he did not really hear the praying voices because he *was* the prayer now, a single last plea too sad to be spoken, rising in blackness and dying into silence.

Mick Congar's four trucks were rumbling along the road between the university lodge and the Carrolton Institute. Congar was actually four minutes behind schedule. The uniformed attendant at the gate was waving the trucks through when an older man had come out of the lodge. He wanted to know who they were. Anyway, why were they delivering stores to the canteen on a Saturday morning? The canteen was closed. Congar had wasted several minutes arguing about this, and in the end the old man still hadn't been satisfied.

He'd have to call the bursar's office. As he turned back into the lodge, Congar shot him in the back. After that it was necessary to kill the younger attendant too, and sever the telephone cables leading to the lodge. All time lost. Time that would have to be made up by extra speed in unloading the guns and missiles from the trucks. Once they were in place, the Carrolton Institute would be totally isolated: held in a ring of fire and steel.

Just before Congar's squad started to unload their trucks, Hibernian Helicopters had landed a Sikorsky 61 at a point about a hundred yards from the Carrolton Institute. Martin Leach had been waiting for it to arrive. He was glad the time for action had come at last; these last weeks in this damp and deadly land he had suffered such feelings of blankness and futility that he'd almost wished he were addicted again.

He was interested to observe the skill with which the pilot brought the ship down onto the right spot. To Leach's surprise, the pilot was the general manager of Hibernia, the tight-lipped Fergus Daimon. "Oh, Saturday morning, old boy. That explains everything, what? My overpaid sods wouldn't dream of working at the weekend."

Daimon sounded resigned rather than surprised when Leach held a gun to his head and told him this was a hijack.

"Oh, my God—*really?* Oh well, suppose it had to happen sometime . . ."

❦ ❦ ❦

Ten minutes after Barbier had first released his dogs, all lines to the Castle were blocked with calls—mostly from members of the public protesting anger, alarm, and sheer incredulity at what was happening in the streets.

In the assistant commissioner's room a special conference had been called. In addition to the commissioner there were two senior superintendents, Thomas Murphy and William Leetham, and two inspectors, Liam Clarke and Sean Brannoch.

The assistant commissioner explained that twenty police marksmen would have by now taken up their positions at windows commanding all the main streets, but he doubted whether this could really contain the threat. The remaining dogs could wander a long way in a short time. They could survive for days, lurking in alleys and back lots.

"Thinking aloud as it were," the assistant commissioner said, "I wonder would it be any good tracking down these brutes with other dogs? Blood-hounds, who could take up the scent and lead us to them."

The others made polite noises of agreement.

"One could put some of our marksmen on motorbikes and have them follow the bloodhounds . . ."

The assistant commissioner's voice trailed away as his mind lost impetus. He was a man popular with his subordinates and yet even at this moment of crisis Inspector Clarke couldn't help feeling that he looked like a huge white rabbit, blinking in strong sunlight.

"What do you think, Clarke?" he demanded, as if he'd read Clarke's mind.

"About bloodhounds, sir?"

"No, the er—general situation . . ."

"I think it represents some kind of assault on public morale, sir."

"Yes, I agree," chimed in Superintendent Leetham. He was possibly irked that the assistant commissioner had asked a junior officer's opinion first. "This is obviously part of some general strategy. We must expect more develop-ments of some kind."

Superintendent Murphy said, "I think there should be some authoritative pronouncement at once, preferably by the taoiseach. To allay public alarm."

"Get through to his office, will you?" the commissioner said. "Oh—of course, he's at the Carrolton Inauguration. He lifted the telephone. "Get through to University College, Dublin, will you . . . ? Yes—UCD. Get me put through to the Carrolton Institute . . ."

After a moment or two of uneasy silence, the assistant commissioner lifted the phone again. "Any luck yet?" He listened, frowning. "Good God . . . they're not, are they?" He looked up; replaced the receiver. "The lines are all out of order—and the Post Office engineers say they must have been cut."

Inspector Brannoch hadn't spoken since the meeting started. Now he said, "Doesn't it occur to anyone that it's all connected? Those booby-trapped dogs and the American president coming to Dublin?"

The assistant commissioner stared at him. He nodded slowly and opened his mouth to speak.

At that moment there was an explosion. It came with the savage, rending effect of a huge paper bag bursting, and in the echoing, deafened seconds that followed, the glass in the shattered windows of the assistant commissioner's office began to drop out with a gentle tinkling sound.

☘ ☘ ☘

The president paused. "I'm nearly through." He had drawn the threads of his speech together and now he was going to tie them up in a neat bow. And yet "neat" wasn't quite fair, Slowey thought. That implied glib and that this man was not. His sincerity shone through the conventional phrases he used.

The president continued: "But before I let you go—one more quotation. Yes"—he grinned—"it's from the Bible. I believe it sums up what we look for from this, the Carrolton Institute—and indeed, what we shall be looking for from the Isle of Man Conference that starts the day after tomorrow . . ."

Slowey's attention wavered, caught by a sound as light as the rustle of a leaf. But he heard it, and suddenly his senses were taut, alert.

He didn't know where the sound had come from. He stared at the faces of the honor guards. They looked as dignified and as immobile as wax dummies. Slowey wondered about the youngish men in business suits sitting up there on the platform. Secret service, guarding the president?

Three shots rang out somewhere at the back of the hall. A woman screamed. Slowey turned to look behind him; could see nothing.

Elegant automata no longer, the Honor Guards had broken ranks and now encircled the president, the taoiseach, and all the other eminent guests on the platform, covering them with their carbines. All the eminent guests were holding their hands above their heads and there was a look of shock and bewilderment on their faces.

Two of the Guards were disarming the husky young men in business suits, throwing their surrendered handguns into a burlap bag. It was hard for Slowey to see from where he was sitting, but another section of the Honor Guard was apparently covering the main entrance. He realized that the design of the hall had greatly facilitated the coup. A handful of guards at the doors could prevent anyone from entering or leaving, while anyone sitting in the body of the hall could be picked off at will by any good shot up on the platform. All the same, he wondered why there had been such a complete absence of resistance. Presumably because Lang had everyone sewn up—including the Special Branch men Glinn had told Slowey were committed to the coup. Slowey couldn't see any of them: they must be among the audience.

He glanced at Frankie McNagan, sitting beside him. She showed no emotion, but she must be bitterly reflecting that Lang had manipulated every weakness of the republican movement, making the members of the Wednesday Committee dance like puppets at his urging.

Slowey looked again at the people on the platform. The taoiseach wore his mask of tragedy with dignity: he didn't look afraid. Some of his cabinet did, especially the minister for economic affairs, who kept moving about uneasily, shifting from one foot to another, till one of the Honor Guards shouted at him to keep still.

Aside from the others, as if somehow less involved, stood the president. He didn't look frightened; only intensely curious.

Now the silence inside the hall was total, carrying a mounting pressure within it that grew unendurable.

A tall fair man was mounting the platform. He was followed by a girl whom Slowey identified as Leni Reffenstab, who (he had learned from the Kommissar only this morning) had a record of murder with the Movement Second June. Then came a man with gray hair. He fitted the description of the Irish-American, Malachi O'Farrell, the "assistant director" on Lang's bogus film unit.

Lang stood quite still, regarding the audience. What impressed Slowey most was the air of calm he projected.

☘ ☘ ☘

The meeting in the assistant commissioner's office broke up when the bombs started. The explosion that had shattered the windows had been the first: a bomb planted in an old Rover parked on Werburgh Street near the Castle. The next went off on Nassau Street beside Trinity College.

Within the next eight minutes car bombs exploded on O'Connell Street opposite the General Post Office; outside the Bank of Ireland on College Green; and in the courtyard of Trinity College. Smaller bombs (activated by timing devices) had been planted at the offices of Aer Lingus, CIE [the Irish state transport monopoly], and of the three Dublin daily papers—the *Irish Press*, the *Irish Independent*, and the *Irish Times*. A little later there was a much larger explosion at Leinster House [the Irish Parliament]. Then more bombs at the National Library and at the main railway stations.

By now a thick pall of smoke hung over central Dublin. In the last half hour more than sixty people had been killed and many more injured; the Mater and Jervis Street hospitals were feverishly trying to cope with all the casualties. Following as it did on the terror of the booby-trapped dogs, this series of explosions bludgeoned most Dubliners into a state of unreasoning panic. What was going to happen next?

At this stage, however, the police were so preoccupied with events at the Carrolton Institute that they had little time to spare on public anxieties. Now it was known that the institute was in the hands of a group of terrorists led by a man who had posed as an American film director: Rex Lang.

When it proved impossible to establish contact with the Carrolton Institute, the assistant commissioner had dispatched three patrol cars there.

The first car had driven straight up to the institute. Getting within two hundred yards, it had been destroyed by a bazooka-type missile just as the police Land-Rover at Kilhassig had been. The other two cars had stopped short when they saw their comrades killed. They had radioed back that the institute now stood at the center of a perimeter of guns and missile launchers that concentrated an enormous firepower within one or two square miles of campus.

As soon as Lang's name was mentioned, Inspector Garvin had suggested the assistant commissioner speak with Superintendent Slowey, as he knew Slowey had been pursuing a line of inquiry with regard to Lang. But when the assistant commissioner rang Slowey's extension, there was no answer. Inspector Brannoch went down to Slowey's office and was shocked to find, not Slowey, but the dead body of Mickey Glinn, sprawled across Slowey's desk, in one hand a Walther automatic and in the other, loosely twined rosary beads.

Slowey's driver, Guard McLintock, said he had driven Superintendent Slowey and Inspector Glinn to the Carrolton Institute just over half an hour ago. The superintendent had gone into the building, but on his instructions McLintock had brought Inspector Glinn back to the Castle. The inspector hadn't looked well at all, he added.

"My God." The assistant commissioner shook his head wonderingly. "So the Blessed Cormac's inside there." None of the other officers present had realized he even knew Slowey's nickname. "Well, this is his chance to achieve full canonization at last."

During the fifteen minutes that had passed since the takeover, Lang had spoken to the assemblage only once. His words had been cold, noncommittal: "Please remain seated. Control your emotions. Wait for an announcement."

There had been a lot of coming and going in the fifteen minutes. Colonel Darrell and a few of the Honor Guards remained on the stage, but a squad of twelve men in dark shades and combat fatigues now came forward. They were obviously members of Lang's group: Slowey remembered Glinn's words: "Lang calls them his Tontons Macoute." Others of them took up places beside the Honor Guards at the entrance of the hall. Colonel Darrell stayed where he was, unmoving as a statue, but now he appeared outflanked, diminished, surrounded as he was by Lang's sinister-looking personnel.

The taoiseach and his cabinet had been herded over to the left of the stage, where they stood huddled together. The president was not being held at gunpoint; he stood aside from the others, on the extreme left, not far from Lang.

One of Lang's men was tinkering with the microphone. Others were setting up television cameras taken from the RTE newsteam. (The Honor Guards had already smashed video gear belonging to NBC, Télévision Française 1, and BBC teams.)

The man stopped tinkering. Lang stepped forward. "Just making sure we've gotten our television link established." He looked down at the sea of tense, silent faces. "So—just go on sitting there, all of you. Don't move. Don't speak. Don't stop being frightened. You've got plenty to be frightened about." He smiled. "Any one of you could so easily die within the next few minutes."

The silence that followed seemed even more absolute than before. Slowey was gripped by a terrifying sense of inevitability, as if he had died and found himself acting out a familiar nightmare in the next life.

Still held by the nightmare, Slowey saw a red dot of light appear on Colonel Darrell's forehead. The dot lingered there, with an effect of leisurely precision—and then Darrell's face disintegrated into a bloody pulp and he crashed forward. Lang's men were firing. The Honor Guards on the platform went down: one, two, three . . .

The laser 180 again—the legendary submachine gun, firing nine hundred .22 bullets a minute, used by the Israelis at Entebbe—which Slowey had first seen in action at the old burial ground at Kilhassig.

He guessed that Darrell's Honor Guards at the entrance had been killed too—without being able to fire a shot in their own defense. Through all this he had heard no sound of firing: the 180 made no more noise than a typewriter.

The bodies on the platform lay where they had fallen. Lang stepped over them as he took up the microphone again.

"That had to be done anyway," he said. "But—see what I mean?"

The television cameras and sound gear had now been set up at the right-hand corner of the platform, near the narrow causeway that spanned the main body of the hall.

Lang's false smile was more threatening than anger or bluster could have been. He apologized: "I'm afraid this delay is typical of the hassle you get mounting any TV production—and this is gonna be a major production! We hope to go out by satellite—we're just awaiting final confirmation that the link is established. Europe, North America, part of Africa—they're all about to see us."

Two of his men were testing the lights. Lang's coloring made him look unreal, evanescent in the glare.

The harsh lighting was switched off again and Lang continued: "I may as well use these few minutes to give you a total picture of this situation. Tell you some things I don't have to tell the world outside—because it is already aware of them. Like, for instance, the fact that this building is ringed by artillery."

The assistant commissioner's car was stopped about a mile beyond the perimeter of the Carrolton Institute—well within the range of Lang's guns and rocket launchers. The total of assembled troops, police, and media people grew larger by the minute. Lang had only to order his men to open up and hundreds would be killed. But so far the only offensive action had been the firing of a 152 mm shell at an army helicopter that flew over the institute. Its crew reported seeing a Sikorsky 61 parked inside the perimeter.

About a half hour earlier, the Castle had received the news that Lang's guerrillas had also taken over the television center at Donnybrook and were holding twenty of its staff hostage there. Shortly afterward Garda technical experts informed the assistant commissioner that a TV link had been established between Donnybrook and the Carrolton Institute. So now the assistant commissioner and Inspectors Garvin and Brannoch were sitting in the commissioner's official Mercedes staring at the screen of a portable television set. It offered a signal that perhaps reflected Lang's grotesque sense of humor: a man wearing a child's plastic mask of a werewolf with long fangs. At intervals the injunction was repeated: Wait. Stay tuned. An announcement will soon be made.

Inevitably, at this time of tension compounded by boredom, the three men discussed Mick Glinn's suicide.

"Overwork, I suppose," the assistant commissioner said. "That's the only explanation for a man doing such a terrible thing."

The two inspectors nodded. Whatever they knew, or suspected, they weren't about to reveal it to the assistant commissioner.

"Of course he was conducting his investigations under the eye of the Blessed Cormac," the assistant commissioner went on. "A fanatic, that one. Should have been an old-fashioned Redemptorist putting the heart across people at the annual Lenten mission."

Now the screen went suddenly blank. Schoolboylike, the assistant commissioner nudged Garvin. "Now we'll see what the bastards want."

❧   ❧   ❧

Tom was sitting to the right of the platform, immediately below the cause-way along which the various establishment figures had made their way onto the platform (that seemed a long time ago now). From where he sat Tom got a good view of Lang. He tried to imagine how he would look to the millions of people who were now seeing him on TV. How would they react to that hand-some face and that cold, deadpan voice?

This was the greatest hijack in history (Lang said). Never before had the actual government of a country been held hostage as the taoiseach and the other members of the Irish Government were being held at this moment. And, Lang added, this was a great first for television too. Never before had an act of mass terror been dramatized like this: the extremities of life and death brought so vividly to everyone's fireside. Lang said, "You're not just gonna see actors this time. You're gonna see the rich and powerful of this earth brought low. Down on their knees begging for mercy—and not getting it!" He paused. "Terror is theater. Enjoy the show."

The taoiseach and his cabinet still stood on the left of the platform. They had been roped together like cattle, hobbled around the ankles, so that they could only walk with a topheavy, shuffling movement. The president still stood aside from them, and now his expression was of concern rather than curiosity.

"Bring them forward," Lang ordered. He indicated that the TV cameras should take in the shuffling progress of the taoiseach and his ministers. "Come on—move it!" Lang snarled and one of the Tontons Macoute prodded Conan O'Kelly with the muzzle of his 180. O'Kelly lost his balance and went crashing down, dragging the others with him. Lang stood smiling as they laboriously struggled to their feet: six panting, sweating, aging men whose once immacu-late morning-dress was already crumpled and disheveled.

"May I present—one head of state and his ministers!" Lang proclaimed in parody of the compere at a fashion show as the camera moved along the six haggard faces. "Take a good look at them," Lang added. "I'm sure you'll agree they're worth keeping alive."

Both the American Government and Ireland's fellow EEC members would be relieved to hear that his demands were very simple, Lang said. Very prac-tical. No demand for the release of any guerrillas from prison. No political demands, in fact, of any kind. He just wanted money. He'd repeat that. Money. Plus, of course, a guaranteed escape route for himself and his associates.

Now (he continued) he would lay it on the line for the relevant agencies in each country.

Impossible to overemphasize the strength of his, Lang's, position. This was the eve of the Isle of Man Conference. Probably the most important, and the most delicate set of negotiations since the Anglo-Irish treaty of 1920. How could the Republic of Ireland negotiate there when—put blunty—its prime minister and all his cabinet were dead? The conference would collapse, and that seemed a pity. And—talking now to Ireland's fellow EEC members— could they really envisage the administrative chaos that would result from a member state being decapitated in this way?

Addressing himself to the Americans, Lang wanted to ask them one thing. Did they feel happy about their president being in the hands of urban guerril- las? He, Lang, was making no threats to the president's person, but you never knew what might happen in this kind of situation. Did the American people really relish the prospect of the vice president guiding their destinies through the remainder of the presidential term? In the present threatening climate? They'd had vice presidents take over the Oval Office before, remember?

"So," Lang said, "now I speak directly to the vice president of the United States and to the State Department. And to the heads of state of the European Community. My demands are made to you, individually and collectively, to be met between you as you think fit."

The price for the release of all of the hostages—the president of the United States, the taoiseach of Ireland and his ministers, and such other hostages as Lang chose to take—would be two hundred million dollars. "Cheap at the price, right? Peanuts in international monetary terms. But"—he smiled cold- ly—"the dollar has had problems lately. In fact, if this wasn't a Saturday, it would be tumbling right now—on account of what's happening here in the Carrolton Institute." He paused. "So I'm afraid I have to ask for payment in gold. Two hundred million, right?" He shrugged. "But before I tell you how you are about to pay me, we'll have a little demonstration of what might happen if you don't."

He walked slowly down the line of hostages, the camera following him. Finally he stopped in front of Tomas O Gubain, the minister for education. Small and bald and tub-shaped, he looked in the worst shape of any of the six ministers. He was trembling and the sweat rose and glistened on his forehead. Lang let the camera play on him for a moment. Then he said, "Untie him."

Two Tontons Macoute did so, releasing O Gubain from the looped rope that linked him to his fellow cabinet ministers. Lang's men stood holding him between them, while another man placed a large asbestos mat at a point on the extreme right of the platform. O Gubain was dragged across and made to crouch on this mat. At a signal from Lang the two men grabbed him again and stripped off his morning coat. Then they forced him into a long canvas garment that reached just below his knees, pinioning his arms exactly as in an old-fashioned straitjacket. When they had finished, he looked swollen, inhuman, more like a dummy than a man.

Lang nodded his satisfaction. "Yes," he said to the cameraman, "show the people."

The camera held on O Gubain for a long moment. Lang said, "That garment he's wearing—it's made on the principle of an old-style lifejacket for use at sea. There's an inner lining and the space between that and the outer coat is padded out with fibers soaked in napalm. Yes—*napalm!*" He smiled. "A word with happy associations for any American, right? Now, inserted in the fibers is a fuse, activated by a tiny electronic device—it's adapted from the kind of remote-control unit that lets you switch on a TV or change channels from a yard or two away." The camera centered on the switch unit he held in his hand. "You're with me so far?" he demanded. "Sure you are—I guess you're ahead of me. Yes—when I press this switch I hold, the fuse in his jacket is ignited and he burns. Yes"—and suddenly his face distorted: he was snarling, shouting— "*burns!* He becomes a human torch, like those Buddhist monks you heard about."

Lang's expression changed again. Now his voice was soft, discursive. "I have to remember that a lot of you folks that are viewing won't ever have seen a man burned alive. Well—remember how they used burn nigras in a tar barrel down in Dear Ole Dixie? I never did see that, but I've seen gooks burn in Nam. It's kind of a great flash and glare and then you can see their skeleton outlined just like an X-ray. And then the fire dies down and they're still there. Or that's what you think, for a second. Really, they're just ash, ready to fall into dust."

Tom tried to detect some expression on O Gubain's face, but there was none, only a trancelike blankness.

"Two hundred million," Lang said. "In gold. If I don't get agreement on my proposal in thirty minutes, then Mr. O Gubain will burn. If, in another twenty minutes, we still don't have agreement, then Mr. Conan O'Kelly will burn. Ten minutes more and no agreement? Then a third cabinet minister will burn— right there on your television screen."

Lang looked around him. "Ten Little Indians—except there are only six of them. Obviously, the taoiseach will be the last to go." He smiled. His voice grew suave, persuasive. "Of course all this has got to be purely academic. It would be monstrous if anyone had to die. What is mere money against the lives of men like these? Men of integrity, of achievement. And, as I say, two hundred million is trifling when you consider the debts between nations."

Now Lang had the camera move over to the president, who looked—as

Tom remembered he had often looked during public appearances in the past—slightly perplexed but resolute.

"Of course," Lang said. "I make no threats against the president. But he is here with us today, and it would be foolish to pretend he is not in danger." Lang grinned. "You all are."

❧ ❧ ❧

The assistant commissioner and the two inspectors were still sitting in the Mercedes, their eyes fixed on the television screen. Now it carried again the werewolf mask, adding a touch of grotesque mockery to Lang's threats.

Twenty-six minutes had elapsed since Lang had announced his terms. So far there had been no indication of what the response of either the American vice president or the EEC heads of state would be.

Four minutes to go. Time was running out.

Having exhibited O Gubain trussed and ready for burning and taken his sinister side-look at the president, Lang had gone on to outline the arrangements for paying the ransom, although these would naturally follow agreement in principle being reached. Once he had that agreement, Lang would set a further deadline for the implementation of these arrangements.

The actual weight of the two million dollars' worth of gold would be calculated at the previous day's New York price. When the gold was ready—and, Lang said, he wasn't in the least interested how the required amount was gotten together: that was their problem, not his—it was to be placed aboard a plane at Dublin Airport. The plane had to be crewed and fueled in readiness for takeoff. Lang had pointed out that a TWA DC9 was due in from Shannon and might be used for this purpose.

Acceptance of Lang's terms and discussion of arrangements deriving from them would be conducted by radio on a frequency Lang had announced. The chief commissioner of the Garda would communicate with Lang on this frequency, acting on behalf of the Irish Government who were, in turn, in contact with the American State Department and the EEC Secretariat in Brussels.

Meanwhile the minutes were ticking away. Now the three policemen weren't even talking with each other anymore. They just sat in a torpor of anxiety, watching the screen.

Suddenly the light glowed on the radiotelephone set on the dashboard. The assistant commissioner lifted the receiver. Somebody was talking very fast at the other end. The assistant commissioner kept saying "Yes" and "Really?" Finally he nodded grimly and put down the receiver.

"The bastards are quarreling, wouldn't you know it?" he said. "The Germans want to agree. Give Lang the plane and the gold. The French are holding back, though. They say how do we know we can trust Lang?" He gestured irritably. "Of course we can't know—but do we just wait and have him kill the hostages?" He shook his head. "That's the Frogs all over!"

"What about the British?" Brannoch asked.

"They're talking about a Mogadishu-style operation at Dublin Airport. They've even offered the same fellas who helped the Germans there. Remember they blew the plane's doors open with special grenades?" He shook his head again. "We daren't risk it."

"And the Yanks?" Garvin demanded.

"Fair play—they've offered to provide the gold. Out of their reserves held in Europe. It can be in Dublin within the next half hour. But, as I say, the French are arguing. About how the debt is to be divided among the EEC partners; about the arrangement with the Yanks—you name it, the Frogs are arguing about it!" The assistant commissioner shrugged furiously; then looked at his watch. "Well—that's his deadline gone, anyway."

☘ ☘ ☘

The hall of the Carrolton Institute was well ventilated, had perfect air conditioning, but as the minutes passed, Tom felt the atmosphere was being slowly poisoned by the fear and tension around him.

Lang's first deadline had been passed—by three or four minutes. He announced the fact without comment, although the unfortunate O Gubain had been hauled to his feet as if in readiness for his exquisitely painful and public death. Now he stood motionless on his asbestos mat, staring fixedly before him.

Lang had to be in some kind of telephonic or radio contact with the outside world. Tom noticed that there seemed to be a system of signals going between him and a youngish, balding man who appeared at the door of the administrative offices from time to time (presumably the telephone or radio transmitter was in there). Twice in the last ten minutes Lang had left the platform to walk along the narrow causeway to the offices. Each time his two lieutenants, Malachi O'Farrell and Leni Reffenstab, appeared ill at ease, as if they needed the authority of Lang's presence.

Tom wondered again whether Frankie had gained entrance to the hall. Anyway, she was unarmed: she had rightly anticipated the weapons check at the door. So what could she do? What could anyone do?

What about himself, though? The ex-grunt from Nam? Had he nothing to offer at this moment? Had his morale caved in like a rotten apple when he returned to the States? Before he came to Ireland with old Seamus, he had sometimes feared it had.

Strangely, Tom noticed the keen edge of his fear was becoming blunted. Was this the euphoria hostages were said to feel at a certain stage of a hijacking?

He had to fight against that. Like a man struggling against the fetid, poisoned air of some loathsome cave. He must keep the will to act.

Act? How? The slightest hint of a hostile move and Lang's men would open up. Sitting in row upon row around the central platform—sweating, openmouthed, totally cowed—everyone in this assemblage knew they would go down like clay pigeons before the laser sights of Lang's Tontons Macoute.

So. To act meant to die.

To die? But suppose you accepted that? You accept that in war. As a possibility—even a probability. An appointment in Samarra looms from the first day at bootcamp. Once in Indochina, Tom had believed his own imminent death to be certain: something to be parlayed, postponed maybe, but never averted finally.

For Tom the miracle had been wrought of course. He had returned alive. But suppose he accepted that challenge, that certainty again? Better than to sit here passive, lamb for the slaughter, waiting for the chop.

What *could* he do? Embracing death as a certainty, a man finds his options wonderfully extended. What about Carl Austin Weiss, the young doctor who walked right up to Huey Long on the steps of the Alabama legislature and just pulled a trigger? The guy must have known he couldn't escape Long's bodyguards. The officers' plot against Hitler would have succeeded if there had been just one kamikaze type willing to sit on at the meeting, nursing the bomb.

Now Tom knew what he was going to do. He'd known, at the back of his mind, ever since he had observed Lang walk to and fro along that catwalk. Twice in the last fifteen minutes Lang had given Tom the chance to act. Sitting there, seeing Lang pass only a few feet above him, Tom hadn't really formulated the thought, but he did now.

Something was happening. The youngish, balding man walked along the catwalk and onto the platform. He spoke with Lang for several minutes.

Lang said, "I have to congratulate you. All of you. The American vice president and the EEC heads of state have agreed, jointly and collectively, to meet our terms. A little late," he added, "but that was to be expected."

His terms had been agreed in principle. Now he had to spell out how they were to be implemented. The DC9 at Dublin Airport had to be fueled and ready for takeoff to an unknown destination. The ransom of two hundred million in gold was to be loaded aboard the plane to await Lang's arrival. In addition the entire airfield had to be cleared for more than a mile's radius of the escape plane.

When Lang got confirmation that all was in readiness, he would leave Carrolton in his command helicopter—along with the hostages. Arrived at the airport, he would weigh and check the gold, and then await the rest of his group. They (he explained) would gradually evacuate the Carrollton Institute and be brought section by section to the airport in Irish Army helicopters. There they would join Lang in the escape plane. Once they were all safely aboard, the plane would leave with the gold, Lang and his group, and the hostages.

"I know what you will be thinking," Lang said, clearly addressing himself to the world outside of the hall. "You will be thinking this is a one-sided kind of a deal. You will be asking: 'When do we get the hostages back?' To which I have to reply: You have to trust me. You have no option if you want to save these people's lives. The hostages will be freed when—and only when—we know we are safely out of reach of your treachery, your reprisals." He paused. "When two parties are negotiating and one of them has all the advantages, the other party has to take a lot on trust. In these negotiations I am the one with all the advantages. That is why you have to trust me."

He went on to say that although his terms had been accepted, he and his group were vulnerable to treachery at every stage. "I don't want anyone to get any smartass ideas," Lang said. "Like that once I'm aboard the plane at Dublin Airport, anyone can do a Mogadishu—or even an Entebbe. Let me remind you of three factors. One, we command rather more muscle than Yousef Akache at Mogadishu or Bouvier at Entebbe. Second, we have a much smaller number of hostages, and we can kill them much quicker. In fact," Lang added, "they will be handcuffed together, only a foot or two away from me. I will kill them personally if necessary." He paused. "Three, we shall be in touch by radiotelephone with my personnel still holding this building. Any sign of hostile action towards me or any of my group at Dublin Airport or en route to it, and this building will be evacuated instantly by my men—who will then reduce it to rubble by the use of missiles, killing everyone inside it. For—don't forget—every man and woman inside this hall is also a hostage and will remain so even after the last of my personnel has left. Because before they do so, they will have planted bombs at various points. You will remain where you are and do nothing till I give you the all-clear or those bombs will be activated by a radio signal from me—again, killing everyone in the hall. So," Lang concluded, "that's the deal and you just have to take it. Just let anyone even *think* treachery and a lot of people die!"

Watching Lang at this desperate moment, Slowey reflected that if he were true to the ideals he still professed, he would pray for this man. But how do you pray for someone with a contempt for human life as cold and blank as the pennies on a dead man's eyes?

Lang appeared to be prolonging his moment of triumph. He had the television cameras briefly take in the taoiseach and Conan O'Kelly, and then linger on the president, who looked grave, unsmiling, but not obviously afraid.

Lang nodded and the taoiseach and Conan O'Kelly were freed from the ropes that tied them to their colleagues. They waited, haggard and disheveled, on the edge of the platform. O Gubain continued to stand on his mat, motionless, zombielike. Tom had noticed that none of the hostages ever looked at each other.

"Okay," Lang said, "the hostages go aboard the chopper now. The taoiseach; Mr. Conan O'Kelly, minister for internal affairs; the president of the United States of America."

He ended on a flourish, and the camera followed the three down the catwalk toward the helicopter, one guard ahead of them and one following.

Lang was talking to Malachi O'Farrell. Leni Reffenstab stood sulkily to one side. Lang turned and gestured for the camera to push in on O Gubain.

"I think we'll leave him where he is," he said. "Leave him wearing the shirt of Nessus. Then—if anyone in this hall steps out of line after I've left—I'll know it and this guy will burn!"

He turned; started across the platform; then stopped and spoke with Leni Reffenstab.

Tom figured that once Lang started down the catwalk it would take him about five seconds to reach a point some four feet to the left of where Tom was sitting, passing some eight feet above him.

That would be Tom's moment, one that would not come again because Lang was going aboard the chopper to fly to the airport.

Tom's chance—and he would take it. The margin during which Lang's men could hit him was tight—two or three seconds maybe—but during those few seconds he would offer them a perfect target. The only thing that could save him would be the element of total surprise. None of Lang's men would believe anyone could be as kamikaze-crazy as this.

Lang started down the catwalk.

Tom shifted himself in his seat so that the weight of his body was resting on his heels. This would be a steeper, higher jump than yesterday's onto the Liffey Weir—he had to go quicker and farther with even greater precision.

Lang was nearly there. Now Tom crouched forward, seeing the image of himself jumping as a cat jumps, praying for a tensile strength in his legs and thighs he wasn't sure he possessed.

Now! Tom catapulted forward and upward. For a second he thought he'd misjudged, was going to go right over the catwalk into the audience the other side. But he landed where he'd intended, grabbing Lang by the shoulders and spinning him around so that he faced the guns of his own men.

No one had fired.

Now Tom had Lang in a wrestler's grip, holding him from behind, grasping his neck, his left leg interlocking with Lang's right leg. He figured he had the correct hold—a sudden contrapuntal jerk and he could break Lang's spine.

And for the moment he could use Lang's body as a shield. Of course Lang's men were all around the hall. Tom knew he could only hold him for a few moments.

"Okay!" he shouted. "Anyone fires and I'll break Lang's back. Even if you miss him and get me, I'll still do it."

Tom knew an expert marksman could shoot him through the head and not harm Lang, but the shot he expected didn't come.

"All right, Dillon." The harsh voice from the platform was Malachi O'Farrell's. "Nice one—but it won't work. You can't hold that grip for more than a minute. Let him go, Dillon, and I might just let you live."

Tom gritted his teeth; didn't answer. He was almost out of breath. O'Farrell was right; the strain of holding Lang like this was too much; he couldn't go on. Even so, Tom realized that what he'd done was effective. Otherwise they would have shot him. But his arms were aching; he closed his eyes to stave off the dizziness that assailed him.

"Tom! Keep holding him. Just one minute more."

Frankie. She had climbed onto the platform and was standing near where the catwalk began. She was covering Lang and Tom with a submachine gun.

"Tom," she said. "Just do exactly as I say, right?"

Still covering them, she fumbled in her pocket and took out a Walther .22 automatic. "Okay," she said. "I want you to let him go. Just for a moment, while I throw you this gun. I'm covering him, so if he tries anything I give him a burst. *They* know that," she added, indicating Malachi O'Farrell, Leni Reffenstab, and the other Lang aides on the platform.

Tom released his grip on Lang, doing it gradually so that the sudden reaction of tortured muscles wouldn't send both of them crashing down into the audience.

Frankie was still covering them with the submachine gun. Then, the moment Tom stood up, straightening his agonized back and legs, she threw him the Walther. With an effort he caught it, nearly losing his footing as he did so.

"Thanks," Tom said. He leveled the gun at Lang's forehead. "Now we can stay like this forever."

Released from Tom's grip, Lang spoke for the first time. "Okay, okay—just don't get drunk with power, that's all. Let me remind you of one thing: we've got the hostages." He paused. "They're out there in that ship, custody of the pilot, Martin Leach. One signal from Malachi there and we can take them anyplace we decide on. Or kill them. Just as you like."

Tom said, "Lang—we can kill you too."

"So?" Lang demanded.

"So it's evens. You've got them. We've got you."

Lang shrugged. "You want to talk?"

Tom said, "A straight exchange? We let you go—you let everyone else go?"

Lang shook his head. "What about the two million? Anyway, like I said, don't get drunk with power. You may have a gun to my head—literally—but there are a lot of other factors. Like, for instance—I keep telling you—you kill me, you get killed yourself. And not only you. Frankie too. And the hostages."

"A lot of threats!"

"And those bombs I mentioned. Planted all around this hall—and you'd better believe it, if you kill me they're gonna go off."

"Fact remains: I pull this trigger, you're dead."

Lang shook his head. "Dillon—it's not that simple."

"No—it's not!" Frankie said sharply.

There was a new, harsh note in her voice Tom didn't recognize. "Who the hell are you two, to agree to a deal? What *right* do you have?" she demanded.

She moved to the center of the platform; now the submachine gun was covering Lang and Tom again. "You, Lang, you are a robber, a bandit. The Wednesday Committee trusted you. We gave you money, arms, personnel to bring about a new and better Ireland—and you betrayed us. You killed Duane; you've just killed Darrell . . . And now you have taken those hostages to get yourself two million dollars in gold." She shook her head in disgust. "Tom—

you're a brave man. I admire your bravery. You're honorable—but dumb. You'd put your life on the line for an establishment that will only use you for its own ends."

Tom kept his gun pointed at Lang, but inwardly he was baffled, reeling. What had gotten into Frankie?

"So," she said. "*I'm* going to make the terms. As an Irish republican, I have the right!" She paused. "In the name of the Wednesday Committee, I demand those hostages. You, Lang—you duped us, betrayed us, murdered our members. Even at this moment the senior members of the committee are waiting at a secret rendezvous for the call to come to Dublin to form a new government. For them this morning was the brightest that ever dawned. It offered them the chance of the Ireland they'd always dreamed of—Eireann Amhain: One Ireland, United, Gaelic, and Free." She paused again. "But you betrayed us, Lang. Those members of the committee are going to wait a long time, aren't they?—and sooner or later the police will track them down and throw them in jail . . . *But not if we hold the hostages.*"

Lang was sneering: "You take the hostages? What kind of crazy shit is that? Where could you take them?"

"Lang—you know where we could take them. And if we held them there, we could make a deal with the government. The president of the United States! The taoiseach! Do you think if we had them, we couldn't get ourselves a deal? We could make our own terms."

Lang said, "Talk away, Frankie. Doesn't alter a thing! Like I said to Mister Purple Heart here: you may have a gun to my head but I have everything else." He grinned. "So I fooled those crazies on the Wednesday Committee? Tough shit!"

"You still with me, Tom? Despite what I said?" Frankie asked.

He nodded. "Sure."

"Take Lang over there. Yes—there." She indicated where O Gubain still stood immovable as a statute on his asbestos mat.

As Tom made Lang walk over to O Gubain, Frankie covered every inch of their progress with her submachine gun. When they stopped beside O Gubain, Tom said, "Good idea, Frankie. Come on, Lang—give me the control switch." After a second's hesitation Lang handed it over. Tom nodded. "You know what we got to do, Lang. Let's do it."

"This is ridiculous!" Lang protested. "What do you get out of this, Dillon?"

Tom made Lang undo the long tapes that held O Gubain's grotesque-looking jacket in place. Then he made Lang grab each sleeve and pull the jacket off the hostage in a single movement.

Freed, O Gubain tottered to the corner of the platform and started to throw up. Then he slumped to the floor, trembling, his face in his hands.

"Look, Dillon—" Lang protested.

"Go on, Tom," Frankie urged. "I'm covering you."

Tom pocketed his gun. He grabbed Lang's wrists, forcing them into the long sleeves. Then he pulled at the tapes, drawing the jacket tight around Lang.

"Okay," Tom said, weighing the control unit in his hand. "Better than a gun, right?"

Lang said, "Shoot me or burn me, what's the difference? You and the hostages—you all die just the same!"

Frankie said, "The shirt of Nessus, Lang. Now you're wearing it, maybe we can get a deal."

A half hour later they had a deal. To Tom, standing beside the grotesque, padded figure of Lang, those thirty minutes had seemed endless. And, although he was still a little dazed to find that his kamikaze-style assault on Lang had succeeded, he was troubled by the change in Frankie. He had known of her political beliefs—of course: he had taken them for granted, really—but this cold, fanatic stranger?

All the time she seemed to be seeking a confrontation that would be mutually destructive. They—she and Tom—could kill Lang by merely clicking a switch, but then Malachi O'Farrell and the others would instantly kill them, and of course the hostages. Tom grew weary of this murderous equation, endlessly repeated in the bargaining between Frankie and Lang. At times he had the feeling that only Frankie and Lang existed, of all the people in that huge hall. Certainly everyone's attention was focused on them with hysterical intensity. At Frankie's request, the events within the hall were no longer being televised, so the outside world must be in total ignorance of what was going on in here.

The argument about the hostages had spun on and on. Lang wanted them, as he'd said earlier, as a guarantee of safe conduct till he was far out of the reach of capture or reprisal. Frankie demanded the hostages as a safeguard, a bargaining counter against the capture and reprisal that must await all the members of the Wednesday Committee after the failure of the coup. She kept reiterating that with the president and the taoiseach at "our headquarters" the committee could hold out for a favorable deal. "Our headquarters" of course meant the island in Lough Ree where what Seamus called "the elders" were sweating it out. Tom wondered if Seamus was with them.

The break had come soon after Malachi O'Farrell had called out, "Hey, any progress over there?"

Lang said, "Still trying to make her see reason."

Then he had smiled at Frankie, but with no hint of emotion behind those greenish empty eyes. It was strange, Tom thought, how the power of this man's personality transcended the grotesque straightjacket that pinioned him.

"You know what?" Lang said. "Malachi's getting nervous. I read the signs. And that's worrying, that's very worrying. Malachi is one unpredictable guy."

Was Lang doubtful of his group's ability to endure the frustration of his long and theatrically public wrangle with Frankie much longer?

Suddenly Lang had said, "Okay, you got a deal."

The essence of their agreement was that Lang got the two hundred million in gold; the Wednesday Committee got the hostages. For the past forty minutes the DC9 had been waiting at Dublin Airport with the gold aboard; ready, fueled, and crewed for takeoff (as Lang had originally demanded). Confirmation had also been received that his other demand had been fulfilled: the whole airfield had been cleared for more than a mile's radius of the escape plane.

The arrangement now was that Lang, Malachi O'Farrell, Tom and Frankie, and the hostages would leave in the Sikorsky 61 Lang called his "command ship." The pilot would be Martin Leach. They would go first to Dublin Airport. There Lang and Malachi would board the DC9. While Lang and Malachi were checking the two million in gold, Leach would take Tom and Frankie and the hostages on to the secret headquarters of the Wednesday Committee. Its location was never referred to, but Tom knew—as did Lang—that this was the island on Lough Ree. Then Leach would fly back to Dublin Airport where he would rejoin Lang and Malachi o'Farrell.

A focus for argument had been the question of escape for the other members of Lang's group and the release of the audience in the Carrolton Institute.

Lang had originally asked for his personnel to be ferried section by section to the airport by Irish Army helicopters—their immunity being guaranteed by Lang's possession of the hostages. This procedure would still be followed, the difference being that it was now Frankie, in possession of the hostages, who would guarantee the safety of Lang's personnel.

Lang had held out for a long time against releasing the audience in the Carrolton Institute. Thanks to the bombs planted in the hall that could be activated by radio from a considerable distance away, they represented several hundred extra hostages for him. But eventually he had shrugged; agreed that the Carrolton audience should be allowed to leave before and not after his personnel started going aboard the army helicopters. Lang would guarantee their passage through his "ring of fire" of guns and missiles that circled the institute. (Incidentally, all this armament would be abandoned by Congar and his men when they boarded the chopper to take them to the airport. So much for the laboriously built-up foundation, which had cost millions of dollars, thought Tom.)

Lang had fought, too, to make it a condition that he be freed of the grotesque jacket that held him enclosed. Frankie had refused, arguing that Lang's physical helplessness was a protection against his double-crossing him. To, as Lang put it, "redress the balance," she had agreed that Malachi O'Farrell should come along—and of course Lang's man Martin Leach was piloting the chopper.

Now they were ready to go. Some of Lang's Tontons Macoute had begun to sullenly corral a section of the audience near the main entrance, preparatory to letting them through. Then Frankie said, "I have a statement to make."

Frankie began by identifying herself as an Irish republican, a member of the illegal Wednesday Committee. She had a particular right to call herself a republican (she said) because not only had she been born the daughter of one, she had also married one. Both of these men, her father and her husband, had suffered for their beliefs.

And the members of the Wednesday Committee were also ready to suffer. "Do you think any one of us is not ready to make the supreme sacrifice—the sacrifice of blood?" Frankie demanded. "Like Pearse and Plunkett and the other signatories of 1916. Today, thanks to Lang's treachery, we may have suffered a defeat"—Tom realized that most of the audience couldn't possibly know what she meant—"but we have not surrendered. We are in fact in a position of considerable strength thanks to our possession of three hostages— the president of the United States of America, the taoiseach, and the minister for internal affairs. We are about to take them to a secure and secret destination—a strongpoint that can never be reached—and we shall continue to hold them there until our conditions for their release are met. Those conditions are—

"Complete legal immunity for all members and associates of the Wednesday Committee in connection with these recent events.

"Abandonment of the Isle of Man Conference and all its aims.

"An amnesty for all Irish republican prisoners serving sentences in Irish and English jails."

The chopper crossed Dublin, traveling almost due northward since the University College campus at Bellfield lies to the southeast of the city and Dublin Airport six miles to the north.

They flew in almost complete silence. Tom sat beside Lang, and Malachi O'Farrell sat on the other side of him. Frankie guarded the hostages. They looked tired and apathetic now. The president had lost his look of sharpened alertness and sat slumped and dejected. The taoiseach no longer had the energy to maintain his tragedian's mask: he looked simply a weary old man. Of the three, Conan O'Kelly managed to look most himself, but even his chubby features were haggard and strained.

When they entered the chopper, Lang had again asked to be released from the incendiary jacket, and Frankie had again refused. "Shit," Lang had protested. "You know very well, you press that switch to burn me, you send this chopper up in flames. So what the fuck—?"

Frankie simply told him that he could endure to wear it a little longer. Once they got to the airport, that was it. She grinned. "Anyway, I feel safer when I see you with that around you." Tom noticed she seemed more relaxed, more her old self, despite the extraordinary tension of this flight.

They were approaching the airport now. Tom was sitting in a left-hand seat by a window. He craned forward, trying to locate Lang's escape plane. He couldn't see it, but in a moment or two he would.

And then he did see it—what had to be it—tiny, toylike, on the main runway. The only thing was, the whole airfield was to have been cleared—to a radius of a mile around the escape plane, wasn't it? That had been one of Lang's conditions, which was still being met.

There was the DC9 on the runway all right, but far from being alone, isolated, it seemed to be at the center of a whirl of frenzied, antlike activity. From this height people didn't even look as big as ants, but those black shapes had to be vehicles—military vehicles, tanks or armored cars—

"Holy shit!" This from Martin Leach.

The helicopter had been going down fast, as Leach had intended to land on the runway close beside the plane. Now he pulled on the controls and sent it soaring skyward again.

"Jesus!" Lang cried. "Looks like the goddamned May Day parade in Red Square! Tanks, guns—the whole schmear . . . This has got to be a double-cross."

"Judas was an Irishman," Malachi said and leveled his heavy Mauser automatic at the back of Tom's neck—only to realize that Frankie, in turn, was covering him with her submachine gun.

🍀 🍀 🍀

The thick, scrubby bushes overran the shore of the island, growing down into the lough: a prodigious nesting and gathering place for the hundreds of wild duck, waterfowl, and other birds whose names Slowey would never know. But at this moment he tried to soothe his jangled mind by pretending to know them, rummaging back into memory in an attempt to guess what they were.

An army helicopter had brought Slowey and twelve other Special Branch men to this island at the northernmost end of Lough Ree. The twelve men had been quickly picked, but he could trust them—he knew that from what Mickey Glinn had told him during that last talk they'd had on their way to the Carrolton Institute.

They had been here for the last fifteen minutes, and now his men were deployed in a rough circle around the only piece of ground on which a helicopter might possibly land. The island was about two hundred yards long and shoe-shaped: the possible landing strip was at the heel; the ivy-encrusted shell of the old Benedictine monastery nearer the toe.

The elders of the Wednesday Committee had been here when Slowey and his squad arrived: Glinn had spoken that much truth anyway, when he said they would be assembled here this morning, waiting for the call of History in the shape of a helicopter that would whisk them away to Dublin to figure in a revolutionary government. This morning, as they sheltered behind the ivy-encrusted walls of the monastery, it was hard to see them as custodians of the rebel spirit. They simply had the rather vulnerable dignity of any group of elderly people. And yet, Slowey reflected, An tAthair Muiris, Liam O Docartai, Sean MacSaoirse, Catherine Cudahy, and others *had* kept that spirit alive in the last twenty years. If Slowey had always been their implacable opponent he could still enter into their chagrin this morning: savor the tragedy of a dream dying forever in these old hearts. He wondered where Seamus Dillon was, the fiercest and most tenacious dreamer of them all.

Their tragedy, Slowey thought, as he trudged aimlessly around the island, crashing through sodden undergrowth: sure to God, it's going to be *my* tragedy too—and what have those old ones of the Wednesday Committee got to lose compared with me?

Every minute or so he looked upward, even though he knew he'd hear the whir of a chopper before he'd see it

He thought with a curious detachment that this might well be his last day as a policeman. As an active, responsible officer with a job to get on with. Oh—

he'd still be a member of the Force: at the worst suspended; at the best shunted off to Mayo or West Kerry to perform office boy duties.

Suspended. Yes, they would almost certainly suspend him, more in sorrow than in anger—although who knew what grudge-holders were waiting in the thickets?—and then mount some kind of internal inquiry. And what could he tell such a body? He wouldn't be explaining any ordinary blunder, an error of judgment which an officer with his record might be allowed just once in a career. He would be seeking to justify behavior so bizarre as to defy rational explanation. Yes (he'd say) I gave her two weapons, a nonissue automatic and a submachine gun. *Why*, Superintendent, *why?* You know the use McNagan subsequently made of them?

Yes, Mr. Chairman (Slowey could hear himself answering), she used them to kidnap the president of the United States and the taoiseach and the minister for internal affairs . . .

Impossible to explain that Tom Dillon's leap onto the catwalk in the Carrolton Hall had created such an opportunity that Slowey's mind had leaped forward with him. More than ever before, this time Slowey had acted on intuition, on blind faith. It seemed to him that the only person who could exploit the situation Dillon had created was Frankie McNagan. That was why he'd given her the arms. They'd only had time for a few minutes' whispered colloquy—so hurried that Slowey wasn't sure he and she had even really understood each other.

In her public utterance she'd talked of a "secret destination," a "strongpoint" to which the hostages would be taken. If his faith in her was justified, she had meant this island, where she knew he would be waiting (Glinn had told him about the committee's rendezvous here). He tried to convince himself that Frankie had spoken with such emphasis to indicate that she was trying to get a message through to him.

He hoped, but each minute that passed without sight of Lang's helicopter made it more likely that she'd double-crossed him. A trick within a trick. She was blood and bone an Irish republican: those people never changed. He would always be an enemy to her.

Slowey felt despair coming down on him again. (Blind faith, Superintendent? In a young woman of these known views?) He felt too numb even to pray.

He had to keep going. Best thing to do was check once more that all his men were deployed to the best advantage and were not visible from the air.

☘ ☘ ☘

"Shit!" Martin Leach said, and then, "Decision time! This here fuel gauge tells me we're about to have to settle where we're gonna land. So—make up your minds!"

No one answered him, but Tom thought: anything to break the deadlock. Frankie and Malachi O'Farrell were no longer pointing guns at each other, but when Frankie had told Leach to take them to the island on Lough Ree (after Dublin Airport had been seen to be full of waiting troops), Lang had blocked it. "You may have me trussed up like a chicken," he said, "but Martin still does like I say. Right, Martin?"

Leach had nodded uneasily. "Yeah . . ."

"Sokatsu! Martin was an addict, maybe you didn't know that? I saved him. He'd be dead now, except I saved him by the power of Sokatsu. So he goes where *I* say, right, Martin?"

"That's right," Leach said reluctantly.

"Suppose I hold a gun to the back of his head," Tom said. "That change his ideas any?"

"Dillon," Lang said, "you're stupid and earthbound, you know that? If I tell Martin to take us down, crash this ship, kill us all, he does it, right, Martin?"

Leach didn't answer.

"You say it for me, Martin. You crash the ship. You kill us all. Say it, Martin."

After a moment Leach said slowly, "That's bad karma, Lang."

"Take us to the island," Frankie said. "At least we'd be safe for the moment."

Apparently confused, Leach said, "All of you, you gotta make your minds up. You gotta agree. I keep going till you do."

And so he had kept going, in what appeared to Tom to be ever-widening circles around the outer perimeter of Dublin. More than once they'd passed other choppers, but no one interfered with them. Probably there was some sort of identification out, Tom thought. It was naive to think they could keep on like this and not be pinpointed, followed.

"Go to the island," Frankie said. "It's the only place. We're safe there," she repeated. "Even if they would find us, we've got the hostages, we can do a deal—"

"Like this deal?" Lang snarled. "Martin, baby—you don't land on that island, hear?"

"Aw, cut out that Sokatsu shit, Lang," Malachi O'Farrell said. "She's right. Where else is there to go? You wanna come down in a field? Have the pigs around you before you can get out of the ship? Go to the island—we have to."

Coming down to the island, Frankie could see the elders of the committee assembled near the edge of the landing strips; could distinguish the tall figure of An tAthair Muiris, the tiny birdlike figure of Catherine Cudahy, and the thick white curls of Liam O Docartai.

Malachi O'Farrell said mockingly, "Just look at them, will you? Conspiracy freaks! Old and fucked-over and finished—and all for Mother Ireland!"

Leach eased the chopper skillfully down onto the narrow strip.

Lang was staring out the window. "Hey, Frankie—this is your 'secret head-quarters'? There isn't even shelter, for Christ's sake! Those old folks there—they've been out in the rain all morning. They're *wet*."

Frankie said, "They've been out there waiting for us. There *is* shelter. In fact there are huge underground cellars under the monastery ruins. Very few people know about them. Actually this is the ideal place. A lot of people could hide out here for a long time. It's remote—and for some reason it's off the tourist track."

"Yeah," Lang said doubtfully. He frowned. "Say, Malachi! Those old-tim-ers—they're standing there like dummies. Not talking to each other. You see that?"

"Shit, Lang," Malachi O'Farrell said. "Get to be as old as that and you got nothing left to say."

Lang snarled impatiently and shook his head. "Let me out of this thing, for Christ's sake!" Tom noticed that Lang suddenly appeared much more aware of the jacket that held him. Now his frustration seemed intense.

"Okay," Tom said. "But let's get onto solid ground first, right?"

"Why?" Lang demanded. "I don't know I want to get out. Bad vibes from this island!"

"We have to get the hostages out, anyway," Frankie said. "We have to keep *them* alive. Time we gave them a drink."

Lang didn't answer. Covered by Frankie's submachine gun, the president, the taoiseach, and Conan O'Kelly descended from the helicopter. They moved stiffly, with the slow-motion effect of great fatigue.

Gently but decisively, Frankie got them to stand a few yards away. Glancing over to where the members of the Wednesday Committee were assembled, Tom became aware of what Lang meant. They did appear extraordinarily glum and silent. They had watched the hostages descend from the chopper with the distrustful fascination of aborigines viewing their first white man. Presumably they were all burned up about the failure of the coup?

"Lang," Frankie said. "Get down here and we'll let you out of that thing."

Why? Tom wondered. But then he supposed they couldn't keep Lang trussed up forever.

Slowly, clumsily, but with his usual agility not quite extinguished, Lang climbed down onto the ground.

Frankie was standing by the door of the chopper. Having helped Lang get out, Malachi O'Farrell remained just inside it. Leach was still at the controls.

Somehow (it seemed to Tom afterward) the sight of Lang's grotesque figure waddling forward acted as a signal.

Suddenly propelled into frantic life, Liam O Docartai rushed forward, his arms waving, shouting, "Take off again, you fools! 'Tis a trap—a trap—the fucking police is here . . .

At that moment Malachi O'Farrell jumped out of the chopper onto Frankie's back, knocking her down and starting to struggle with her for possession of her submachine gun. A second later he'd grabbed it and was covering the hostages.

"Go on," he ordered. "Get back in there. Go on—move it!"

His words cut across Slowey's "Drop it, O'Farrell. You haven't a chance."

Slowey and his men were advancing across the landing strip, fanning out as they came. Slowey was covering O'Farrell, but it was stalemate—neither dared shoot with the three hostages ranged between them.

Then Tom saw that Lang was moving. Edging in a clumsy, sideways fashion toward the president.

Slowey shouted, "Lang—stop where you are. I'll kill you, Lang!"

But he was bluffing. It would be hard to shoot Lang from this angle without hitting the taoiseach. Lang kept coming.

Then Tom remembered.

For a second he thought the remote-control switch hadn't worked. Then he saw Lang stop, sway a little, and then turn back toward the helicopter. He saw the black smoke rising from the front of Lang's jacket. Then, as Lang still kept moving, the smoke began to pour out, swirling around him.

Malachi O'Farrell was back on board the chopper and Leach had the engine going.

Lang had nearly made the chopper door when he burst into flame: a grisly scarlet flower of incandescent heat and pain. Tom had no time to see Lang melt like a candle, for he had just realized the danger.

"Down! All of you—down!" he shouted and threw himself flat on his face, just before the roar of Lang's burning ignited the Sikorsky's fuel tanks.

The echoes of the explosion came hitting back from the shores of the lough like great iron gates closing, startling the birds of the island into a frenzied chorus of mourning.

☘   ☘   ☘

Everyone agreed that a great job had been done on the UCD campus. Only four days after the Carrolton siege and the idea of a gun or rocket launcher in these peaceful groves of academe seemed an aberration. Tom said as much to Frankie as they walked along the road that led to the Carrolton Institute.

"That's the whole idea of terrorism," she said. "The familiar suddenly becomes the frightening."

Neither spoke for a moment. Then Tom said, "Will you come with me to Seamus' funeral?"

She nodded. "Of course."

"I think he'd have been glad—to die in Ireland, I mean."

" 'May you die in Ireland,' " she quoted. "Yes, I'm sure."

"I'd have loved him to be buried in Kilmainham," Tom said, "along with all of the heroes. But of course that's just a fantasy."

"Yes." After a moment she said, "I shall be glad of your protection at the funeral."

"What do you mean?"

"A traitor to the movement—like me. A Judas bitch, that's what they'd call me. For what I did."

"To *Lang?*"

"That doesn't matter. I helped the police. My days as an activist are over." She shrugged. "Never mind. I suppose I've come round to seeing it doesn't work anyway." She paused. "Violence, I mean."

He pulled a copy of the Dublin *Evening Herald* out of his pocket. The headline ran, "Isle of Man Conference Runs into Snag."

She smiled wryly. "You know what the man said: 'Jaw, jaw, jaw, is better than war, war, war.' "

"An Irish republican quoting Winston Churchill?"

They walked along in silence for a moment. Then Frankie said, "Mind you, when I was announcing my ransom terms—amnesty for all republican prisoners in English jails—I thought of the Other Frankie and wished it was for real." She paused. "It wouldn't have worked, though"

They walked on. Tom was thinking of the Other Frankie. He was a name—a ghost—but he was a ghost that would always come between them. Tom and Frankie had been close these last days, but now Tom sensed a blankness. Somewhere along the way there was something he could have said that would have kept them together forever.

Tom knew he could never say the magic words now, whatever they were. She might no longer be an activist, but she would go back to visiting the high-security wing at Parkhurst: faithful to the Other Frankie to the point of self-immolation in the best Irish tradition.

Something made him say, "You know Seamus had a Gaelic saying—something about floodtime . . . Do you know it?"

She smiled and said, "Is mairg a bhaidthear in am an anaithe mar tagann an grian i indiaid na fearthainne," and then translated, "It is foolish to drown at floodtime because the sunshine always follows the rain."